The Alchemist Who Survived
Now Dreams of a Quiet City Life

Usata Nonohara
Illustration by OX

05

YEN
ON
New York

The Alchemist Who Survived Now Dreams of a Quiet City Life 05

Usata Nonohara

Cover art by OX   Translation by Erin Husson

IKINOKORI RENKINJUTSUSHI HA MACHI DE SHIZUKANI KURASHITAI
Volume 5
©Usata Nonohara 2019
First published in Japan in 2019 by KADOKAWA CORPORATION, Tokyo.
English translation rights arranged with KADOKAWA CORPORATION, Tokyo through TUTTLE-MORI AGENCY, INC., Tokyo.

English translation © 2020 by Yen Press, LLC

Yen On
150 West 30th Street, 19th Floor
New York, NY 10001

Visit us at yenpress.com
facebook.com/yenpress
twitter.com/yenpress
yenpress.tumblr.com
instagram.com/yenpress

First Yen On Edition: December 2020

Yen On is an imprint of Yen Press, LLC.
The Yen On name and logo are trademarks of Yen Press, LLC.

Library of Congress Cataloging-in-Publication Data
Names: Nonohara, Usata, author. | ox (Illustrator), illustrator. | Husson, Erin, translator.
Title: The alchemist who survived now dreams of a quiet city life / Usata Nonohara ; illustration by ox ; translation by Erin Husson.
Other titles: Ikinokori renkinjutsushi ha machi de shizukani kurashitai. English
Description: First Yen On edition. | New York : Yen On, 2019
Identifiers: LCCN 2019020720 | ISBN 9781975385514 (v. 1 : pbk.) |
    ISBN 9781975331610 (v. 2 : pbk.) | ISBN 9781975331634 (v. 3 : pbk.) |
    ISBN 9781975331658 (v. 4 : pbk.) | ISBN 9781975310455 (v. 5 : pbk.)
Subjects: | CYAC: Fantasy. | Magic—Fiction. | Alchemists—Fiction.
Classification: LCC PZ7.1.N639 Al 2019 | DDC [Fic]—dc23
LC record available at https://lccn.loc.gov/2019020720

ISBNs: 978-1-9753-1045-5 (paperback)
          978-1-9753-1046-2 (ebook)

10 9 8 7 6 5 4 3 2 1

LSC-C

Printed in the United States of America

The Alchemist Who Survived

Now Dreams of a Quiet City Life

05

Hey!
The Japanese edition
of this novel begins with a
manga section. To preserve the
right-to-left reading orientation of the
material, we've moved that section to the
back of the book, so flip to the end,
read that first, then come back
here to enjoy the rest of
the story!

The Alchemist Who Survived Now Dreams of a Quiet City Life

05 Contents

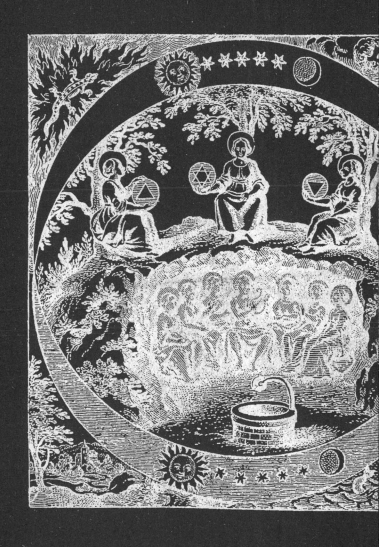

PROLOGUE

The City with a Labyrinth

01

There was a labyrinth in this city.

When the sun hung low and cast the sky in red, adventurers who had finished their day's work received money for the materials they had obtained by defeating monsters. Then some of them would head to the bars with their companions, while others hurried home, where their families awaited their return. People returning from work scoured the marketplace and open-air stalls for dinner ingredients. Stall owners advertised their prized dishes in loud voices, and their wares sent delicious smells wafting toward potential customers. Even children who hadn't had their fill of playtime were driven home by their empty stomachs, wondering all the while what the day's dinner would be.

This peaceful, mundane sight could be found in any city. An evening scene that might unfold anywhere, regardless of time or place. Some might even watch it play out with a fond nostalgia. But unlike those other cities, this one had a labyrinth.

Could there have been pots of soup steaming in the houses awaiting the return of their occupants? Perhaps there was a basket of bread on the table, along with plates of meat or fish.

This city was surrounded by a sturdy protective wall to keep out the monsters of the Fell Forest. Similarly, each house was surrounded by a stone wall in case of the unthinkable: a monster invasion. People ate heartily in these secure homes, then went to bed without a care.

Greeting another day of safety and hoping for a happy future beyond these ordinary days: everyone in the city wished for the same thing. From the rich to the poor, the happy to the unhappy, the young to the old, everyone held the belief that the sun would rise and tomorrow would come.

This was despite the fact that the place they lived, the foundation of their livelihood, was situated directly above a labyrinth that went down more than fifty strata. No matter how high they built their walls, a veritable hell of a maze, crawling with monsters, lay just underfoot.

The boss of the Labyrinth had long ago devoured the spirit Endalsia, a former guardian of this land, and what little remained of her existence was beginning to vanish. The lives of the humans Endalsia dearly loved now rested on what might as well have been a thin layer of ice, although only a few people knew the troubling truth.

Yes. This was the Labyrinth City.

There was a labyrinth in this city, which was both an important part of everyone's daily life and absolutely incompatible with it.

02

"Hrm, a monster ate this patient's leg. Tore it clean off and crushed it into bits of meat and bone. When it was healed, it was shorter than it had been originally. A high-grade specialized potion was used..."

Robert muttered to himself as he read diagnosis and treatment records from the Labyrinth Suppression Forces' medical team with great interest. These documents detailed information on soldiers who'd been treated with multiple high-grade specialized potions by Nierenberg and others. Back then, there had been an extremely large number of injured soldiers, and the treatment for this particular one had been postponed as a consequence. The limb had been connected only by the bare minimum, just enough so it wouldn't rot, and treatment was administered at a later date. When the injured man finally received proper care, the soldier's provisionally attached leg was so *damaged*, it was beyond the healing capabilities of a high-grade potion.

To start, the amount a potion restored was determined by its rank. For missing limbs, perhaps one could think in terms of the flesh, bone, and blood that had been lost. Generally speaking, a special-grade potion could restore a full limb's worth. However, that didn't mean a soldier with a missing arm who drank such a concoction would grow a new arm. It meant the potion could be applied to the wound while pressing the severed limb against it to compensate for the missing tissue, thus attaching it to the body again.

If the wound was smooth—if, for instance, the limb had been severed by a sword—a high-grade potion was probably all that was required to reconnect the limb. However, if the teeth or claws of a monster had torn the limb from the body, there wouldn't be an even cut. The skin and muscle tissue would be shredded, crushed by fangs, or even chewed. Both the bones and the muscles would have lost their natural shape at that point, having been split vertically or smashed. The wound itself would also be messy. So even if the arm or leg was recovered, flesh from the wound was already sitting in a monster's stomach or rotting on the ground in the Labyrinth somewhere. Treating something in this condition required a substantial amount of healing ability to both restore tissue and reconnect the limb.

When someone who'd lost an arm drank a special-grade potion, it could heal the complex network of bone, blood vessels, nerves, muscles, fat, and skin tissue to a satisfactory degree. This was only if several centimeters were able to grow back, however. Unfortunately, the exact number of special-grade potions needed to induce this kind of healing was unknown. Moreover, the more time that had passed since the injury was sustained, the more the body would forget its previous natural state, decreasing the chance of being able to regenerate the lost limb.

Then there was the subset of potions known as specialized potions. Such potions had been known to restore gouged muscle, even if those concoctions were only of high grade. Ones specialized for bones could heal compound fractures and even completely restore missing bones. With specialized high-grade potions already carrying such efficacy, if one used multiple specialized special-grade potions, it wasn't impossible to completely regenerate missing arms or legs. One such mixture had healed Sieg's Spirit Eye, after all.

The ingredients for such draughts were more than a little difficult to acquire, however. Considering the materials that went into them, ten gold pieces for a single specialized special-grade potion seemed almost too reasonable.

Mariela was just now becoming able to make specialized special-grade potions, but how many people in the Labyrinth City had lost hands or feet? The boss of the Labyrinth would most certainly take control of the ley line and destroy the Labyrinth City before all the necessary potion materials could be gathered and the resulting concoctions could be distributed to everyone who needed them.

That was why the Sage of Calamity's ordering Nierenberg and Robert to treat everyone in the slums seemed a truly insurmountable task at first. However...

"So, by deliberately breaking and crushing, then using a specialized potion, you forced it to heal and compensate for the deficiency? I see. This says a lot about how specialized potions restore tissue."

The medical team—particularly Robert and Nierenberg—had been having a fervent discussion about some new methods.

"If this is possible, couldn't you take about half of what you need from healthy parts of the body, add that to it, and then restore it?"

"But how would you add to it? If you leave it cut open like that, it would likely start to decay."

Actually, the only ones engaged in heated conference and conjecture were Nierenberg and Robert. All the other members of the medical team were more or less being dragged along for the ride.

"...Cut into healthy parts of the body?"

"...'Add to it'..."

Other members of the medical staff muttered to one another as they slowly moved away from Robert and Nierenberg. If there was an injury, it was to be healed using magic or potions. That much was common sense to them. Cutting open a perfectly healthy body and deliberately creating more wounds seemed nothing less than pure madness.

"A Proxy... No, there are medicines that will let a body survive for a fairly lengthy bit of time even when it's cut open. If we put those to use, we can probably utilize the restorative effects of special-grade potions and the reparative effects of specialized high-grade potions to reconstruct the tissue."

"I see. Surely if we go that route..."

Proxies. These were the living dolls Robert had once used through the black arts. Robert had hit upon a method he called "black new medicine," which allowed the Proxy to take on the medicine user's wounds. Although such things were considered heresy to most, the techniques he employed had inarguably practical uses. Even so, it was hard for most of the medical team to accept. Excluding Nierenberg, of course.

This was the birth of a truly dreadful duo.

Nierenberg, who gleefully opened soldiers' wounds to administer treatment, was scary enough, but Robert had provided a supplement to Nierenberg's methods. The two had a frightening synergy. Without a doubt, this dark collaboration would cause Labyrinth City medical treatment technology to spiral up in the coming days like dragons climbing into the heavens. Their revolutionary method would almost certainly have brilliant effects, but normal medical engineers absolutely couldn't keep up with it. Before the paradigm of the medical community could adapt, the changes might simply collapse the entire thing.

The medical engineers watched Nierenberg and Robert in shock as the two smiled slightly and the fervor of their conversation increased.

"That's the act of a demon. Nobody could ever hope to pull it off..."

Robert ignored the scornful comment.

This is not the work of some fiend. That woman is far more vicious than any such creature...

In the short time since he'd been taken under the wing of the Sage of Calamity, Robert had become painfully aware of the futility of searching for a reason why he couldn't do something.

03

Robert was at a loss for words the first time he saw the thing in the temporary atelier.

"That's why you generally use a nozzle to focus the stream, and then the drops of water pop. Ah, while you're at it, freezing them might make it easier. You don't exactly *make* them get colder and freeze them. It's more like you *let* them get colder and freeze."

The girl spoke as if she was telling Robert how to do it, and although he understood the words she was saying, he didn't comprehend her meaning at all.

"Ohhh, we've discovered a new technique!" the girl exclaimed as she extracted lunamagia without the use of any tools. This was the girl from the apothecary who was friends with Robert's younger sister, Caroline.

The older brother might have doubted anyone who'd said that the owner of Sunlight's Canopy was harmless and innocent at first. But even if he had, and he had gone to confirm it with his own eyes, he would have quickly arrived at the exact same conclusion.

The girl called Mariela was the epitome of ordinary.

Incidentally, Caroline had casually confirmed that Mariela had also been in the cellar where Estalia had slept at the time of Robert's arrest.

Back then, the once-cursed man had most definitely shouted things like "Where?! Where are they?!" and "Hand over the alchemist!" at the top of his lungs. Ironically, the alchemist he sought had been right there all along.

I didn't even notice her...

How disgraceful. The mere thought of it was torture to Robert. His humiliation over the mistake was so great that he would rather have returned to his lonely cell than endure it.

It's too late now, though. I sold my soul to the flame devil. It's been ordained that my body will burn in eternal suffering...

Even that might have been preferable if it were true. However, in reality...

"Rob, we're out of ice. Don't just stand there! Go make some more, lickety-split! Work for that money you borrowed."

The woman Robert thought was a flame devil was apparently called the Sage of Calamity and was the alchemist's master.

Thanks to the miraculous seal the Sage of Calamity had burned into the back of his left hand, Robert had been able to spirit Caroline away without anyone noticing—a feat that had saved her life. However, neither his life nor his soul had been taken in exchange for the power to accomplish it.

Instead, this seal was a favor in return for a debt the sage owed Robert's ancestor. Thus, it had come free of charge, despite being so incredibly rare.

Thinking it would claim his life in payment, and due to the urgency of other matters at the time, Robert hadn't transcribed the mark. However, he soon discovered that he would continue living even after the mark had faded. Yes, Robert was still alive, and part of that life was the shame of being forced to witness someone propose to his sister while he was frozen in an idiotic pose.

If only I'd thought to draw what that seal looked like...

It was a complex design, so Robert probably wasn't expecting a copy to have as great an effect as the original, but at least it would let him vanish whenever he felt the embarrassment of that memory.

"Rooob, haven't you made the ice yet?" The Sage of Calamity clinked the rim of her glass with a cocktail stirrer and urged him to get on with it. If the red-haired master were not so loud, she could have been a beauty who caught every eye in the city. However, her habit often left her drunk in the middle of the day, and her crude tapping on the glass did little for her charm.

Even knowing the kind of person she was, Robert could have accepted his servitude to her if it were compensation for the seal she'd granted him. Instead, however, the golden-eyed sage claimed the reason was "a debt of five silver coins, plus interest." Normally, if a steward of the Aguinas family were ordered to return such a piddling amount, he wouldn't be asked to work it off, because the family's assets belonged to Caroline now. However, the sage had demanded that Robert earn his own keep.

I'm not working for a devil, or to compensate for the seal, but as collateral for a debt... This is depressing. I want to disappear.

Sulking, Robert used ice magic to fill a bucket with the stuff.

Perhaps because of those feelings of melancholy, residual curses leaked from his body and into the ice.

"Aah, what do you think you're putting in there?! **Fire!**" the Sage of Calamity shouted with some delight as a blaze engulfed Robert.

Ugh, she burned me again...

Although he hated her forehead poke attack, he hated when the sage burned him, too. It gave him a feeling of extreme discomfort, as if countless years' worth of deep stains were being forcibly cleansed. Or perhaps it was more like being stripped naked and washed from head to toe. Either way, every time the Sage of Calamity used this magic on him, Robert also noticed the residue of curses he couldn't completely control—curses he'd thought had seeped deep into his body and soul—fading more and more with each lick of the flames.

Unbelievable. Nothing but unbelievable things happen here.

"Good job, Mr. Robert! Now, Master, I'm done for today, so we're going home." Apparently, Mariela had finished making high-grade potions while Robert was dawdling. She grinned and gave a thumbs-up at seeing that her master had imbibed less alcohol than usual.

"Whaaat? Mariela, you still have magical power left."

"I do, but I have no more materials. Now let's go home and practice special-grade potions!"

Mariela wore an expression of triumph, while Freyja clung to her bottle. The soldiers guarding the alchemist smiled and asked things like "You don't need a nap today?" while apportioning the completed high-grade potions into storage vials and carrying them out.

Speaking of the quantity of those high-grade potions...

Why is everyone so comfortable with all this?! Robert wondered.

Everything related to Mariela's work in this temporary atelier was terribly bizarre, from the making of high-grade potions with no tools to the immense amount of magical power the girl possessed. It was also strange that the alchemist worked every day until she ran out of magical energy and collapsed, although she hadn't done so today.

When young children ran themselves ragged playing, they could suddenly pass out even if they were in the middle of eating. Kids that young didn't feel bitter or get upset about that kind of thing. Even though Mariela was in her late teens now, she continued to do alchemy and wear herself out like a child.

When Robert learned from Caroline's letters about the start of potion sales, he'd thought there were several alchemists involved. Technically, there were two: a master and a pupil. However, only the pupil was actually making the potions, while the master was content to simply tease and agitate.

It was completely absurd for Mariela to be training to make special-grade potions, or so Robert had thought. He had judged Mariela as utterly average, but after seeing her perform alchemy once, that evaluation was proven completely inaccurate. She boasted a large quantity of magical power and incredible skills. If Mariela ordered magical tools used for making special-grade potions from the imperial capital, she would probably be able to craft the difficult draughts right away. No, Robert was certain she could do so even with the old magical tools left sleeping in the Aguinas family storehouse. Mariela's ability exceeded the need for the latest technology from the capital.

However, when Robert tried to tell Mariela this, the sage had quickly silenced him with a forehead poke attack. He even tried asking the Sage of Calamity about it when Mariela wasn't around, but all Freyja did was laugh meaningfully and evade the subject. Robert had asked the fiery woman this question several times now and had only once gotten an answer of any real substance.

"Humans are free yet bound by chains. They can go anywhere they want, become anything they want, and decide everything themselves, including the place they belong and what their own limits are. So, Rob, that's why you shouldn't decide your own limits by saying things like 'It's difficult; I can't do it; this is all I can do.' Remember this: If you tell yourself you can do something, you just might surprise yourself and manage it."

The speech opened his eyes a little to the drunkard sage's extremely unorthodox methods. Robert couldn't figure out exactly what she wanted to make Mariela do even if he tried, but Freyja probably had a goal that could only be reached if she pushed Mariela like she'd been doing thus far.

Perhaps the Sage of Calamity's seemingly absurd guidance had some merit, because in the span of just a few days, Robert witnessed the young alchemist learn to process ley-line shards without any tools whatsoever.

This Sage of Calamity is more wicked than any demon...

From Robert's perspective, dissolving ley-line shards in Drops of Life using skills alone was not the work of a mere mortal. And the next thing he witnessed Mariela do—*Crystallize Medicine*—was something he'd only seen in ancient texts. He had always thought it was some old fabrication, a fairy tale.

Even Mariela herself seemed surprised, proudly crying, "Oh hey, I did it! It's so pretty!" after using *Crystallize Medicine* on every material she had. The young alchemist then promptly put them into vials and placed them on a shelf. She was laughing like a preschooler collecting beads; such an accomplishment was hardly the time for such a childish display. Robert's evaluation of Mariela came full circle, and the girl returned to looking rather mundane in his eyes.

In many ways, it was foolish of me to take her so seriously in the first place.

Robert, who knew firsthand that it was meaningless to search for reasons he couldn't do something, researched ways to heal the injured of the Labyrinth City with the skills and potions he had now.

Of course, he had no plan to use evil methods such as curses and other taboos. If he did, he was positive fiery calamity would come running on two legs and unleash a combination of flame and forehead pokes.

"If you go to the Labyrinth Suppression Forces, they can heal your lost limbs. I heard they even let you start a tab if you can't afford to pay up front." It didn't take much time for such rumors to spread throughout the Labyrinth City. A chance to heal grievous injuries and descend into the Labyrinth again was a tempting offer. When it became apparent that people who'd resigned themselves to their lot in life now had a chance to start again, the number of people who wanted to follow in their footsteps increased.

Denizens of the City who had long since given up and forgotten their desire to leave the slums regained their drive when they had their limbs back. Renewed, they took up their old swords and began venturing into the Labyrinth once again.

Another day had ended, and the sun was setting. The sky was the same deep red it always was at that time. Did the people of the City now see a bright future in the dusk, where before they'd only waited for darkness?

There was a labyrinth in this city.

A fearsome thing that had taken their limbs, their futures, and the lives of their comrades. It threatened their way of life, even now.

However, the people were now able to stand against it on their own two legs again. They believed a peaceful tomorrow would come after they weathered the battle.

CHAPTER 1

Red Dragon Subjugation

01

"Oh, come on! *Whyyy* have we come to the snow field again?!!" Edgan's cry reverberated across the sprawling, icy landscape. "Normally, if someone says, 'Edgan, I need you,' this isn't what they mean, you know? When someone says something like that, it means feeding each other the fruits of the autumn harvest and keeping each other warm on chilly nights! Siiieg!"

"It's all right, Edgan. If you catch a lot, the ladies will consider you reliable."

Edgan, as was so often the case, whined while Sieg gave him empty comfort. People often said that what happens twice will happen thrice, but who would have actually thought the adventurers would visit these frigid wastes for a third time?

How this came about was simple. Right when Sieg was asked to go to the Labyrinth for some harvesting, the door of Sunlight's Canopy had flown open with a bang, and Edgan had come bursting in.

"My beautiful amour! It is I, your poor servant of love! I've returned to the Labyrinth City!" he proclaimed as he intruded upon the store.

Such was the so-called Lost Child of Love. He'd returned from wherever he'd managed to wander off to, though Freyja had likely never noticed that he had gone anywhere at all.

"Ohh, it's been a while! Umm, err, uhh…ah! Edgan! Perfect timing. I actually think I need you for something!" The unnaturally long pause before remembering Edgan's name was a new level of cruelty for Freyja. Her golden eyes shone with an unusual light. Although she directed her gaze toward Edgan, she appeared to be looking right through him at something else.

"Master, that's not something worth searching through the Akashic records for…"

"Unbelievable… Using such a transcendent skill just to remember someone's name… I guess I shouldn't be surprised…"

Mariela watched her master and muttered in exasperation, while Sieg tried to deny what he was seeing but quickly gave up. Mariela had described this woman as being completely over-the-top in intelligence, personality, and actions, and Sieg already understood her better than he would have liked. The golden-eyed sage never held back; she used her full power even for something as trivial as remembering a name. It made her rather difficult to deal with at times.

However, poor Edgan—whose name Freyja had well and truly forgotten—was ecstatic at hearing the words *I need you.*

"Of course! If it's with you, I'll do anything!"

"Oh, actually, Sieg's the one who'll be going with you. I'm counting on you!"

"So cold! You're clearly my femme fatale!" Edgan used a phrase he'd clearly learned in the imperial capital.

"Hey, Sieg, what's a 'femme fatale'?"

"A woman someone is destined to be with, but who has a strong sense of danger around her. A devilish woman who invokes ruin."

"Ohhh. Master is cold to Edgan, but Edgan is also obsessed with her. It fits, I'd say."

"Yeah. Well, see you later, Mariela."

Mariela smiled, pleased with the thought that maybe she'd said something smart. Sieg said good-bye to her, then turned toward his lovesick friend.

"Let's go, Edgan."

"Right! Uh, so where are we going?"

"Fishing."

And that was how Edgan was roped into Sieg's errand and ended up in the stratum of snow and ice.

Accompanying the two was the entire regiment of the Black Iron Freight Corps, having been coerced into participating. Of course, this was because the Corps's new captain, Edgan, had told them to come, even though they should have been taking the day off in the Labyrinth City.

Had Captain Edgan's tyranny turned the Black Iron Freight Corps into an exploitative workplace?

"Shut up, Edgan. You'll scare the prey away."

"Indeed. Fishing is something to be done quietly." The other members' responses were colder than the raging wind.

The group was in the Labyrinth's thirty-third stratum, where Edgan's charges treated him in a manner that suited the mid-winter temperatures. This level was known as the Sea of Ice Floes. It sat one level below the floor where Edgan, Sieg, and Lynx had gathered aurora ice fruit in the past. Its defining characteristic was its sea of deathly cold, with a great many gigantic ice floes floating on it.

Although these were not true ice floes; they were really just large masses of ice floating in a conquered stratum, an enclosed space. There were no ocean currents or the like, so the ice developed steadily over time. Likely, the floating chunks had probably cracked, risen, and frozen in place again on countless occasions due to battles between monsters and adventurers. The great frozen chunks weren't all flat, either; many had protruding lumps of ice larger than people but smaller than hills. The thickness of the mostly flat piece of ice the group was currently positioned on depended on where one stood.

The members of the Black Iron Freight Corps had made holes in places where the ice underfoot was thinner, or they dangled their fishing lines off the edge of its floating mass. The adventurers passed the time doing as they pleased while they waited for a catch. At first glance, it might've looked like they were just relaxing.

Sometimes a dart-shaped fish—an epelfish—would jump from the water like an arrow. Even such a seemingly dangerous creature fell into the category of "recreational fishing" in this stratum.

"Heave-ho!"

Grandel used the pot lid in his hand to ward off an epelfish that had leaped at him, and Newie swiftly disposed of it as it flopped around on top of the ice. These ferocious fish flew out of the water toward animals on land to pierce and eat them, but they technically weren't monsters. That was why they left the bodies behind after they'd made their kill.

An epelfish was about the size of a cooking knife, with thick skin and few edible parts, but the parts that were edible were extremely delicious, making it a high-class catch. Its body was made of fatty white meat; in fact, the creature had too much fat when eaten raw, and people felt it was too rich. When boiled or roasted, however, the fat would ooze out and the fish lost its prized deliciousness. The best way to cook such a pesky morsel was to make it into fritters. If one deep-fried an epelfish without breading or batter, it proved difficult to get the temperature of the oil and the frying time just right to retain the perfect amount of fat. But when an epelfish was coated before being fried, even a chef's apprentice like Newie could cook it without much trouble.

Grandel, the gourmet, and Newie, the gourmand, couldn't overlook the chance at such a dish, and the pair had been industriously working to catch a number of fish for a while now.

As for the other slave, Nick, he seemed to have taken a great liking to the magical rotating and cutting tool the Corps had purchased to make holes in the ice, and he was diligently searching for areas thin enough to do so. The tool consisted of a cylindrical saw and a support, and if you fixed the support in a spot where you wanted to make a hole and activated it, the teeth of the saw rotated at high speed and sank into the ice. Once the tool reached the bottom, the ice could be pried loose like the stopper of a bottle being uncorked.

The healing magic user, Franz, and the man in charge of carriage maintenance, Donnino, enjoyed the leisurely task of fishing, dangling their lines and sipping the hot tea Yuric had brought.

Despite what one might have thought if they observed the group, the day's target wasn't epelfish. It was a transparent creature called a philoroilcus larva, which looked like a cross between a jellyfish and a fish. The bottom edge of a parasol-shaped section that spread out from its transparent body and the short, swaying tentacles were the parts reminiscent of a jellyfish. However, the area from about the middle of the parasol upward was constricted and bulged, making the creature vaguely resemble a fairy in a skirt. Its buoyant, drifting body was a beautiful sight.

Exactly how such a creature survived was still a mystery. Its name contained the word *larva* because when this creature was captured and raised, the parasol grew long and narrow, and the fish acquired the shape of a snake. Thus, the more immature form was dubbed a larval stage.

Incidentally, the diet of this strange, apparently unnatural creature seemed to change once it had assumed that long and thin stage, because the larvae the researchers were raising all died. As such, its forms beyond this one were still unknown. A philoroilcus larva had neither a mouth nor digestive organs; rather, the surface of its body absorbed magical power directly. So if one dangled a fishing line with a magical gem attached to it as bait through a hole in an ice floe, then a lucky angler might reel up a philoroilcus clinging to the gem.

However, only Franz and Donnino were enjoying this leisurely fishing style. Sieg moved between standing at the edge of the ice floe and posting himself at different holes, loosing arrows with strings tied to them at the philoroilcus that approached the dangling magical gems.

Despite the light refraction, currents, and overall resistance the water provided, Sieg could easily strike such slow-moving creatures, even with his Spirit Eye hidden behind an eye patch. He pierced several at once with one shot—extreme overkill, perhaps—but since Sieg was the only one seriously hunting the philoroilcus larvae, he had no time to take it easy.

All Edgan did was shout, making him the least helpful of any in the group. The aggressive epelfish reacted to his voice, flew from the water with a splash, and almost stabbed him. Unfortunately, this startled and chased away the philoroilcus larvae that had eaten the valuable magical gems.

Edgan was a complete and utter nuisance. Few would have minded if the pointed snouts of the epelfish had sewn his mouth shut—though the man quickly proved that he wasn't bordering on the edge of being an A-Rank adventurer for nothing. The Lost Child of Love cleanly sliced the epelfish that took aim at him into three pieces, and the bits tumbled down onto a platter that had been placed on the ice.

The group had made careful use of midgrade monster-warding potions for this excursion, such that the monsters that infested this stratum gave them a wide berth. For just about all of the adventurers, it might as well have just been a day off.

"Is this enough?"

While Edgan was busy not catching a single philoroilcus larva, Sieg had acquired all they needed. These larvae were an ingredient in the Ice Spirit's Protection special-grade potion. Ice Spirit's Protection produced a thin membrane of ice to protect against heat. Such a defense was mandatory for the hunting of the red dragon that dwelled on the fifty-sixth stratum.

With Sieg and Voyd participating, long-distance attacks and protection against the dragon's breath would be possible, meaning there was a proper chance of success in their mission to eradicate the red dragon. However, the stratum boss, the Walking Mountain of Fire, also awaited them there. Last time, Mariela hadn't been able to make special-grade potions, and Weishardt had protected them from the heat using magic. Now, the safety that an Ice Spirit's Protection potion would afford was far superior.

Sieg filled a large bottle with the philoroilcus larvae he'd caught, along with some crushed ice. Then he wrapped the bottle several times with cloth and stowed it in a bag. Ultimately, he was the one who did almost all the work.

After he considered it for a moment, though, Sieg realized that wasn't entirely the case. Nico had helped by cutting holes. He'd given Sieg more spots from which to shoot at his quarry and had made it easier for him to collect crushed ice. Grandel and the others had dealt with the epelfish so that he was able to focus on the philoroilcus larvae, and he was also thankful to Yuric for offering him tea. So really, the labor had been divided up. In its own way, it'd been a kind of teamwork.

The only exception was Edgan, who'd been yelling about love in the bitter-cold snow field for a while now.

"Hey, Edgan. We're done here. We have a lot of epelfish, too. Let's get going."

The hapless lover turned at the sound of Sieg's voice. His nose was red, perhaps from the cold, but curiously, the rest of his face was red, too.

"Siiieg, you got on Mariela's good side in nooo time after you two met, right? And you even live with those two under the same rooooof."

"Yuric, did you give him alcohol?"

"He didn't get anything from me."

Edgan was a lightweight when it came to alcohol. He got drunk quickly, and it showed clearly in his face and subsequently behavior. Sieg, seeing how plainly inebriated Edgan was, suspected Yuric had given the man some drink. Yuric, however, merely gave an exasperated reply as they made preparations to leave the stratum.

"This wasss! A preeesent from my beautiful honey! Yeeeah, she gave it to me!"

Surprisingly, the small bottle of alcohol Edgan held seemed to be one Freyja had started but not emptied. The foolish lover had managed to move past annoying and now just seemed pitiful: a strange accomplishment.

Sieg was unsure whether it'd be worth trying to talk to Edgan in this state. The other members of the Black Iron Freight Corps were content to pay him no mind and quickly continued preparing to depart.

"Ohh, I know! Century ice! I'll express my love with a huuuge block of ice!" Edgan shouted. He unsheathed his dual swords and began running toward a smallish, hill-sized iceberg a short distance away.

Sieg didn't know what kind of woman would be happy to receive ice as a gift. There was a certain alchemist pupil somewhere who would happily accept it as a material for her potions, but Sieg liked to think she was already spoken for.

"Raaaaah!" Edgan focused his attack on a single fracture point to break the ice. He drove his two swords into a spot near the middle of the block, just a hairsbreadth apart.

Crack.

Unfortunately, it wasn't the iceberg Edgan attacked that cracked, but rather the ice floe he was standing on.

"Edgan, run! It's going to—!!!" Sieg's cry of warning was drowned out by the thunderous sound of the ice giving way to the lover's weight.

The Black Iron Freight Corps, who'd gotten a head start on departure, were already in the safe zone near the stratum stairs, so they were free from harm. However, the ice floe between them and their leader—where Sieg stood—shook like a small boat in a storm, and the hunter barely kept his footing.

That was to say nothing of Edgan; if he hadn't been gripping the swords he'd thrust into the ice, he would have promptly been thrown into the sea and lost his life to the freezing cold.

"Hup, har!"

Edgan twisted his dual blades back and forth and wrenched them from the block of ice sinking into the sea, then kicked off to leap in Sieg's direction. Despite the damp, slippery footing and the shaking of the ice floe, he nimbly landed with only a slight wobble and with both swords at the ready. He glared at the spot where the ice floe had sunk.

All present beheld what gradually rose from the water's surface.

It would've probably looked like a snake if seen from far away. But the thing was so thick, even the arms of several adult men wouldn't have been able to encircle it completely. The creature's sickle-shaped neck was so gigantic that they had to crane their own necks back just to see it.

Most startling of all, however, was the creature's head.

The smooth tip at the end of the neck had nothing resembling eyes or a chin. Instead, it had what looked a pointed earthworm mouth. The strange head opened as if the skin was ripping, or as if it was being turned up from the inside and aimed to swallow the prey before it.

"Crap, it wasn't because of the ice breaking. It was because of that giant worm!"

The creature slowly raising its head from the sea was more of a worm than a snake. It had likely suffered a rude awakening at Edgan's attack. The hapless lover had probably survived only because of parts of the creature's body were still frozen, keeping its movements sluggish.

Doubtless, the creature sought prey with warm blood to fully revive itself. Its mouth descended toward Edgan, threatening to engulf him, but he lightly sidestepped and slashed at it with his dual swords right before leaping back.

"Shit, that didn't do anything!"

The worm's body was in a semifrozen state, as if below the thin skinlike surface the thing consisted entirely of fine pieces of ice instead of flesh or fat. If the enormous beast had bones or bodily fluids, none of the adventurers could perceive them. Because its entire body was like partially frozen jelly, it was easy to slice, but any cut closed as quickly as it was made, and the creature didn't seem to mind when it happened, either. It twisted its body to close the pustulant wound, which then froze over. As if unaware of both Edgan's dodge and its own injury, the worm plunged into the ice floe the man had been standing on until just a moment ago. The ice split, crumbling under the force of the great creature with another resounding boom, and the creature dove back into the sea.

"I'm the one it's after! Everyone get out of here while you still can!"

Though normally a shallow person, perhaps Edgan had inherited some of the dignity and responsibility that came with captainship of the Black Iron Freight Corps. To save his comrades and give them the time they needed to escape, Edgan focused his strength into his grip on his blades and prepared to confront the unfamiliar ice worm again.

How did the stalwart members of the Black Iron Freight Corps respond in the face of such a gallant and noble gesture?

"I'd do that even if ya didn't tell me to, y'know?" Yuric retorted, cold as ever.

"Ho, ho. Well then, we shall go on ahead. Newie, I'm looking forward to your epelfish cuisine." All Grandel could think about was food.

Meanwhile, Newie acted as if he hadn't heard Edgan and simply nodded.

"Get back before dinner," said Donnino curtly. "If you're late, we'll start without you. Nick, after you're done putting the baggage in the base, come join our celebration at the Yagu Drawbridge Pavilion."

Nick nodded.

"Edgan, be sure to finish it off before you return so it doesn't cause trouble for other adventurers." Franz's comment served as the finishing blow.

"Whaaaaaaa?! You guys are so cruel!" Edgan shouted at his quickly fleeing companions, who seemed content not to give a second thought to the worm. Sieg found himself unsure whether he should go back with the Black Iron Freight Corps or wait for Edgan.

"Siiiiiiiieg! Don't leave! Don't leaaaaaave! We're friends, right?!"

"...Fine. Hurry and clean up that giant thing, Edgan. It's approaching from your rear."

"'F-fine'?! I told you... I can't...do anything...to it!"

The ice creature was enormous, and although Edgan deftly jumped from floe to floe as he attacked, it seemed each blow was for naught.

"Hey! Sieg! Let's team up! Just help me a tiny bit!"

The ice worm had emerged from the sea again, and it raised its head, towering over the ice field like a huge tree. Edgan begged for Sieg's help as he clung to the terrible creature. The hapless adventurer then nimbly climbed the length of the worm as he attacked it again and again. One had to admit, Edgan was nothing if not dexterous. The onlookers likened him to a new kind of monkey. Or perhaps, given that he was clinging to chunks of ice, a yeti.

"I could shoot my bow once as cover fire, but..."

Sieg was surprisingly calm about the whole situation as well. He watched Edgan's tree-climbing—er, battle—as if he wanted to say "What am I going to do with you?"

It was clear from the reaction of the Black Iron Freight Corps, who had gone home, that the ice worm was a foe they believed Edgan could defeat by himself. Sure, the fiend was gargantuan, and attacks weren't particularly effective, but that was all. Things like a large size and a resistance to attacks were common characteristics of a strong monster. That was not to suggest that it was an opponent novice adventurers could take down, however. In terms of rank, the worm was probably around B. Perhaps A, if you factored in the environment. A freezing sea and unstable footing made for difficult terrain.

This stratum had enough ice floes that tumbling into the water wasn't too much of a problem at least. Plus, considering Edgan was on the higher end of B Rank, the worm's movements were relatively slow. What was more, it seemed capable of only physical attacks. Edgan could escape at any time if he wanted to. However, even if this was the Labyrinth, leaving such a giant monster alive and well could prove problematic for someone else in the future. It was just good manners to send caught monsters back to the ley line. Since Edgan had gone out of his way to stab and wake the frozen, sleeping worm, he had the responsibility to get his act together and bring down the great beast. Sieg was ready to step in if he truly had to, but it was obvious Edgan wasn't actually trying all that hard.

"Sieg! Hey! Come on!"

Edgan, abandoned by his comrades in the Black Iron Freight Corps, developed Lonely Man Syndrome and completely neglected his attacking, choosing instead to call for Sieg with all his might. At this rate, Sieg didn't know how long it would be until the worm was defeated.

It wasn't that he thought Edgan was incapable, but the planned epelfish cuisine party at the Yagu Drawbridge Pavilion was likely to end while the foolhardy lover took his time making an ass of himself.

Freyja, who was always causing trouble for Mariela and Sieg, had thrust Edgan upon the hunter… Though, knowing Edgan, he likely would've happily volunteered himself anyway. However, Sieg's plan to spend time with Mariela eating epelfish would be ruined if he didn't step in and end things quickly.

"I guess I don't have a choice."

Sieg assumed a stance with his bow and focused his awareness on the Spirit Eye hidden under his eye patch. He was content not to use the eye to increase his attack power against the worm—he still thought it was Edgan's job to ultimately kill the thing, after all. But if Sieg found a weak point, he could probably shorten the time needed to bring the creature down.

"There. Is that why it woke up?"

Although he found just such a vulnerable spot by using his Spirit Eye, that didn't mean he physically saw it. It was more like Sieg simply somehow understood where it was. The sensation was like walking along a dark road at night, coming upon a crossroads, and somehow sensing which path was dangerous. Most likely, the place where Sieg sensed the worm's core was exactly the same spot Edgan had pierced with his swords when it had been sleeping in the ice.

"Edgan, its vitals are in the place you hit before! That's why it woke up even though it was frozen!"

"Easy for you to saaay. This thing keeps moviiing. And my dual swords are tiiiny compared to iiit."

Even though Sieg had gone through the trouble of spotting a weak point, Lonely Man Edgan merely gave excuses while glancing back at his friend. He repeatedly stabbed at the thing here and there to virtually no effect. Suffering the whiny excuses of a grown man was getting a bit irritating to Sieg.

"Rgh." This was inconvenient for the hunter. At this rate, the party was going to end without him. Even if Sieg didn't use his Spirit Eye, it would be possible for him to defeat an ice worm with the mythril sword at his waist, but thanks to Edgan's "but, but, buts," Sieg had no inclination whatsoever to join the battle. His sword was now nothing more than a decoration.

Still, Sieg needed this to wrap up quickly. After desperately racking his brain, he turned toward the other man.

"Edgan! Lady Frey said she wanted to warm up together when you got back!"

With alcohol, of course.

However, inside Erotigan's brain, swimming in alcohol and drowning in love, a field of neon-pink flowers—no, a love garden and a paradise of pleasure were locked in a wrestling match and writhing around.

"What?! What did you saaaAAAaaay?! I'm! Going! Right nooooooow!" Edgan shouted without taking a breath and started running. His eyes had a wild gleam in them now, and he was brimming with determination.

"I'll consign this lump of ice to oblivion!" he cried, then chanted to use a skill that even Sieg had never seen before:

"My left arm is a pedestal for flames, my right arm a pedestal for thunder. Abide in me! Dual Sword Elements!"

"Wha...?! Two elements at once?!"

Where had Edgan's useless and defeated attitude gone? As though he were an awakened hero, Edgan charged his left sword with flames and his right with lightning. The adventurer dashed up the towering ice worm, an incline so steep it was nearly a sheer vertical drop.

The act itself of putting magic in a weapon wasn't difficult, and adventurers who were at least at intermediate level could put that to practical use by sending the magic forth from the weapon. However, handling two elements at once wasn't easy. The technique was just barely doable through a combination of innate talent, substantial power of concentration, and high skill. Perhaps the best indication of just how unusual a scene was unfolding...

"Ohh?"

...was Sieg's own exclamation of surprise.

"Rrah!"

Edgan drove the blazing sword in his left hand deep into the wound he'd first inflicted on the monster, a little under the head, where the neck or throat might've been were the monster a snake. The sword, wreathed in flame that burned despite the cold body of the worm, slowly and steadily melted the creature's flesh as Edgan buried the weapon to the hilt. However, this was likely little more than a needle prick to such an enormous worm. The tip of the blazing sword had no hope of reaching the worm's core. But then...

"This is the end for you!"

...Edgan released the fiery sword from his left hand, twisted his body around in one full rotation for momentum, and struck the hilt of the buried blade with the lightning sword in his right hand.

The blazing sword pierced the worm even deeper, and an electric shock traveled down its blade and through to the monster's core.

The worm, now without a core, writhed in its death throes. Its open mouth pointed straight up as if it was about to devour the heavens, or perhaps was merely seeking air, then turned up from the inside and split into four. To Sieg, who watched the spectacle from a safe distance, the monster formed the vaguest shape of a flower.

The worm trembled slightly, then sank into the sea as if withering from its foundation upward.

"Now let's go, Sieg. Freyja's waiting for me." Edgan emerged from the surrounding frost with the hazy spray of water from the worm's fall behind him. With the way he calmly returned his dual swords to their sheaths and the confident, nonchalant smile on his face, he might have won a few hearts. That was, if they could ignore the way he was walking. It made him look like someone who needed to get to a restroom right that second.

"Uh, yeah. Let's go. What on earth could that worm have been?"

Sieg joined Edgan, and the two made their way toward the stratum stairs. Quite suddenly, an answer came from a most unexpected source.

"That was a full-grown philoroilcus."

"Freyja!" Edgan said with a gasp. "Did you really come here to meet me?!"

With timing that could only have meant she'd been watching

them, Mariela's master appeared from the stratum stairs and revealed the worm's true nature. For some reason, Mariela was there, too.

Edgan rushed over to Freyja and said, "Please warm my freezing heart and bodyyy."

"Hmm? You're cold? Here, **Fire!**" she replied, likely reducing his heart to cinders more than anything else.

Leaving poor Edgan behind, Freyja led Mariela and Sieg toward the adult philoroilcus, which lay dead atop an ice floe.

"The philoroilcus is an unusual creature. Out of trillions of sporophytes, it's possible not even a single one will reach the adult stage. At the larva stage, they only absorb magical power—they don't start feeding on prey until early adulthood. After that, they grow through the middle adult stage, the late adult stage, and finally the mature adult stage, all over the course of several decades. Their habitat steadily moves deeper into the ocean as they get older.

"Few people know about this form because it only returns to the sea's surface to spawn. Well, it's closer to producing sporophytes than spawning. They reproduce asexually. In a real ocean, emerging from the depths and generating offspring usually kills the parent. But since this is a labyrinth, the water isn't as deep, and this one survived because it froze and entered a state of suspended animation before it could die."

As Freyja unloaded her extensive knowledge, Mariela trotted behind her, saying things like "Whoaaa, it's so cold."

The sight of her in fluffy winter clothes reminded Sieg of the era of Chubby-ela, when the young alchemist had gained weight. Mariela looked positively lovely to him, and Sieg accompanied the two women while making sure that Mariela didn't take a tumble.

"Here, Mariela. Use *Crystallize Medicine* on its body fluids."

At her master's prompting, the alchemist gingerly touched the philoroilcus.

"But this is the first time I've... Huh? This is...! But it's extremely dilute."

"That's right. This thing is a dragon, though not much of one. Only a philoroilcus that acquires a dragon element has that one-in-a-trillion chance of surviving. Even the lowest members of dragonkind are strong, so this thing's blood is a thousand times more dilute than the blood of a low-ranking earth dragon, right? These guys get pretty huge, and most of their insides are fluid, so there's a lot of the stuff. But usually when one of these guys procreates, that element vanishes from its body in the process. With *Crystallize Medicine*, you can extract medicinal crystals of water dragon blood from this big thing. There won't be any other opportunities to get water dragon blood this easily, so hop to it, Mariela. Treat it like earth dragon blood."

"Okay, Master."

After Mariela's *Crystallize Medicine* removed the dragon element from the carcass, the philoroilcus corpse transformed into small ice beads that gently flowed into the frigid sea.

If viewed from underwater, the fragments that sank into the dark ocean might have looked like powdery snow. Philoroilcus larvae drifted gently to shallow spots in the water to absorb the magical power dwelling in the corpse. The little things looked like a group of sea sprites in a beautiful dance.

Surely this was the same as the natural process that befell a mature philoroilcus in the wild. It would die, having expended all its energy; then its body would nourish the offspring.

"Well, let's head home right away and warm up! Hey, you too, Edgan!"

As soon as Mariela was done using *Crystallize Medicine*, Freyja urged everyone not to stay longer than they needed to. After all, if they didn't hurry back soon, all the epelfish fritters would be eaten.

Mariela obtained fewer dragon blood medicinal crystals from the giant worm creature than she would have from a single earth dragon. The young alchemist gazed at the little blue fragments, which resembled the ice floes in the stratum they had come from. Then she carefully deposited the vial of crystals in the pouch at her waist.

"Oh, right. There are still philoroilcuses sleeping here, and all of them should be exterminated. You can start tomorrow. It should hardly be a problem for someone who so skillfully struck one's weak point and woke it up. I'm counting on you, Edgan."

After Freyja's merciless request, the Black Iron Freight Corps enjoyed an extended holiday in the Labyrinth City while Edgan began daily excursions that froze his body and soul to the bone. Sieg participated too, of course, though only after much begging from the hapless lover.

Edgan continued to awaken and bring down philoroilcuses, creatures that were—despite being the lowest in the order—technically a kind of dragon. He was promoted to A Rank in recognition of his service.

"I…want love more than I want A Rank…," he muttered with a distant look. As usual, Sieg comforted him with a baseless claim: "A-Rankers are popular!"

02

"All riiight, let's make Ice Spirit's Protection!"

It was morning, and Mariela had begun making potions in the second-floor atelier of Sunlight's Canopy. Since Ice Spirit's Protection took time to make, today was bit of a break from Mariela's potion-making in the room set up for her at the Forces' base. It might have been the first relaxing day off in a while for Mitchell and his crew, too, as Freyja was always taking advantage of them. However, it was not a day off for Sieg and Edgan, who were busy hunting philoroilcuses again.

Two large pails had been placed in Mariela's atelier: one contained philoroilcus larvae, and the other contained century ice they'd taken the opportunity to collect while on the freezing sea of the Labyrinth's thirty-third floor the other day. In addition, plates with aurora ice fruit, magical gems of ice, and ley-line shards had been set out. There was also some funnel-like glass equipment, giving the impression that perhaps Mariela was going to start cooking. The beachy scent wafting from the philoroilcus larvae made Freyja restless. She looked like she wanted to drink.

Ignoring her master, Mariela focused on the materials. Usually, she would have completed the processing of the ley-line shards in advance, but many of these materials would melt or spoil after being taken out of the magical tool for freezing. As such, Mariela had to complete their processing first.

Incidentally, the alchemist was using glass equipment this time. Freyja had been the one to insist that Mariela use it, which was odd for the woman who typically made Mariela do everything with alchemy skills alone. The equipment was made up of three deep funnels stacked on top of one another and connected vertically. The side that came in contact with the open air had a hollow dual structure, apparently to help keep the inner temperature constant. According to Freyja, the way heat transferred varied depending on the object. This tool's structure created several layers of air and supposedly slowed the loss of heat.

Padding had been lightly stuffed into the funnel openings so the materials wouldn't fall through. Mariela put aurora ice fruit, coarsely crushed and still frozen, in the lower layer and filled the middle section with equally coarsely crushed magical gems of ice. The top layer contained century ice. The ice had been broken up just enough to fit into the equipment and no further.

Plink, plunk.

Drops from the slowly melting century ice dripped into the layer with the magical gem fragments, permeating them and spreading out. Those fragments then dropped into the layer with the aurora ice fruit. The cold, newly melted drops of water slowly dissolved the ice fruit, mixing with the juice of the fruit before dropping into a container placed under the bottom layer of the glass device.

Plink, plunk.

The work required a lot of patience, though perhaps *work* wasn't the right word for it. After setting the materials in place, all Mariela had to do was add century ice at fixed intervals and keep one eye on the whole setup.

"Master, if the ice is melted slowly, wouldn't it have been better to control the temperature in a Transmutation Vessel? Do the materials have to melt slowly like this? I can't tell the extraction temperature or speed. Can't it be extracted all at once after the ice melts?"

"Are you saying it doesn't matter how the ice melts? You don't get it, do you, Mariela? This ice was frozen for over a hundred years. An entire century has been gathered in the crystals of that ice. That's why you let it melt slowly and naturally like this," Freyja answered while clinking her own ice as it bobbed in a cup of booze.

"Wha—? Time melted into the ice?!"

"Nah, it was just a metaphor. You've got no sense of playfulness, Mariela."

Freyja swirled the contents of her glass as she watched the century ice slowly melt and permeate first the magical gems, then the aurora ice fruit.

"Wait, what are you drinkiiing?! When did you get that?!"

"Hey, the philoroilcus larvae will melt if you look away."

"I really can't take my eyes off you for a second…"

Freyja leisurely sipped her alcohol as she watched the alchemical setup. Mariela left her master as she was and faced the pail containing the philoroilcus larvae. Just as Freyja had said, those larvae would melt into a gooey liquid if they weren't kept cold.

The only part of a philoroilcus larva's body used as a material for Ice Spirit's Protection was a pale pink portion. The larva, strangely, had no bones, muscles, or internal organs. Its body was squishy, not unlike jelly, except for the firmer center. This harder portion of the creature was a dull pinkish color. Perhaps that center bit might've been what became the philoroilcus's core when one matured.

Mariela deftly prepared the many larvae and transferred their cores to a separate container.

The half-frozen larvae were extremely cold to the touch, and Mariela's hands turned red while she was handling them, as if she'd gotten frostbite.

"Cooold..." Mariela exhaled on her hands and rubbed them together.

"You still get frostbite pretty easily, huh? Lemme see those," Freyja said, nostalgia in her voice, then beckoned Mariela.

When Mariela approached Freyja and held out her hands, Freyja took them in both of hers and massaged the young alchemist's fingers, which were puffy from slowed circulation.

"Your hands are as warm as ever, Master."

When Mariela was young and still at the orphanage, she would get frostbite during the winter, which made kitchen work extremely painful. Every time her hands had swelled from the cold, Freyja had massaged them like this. Maybe she just wanted to touch the child's puffy hands, but Freyja's hands were very warm, and when she rubbed Mariela's like this, the frostbite curiously vanished quite quickly. A low-grade potion could've cured the frostbite in an instant. However...

That's...not the case, is it?

Mariela pondered as she gazed at her hands, now warm thanks to her master. The century ice next to Mariela dripped very slowly as it melted, and she somehow felt that she understood why her master didn't let her quickly process it using alchemy skills.

If Mariela had slowly heated the philoroilcus larvae's cores in a Transmutation Vessel, they would've lost their shape and taken on a gooey consistency. If she added about half the cores' volume's worth of water infused with Drops of Life, it would stay a liquid even at room temperature.

After that, she would just have to mix the extract with century ice and the base material made from processing ley-line shards, but Mariela felt it would still take time for the century ice to completely melt after that was done.

"Sieg and the others are probably cold. Today I'll cook some stew, even if it takes a while to make."

Surely a soup with slow-cooked meat that melted in the mouth would warm their chilled bodies.

Mariela divided the morning between preparing the ingredients for the stew in the kitchen on the first floor, taking century ice and aurora ice fruit from the magical tool in the cellar and replenishing their supplies in the device in the atelier, and making a short appearance in Sunlight's Canopy.

Ice Spirit's Protection might actually be easy to make...for a special-grade potion, Mariela thought as she watched the melted ice drip.

Aurora ice fruit was also a required ingredient for polymorph potions. Last time, it had come from the thirty-second stratum, but this time, Mariela was able to use the fruit she grew in the magical tool in the cellar. She needed a lot more of it now than she had for the polymorph potions, but that wasn't an issue since she'd gotten carried away and grown a large quantity.

Century ice, as its name suggested, was ice that had been frozen for a hundred years, and since it had been two hundred since the Labyrinth first formed, ice found there met the requirements. Mariela and the others had taken the opportunity to collect it when they'd gathered the philoroilcus larvae.

The magical gems from monsters that dwelled on the thirty-second and thirty-third strata known as frost trolls—living embodiments of cold—filled the requirement for ice-elemental magical gems. Mariela had been able to obtain these easily rather easily by putting in a request for them at the Adventurers Guild.

What made the Ice Spirit's Protection potion special-grade was the inclusion of ley-line shards, but obtaining the other materials was unusually easy for a concoction of that rank. Holy water was also easy to make for a mid-grade potion, so perhaps alchemical brews that bestowed magical effects rather than healing their imbibers were easier to make compared with the rest of the formulas among their respective ranks.

Mariela had heard that Sieg would be using this potion and participating in the next Labyrinth Suppression Forces subjugation. The fifty-sixth stratum of the Labyrinth, where Sieg and the others would be heading, was a volcano stratum where a fire-breathing red dragon lived.

Please let this potion protect Sieg, Mariela prayed to the drip-dripping water.

Plink, plunk.

The sun was still high, but the century ice hadn't finished melting. It wasn't yet time to head out to the Labyrinth to use *Crystallize Medicine* on the water dragon blood from the philoroilcuses, either.

Plink, plunk.

Perhaps Freyja had gotten tired of watching the century ice melt, because she seemed to be teaching some useless thing or other to the children who'd come by Sunlight's Canopy after school.

Mariela retrieved a largeish piece of monster leather and

several magical gems and minerals from a corner of the atelier. The leather had been processed like parchment so it could be written on, and she crushed the magical gems and minerals and mixed them into ink.

Prayers and wishes were useless if nothing carried them. No matter how much Mariela felt something in her heart, that alone wasn't enough to help Sieg. The least she could do was use a magic circle to put magical power into her wishes and hopes to make them manifest.

Mariela dripped her blood into a dish she'd put the custom ink in. By adding blood, one could charge a magic circle itself with power. However, the ability to invoke such a magical circle was limited to the person the blood belonged to.

That would hardly be a problem for this particular circle, because activating it required an enormous amount of magical power. Only someone with an absurd capacity, like Mariela, could manage such a task.

Mariela had also been told the strategy for subjugating the red dragon. The plan was for the group to slip through the breath of the dragon that flew in the sky; then Sieg would use his bow to pierce the dragon's wings.

The fifty-sixth stratum of the Labyrinth was a place of scorching heat, where lava spurted everywhere. Ever since the previous subjugation attempt, the red dragon had been keeping constant guard around the stratum entrance. If the great creature caught sight of anything, it spewed its fiery breath. Even if you skillfully avoided its first attack and managed to come within range of it, the pools of lava everywhere made maneuvering extremely dangerous. Moving through the stratum was difficult, and there was almost nowhere to hide.

No matter how many potions of Ice Spirit's Protection the incursion group had, was it possible to successfully shoot with a bow while avoiding the dragon's breath *and* dealing with such an unforgiving environment? A-Rank adventurers had very high physical abilities—even their running speed far outclassed that of someone like Mariela—but no A-Ranker could rival the speed of a dragon flying overhead.

That was exactly why the young alchemist planned to use this magic circle.

It was a parting gift from her master that Mariela had received a little over two hundred years ago, after Freyja had made her complete the Magic Circle of Suspended Animation. Back then, the young alchemist had whined in anger, "When am I gonna use a magic circle like this?! Master only Imprinted it to knock me out! Grr!" Now, however, the girl felt that surely her master had Imprinted it in preparation for this day.

If I asked her, she'd probably dodge the question, though.

Plink, plunk.

The ice that had been frozen for a hundred years continued to melt.

Please let Sieg come home safely.

Mariela's efforts with the enchanted array would give that wish a tangible form. As she listened to the sound of the century ice slowly warming and dripping, Mariela patiently and carefully drew the magic circle.

03

This morning was the same as every other in the Labyrinth City. Peaceful daybreak air mingled with the smell of newly baked bread rising from the bakeries, and all around, houses stirred with life. The animals in the section of the city where yagus and livestock were kept had woken even earlier and were clamoring to be fed.

In the residential parts of town, more dense with people, the morning was about as quiet as the boisterous birds would let it be. Even so, one could feel the radiating life of the City just from observing the early activities of its residents. The aromatic scents of meat cooking for breakfast, or perhaps for boxed lunches, coupled with the smell of coffee wafted from windows opened to let fresh air in.

As the sun rose little by little, the early hours of the day grew noisier.

Adventurers eager to earn as much money as possible headed quickly for the Labyrinth while gnawing on large pieces of bread, and stalls catering to those adventurers by selling smoke bombs, monster-warding incense, and portable meals were opening one after another. Among them were shops that dealt in low-grade potions, so that even at such early hours, adventurers could enter the Labyrinth with magical concoctions.

The retail sale of low-grade potions had begun a little while after the conclusion of the first attempt to put them on the market. The merchants carrying them were chemists who held contracts with the Merchants Guild for delivery of medicinal herbs for use in potions, at or above a fixed quantity. Since the wholesale price, selling price, and sales quantity of potions had been uniformly established at this stage, the chemists were only able to make a fixed profit. However, the ability for the people in the City to buy low-grade potions at the same apothecaries they had already been using gave them a sense of security. Knowing that they could obtain potions at any time was comforting for many adventurers. What was more, the system kept apothecaries from losing the customers they'd had up to that point, and the businesses were able to take the opportunity to sell goods such as smoke bombs and incense as well.

Most adventurers of mid-rank or above earned a steady income and were already on their way to the Labyrinth around the time most of the stalls were open. They were after the mid-grade potions being sold within the great subterranean maze. Most of them had healing magic users in their parties, but mid-grade potions only made it that much safer to go hunting.

Today, the area around the Labyrinth entrance was just a little more rambunctious than usual.

"What, really? We can get high-grade potions?"

"Apparently, it's one per person, first come, first served."

"How much?"

"One large silver coin. Tch. I don't have that much on me. Gotta rush home to get it."

To the public, this was a "trial sale." But in fact, it was a measure to minimize casualties in the unlikely event the red dragon subjugation failed.

*   *   *

"Sieg…come back safely."

"Of course. Mariela, take good care of this eye patch for me."

Mariela accepted the eye patch from Sieg and carefully deposited it in her bag. Lynx had given it to Sieg as a present, and he cherished the thing, along with the short sword Lynx had lent him, which he would never be able to return.

The pair stood together in the fifty-fourth stratum, a series of ocean caverns once controlled by the Sea-Floating Pillar.

Although Sieg had removed his eye patch and was looking around with his Spirit Eye, only here and there did he see the light of extremely small, weak spirits floating upward. They didn't appear en masse, as he'd witnessed them in Sunlight's Canopy.

"The energy overflowing from the ley line nourishes the spirits. They feel ill at ease here because the Labyrinth devours that energy. In this city, they are weak, and there aren't many of them left." Freyja spoke as if to no one particular while she dipped her finger into one of the nearby lights. Mariela's master had once said that spirit magic couldn't be used in the Labyrinth because the power of the spirits was so weak, and the frail state of the little things that Sieg saw through his Spirit Eye supported that explanation.

However, it was doubtful that Freyja, known even two hundred years later as the Sage of Calamity, was powerless in the Labyrinth, even if it was true that she wasn't able to use spirit magic in its depths. Or rather, Mariela couldn't imagine her master so defenseless in any situation.

Back when Leonhardt and Weishardt had asked for Freyja's cooperation, she'd said, "Weishardt would be more helpful." In other words, even without spirit magic, Freyja had probably been hinting that she could use A Rank–equivalent magic, the same as Weishardt. Freyja had insisted that Mariela be nearby for the red dragon subjugation, even offering to protect the alchemist herself. Perhaps wary of the sage's own power, Leonhardt and Weishardt did not risk barring Mariela from accompanying them to the fifty-fourth stratum.

Other than Mariela, Sieg, and Freyja, the only people there were Leonhardt, Weishardt, Mitchell, and several escorts who knew Mariela was an alchemist. The other members of the red dragon subjugation group had gone ahead to the fifty-fifth stratum and were awaiting orders.

Mariela hadn't come this deep into the Labyrinth just to see Sieg off. The young alchemist produced both Ice Spirit's Protection potions and the magic circle she'd finished, and she spread them out in front of Sieg.

Please protect him. The girl had put all the magical power she had into the magic circle.

The array incarnated a spirit and allowed it to manifest until it exhausted the supply of magical power put into it. This was the seal that Freyja had Imprinted on Mariela after the young alchemist completed the Magic Circle of Suspended Animation two hundred years ago.

The magic circle served to give a spirit a physical form, albeit a transient one. Although not as complex as the Magic Circle of Suspended Animation, it was still quite an advanced array. However, there were difficulties beyond just the complexity of the magic circle itself: In order to activate the seal's power, you had to pour an enormous amount of magical power into it. Enough for an incarnation, in fact. Even if you successfully activated the circle and summoned a spirit, the spirit would remain only until the supplied magical power ran out. Taking the rank and the physical abilities given to the spirit into account, such an incarnation might not last even two hours. That was even factoring in that Mariela had poured her massive stores of magical power into the thing twice: once when she'd drawn the circle and again when she'd activated it. This short time limit was why Mariela had come all the way to this stratum.

To complicate matters, the magic circle couldn't manifest just any spirit. It needed to be one with a connection to the person activating the magic circle, and it wouldn't respond if it wasn't the kind of spirit that regularly lent its power when called upon.

Only one such spirit had always freely helped Mariela. Or perhaps it did so—even going so far as to give her a ring once—because Sieg was with her, not because of Mariela herself. However, that was precisely the reason why Mariela thought the spirit would help.

"Mariela, call to mind what you want it to do, what form you want it to take," Freyja instructed.

I want it to help Sieg. There's a scary dragon flying and breathing fire from the sky in the place he's going. So if he's in danger, I want it to take him and run. Like the raptor that took me on its back and escaped when we faced the horrible death lizards.

When that image solidified, she felt a click, as if it was the key that would open the magic circle. Mariela poured all the magical power she had into the circle and summoned the spirit.

"Come forth, spirit of flames, salamander!"

The ring on Mariela's middle finger sparkled, and the magic circle erupted in fire. The grand, towering blaze cast a strong light. Its perimeter burned yellow and red, but the center was a mass of dazzling white light. A tremendous amount of energy was clearly gathered there. It looked hotter than anything most had seen in their lives. Surprisingly, the heat wasn't a burning intensity, but rather a gentle warmth. The kind that would protect people from monsters and beasts in a forest at night.

The billowing pillar of fire shrank to a size only slightly larger than a human. The change in size did not alter the fire's warmth. As the flame took form, a raptor emerged, shining white-yellow like steel heated at a temperature of over a thousand degrees.

Upon closer inspection, not just the beast's color, but its eyes, its toes, and the tip of its tail differed from those of a normal beast. The strange creature resembled a salamander that had assumed the shape of a large raptor.

From Mariela's point of view, the conjured creature appeared quite powerful. Having exhausted so much magic energy, the young alchemist now clung to consciousness by a thread. She managed a smile from the joy of successfully executing the technique as she looked at Sieg and the salamander.

"Mr. Salamander, thank you for coming! Please prot—"

"Grar! Rar rar rar!"

Before Mariela finished speaking, the salamander nestled up to Sieg. Already quite feisty, the summoned creature wagged its tail as though it were a dog. Since the tail was so long, the centrifugal force was whipping its whole body around.

"Whoa, calm down. Whoa, boy."

Although the hunter successfully soothed the salamander, the tip of its tail still swayed in delight, and the odd creature seemed very happy to let Sieg ride it.

When a member of the Labyrinth Suppression Forces approached to put a saddle on the creature, it growled and bared its teeth threateningly, appearing quite feral. After Sieg scolded it, however, the salamander became more or less obedient, but it still wouldn't let anyone else touch it—meaning Sieg was forced to saddle the beast himself.

"Lady Sage, what on earth is that?" Weishardt asked Freyja after observing the summoning of the salamander from a distance.

"Ahh, that's a magic circle I drew that gives form to a spirit for a fixed period of time. Making it that big eats up an absurd amount of magical power. You can only call a spirit you have a connection with. What's more, if the summoner doesn't have an intimidating air or a dominating power of will, the conjured spirit ends up acting a bit wild."

"I see..."

Leonhardt and Weishardt had lit up when a creature they first believed was a perfect cavalry animal had appeared from within the flames, but the brothers' hopes were quickly dashed. The instant they saw the salamander's wild behavior, Leonhardt and Weishardt deigned it unsuitable for use in battle on a large scale. Weishardt, of course, showed no emotion, but it was clear the two siblings were thinking the same thing. When he was next to his brother, Leonhardt, Weishardt's expressionless face made the two of them all the more amusing.

Other than saying she was the one who had drawn the magic circle, Freyja had been entirely truthful. Spirits did what they liked by nature. As such, they wouldn't behave like properly trained animals. If a spirit was given physical form, it simply frolicked about however it wished unless the summoner exerted powerful control over it. Everything in the world was curious and fun to the mysterious creatures, and they enjoyed themselves to the utmost whenever they could, not unlike a kitten or puppy. Whether they could be summoned in the form of a trained, full-grown creature depended on the nature of the one who summoned them.

Mariela didn't exhibit a fraction of any sort of dominance, even over Sieg, whose will had once been bound to hers. It would've been impossible for Mariela to control the likes of a spirit. That was why the salamander had manifested in its natural, carefree state.

Sieg had the Spirit Eye, and the spirits loved him unconditionally, so even Mariela's wild salamander wasn't likely to give him any trouble, but to normal humans, the spirit was sure to prove far more meddlesome than it was worth.

"Lady Sage, is that magic circle something I can use?" Weishardt asked.

To which Freyja responded, "I'll teach you once there's a spirit you're friends with."

A question like that was the exact reason Freyja pretended to be the one who had drawn the magic circle. Spirits wouldn't help someone who wanted to use the magic circle—to use the spirits themselves—like a tool.

Weishardt, understanding the true meaning behind the answer, simply replied with "I see," nodding regretfully.

"Hey, Mr. Salamander! Make sure you protect Sieg!"

"Grar! Grar!"

"One 'yes' is enough!"

"Grar!"

Although they shouldn't have been able to communicate, Mariela appeared to be conversing with the salamander to a very convincing degree. The young alchemist had put plenty of magical power into her wish for the fiery creature to protect Sieg in order to make sure the spirit would manifest. Perhaps her wish was so strong that some of it had been imparted to the salamander in raptor form.

"Well, I'm off."

"Okay. Come back safe!"

Mariela smiled and waved, and Sieg responded in kind. The salamander, trotting alongside the hunter, also waved the tip of its tail as if to say "See you."

I'm glad I could see him off with a smile…, Mariela thought as she waved to Sieg and his unusual companion. The young alchemist watched as Sieg descended into a place of extreme danger. In truth, Mariela had been on the verge of tears until just a moment ago. Even now, she was painfully worried about Sieg. The red dragon he was off to fight was dozens of times stronger than those death lizards had been. When Mariela thought about the day they'd lost Lynx, she grew terrified and very nearly started to cry.

"Graaar, graaar."

The salamander swayed from side to side as it made a great effort to descend the stairs. A raptor's two back legs were well developed, but the front ones were considerably shorter. When it ran at high speeds, it raised its tail and lowered its head; in other words, it looked like it was going to pitch forward. It wouldn't, of course, but if such an animal tried to go down stairs in that kind of posture…

"Graaar!"

Tumble-tumble-tumble-thud.

Falling would be inevitable.

"…Are they really gonna be okay?"

"They'll be fiiine."

Mariela's source of worry had changed entirely, thanks to the salamander's foolishness.

"All right, Mariela. Let's get back to Sunlight's Canopy. That way, Sieg can fight without any concern."

"Okay, Master."

Mitchell and the handful of other escorts accompanied Mariela and Freyja as they climbed the stratum stairs. Meanwhile, Sieg, in a fluster, rushed after the fallen salamander.

Thanks to the summoned spirit, Mariela and Sieg had parted feeling that today was nothing more than a routine hunting trip.

The salamander tumbled all the way down to the fifty-fifth stratum, where the other subjugation members were waiting. The spirit slid to a halt, landing next to Leonhardt, who had just alighted himself. Sieg met the man's eyes and felt an unease take hold of him.

In today's subjugation, Sieg would be the only one on a mount. Even Leonhardt's splendid horse couldn't withstand the scorching-hot ground of the fifty-sixth stratum. Sieg was likely the lowest present in terms of both social position and adventurer rank. Although he'd been a penal laborer under false charges, his former status as a debt laborer was legitimate, and he'd only just recently reached A Rank.

Feeling awkward riding a mount in flagrant disregard for the higher-ranked members of the incursion, Sieg indicated the salamander to Leonhardt. "Your Excellency. If it pleases you, I would offer this salamander for you to ride."

"No, that's your mount. It's essential to the operation. No need to force yourself to adhere to convention. More important, it seems quite attached to you."

"Graaar."

Leonhardt gently declined Sieg's suggestion as he glanced at the salamander, which had quickly recovered from its fall and was now rubbing its head into Sieg's hand.

"Yes, sir. Thank you very much."

What a generous person, Sieg thought. He bowed and also pushed on the salamander's head to tell it to bow, too. Clearly, the salamander just thought it was getting its head stroked, though, and trilled happily.

"...Brother, about the magic circle that manifests spirits..." Weishardt spoke to Leonhardt quietly enough that no one else would hear.

"We don't need it. It's not suited for warfare anyhow."

"Agreed."

Whether because of the salamander's embarrassing tumble down the stairs or because of the wild demeanor the spirit exhibited, Leonhardt and Weishardt reached the same conclusion.

It was up for debate whether that decision saved more work for Mariela, the one who'd made the circle, or the brothers themselves. Though with the art of spirit magic lost to the world, perhaps the answer was obvious.

"Grrraraaar."

Leonhardt and Weishardt approached their assembled troops, with Sieg and the salamander following them. Although the spirit had made an impressive show of falling over, it now acted like nothing had happened. Despite the salamander's physical form being only temporary, its body seemed quite sturdy. Sieg greeted his cohorts with no small amount of embarrassment.

Just like on the first attempt, the other members were Leonhardt; Weishardt; Dick, who'd only recently returned to the

Labyrinth Suppression Forces; and the same five A-Rankers from the Forces as last time. Filling out the ranks on the Adventurers Guild side were its guildmaster, Haage the Limit Breaker; Elmera the Lightning Empress; Elmera's husband, Voyd; and Sieg. Altogether, they made a group of twelve.

"Allow me to make the introductions. Siegmund is a new A-Ranker. He's a bow user with a Spirit Eye. And this is the Isolated Hollow, Master Voyd."

The Isolated Hollow. Not a single person was unfamiliar with the name of that S-Ranker.

Sieg knew of Elmera's status as the much-beloved Lightning Empress, but he would never have thought her husband was the Isolated Hollow. When Sieg had reached the current stratum, he'd thought Voyd had merely come to see off his wife, not unlike Mariela had done for him. With neither eye concealed behind an eye patch, Sieg beheld Voyd in utter amazement.

"Hello. It looks like using a bow does suit you better after all."

Voyd, however, didn't seemed bothered in the least by Sieg's unusual eyes or by the mysterious raptor at the hunter's side. He greeted Sieg as calmly as he had the day the two first met in the city, then smiled at Elmera next to him with a serenity that belied the coming battle.

Elmera returned her husband's smile, saying, "I look forward to fighting together." Her hair, which was normally kept tied up in a bun, was loose today. Elmera had also donned a tight-fitting suit of monster leather. The woman made a far greater impression than Voyd to say the least.

"Hey there, Sieg. We'll be counting on you!" Dick called, along with the other commanding officers. They were all familiar faces Sieg had met during the hunts for earth dragons.

"You've grown into a fine adventurer!" a certain guildmaster praised him.

"Thank you. It's because of your guidance, Master Haage."

"Oh, stop. I didn't teach ya the bow!"

"Grah?!"

Glint, sparkle.

Haage greeted Sieg with his usual thumbs-up, and the salamander reacted to the man's gloriously shining cranium.

No one pointed out that Sieg's right eye had been healed and was a Spirit Eye, nor did they thoughtlessly react to learning that Voyd was the mysterious S-Ranker known as the Isolated Hollow. Everyone had made a magical Vow that anything they learned on the fifty-fifth stratum and below about their party was the highest level of classification and was never to be disclosed. The identity of the Isolated Hollow was the likely to be the biggest bit of news if it ever got out, but even some of the assembled A-Rankers preferred to keep things like their unique skills and techniques a secret. Even if the twelve hadn't made the Vow, no one was likely to do something as crass as disclose such information anyway.

The members who made up this group were among the strongest in the City. Yet as they made their way down toward the next stratum, they knew it wasn't out of the question that they would die for their efforts that day. The fact that everyone had returned alive the previous time was a miracle.

Perhaps Lynx's death had been the price they paid for that. If he'd survived, surely Lynx would've been joining them now. He was a resolute young man brimming with intelligence, and no doubt he would have become their stalwart comrade.

These warriors weren't glad they'd survived at the expense of someone else's life. No one like that would've dared return to this decisive battle.

Each of the twelve had their own reasons for gathering here. Different though their motives for fighting were, they were comrades bound by their conviction to kill the Labyrinth.

Leonhardt gave a speech as he met the eyes of all the other members of the incursion one by one. "'Kill the Labyrinth.' You hold this missive in your hands. 'Kill the Labyrinth.' You carry the conviction of your comrades with you. Even if my life is lost, this determination must remain. This is the land where we live, where our children live. We cannot let the flames of those lives be extinguished." Leonhardt's voice was very calm, yet full of an unyielding strength. "If the ruler of the skies is an obstacle, we shall lop off its wings. If a mountain towers over us, we shall break it and move onward. We will never stop. Onward, everyone. To defeat the red dragon and the Walking Mountain of Fire!"

"Ho!!!"

Kill the Labyrinth: a goal that united them all. In unison, the assembled people gave their answer to Leonhardt and marched toward the Labyrinth's fifty-sixth stratum, the site of their decisive battle.

The Labyrinth City, far above the coming war, welcomed the morning as it always did.

Would it soon be time for the children to go to school?

Voyd usually saw Pallois and Elio off, but today they were sent off by their great-grandfather Ghark.

Amber, who usually went to buy freshly baked bread first thing in the morning, didn't show up at the bakery. After finishing her breakfast of leftovers from yesterday, she left her house a little earlier than usual to prepare to open Sunlight's Canopy.

At the Aguinas estate, Caroline muttered, "I wonder if I shall be able to see Lord Weis today," as an attendant beautifully arranged the maiden's hair. The fact that near every other word out of Caroline's mouth these days was *Lord Weis* made her older brother desperately want to leave. Robert hastily departed the estate a little earlier than usual to head for Nierenberg's clinic.

The Adventurers Guild was silent. This morning, the nuisance that was the snappy guildmaster, who usually had to be forced by his subordinates to do any real work, was nowhere to be seen. Most days, staff members at the guild had to work extremely quickly, having time to concentrate only during the brief moments when their guildmaster was elsewhere—working to maintain security somewhere else in the city. Today, they began to prepare for work amid a somewhat different, tense atmosphere.

It was the same for the Merchants Guild, where Leandro, who usually showed up barely on time, arrived an hour earlier than usual and allocated the day's work.

Among the Labyrinth Suppression Forces, each unit's two lieutenants directed the morning's training as they'd done every other day, but the captains of six of the eight units, normally present for the drills, were conspicuously absent. The soldiers joked during their training sessions that the captains might be having a private get-together.

In each place, something was a little different, just the tiniest bit off. If viewed from a distance, the morning scene looked the same complete picture it always was, but up close, a few strokes were different. Those missing portions were gathered here, in the Labyrinth. Would the day come when these wayward pieces would be returned to their proper spots in the morning routine of the Labyrinth City?

The red dragon breathed a terrible cloud of flame to reduce the intruders to ash.

04

In response to the invasion of many creatures with high magical power, the dragon with wings of crimson lifted off from its bed, the crater of the Walking Mountain of Fire.

Anyone would try to kill troublesome insects that invaded their home. The red dragon's reaction was similar, and the power differential between the great monster and the Forces was comparable to that of a group of bugs and a person.

However, one would be foolish to make light of insects. Some carried disease, or deadly venoms in stingers. There were also insects that descended in swarms and left behind nothing but the bones of beasts they'd devoured. Simply being small didn't always mean something was weak.

The fifty-sixth stratum of the Labyrinth had only one entrance, leading from the stairs and quickly opening up into the large area rife with lava pools, where the red dragon awaited.

Rather than being buried under rubble, as would have been the case from a normal monster attack, the entrance was melting and expanding due to multiple hits from the red dragon's flames. One person charged forward from that molten entryway, speeding like an arrow.

That one insect who'd somehow safely slipped through the passageway to the fifty-sixth stratum quicker than the dragon's breath could hit them didn't make for the dragon; instead, they headed toward the Walking Mountain of Fire.

The red dragon had lived in this stratum all its life. This was only the second time it had seen this type of creature.

Moving at a speed far greater than last time, the creature seemed to be riding some kind of beast that the dragon had never laid eyes upon.

The red dragon fluttered its wings, holding its position in the air, then opened its mouth and loosed a volley of fiery blasts. It had learned from last time that this method made it easier to hit the little fleas that hoped to infest its home. They were fragile and couldn't go in the lava pools; thus the dragon reasoned that by using its breath to drive them toward the pools, it would probably win easily. The red dragon had to protect the Walking Mountain of Fire. These small things didn't seem like they could harm it, but the winged fire-breather disliked the idea of them getting close anyway.

Such thoughts were likely what directed the red dragon to breathe at Sieg, who was urging on the salamander. He'd been heading straight for the Walking Mountain of Fire, but the incessant rain of dragon fire forced him to change course.

No matter how many times he spurred the salamander toward the Walking Mountain of Fire, the dragon swooped around and cut in, then blocked the way with its flames.

Again and again, Sieg advanced toward the walking mountain, only to find his progress barred by deadly blasts of flame. To avoid the enormous pools of lava, Sieg was forced to take a wide detour, but he quickly resumed his course for the Walking Mountain. The red dragon pursued him and rained its breath down ahead of whatever path would take Sieg to his goal the fastest, trying to obstruct the hunter's advance.

Sieg had first made straight for the Walking Mountain of Fire when he'd burst from the stairway to the fifty-sixth stratum, but his course had immediately become more complex. Dodging deadly gouts of flame was bad enough, but avoiding the pools of molten rock that dotted the landscape only made things even more difficult. Far from closing the distance between himself and the living mountain, Sieg was actually now farther away. In fact, he found himself now approaching the stratum entrance.

Did the red dragon enjoy toying with prey before striking? Was it the monster's confidence in its own power that kept it from noticing the unnatural way its quarry simply ran about, escaping but never attacking?

The dragon drove its prey toward the edge of the stratum. This meant that the great flying creature itself was en route to collide with the natural wall of this level. However, a lava pool the size of a pond spread out along the edge. Could the dragon have been intending to trap its quarry on a path with no escape before finishing it off with an especially large jet of fire?

After driving Sieg and his mount along the straight path toward the lava pool, the red dragon bent its tail, tilted its wings, and turned several times to avoid crashing into the wall.

Perhaps if the dragon had been craftier and hadn't taken

its eyes off its prey until it was dead, it would have seen what unfolded next.

The salamander Sieg rode didn't care about the lava; it ran over the pool just as easily as it ran on land. The molten rock ahead of the scampering raptor-like creature cooled and hardened to become a foothold to support its feet.

Sieg's mount was a fire spirit. Heat and flames were its domain. Even though this lava resided within the Labyrinth, that didn't mean the salamander couldn't control the heat around its body.

If the red dragon had had its presence of mind, rather than the excitement of hunting down its prey, it surely would have noticed. Ever since the last battle, when the red dragon had suffered that humiliating strike from the Lightning Empress's Heavenbolt and been forced to crawl on the ground, it had maintained an altitude that even a bow couldn't reach. However, the dragon's repeated turns chasing Sieg had gradually worked to lower its altitude.

It spread its wings in an arrogant display, but that made it nothing more than a target to Sieg, who circled and took aim at them. Siegmund drew his bow as far as it would go.

The arrow he nocked was made of mythril. He charged the bow and the arrow with magical power and took aim, the Spirit Eye reinforcing his movements all the while.

The dragon's wings were disproportionately small compared to its body, and magical power helped it fly. Sieg could perceive the gap in the magical barrier that stretched thinly across the surface of the red dragon's body. Slight distortions surfaced here and there due to the monster's flight movements.

"There."

One shot, then another. Five arrows sped in rapid in succession, piercing the red dragon's exposed left wing with perfect accuracy.

To a dragon's wing, a normal arrow felt like little more than a needle, but these arrows, wreathed in magical power and strengthened by the Spirit Eye, struck to cause more than enough disruption to the membrane of the wing.

In particular, the red dragon had been turning with the wind caught fully in its left wing. When the arrows tore that wing, it was no longer able to withstand the wind pressure, which threw the dragon entirely off-balance. Finally realizing what the gnat was up to, the red dragon twisted its neck around and glared at Sieg as if to express its annoyance.

What it saw was a man with a Spirit Eye who was nocking another arrow and aiming at the dragon's face. Did the man mean to pierce the skull of the unsteady dragon?

Perhaps to declare that it could chew up and spit out such a shoddy missile, the red dragon caught the steel shaft of Sieg's arrow in its mouth. That was when it happened.

An especially large bolt of lightning pierced the heavens and shot down toward the dragon.

"Heavenbolt!"

The energy of the enormous lightning bolt that coated the stratum in blinding white pierced the arrow Sieg had shot, the one that was currently clenched in the jaws of the dragon. Surging, wild energy shot through the dragon's head.

White smoke rose from the falling monster, which had already lost consciousness. Its left wing, which should have caught the wind and weakened the impact of the fall, was too torn to do so.

Gravity continued to pull the red dragon down. Unconscious,

the mighty creature was little more than an enormous hunk of meat falling faster and faster. If this prideful monster hadn't been completely engrossed in chasing its tiny prey and had paid attention to its surroundings, it probably would've noticed it wasn't driving its quarry, but rather being led by it.

However, the dragon had always lived in this stratum, distant from the outside world, accompanied only by the eternally silent Walking Mountain of Fire. The monster hadn't even recognized that several humans had appeared from the same hole its prey had rushed out of and were hiding in the shadows of rocks.

With a great rumble, powerful enough to shake the stratum, the red dragon hit the ground.

"Hurry! It could wake at any moment!"

At Leonhardt's order, the soldiers hidden among the rocks charged from their hiding spots. They all wore masks to ward off the poison gas of the stratum, though that didn't mean breathing wasn't difficult. However, thanks to the effects of the special-grade potion known as Ice Spirit's Protection, drawing breath stung no more than it would on a hot summer's day. The concoction's veil of cold also afforded them protection against the ambient heat from the lava, keeping it from burning their skin.

Leonhardt and the others rushed toward the dragon with far greater urgency than during the first attempt. It might have crashed to the ground, but their enemy was still a top-ranking dragon. Furthermore, it appeared that the monster had acquired some amount of resistance to lightning attacks during the previous battle, as it regained consciousness before Leonhardt and the others even had a chance to attack. The furious, gigantic creature struck at the intruders with its torn left wing, hoping to mow them down.

"Limit-Breaking Cleave!!!"

It was Haage who first met the enemy with his sword. However, by all appearances, the trajectory and length of the blade he swung weren't enough to turn back the dragon's attack. Yet the space past the tip of Haage's sword—where there should have only been empty air—clashed with the dragon's left wing. The invisible force ground against the appendage, magnificently diverting the creature's path to protect Leonhardt's forces from a direct hit.

"Phew, that thing really is tough! A real blade wouldn't stand a chance!"

This sword technique was the source of Haage's alias, Limit Breaker. It allowed the guildmaster to go beyond the length of the weapon he held to unleash an attack. The ability worked with any weapon; the real advantage was how the difference between the observable length of the weapon and that of the actual range made it difficult for opponents to guard themselves.

By his own admission, even the man who wielded the technique didn't really know whether this was due to magical power or a combination of spells. Haage seemed content to settle what it was with three words: "It's fighting spirit!" In truth, the skill's strength and size did actually vary based on the intensity of his fighting spirit when he used it, so he wasn't necessarily wrong.

After Haage's strike to its left wing, the monster raised its right faster than Haage could flash a thumbs-up. This membrane was still intact, and the dragon attacked Leonhardt and the others with the wing itself along with a surge of wind it gathered via magic. Despite the fearsome attack, Sieg didn't overlook this opening.

The right wing caught enough air pressure beneath it that the dragon could have taken flight if both wings were intact, but Sieg's arrow tore straight through it. Then, to make matters worse, a single spear left another hole in the membrane.

"Rising Dragon Spear!"

Struck by Dick's spear and Sieg's arrows, the red dragon had finally lost the power of flight.

"Rrraaaaaah!" The earth-shaking roar assailing the subjugation force was anger made tangible, and the stratum started to shake as if in answer. Everyone plunged their weapons into the ground to endure the violent tremors.

The volcano had started to move.

The lava surged upward with loud booms, while the temperatures around it grew even hotter. The soldiers, despite their alchemical protection, felt the searing heat on their skin. Worst of all, breathing became more difficult than ever as clouds of noxious gasses issued from the molten rock, diluting the surrounding oxygen. The masks were only barely sustaining them.

Rrrrrrrumble, rrrrrrrumble.

The footsteps of the volcano reverberated in the distance. Was it moving toward the dragon and the invaders? Eight legs, visible in the distance, lumbered forward like a turtle with the bizarre monster on its back. The small volcano the size of a hill, bearing nothing resembling a head, spouted ash and smoke from its top as it advanced slowly but steadily. Clinging to the thing's side were five soldiers, with Weishardt leading them.

"Eat this!"

"Huuu-ra!"

Four unit captains drove giant steel piles one after another into the side of the living mountain at a point about a third of the way down from its summit. The weight of the piles and the collective skill of the soldiers driving them in served as a testament to their strength.

"Why're we pretending to be combat engineers?"

"Can't do nothin' about it. This is also revenge for that young guy. Dick assigned this to us."

"Besides, he's terrible at magic."

"When we get back safe, let's have a round of drinks on Dick's coin!"

After driving in all the piles they'd been able to carry, the four captains dashed toward the crater. There, Weishardt and the fifth captain, a magic specialist, were busy crafting a large-scale spell together.

"We'll help!"

The four captains who joined up with them also poured in magical power to assist. The technique they were building gathered together a large mass of a certain something this stratum was full of.

No matter how many piles they shoved in, the Walking Mountain of Fire seemed unbothered and kept walking. As if building up energy for an eruption, it simply absorbed the lava at its feet and continued its slow, thundering march toward the red dragon. It was evident to all that their party would need something of a suitable mass to defeat this stratum boss.

Rrrrrrrrumble, rrrrrrrrumble.

The Walking Mountain of Fire shook the earth with each step. The group was only going to get one shot at defeating it, and they were going to need more time.

05

One could harvest expensive materials from dragons. In the case of a high-ranking dragon, this was not limited to just its leather and fangs. All sorts of parts, ranging from a single scale to a tiny drop of blood, were valuable and could be used to make highly effective medicines. This was true even for materials taken from the bodies of dead dragons.

Why would one assume a living, moving dragon was weak after merely losing its wings? Perhaps a spurt of lava had helped push it back up onto its feet, as the red dragon now stood on its two hind legs. Enraged, the crimson monster thrashed about with its powerful tail.

The only ones able to dodge were the Lightning Empress Elmera, whose physical abilities had been bolstered through electrical power, and Voyd.

Haage was in the tail's trajectory and avoided a direct hit by using his Limit-Breaking Cleave, but he was still blown about ten meters away. Likewise, Dick timed his Dragon Spear Attack to coincide with the moment the dragon's tail collided with him, reducing the impact enough to withstand. Though perhaps *withstand* wasn't the right word. Haage had taken a weighty blow, and blood trickled from his mouth. Likewise, although Dick successfully negated the attack's impact, both of his arms were bent in unnatural directions from ramming his spear into the oncoming blow.

Even with such wounds, they were probably very lucky simply by the fact that neither had fallen and met their immediate end in a pit of lava.

Leonhardt, who had also used his sword to avert the attack, was knocked toward a lava pool, and Sieg rushed over to catch him, just barely arriving in time. Well, catching him was perhaps a bit optimistic. Leonhardt was a large man, too large for Sieg to catch on a mount while keeping his own momentum, and in the process, they very nearly crashed into the lava pool together.

"Grarar!"

The reason the two only ended up with some fractures and burns was because the salamander slid between Sieg and the lava hardening the molten rock around them.

"You saved me."

"No, someone else came to my rescue as well."

"Grar!"

The two smiled ruefully at the salamander, who seemed to say, "Don't worry about it!" Even in the face of such a powerful enemy, Sieg and Leonhardt still seemed hopeful of victory.

"Just to be sure, let's use Ice Spirit's Protection. It's coming again."

"Yes, sir."

The two used special-grade heal potions and Ice Spirit's Protection, both of which they had plenty of, and immediately returned to the battlefront.

Both Dick's arms and Haage's internal organs had been severely damaged but recovered in an instant, thanks to the special-grade heal potions. Everyone who would have otherwise been out of commission was able to resume the fight.

The crushed insects were beginning to move again, and the discontented dragon opened its jaws and breathed an inferno to reduce the defiant creatures to nothing.

"Hollow Rift."

Yet even such absolute firepower was swallowed by the rift that expanded in front of Voyd. The flames were consumed without so much as singing a hair.

"Groooooooar!"

The dragon seemed to shift its focus. If it couldn't reduce its opponents to cinders, it would just eat them. Thankfully, the enormous maw aiming for Voyd never reached him because Hollow Rift—the mosaic-like space where tiny fragments of light and darkness were at odds—had thwarted it.

The red dragon loudly gnashed its teeth. Elmera fired her lightning at its head, and Sieg fired his arrow at the monster's left eye. The flash of lightning slowed the dragon's reactions for a split second, and Sieg's arrow found its mark with exquisite accuracy. When the red dragon threw its head back in pain, Leonhardt, Dick, and Haage charged with their weapons and pierced its throat and stomach in rapid succession. The gargantuan monster tried to shake them all off with its tail. Some avoided it, while others who flew back and coughed up blood returned moments later. The red dragon's breath was extinguished, and its left was eye crushed. Its body was weakening more by the second.

What was the dragon thinking as the storm of attacks bound it to the earth? Did it seek help, seek hope from the slowly approaching Walking Mountain of Fire? At that same moment, the mountain the red dragon was supposed to be protecting was similarly nearing its final moments, right before its guardian's eyes.

"It's done. Now!"

As Weishardt gave the signal, the block of ice they had gathered and formed with a large quantity of magical power was dropped. The enormous block was just ice magic. To be exact, only the surface was frozen; the inside remained water.

The mass of liquid encased in a thin frozen layer was constructed by gathering steam from the water that had been steadily leaking down from the fifty-fourth stratum two levels above, the stratum of sea caverns.

The size of the block was unbelievable. At Weishardt's signal, the unit captains retreated all at once, and behind them, the enormous block of ice slowly fell toward the caldera. The volume of water might have been a full third of the size of the entire mountain.

Volcanos are known to suffer tremendous explosions when water vapor builds up inside them. The degree of the blast is said to be determined by the ratio of water to lava. According to volcanologists in the imperial capital, the most violent explosions came a volume of water that was 30 percent of the lava's volume. That was exactly the proportion that Weishardt's group had used.

To those present, the ensuing sound was difficult to describe. Their eardrums had already ruptured from the thunderous roar of the explosion that swept over the area, and the only thing they had to go on was the tactile, the impact of the small rocks that hurtled at them along with the searing, steaming wind.

The incursion had driven piles into one side of the Walking Mountain of Fire specifically to make sure the force of the explosion would release on the side opposite Leonhardt's group. Their plan had worked, but the soldiers had still been too close when it had gone off.

Even just the blast that had erupted from the caldera was enough to put the nearby people in danger. Although one unit captain, a shield knight, extended his skill to protect the lightly armored Weishardt and the accompanying mage, they were all blown clear off their perches. Their Ice Spirit's Protection potions had long since worn off, and each suffered serious burns beneath their armor. The other unit captains, too, were thrown to the ground and lay completely motionless.

"Hang in there! You're still breathing, right?!"

Weishardt and the mage could only barely move their bodies. Heedless of their own broken limbs, they immediately used special-grade heal potions and Ice Spirit's Protection to restore the other soldiers, starting with the one with the most serious injuries, the shield knight.

"Ugh, phew. That was the most painful thing I've ever felt in my life."

"If you can complain, then you'll be all right. What of the volcano?!"

"How should I know?"

The endless smoke and ash rising from the walking mountain made it impossible to see anything but what was immediately in front of them. Some of the soldiers spied a distant glow of red and thought it might be lava spilling from the collapsed mountain. However, they could no longer feel the tremors from the volcano's earth-shaking gait.

"Groooooooar!" The howl of the red dragon cut through the hazy air. It sounded mournful and furious.

"The volcano has fallen. Let's return to my brother!" Without knowing exactly why, Weishardt was almost certain that the dragon's roar signaled the death of the volcano.

The explosion was severe enough to cause devastating damage to Weishardt's group, but Leonhardt's hardly suffered thanks to the dragon between them and the Walking Mountain of Fire. It blew away Sieg, who had distanced himself from the dragon to use his bow, and once again, the salamander saved him right before he fell into a pool of lava. Thankfully, the injuries weren't serious enough to require special-grade heal potions.

After having seen the thing it was sworn to protect fall before its eyes, the red dragon appeared dumbfounded for a moment.

"Groooooooar!" Did the mighty monster howl with anger or grief?

"I'm sorry." And why did an apology slip from Leonhardt's mouth?

The dragon had briefly lowered its guard, and Leonhardt wasn't about to miss that chance. He lunged at its chest, charged his sword with all the magical power he possessed, and pierced the dragon's heart.

The steam and ash that erupted from the volcano cast the entirety of the Labyrinth's fifty-sixth stratum in pure white. Amid the thick murk in the air, the light emitted from the lava pools reflected off the floating motes of ash, a sight both dreadful and beautiful.

None of them could see beyond an arm's length in the world

of white, and the low visibility didn't feel confined to this stratum of the Labyrinth alone. Rather, it seemed to be a mist that carried on all the way to the world of the dead.

In that alabaster realm, the dark, towering silhouette of the red dragon crashed to the earth, never to move again.

"Heyyy!"

"Everyone's here. Are you all right?!"

Calling out in concord, one figure, then another emerged from within the cloudy world. The people who gathered under Leonhardt numbered twelve in all. Everyone had managed to return alive.

At the joy of being alive and seeing one another again, they bumped fists, clapped shoulders, and congratulated each other on a good fight. No joy came from the kill, however. Perhaps their sense of accomplishment in that feat had been soured by the mournful cry of the dragon when it lost its companion.

The hunters owed their lives to a nearly endless list of fortuitous circumstances. They had started with skillfully luring the monster and impeding its left wing, then downing it with Heavenbolt. If the dragon's left eye hadn't been pierced, Leonhardt probably wouldn't have been able to make an attack on its chest, even if the great fiend had dropped its guard when the volcano fell. Had they not been able to so narrowly avoid the monster's attacks, the adventurers would have met their end in a single strike. Maintaining pressure on the dragon and rapidly wounding it had proved critical, too. Otherwise, they wouldn't have been able to bring the monster to its knees, and Leonhardt's sword wouldn't have reached its heart.

There was no mistaking that this victory was one that could

have only been accomplished together. Yet even with their many triumphs, Leonhardt and the others who heard the red dragon's howl were overcome with a feeling that today, they'd protected what they loved, but the dragon had been unable to do the same.

Ceaseless rains of ash in the Labyrinth's fifty-sixth stratum were like the voiceless death cry of the volcano and cast the scenery in grays and whites from the stratum stairs to the middle of the cavern.

"Rarar."

They didn't know how on earth it could see in such poor visibility, but under the salamander's guidance, the group finally managed to reach the stairs leading back up. It seemed that searching for the stairs to the next stratum, however, would have to wait until the ash settled.

"Let's withdraw for today."

As everyone began to ascend the stairs on Leonhardt's order, Sieg, who brought up the rear, found himself being licked on the right cheek by the salamander.

"Rar!"

With that last utterance, the spirit burst into flames and returned home. Its magical power had finally been expended.

"That creature was a great help." Leonhardt turned his head at the sound and expressed his appreciation.

"You're right."

It wasn't simply that it had successfully lured the red dragon. The salamander had saved members of the incursion countless times when they were about to fall into a lava pool. The salamander—and Mariela—had protected all of them.

That Walking Mountain of Fire was coming straight this way.

Could it have been trying to protect the red dragon...? Sieg lightly shook his head as if to shake off the thought itself. Even if that were true, there was little choice about what needed to be done.

If they didn't kill the boss of the Labyrinth that awaited them on the deepest level, there was no future in which Sieg or the others could survive in this land. Simply sitting and waiting idly for the day they'd be eaten wasn't an option.

By the time the party returned to the Labyrinth Suppression Forces' base after climbing the stratum stairs, using a Teleportation Circle, and traveling through the underground Aqueduct, the sun hung high in the sky, and it was well past noon.

After washing off the ash that caked their bodies at the base's watering hole, followed by medical examinations from Nierenberg, the exhausted dragon slayers were finally permitted to go home.

Those who had worn masks to protect against the volcanic gases hadn't inhaled the cinders, but some unfortunate ones had removed theirs to drink potions and inhaled a large quantity of the white powder. They needed a bit of time to be treated.

The shield knight's gait was a bit off, and his legs appeared to be crooked. Nierenberg took him away, saying with a smile, "Do you intend to leave them like that? I'll heal them right away." As he was ushered off, the knight seemed even more sorrowful than he had before they challenged the red dragon.

Mariela, Amber, and Freyja—the ones who'd seen the party off—awaited the warriors' return in a room of the base that had been prepared in lieu of a proper waiting room. Apparently, the Forces had very kindly prepared the room and offered it to the three women.

"Welcome back! Sieg, are you hurt at all? Here's your eye patch."

"Thanks. I only made it back because of you, Mariela."

"Good jooob. Sieg, you haven't eaten yet, right? Let's go to the Yagu Drawbridge Pavilion for some fooood."

Freyja's involvement had soured the mood a little, though that was nothing unusual. Next to Sieg and Mariela, Dick and Amber shared the joy of Dick's safe return with a discreet distance between them. The two were adults and newlyweds, so there was no need for them to hesitate to be all lovey-dovey in front of others. Amber seemed to be in the "no public flirting" camp, however.

"Anyway, let's have lunch at the Yagu Drawbridge Pavilion! Sieg, your group should come, too!"

Dick probably wasn't in the mood to return to work. In truth, he wanted to go to the pavilion with Amber. Perhaps Dick thought she would turn him down, though, as he instead proposed everyone go together. Before they all left the base to get some much-needed food, Voyd and Elmera Seele passed them.

"Oh, we're off."

"Good job today, everyone."

The pair passed by with very simple farewells. Per usual, Elmera had her hair tied up and wore her glasses. Similarly, Voyd wore glasses and had a calm look on his face, but the couple's arms were linked, and they happily stuck close together with no regard for what the others might think.

"Say, darling. Let's go on a date before the children get home."

"That sounds nice. There happens to be a restaurant I've been wanting to go to with you."

It had been obvious since that time they'd eaten fried prawns at Sunlight's Canopy, but Mr. and Mrs. Seele had no qualms about public flirting. Dick, seeing how close the couple was, put his left hand on Amber's lower back and glanced at her imploringly, but she took an extra half-step away from him and urged, "Well, shall we go?"

As she watched the newlyweds, Mariela took Sieg's hand in her right and Freyja's in her left and followed the couple.

Together, the five departed for the Yagu Drawbridge Pavilion.

"Captain! I got to A Rank! It might be indirect, but fighting the red dragon would be vengeance for Lynx! I'd like to join you!"

Trapped by a chance encounter with Edgan, Captain Dick couldn't bring himself to tell the eager man that his quarry had already been defeated. Instead, Dick averted his eyes with an uncomfortable expression.

Freyja was about to burst out laughing, while Sieg had clearly forgotten that Edgan had reached A Rank at all; Mariela took both of them and inconspicuously made an escape from the Yagu Drawbridge Pavilion.

Even though he missed lunch, the unchanged hustle and bustle of the Labyrinth City made it clear to Sieg that the battle with the red dragon had been worth it.

CHAPTER 2
The Final Lesson

01

Squish. Mariela took Sieg's face in both of her hands.

At first, Sieg's heart pounded as he wondered if she was going to give him a kiss, but that didn't seem to be the case. Mariela's face wore just a hint of seriousness as she stared fixedly at Sieg's blue left eye and green right eye in turn.

"What's wrong, Mariela?" Sieg asked after she had peered at him for a while and then nodded as if understanding something. Whatever it was likely wasn't anything good.

"Umm, well. When I first met you, you know, I really liked your blue eye. I even thought it was beautiful. But…that was a feeling from Endalsia that had flowed into me from the Nexus."

"That's…"

Contrary to Sieg's expectations, Mariela's answer was fairly serious.

Was the young alchemist saying that the kindness she'd always shown Sieg was only because of Endalsia's influence? Were Mariela's feelings toward him…

"But when I look at them now, I think both are beautiful, and you're still you no matter what the color."

"!!! You mean…"

In other words, Mariela was saying that she was no longer influenced by Endalsia's feelings. What she meant was that her feelings regarding Sieg were her own.

Sieg's mood violently fluctuated, first down, then up. He grasped at the air, unsure whether to place his own hands over hers on his face or perhaps just to embrace Mariela.

"Marielaaa, let's go out to shop!"

"Okay, Master. I'll be right theeere."

As was becoming rather common, Freyja interrupted the two with exquisite timing. Mariela removed her hands from Sieg and deftly escaped his arms. The girl must have had formidable reflexes to dodge an A-Ranker's advance, but of course, Mariela was completely unaware of such things. It had been completely by chance.

Freyja had been in the shop portion of Sunlight's Canopy while Sieg and Mariela were in the living room. The interruption seemed to have come at exactly the right—or perhaps wrong—time. How had Freyja known? Was her sense of timing the reason she was known as the Sage of Calamity?

She did that on purpose, didn't she...?

Despite his suspicions, after hearing what Mariela had to say, Sieg was grinning just a little more than usual. He followed the young alchemist into the storefront of Sunlight's Canopy.

Sieg usually enjoyed brief moments of rest during a normal day at Sunlight's Canopy, but his days with the Labyrinth Suppression Forces were extremely busy.

First, they'd started butchering the corpse of the red dragon, which they'd slain a few days ago now. It was a high-ranking dragon, so not a single drop of its blood could go to waste, and the Forces were unwilling to delay the work any further, as they feared the corpse would start to rot.

Under Freyja's instructions, members of the Labyrinth Suppression Forces harvested materials needed for alchemy, as well as parts that would be manufactured into weapons and armor. They stayed up all night stripping the meat. Red dragon meat was an extremely high-class ingredient, after all.

Now that it was possible to travel through the Fell Forest thanks to monster-warding potions, many people and goods had been brought to the Labyrinth City. An equally large amount of various materials produced in the city was being exported, too, mainly to the imperial capital. That in itself was profitable for both the Labyrinth City and the capital, but such sudden change demanded fastidious guidance from those managing it.

Leonhardt, the current margrave, who was instead devoting himself to subjugating the Labyrinth, had left the responsibilities to his father and wife. They were in charge of social relations with their troublesome fellow nobles in Leonhardt's place. No matter how much the margrave excelled at fighting, he was empty-handed and at a bit of a disadvantage against nobles who resorted to multiple layers of roundabout bureaucracy. Thankfully, the red dragon meat would prove very helpful in negotiations with such troublesome people.

A rare thing like red dragon meat wasn't something that could be obtained with piles of gold. It was the kind of thing that would've normally been presented only to the emperor, and many nobles sought that rare delicacy.

Freyja, who directed the dismantling work, brought a lump of the meat home to Sunlight's Canopy as if it were the most commonplace thing in the world. Mariela, having no idea how much it was worth, cooked and ate it with her master and Sieg, all the while commenting on how delicious it was. If someone had told Mariela the price of what she'd just eaten, no doubt her eyes would've popped out of her head.

"Thanks to the intervention of my wife and our father, we've got a little more time to deal with those nobles. We should be able to focus both time and resources on combating the Labyrinth for a little while."

"Yes, Brother. However, we cannot afford to suffer even the slightest of delays."

"I know that. That's why I've called Marrock."

Leonhardt and Weishardt, a pair who continued to fight on the front lines of the Labyrinth, headed into a council room. There, Kunz Marrock, who governed the dwarven enclave known as the Rock Wheel Autonomous Region, fiddled with the edges of his tidied beard. He had a sour expression on his face. Placed on a desk in front of Marrock was a lump covered in a white cloth.

Marrock, shrewd man that he was, probably had a rough idea of what was under the cloth. The ruler of Rock Wheel was only half dwarven: his father was a dwarf and his mother was a human. His craftmanship was no match for that of pure-blooded dwarves. However, this also meant he possessed keen judgment, which was rare for dwarves. Marrock's sharp eyes could discern the truth behind any sort of shroud, whether an object or a lie.

"I hope we didn't keep you waiting too long, Lord Marrock."

Smiling, Leonhardt amicably offered a handshake. Although he and Weishardt had to have placed it there to show it off, he appeared not to see the mound hidden by the cloth, and this blatant behavior served to irritate the half dwarf. The feeling was akin to when someone gave a drawn-out toast in front of a tantalizing drink.

"There's a reason we called you here. We have ore we would like you to appraise."

Marrock recognized immediately that the words were not literal. The Labyrinth City was a treasure trove of materials. There were enough craftsmen here that the two brothers could ask for ore appraisal.

"It's this, right?"

"Yes. Allow us to show you."

Leonhardt signaled to a soldier waiting behind him, who then approached and removed the cloth cover.

What greeted Marrock's eyes was a mass of unrefined metal with a metallic luster and hardened lava, fused in perfect harmony. Miraculously, the ore hadn't lost its shine even after being exposed to the lava's scorching heat. This was a special quality that mere iron could never possess.

"...It's adamantite. Good gracious, I thought a general would know that much. Let me get straight to the point. What do you wish for Rock Wheel to do with this?" Marrock raised an eyebrow and threw a glance at Leonhardt.

The mountains in the vicinity of the Labyrinth City were rife with mineral resources. They yielded a variety of common metals, like iron. However, when it came to magical metals, the mountains yielded only mythril deposits on a small scale, and no adamantite. Moreover, the ore before the gathered men contained no soil. Instead, there was hardened lava, making it unlikely to have come from a mine. It would've been reasonable to assume that the brothers had procured it in the Labyrinth.

Just as Marrock deduced, the adamantite had been harvested from the Walking Mountain of Fire. This metal with a large relative density came from the bottom of what was left of the monster after the explosion.

Adamantite had a high melting point. It was not something an ordinary blacksmith could refine. Despite its hardness, it also had a low shatter point.

"Hard but easily broken" was a matter of degrees, of course. Adamantite wouldn't break from a blow with a normal steel weapon. More likely, it would just cleave the blade of the weapon in two.

But then, in most battles, a good-quality steel weapon was sufficient. Even though it was stronger, an expensive adamantite weapon wasn't necessary. The type of battle that called for one would be when a lone person was fighting hundreds of thousands of enemies, or when one was facing a monster so powerful that a steel weapon wouldn't be enough.

That was why adamantite was often combined with other metals to make an alloy. This gave the resulting metal compound the durability needed to not break during a long battle. Such a powerful material was treated in accordance with its commendable traits before being tempered into a weapon.

It was not just about the level of the technique used to cast it into the shape of a weapon, either. Only an extremely high-ranking blacksmith could precisely adjust the alloy's composition ratio, heat treatment temperature, and time exposed to heat. Such a level of skill was not an easy one to reach, but working with adamantite was one way to work toward it.

Just coming into contact with and refining adamantite would greatly increase the smithing skills of the Rock Wheel dwarves and bring them closer to their dearest wish: the ultimate sword. Marrock understood this well. And the fact that Leonhardt was showing this to Marrock meant he had an interest in letting the Rock Wheel dwarves handle the material.

"One hundred weapons in twenty days. Those are the details."

In response to Marrock's question, Leonhardt responded only with his objective.

"...You're asking for something absurd. Just remodeling the furnaces would take more than twenty days, even for Rock Wheel."

Marrock responded to Leonhardt's unadorned request by doffing his own social mask and turning down the request with dwarflike frankness. No hidden meaning in his words indicating room for bargaining or negotiation was evident.

"Do the refining in the Labyrinth City. We will provide red dragon scales for the furnaces. We ought to have enough for one hundred weapons." Leonhardt answered matter-of-factly, and Marrock turned to face the man with a hostile gaze.

"...Did you say red dragon scales? Are you sober?!"

"We don't have much time left."

Adamantite had a high melting point. At such a temperature, a normal furnace would melt. However, by lining furnaces with red dragon scales, they would likely be able to hold out long enough to make about one hundred weapons' worth of ingots. It was possible, but it meant wasting the scales on something that seemed utterly absurd.

Marrock made no attempt to smile and hide his true feelings. Even if furnaces were reinforced with dragon scales, Leonhardt's aim to have all those weapons in twenty days made the half dwarf suspicious.

Is the Labyrinth in such a dangerous state? If the worst happened, there's no doubt the damage would reach Rock Wheel. Though being destroyed along with our home would be the measure of a true dwarf.

Digging out minerals from the earth, melting them, removing impurities, adding alloys, hardening them. Casting the hardened metal, turning it red in fire, cooling it, tempering it.

Dwarves created a variety of things, but the process of tempering metal was what stirred Marrock's blood the most. All the dwarves gathered in Rock Wheel probably shared that sentiment.

They weren't the kind of people who could still feel alive if they were to ever depart from the resource-rich Rock Wheel region just to save their lives. Even if the worst happened and monsters overflowed from the Labyrinth and reached Rock Wheel, it was certain that Rock Wheel's inhabitants would gladly die with their home beneath their feet. As he thought on such things, Marrock touched the adamantite.

My decision was made as soon as they revealed this.

Few could say whether Kunz Marrock's decision was motivated by personal sympathies or an understanding for the fate of the dwarven race.

"Rock Wheel will undertake this great task. However, a forge is our sacred ground. That won't change even if we're using the Labyrinth City's workshops. You must let us craft our way."

"You have my gratitude."

"Oh, I should be thanking you. I'm looking forward to this."

Marrock raised his right hand and made a gesture like he was drinking alcohol, then grinned broadly and departed.

Unlike his usual calm self, Marrock quickly returned to the trading company he'd established in the Labyrinth City, then immediately headed for his magical tool for communication and barked excitedly.

"Fellas! Assemble in the Labyrinth City right away! The finest-quality adamantite is waiting for you! It's an excellent item with high purity. This ore's just begging to be hammered and shaped. First come, first served, all right? This beauty won't wait. Get here in five days. No stopping for rest!"

This wasn't like him. Marrock was aware of his own excitement as he called to his comrades on the other end of the magical tool and raised his voice. This feeling was like the day he had first hammered red-hot steel.

"Did ye say adamantite?! Ohhh, I'm goin'! Right now!"

"Hey now, we gotta tell everyone first! Marrock! We don't need beds or whatnot, so just make sure ye got plenty o' booze for us!"

"How much adamantite? Don't forget the copel ingots for the alloy!"

The dwarves back in Rock Wheel on the other end of the magical tool seemed even more excited than Marrock, as he could hear them noisily running around knocking over shelves in their great hurry to get ready.

"At this rate, they'll be here in four days."

Marrock trusted that his people wouldn't forget their work tools, but they seemed idiotic enough to gallop to the city on yagus without eating, drinking, or resting along the way.

"I'll send yagus piled with alcohol and food to welcome them. And then I need to reserve all the smithing workshops in the dwarf quarter of the Labyrinth City. Better get negotiating. Focus on the best furnace and finish remodeling it before those guys get here. May as well buy up all the good booze while I'm at it! The house of Margrave Schutzenwald is going to handle the entire bill. No need for me to hold back! We'll show them our best!"

Marrock laughed heartily as he spoke to himself. He removed his trim jacket and cast it aside. He planned on going to the smithing workshops in the dwarven quarter right away so he could negotiate directly. Both his trim jacket and his polished shoes would just be the way in a smithy. Marrock took his familiar work clothes from the luggage he'd tucked away and began to change.

Beneath the stiff fabric of his clothes, he wore a cotton long-sleeved shirt and long johns that went all the way to his ankles; there wasn't an ounce of style to be found here. More importantly, the cloth wouldn't burn or shrink in heat that otherwise singed the skin, and they also absorbed sweat well—indispensable underwear for those who worked with fire. Additionally, Marrock had fire-resistant leather coveralls along with his familiar leather boots with steel plate inserts. This crude outfit was quite different from Marrock's usual refined image, but when he donned it, every piece fit perfectly.

"No self-respecting dwarf would suddenly get defensive after being shown such a fine specimen of adamantite."

As a representative of his nation, perhaps Marrock should've been doing other things, such as strengthening its defenses or making plans to abandon it.

But if I did that, Rock Wheel would be lawless.

If they fled, they would do so after finishing with the adamantite. That was what it meant to be a dwarf. Above all, Marrock himself couldn't contain his desire to witness the forging of the adamantite.

Good grief, it's hard being a dwarf.

Despite such thoughts, Marrock—now made indistinguishable from his full-blooded brethren by way of his clothing—cheerily left for his destination.

It wasn't just weapons that were necessary to challenge the fifty-seventh stratum. The Labyrinth Suppression Forces continued to prepare by processing as much of the material gathered from the red dragon as time and manpower would permit. They worked tirelessly, shaping the resources into weapons and armor.

The Labyrinth City was alive with skilled people and the sounds of the weapons and armor they bore. One person in particular was absent during this time of great effort, however.

The Labyrinth City's alchemist, guided by her master, had departed from the city. She headed into the steep mountains to get the final preparations in order.

02

Precipitous mountains stretched to the southeast of the Labyrinth City. The farther south you went, the steeper the mountain range rose, and even if you could climb partway up, the terrain proved difficult for human feet to cross. The east was the same, still rife with rugged rock. The only difference was that the slopes were somewhat more forgiving. However, the eastern mountains had a spot before the steep summit where huge rocks had accumulated, perhaps the result of a part of the mountain having shifted and crumbled long ago. The only way to get there was to take a detour through the valleys and travel along a mountain road with a relatively gentle slope but poor footholds.

It was a rocky area where few traveled. Maintaining a road was all but impossible, and there were many steps along the way that were as tall as Mariela was. Only creatures like yagus could've willingly lived in a place like that.

The yagus were happily and nimbly making their way along the mountain road. Mariela, on the other hand, had been on the verge of tears for a while now, clinging to one yagu's back.

"We're so high up. I'm scared, Masterrr. I want to go hooome!!!"

"You're fine. You'll be just fine. Not long now, I promise."

"You've been saying that for way too looong!!!"

Mariela sat in front on one of the yagus, desperately gripping its splendid horns with all her strength to keep from being thrown off. Freyja sat sidesaddle behind her pupil, humming a song while enjoying the scenery. Sieg, bringing up the rear on his own yagu, followed the two with clear confusion on his face. If one observed the three as they traveled along the mountain road, they'd probably have a lot of questions.

For example, the yagu Mariela and Freyja rode was smaller than Sieg's, yet it easily scaled the rocky mountain without the slightest appearance of fatigue. The creature moved as if no one was riding it. The yagu Sieg rode, one of the finest in the Labyrinth City, barely managed to keep up. Freyja also sat with her legs to the side, yet she didn't look like she was even close to falling off, despite the extreme swaying. What was more, the road was so bad that a clumsy girl like Mariela shouldn't have been able to hold on for such a long time.

However, to Sieg, who had gotten considerably used to what

was likely Freyja's magic, the most incomprehensible thing was "Why aren't Mariela and I riding on the same yagu?"

"We'll make camp around here today."

"Huh? Master, you said not long nooow…"

The party's yagus came to a stop in a relatively open area. Thanks to the magic Freyja used, she and Mariela hardly swung at all on the yagu's back, and neither of them would have tumbled off even if they hadn't been paying attention. Of course, Mariela hadn't known this and had spent the entire ride clinging to the yagu with all her might. Even now, her entire body was trembling. Sieg helped her down from the creature's back, but Mariela's legs could no longer support her weight, and she fell onto her hands and knees, wobbling like a newborn foal.

"R-Regen…"

Mariela retrieved the Regen medicine she'd brought with her from a waist pouch and swallowed it. The girl's master had been right in telling Mariela to bring it. Had they seen her drinking it so casually, the Labyrinth Suppression Forces, who trained hard every day, shed bitter, envious tears. However, there was a difference between a young man who built up muscle and stamina over time and Mariela, who made potions and had limited free time to exercise. This was a rare Mariela Strengthening Month. Hopefully, the jealous Forces members would understand and overlook the use of the Regen medicine.

"Mariela, why don't you take it easy?"

"Thanks, Sieg."

"Sorry for the trouble."

Even Freyja, whom Sieg hadn't told to rest, left the camp setup to him and stretched out on the ground. Despite it being "camp setup," there were no tents. It was just a matter of spreading thick monster pelts on a relatively flat surface, covering yourself with a blanket, and going to sleep. Sprinkling monster-warding potion around would keep weak monsters away. Thankfully, more powerful monsters didn't live around these parts. As it happened, the actual animals here were probably more dangerous than the native monsters, but they wouldn't approach either, so long as a fire was lit. Sieg was about to go look for firewood to make dinner when Freyja stopped him.

"Mariela, put magical power into your ring. Plenty of it."

"Huh? We don't have a magic circle."

"I'll call take care of that; don't worry. Even if you called it, the salamander wouldn't do any work, right?"

The free-spirited salamander wouldn't want to hear that from Freyja, a woman who basically never did any work. Back during the assault on the red dragon, the spirit, unused to its raptor body at first, had taken a tumble and had a little fun with the new form. Even so, it had played a very active part in helping Sieg.

Freyja laid her hand over Mariela's right hand, where the young alchemist wore the salamander's ring. The sage then chanted some sort of spell and summoned a palm-sized salamander. Today, the spirit had taken the form of a flame-clad lizard, like most other times when Mariela had summoned it.

"It's so small…"

"It's fine. All it's gonna do is keep watch until morning. If it were bigger, it wouldn't last until morning, you know?"

With the amount of light and heat it emitted, disproportionate to its size, the salamander made the place nice and warm just by being there. The group had climbed high enough that there was a chill even with the sun directly overhead. Heat from a salamander to get them through the night was most welcome.

The salamander glanced around nonchalantly, and when it saw Sieg, it shook its tail happily.

"I owe you for back then," Sieg said as he piled up some gathered rocks to make a simple stove. The spirit slowly crept into the little makeshift construct, as if to say "You made me a home!" Rather than a watchdog, the three had a watch-salamander. Since it could move much more freely with the physical body it had now than had it been summoned as a spirit, the salamander would protect them all from beasts and monsters through the night, even if they were asleep.

As Sieg was making a simple meal from ingredients loaded on the yagus, a group of migratory birds with long, decorative feathers flew overhead, chasing the setting sun.

"Wigglertrills. I wonder if that's their first migration."

The migration of wigglertrills announced the arrival of autumn in the Labyrinth City.

During the current season, the migratory birds could only be seen high in the sky from the Labyrinth City. No one knew where they lived. However, after they'd passed overhead, the days shortened, the temperature started to drop, and the leaves began to change color. That was why wigglertrills became known as the harbingers of autumn.

No one knew the exact colors of the birds, as most only ever saw their shadows against the setting sun. But as migratory birds, they were on the smaller side. Perhaps because of the altitude, Sieg and the others could see them more clearly here than they'd ever been able to in the Labyrinth City. Wigglertrills flying in a line with their long, decorative feathers proved a beautiful sight, even from a distance.

Mariela gazed absentmindedly at the sky.

Watching her, Sieg thought nostalgically about how he'd met Mariela during this same season. He nearly remarked out loud how it'd soon be a year since the two had first found each other. Before he could, however, Freyja informed him of the following day's schedule.

"Sieg, you'll be hunting wigglertrills tomorrow. Your arrows will be able to reach them from here." Although their plans had yet been undecided, Freyja went ahead and made the choice for all of them.

"What?"

"Huh?"

It seemed that the second day of Sieg and Mariela's first overnight excursion together would be spent apart, thanks to the young alchemist's guardian exerting her absolute power.

The next day, Mariela reluctantly climbed back onto her yagu, crying to Freyja, "We're so high up, I'm scared, Masterrr!"

The mountain road was much steeper than the previous day's climb. The poor girl's master continued to offer a rather useless reply: *"You're fiiine."*

Meanwhile, Sieg, who had been ordered to go off on his own, drove his yagu at full speed as it carried him away from the mountain road with poor footholds.

"Gh, I never would have imagined wigglertrills were this aggressive…"

As soon as he reached a slightly stable spot in the earth, Sieg turned and readied his bow. Shooting wigglertrills in the sky from the back of a swaying yagu required advanced marksmanship, but with the help of the Spirit Eye, it wasn't particularly difficult.

Thunk.

With a sound like the piercing of tough but thin armor, the lead wigglertrill fell from the sky. Far from flinching, however, the birds that had been following their leader increased their speed, charging toward Sieg. At the rate they were going, the wigglertrills probably wouldn't stop attacking until Sieg brought down the last of them.

It had been a mistake underestimate these migratory birds and shoot the first one in a large group. A far more prudent strategy would have been to shoot the rearmost bird so that the others wouldn't notice. The flock of wigglertrills, noticing their lost companion, had taken a sharp turn to attack Sieg in an attempt for revenge.

Did she designate this place expecting this to happen...?

This was where they had camped last night. The terrain was like a valley surrounded by the crumbling rock of the mountains. Although footholds were hard to come by, there was no fear of tumbling off the mountainside. Also, if Sieg ventured a little farther, there was a place where tunnels had formed from the accumulation of debris, along with many large stray rocks to hide behind. Both made it easy to dodge the flock of wigglertrills descending upon him like a volley of arrows.

Sieg lowered his body to cling to the yagu and plunged into a gap between boulders. The flock of wigglertrills passed by just behind him. The place he'd gone into wasn't a cave, however, but merely a gap between a few close boulders, so the birds immediately circled around the great stones and came at him again. Still, the maneuver had served to put some distance between Sieg and the flock of angered little creatures.

What? They're flanking?!

Evidently, wigglertrills were intelligent. Just by his passing through this same place a few times, they had memorized his movement pattern and circled around to both the front and the back.

Gh. If I can fell two—no, three from the front on the left, I can get away!

Sieg instantly understood the trajectory of each wigglertrill, and he loosed several arrows. How many did that make now? How many more were left?

Riding on the wind and flapping their wings, wigglertrills could fly at both high and low altitudes, and turn at seemingly impossible speeds. These creatures the same size as small migratory birds had wings covered in feathers, and a head and tail with beautiful plumage but no beak. When they opened their pointed mouths, Sieg saw small, sharp teeth, and every time they flew by, he could feel an invocation of magical power.

Impossible... Could a wigglertrill actually be some kind of dragon...?

If not for their proportionally limited stamina, Sieg might not have been able to outdo the relentless little creatures. Sieg saw no chance of victory against that many wigglertrills, aside from defeating them in one shot.

Sieg opened his Spirit Eye wide and probed the swarm's movements from the right, from the left, from behind, from above. He watched their patterns and secured a route. And although he gained distance, Sieg also watched for an opening.

Is this supposed to be training for my Spirit Eye...?

Whether intentionally or not, it proved as such, and difficult training at that. Sieg had thought this was merely some kind of excursion, but it was a one-man boot camp.

I have to defeat them before Mariela gets back.

This was typical of Freyja. She'd circumvented this entire place, probably to protect Mariela from a wigglertrill attack, and sent Sieg off on his lonesome to take care of things.

The hunter imagined himself walking alone on the way back with a large number of wigglertrills piled on the yagu. He shivered to shake off that image and readied himself as well as his bow.

"We're heeere."

"Owww, my rear hurts…"

Freyja nimbly descended from the yagu, and Mariela followed, slipping off the creature. The young alchemist's master had taken Mariela to a cave entrance resembling a natural fissure that had been cleaved by collapsing rocks.

"Light."

Mariela followed her instructor, who had chanted an illumination spell and entered the cave. The alchemist's legs wobbled with exhaustion. The inside of the cave was made up of a truly immense lode: sparkling crystals protruded from just about everywhere the eye could see. After they climbed through the cavern for about half an hour, light from somewhere deeper within became visible. It quickly became so bright that Mariela and Freyja no longer needed magic to see where they were going.

"This is a crystal cavern."

The crystals filling the walls seemed to be of high purity. It appeared to Mariela that anyone who mined here would surely strike it rich. The two eventually came to a more spacious area, where crystals as tall as a person stood packed together, as though only the clearest ones had been polished and lined up.

It was like a museum of shimmering stone. The roof of the enclosure had a hole like it had been blown through, and the light of the sunset beamed down through the aperture. As the sun bobbed lazily into the horizon, it dyed the crystals a crimson shade. How radiant would it have been in broad daylight with the sun shining from straight overhead?

Even now, when it wasn't getting much light, the place seemed to overflow with a mysterious power.

"Seems like no one's come here in two hundred years," Freyja muttered as she surveyed their surroundings.

"Master, was this a famous place?"

"Nah. It's my secret spot. There aren't many spots where you can gather magical power from the moon. Mariela, keep this place a secret. Although, we're gonna take it all with us today, so it'll probably be decades before anyone can get such a large amount again."

Freyja had shared something significant with her pupil in bringing her here. However, Mariela wasn't able to make a trip like this on her own, and the girl had no confidence she'd even remember how to get back decades from now.

What Mariela was going to make with the magical power of the moon was a well-known, exceptionally expensive potion. The alchemist wondered whether there was any simpler way to get a steady supply of this material other than coming to a rocky mountain like this, where it could only be harvested once every few decades. It was said the imperial capital had established a method of cultivating lunamagia. Even Mariela had been able to accomplish something similar, cultivating aurora ice fruit in her magical tool for freezing. As she considered this, Mariela had dinner with her master and waited for the moon to rise.

The moon seemed to have reached the highest point in the sky while Mariela, tired from traveling, was dozing off. When Freyja woke her and she opened her eyes, Mariela took in the sight of the beautiful pale orb visible from the hole in the cave's ceiling.

Moonlight poured in a steady trickle from the perfectly round moon, unobstructed by even a single cloud. In that cavern, awash in the night's glow, the moonlight reflected by the crystals seemed to ever so gently spill over.

Lunar rays gave off no heat. Even if you touched one of the shining crystals, all you'd feel was the usual coolness of a rock. In that cold, unassuming moonlight—rays full of peace—dwelled a power that belonged to no one.

The moon's magical power.

"Mariela, start now."

"Okay, Master."

Mariela produced from her waist pouch a transparent ball that fit in the palm of her hand.

This ball, which Freyja had described as "having passable roundness, considering it took no time to get," had been recovered from a dragon head of the Sea-Floating Pillar in the fifty-fourth stratum of the Labyrinth. Apparently, it was part of a lens that focused the beams of light that had previously given the Labyrinth Suppression Forces a tough time.

The original had been big enough to carry in both arms, but

this was the biggest piece recovered after the battle, an indication of how extreme the destruction had been.

Despite its size, it was a first-class material. In particular, the sphere's nature enabled it to focus and accumulate magical power at a rate thousands of times greater than that of ordinary crystals. This made it perfectly suited to Mariela and Freyja's purposes.

Mariela took the crystal ball in both hands, walked to the middle of the space, and held the small orb aloft in the light of the moon. Both the moonlight shining in from above and that coming from the gemlike pillars converged on the crystal ball Mariela held as if to allow it to absorb the pale glow.

The phenomenon was like water flowing down from the hills, completely different from the reflection and refraction. To an outside observer, it likely would have seemed that the small crystalline ball was the source of the light, not the other way around.

The magical power of the moon had no color and belonged to no one. So if you processed it into a potion, it could give that energy to whoever drank it. This made the power of the moon a key material in mana potions, a mysterious kind of medicine that could restore magical power.

A person could collect the magical power of these crystals only when they were bathed in moonlight. As soon as the moon moved from the highest spot in its alignment, or if it became obstructed in any way, it would be impossible to draw any more of the stored magical power from the crystals.

"Drops of Life."

Mariela raised her free right hand with her open palm facing the sky.

"Wind."

Freyja called upon wind magic at the same time.

Drops of Life rode on the wind and sprinkled throughout the cavern. The droplets changed into particles smaller than mist and came to rest on the crystals. Freyja's winds then carried the vapor back. This was to reveal and gather the remaining magical power of the moon stored in the crystals.

Just as Freyja had said, the crystal ball had taken the entirety of the magical power in the crystals into itself. All that emanated from the little orb now was some flickering moonlight. It looked like a glass ball with shimmering water trapped inside.

"Let's sleep here tonight. We'll meet up with Sieg tomorrow."

Indicating that the cave was safe, Freyja flopped down on a pelt she'd spread on the ground, completely defenseless. Mariela spread her own pelt next to Freyja's and joined her.

"Master, this cave's a little cold."

"Truth is, the temperature hardly changes at all in here. It's actually pretty warm come wintertime. It's because the ceiling is open. Since you can see the moon and the stars, it's not bad as far as the scenery goes, either."

Freyja laughed, saying that alcohol would've made the whole thing complete, and Mariela nestled close to her. The two hadn't slept this close together since Mariela was very young, when her master had first taken custody of her.

"Hey, Master."

"Hmm? What is it?"

"It's been forever since we spent time together like this, just the two of us."

"Oh? Sieg is always out hunting, so it hasn't been that long."

"Mm, that's true, but...there are always people in the city."

"Ahh, I guess it has been a long time since we were totally alone."

In the past, the young alchemist hadn't sensed the presence of other people at all. As she became more proficient in her craft, Mariela started to notice just how many people were living in the Labyrinth City. She really didn't know whether it was the Drops of Life flowing through the Nexus that connected her to the ley line, or the Drops of Life dwelling in and drifting through her surroundings that she had begun to sense. Either way, Mariela was now able to perceive it, where she hadn't before. So...

"Hey, Master."

"What?"

"When I woke up a year ago, I felt like something had awakened in me. Did you experience anything like that?"

"Who can say?"

Just as Mariela had expected, her master didn't give a straight answer.

"Heeey, Master."

"What now?"

"Wigglertrills are a wind-type dragon species, aren't they?"

"That's right."

"Earth-type earth dragon, fire-type red dragon, water-type philoroilcus, and wind-type wigglertrill. We've got all four elements."

"Yup."

These four types of dragon blood were also materials for potions with powerful effects, though different from mana potions. Neither philoroilcuses nor wigglertrills were known by most as dragon species, so it probably would have taken an extremely long time for Mariela to get all four elements without her master's help.

The golden-eyed sage hadn't offered any kind of explanation, but Mariela somehow understood. Everything they had to do was done. Doubtless, everything they needed had been collected now.

"We got them all...," Mariela muttered, and her teacher gently put her arm around Mariela's back and slowly patted her, as if lulling a child to sleep.

"There's still a bit more time. Just about enough to make a Magic Circle of Suspended Animation." Freyja's voice was unusually tender, her tone like that used to speak to a beloved infant. But Mariela calmly shook her head as she answered.

"I can't leave everyone behind to save myself."

There had been people two hundred years ago who treated Mariela with kindness, but she hadn't had any deep relationships with any of them. Mariela hadn't hesitated to escape the Stampede alone with a Magic Circle of Suspended Animation.

Her master had been the sole exception, of course, but Freyja had left their cottage in the Fell Forest three years prior, and Mariela hadn't known where she was. That was why Mariela held no regrets about having put herself into suspended animation back then. But now...

"I'm glad you have so many to care for." Freyja said warmly.

"Mm-hmm..." Mariela had grown sleepy from her master's high body temperature and the hand soothingly patting her back. "...Hey, Master."

"Mm?"

"Don't...disappear suddenly...this time..."

Freyja responded with a gentle smile tinged with chagrin. Whatever her answer was went unheard: Mariela had already fallen asleep. The light of the moon in the crystal cavern gently settled over teacher and student like a blanket.

04

The next morning, Mariela and Freyja departed from the crystal cavern and met up with Sieg in the afternoon. Sieg and his yagu were sitting next to a pile of dozens of wigglertrills. He bore no conspicuous injuries, thanks to the use of potions, though he and his mount seemed absolutely ragged from their efforts.

"Whoa, good job!"

Despite receiving such rare praise from Freyja, Sieg seemed a bit dejected. "I couldn't fully command the Spirit Eye; I felled the last ones with my sword." He appeared to have fought a great number of flocks while healing and resting when he could between each encounter.

"Ahh, that doesn't matter, does it? As long as you were able to beat them. Here, drink up."

Sieg had battled the wigglertrills thinking it was training to master his Spirit Eye. Apparently, all he'd really had to do was catch the creatures. After she handed Sieg a mid-grade heal potion, Freyja told Mariela to use *Crystallize Medicine* on the wigglertrills' blood.

"Ohh?! They're so tiny, but their dragon blood might be pretty thick."

"The strength of a dragon species isn't measured just in terms of offensive ability or the size of the body. These guys have stupidly long lifespans. Though, despite their long lives, they have the same intelligence as migratory birds. All they do is chase the wind."

"Whoa." Mariela gave a vague reply, as if she didn't really understand. The alchemist held out her hands toward the mountain of wigglertrills felled by arrow and blade and gave her *Crystallize Medicine* skill a shot.

The philoroilcus had been so big she'd thought it was an iceberg itself, yet its dragon blood was very diluted. As such, Mariela had gotten a disproportionately small amount of medicinal crystals from it. This necessitated returning to the Labyrinth many times over to get enough just to fill a vial. Conversely, the alchemist was able to get a full vial's worth of medicinal crystals from the small mountain of wigglertrills. After all their blood had been converted to medicinal crystals, the wigglertrill corpses began to transform into something resembling dead leaves or molted husks. In the blink of an eye, the small bodies of the creatures went from soft to dry.

As Mariela watched the abrupt change with astonishment, a strong gust of wind blew between the rocks to lift the wigglertrill corpses and send them scattering like fallen leaves.

They whirled around and around as they rose on the wind toward the sky; then they suddenly reverted to their little bird-like shapes. They loudly *cheep-cheep*ed and fell in line with each other, soaring toward the western sky.

"...They came back to life!"

"Yup. They are like the embodiment of the wind; they don't simply die. Since we extracted their dragon blood, they'll probably stay small for a while, though."

"Whoaaa," Mariela uttered, astonished.

Freyja turned to the alchemist and said, "With this, our task is done."

Recalling the conversation from the night before, Mariela felt a slight twinge of melancholy.

"Okay. Master, Sieg, let's go home."

"Ah, if we hurry, we can get back to the Labyrinth City before the end of the day."

"Whaaat? I don't want another scary ride…"

Although he should have been tired after the battle with the wigglertrills, Sieg wanted to hurry home. He wore an expression of extreme disappointment at seeing Mariela climb onto her master's yagu again, but he would have many opportunities to ride his yagu in the future.

"Since we finished what we needed to do, let's take our time heading back. We can get home before the end of the day even if we take it slow," Mariela said to no one in particular, as if reassuring herself they could make their way home at a reasonable pace.

I don't think it was just me who awoke, Mariela thought as she recalled the previous night's conversation with her master. Though she had no real basis for the supposition, Mariela somehow knew that her days being jostled around on Freyja's yagu were dwindling.

05

"You stink. Take a bath in the bathhouse outside and then come back."

"Heh-heh, sorry, young doc."

Paying no attention to the displeased expression of the young noble sitting in the examination room, a middle-aged man flashed his yellowed teeth in a smile and left the room, dragging his leg behind him. The dirtied man headed for the clinic's reception desk, where he said, "The doc told me to take a bath." The receptionist handed him a ticket of admittance to the bathhouse. The man accepted the ticket with the hand not holding a cane and thrust it into the pocket of his dirty tunic. His cuffs were worn out, and he hadn't washed his clothes in a while, so they were very dirty. The man smelled so bad even he himself could tell.

S'pose I'll wash them, too, while I'm at it.

The Labyrinth's City economy had improved recently, and the man had come into some steady work as of late, so he had a little extra money to spend.

Conveniently, the bathhouse had a place for doing laundry. The man could borrow tools and do it himself, but for several copper coins, there was also a service that would wash his clothes for him while he took a bath. A clean body just out of the bath wearing freshly washed and folded clothes felt extremely nice, even if those clothes were his usual rags. For one who had lived alone for

a long time, putting on clothing that had been washed and prepared by someone else felt extremely respectable and first-class.

The fee for a bath was also just a few copper coins, but a bathing fee, a laundry fee, and the costs of meals and lodging all at
once added up to a considerable sum. That was why the man was
grateful for the free bathing ticket.

The youth treating people in the clinic appeared to be of noble
birth. His arrogant manner of speech, his conduct, and the way
he looked at people made him the spitting image of an upstart
nobleman in the dirty, middle-aged man's eye. The older man had
most certainly been upset by the noble's attitude at first, but there
were escort soldiers waiting behind him. The truth of it was that
the older man's clothes and his body were well and truly unclean.
When he had stood up for himself and defiantly proclaimed, "I
haven't been able to bathe, so I can't help it if I'm filthy," a bathhouse was constructed soon after near the clinic, and he'd been
given a ticket to use it.

Somehow, that young noble didn't seem to be as bad as his
demeanor had first suggested.

Now when the middle-aged man went to the clinic, he made
sure to look as dirty as possible so he'd get a free bathing ticket.
He'd thought he alone had come up with this trick, but it became
clear rather quickly that he was not so unique. Other slum residents who visited the clinic soon began using the same method to
get bathing tickets.

When the man with the bad leg handed over his bathing ticket
at the entrance to the bathhouse, he received a small bar of soap
and a hand towel.

There were cheaper tickets that could be purchased for only
two copper coins, but they didn't come with the soap or the towel.

Still, the place was run by a noble. The ill-tempered young man proved generous and gave people the more expensive bathing tickets. Neither the soap nor the towel was used up in a single bath, and the poor man was free to take them home and use them again.

The once-dirty man didn't know if it was because he was living a more hygienic life or because he'd been eating better as of late, but recently, his health had improved.

"Your leg's grown quite a bit, huh?"

"Oh, it's you. Yep, that's right."

Shedding his dirtied clothes and dragging his leg as he headed for the bathtub, the man was greeted by another person. An acquaintance of his from the slums.

"There wasn't enough of it ta drag before."

"By the by, how ye been lately?"

"Oh, I'm doin' good. Completely recovered."

At the sight of his acquaintance spreading his dominant hand to show all five fingers, the man thought, *Lucky guy.*

If he remembered correctly, the ring and pinky fingers of his friend's hand had been bitten off by a monster. His acquaintance hadn't been able to properly grip a sword with the remaining three fingers, so he'd eked out a living by carrying baggage and such.

The middle-aged man had lost his leg all the way to the middle of his thigh, and it had taken a long time to even get back this much through healing. The other man had comparatively lost far less, only lost two fingers, so he'd quickly healed and been able to return to the Labyrinth.

"I envy ye," the man commented honestly.

"What're ya talkin' about? Ya just got a little while to go before you're all healed up, too, yeah? After all, ya can use magic, and once your leg's back to normal, you'll be stronger than me. How about this: When you're better, let's go into the Labyrinth together."

"It's a deal. Thanks."

The man with the wounded leg could almost wrap his fingers around his recovery now, and that was why he was envious. He had a nagging feeling that if he pushed himself just a little, he could return to the Labyrinth right now, even though he knew he needed to be patient.

Pipe dreams like becoming very rich and living in a stately mansion or becoming an S-Ranker and making a name for himself didn't inspire envy, even if they were fun to imagine. The man knew that strong, honest jealousy was precisely because he had the very real sense that both of his legs would soon be whole again and he would be able to enter the Labyrinth, just like the other man who'd gotten his fingers back.

"I wanna return to the Labyrinth before winter gets 'ere," the man muttered. There was food distribution in the slums, so he wouldn't starve to death, but the winter was harsh. If snow fell, cold water would soak through the holes in his shoes and make his feet ache as if they were frozen through. Even the leg he'd since lost seemed to complain of the cold, as the damaged appendage still felt pain as plainly as any whole limb.

"You'll be fine. But don't even think about doin' things by yourself right after you're cured. You'll find others like us in the Adventurers Guild, and staff members will accompany ya into the Labyrinth; make use of that resource."

"Ohh, that sounds great. I'll do just that," the man answered. Starting to feel a little dizzy, he got out of the bathtub. Once his leg finally healed, he'd be able to take a bath like this every day, and he'd probably be able to afford some better food and a nicer place to sleep.

Until now, the only thing the man had wished was for winter to end early. The way his life had been going, the only things on his mind were surviving to the next day and gathering up any trash he could find that might be useful. But now, the man was surprised to find that even his innermost feelings had changed. He could recall, if only just a little, the feelings from before he'd lost his leg, back when he was still a man full of hopes and desires.

Food, clothes, shelter. These things were necessary, but after having spent the last winter without a leg, holding on to feelings of desire and ambition seemed to be just as necessary to the man as something to eat or drink.

"'Not dying' and 'living' ain't the same thing."

"Yeah, no doubt about that. We'd do well not to forget it."

The man who'd lost fingers agreed with the man who'd lost his leg. Neither person was possessed of great intelligence, but both had realized something important during their struggles.

Unaware that he was giving residents of the slums ambition and the will to live, the young noble in the clinic, Robert Aguinas, breathed a quiet sigh. This clinic had been built on the southwestern side of the Labyrinth using the profits from sales of potions in the City. It had been constructed specifically to treat people living in the slums who could no longer fight because of grievous injuries. However, others who'd suffered injury in the Labyrinth also found themselves at Robert's clinic. Among those, Robert was in charge of serious cases, like those who'd lost arms or legs.

Special-grade potions were crucial for subjugating stratum

bosses. The ley-line shards used as materials in such concoctions were limited since monsters so rarely left them behind when slain. Although the Aguinas family had been building a supply of shards for about a hundred years, that didn't mean the potions made from them were readily used for the people who sought treatment at the clinic.

That was why Robert was putting high-grade potions and the techniques of the black new medicine he'd once manufactured to practical use, regenerating missing body parts over time.

When Robert had begun administering treatment here, he'd found the squalid people of the slums unbearable. They were in such unsanitary conditions that at dinnertime, against his better judgment, he'd complained to his younger sister, Caroline.

"My, an unhygienic environment will lead to infectious diseases! On that subject, I have heard there are public baths in the imperial capital," Caroline had said after listening to him complain. Shortly afterward, the bathhouse was built.

One might've thought it philanthropic work befitting a woman of nobility. However, the construction was, in fact, quite profitable. Construction of the bathhouse helped establish a number of related businesses, including the cheap provision of hand towels from villages near the Fell Forest, the manufacturing of soap sold at the bath (thanks to everything they'd learned making pest control dumplings), and the establishment of a laundry service to clean the terrible stains acquired in the Labyrinth.

The bathhouse itself was popular, but the Aguinas family also improved their reputation by creating new jobs for people who were unable to fight. The future of the family was exceedingly secure, and Robert, dealing with less-than-savory characters every day, found himself in a slight bind.

*   *   *

Robert sighed again. The examination room reeked of his patients.

Human body odor is so unsettling. What would calm Robert's heart was the smell of a library with a large number of books, or the slightly musty smell of a damp cellar.

While he'd been manufacturing the new medicine, he'd come in contact with many materials, but what thrilled his nostrils was the suffocating smell of blood and the odor of chemicals with unique stimuli, not the stench that wafted from the people of the slums and the adventurers who visited him in the clinic.

Why does it smell sour? Sweat? The bodies Robert begrudgingly touched to do his medical examinations were hot, and their hearts pounded.

Many patients took the opportunity during their examinations to make Robert listen to them talk about completely unrelated things—what monster they'd defeated that day, how such-and-such a place had delicious food, how some shop had a cute girl. All of them became more talkative as their conditions improved.

They'd explain how, when their injuries were healed, they'd go into the Labyrinth and make a lot of money. And when they'd earned all that money, they were going to eat the delicious food, or talk to the cute girl, or save up a lot for a home someday. They wanted a house, or to start a business, or to have their parents move here so they could live more comfortably. Over and over, Robert was forced to listen to these stories, and he felt that each and every one of these little anecdotes was truly idiotic. Without exception, these trite, meager wishes were the kind that could be found anywhere.

Two hundred years after the Stampede, these kinds of hopes and dreams were hardly original. They were just like the one the Aguinas family and the alchemists shared, the one that had bound them together.

Every one of the people who had been injured and healed returned to the Labyrinth.

Twenty percent of their earnings was paid through the Adventurers Guild for the cost of treatment, so there was no need for them to pay the clinic separately. Yet still they brought Robert game or some of the items they'd harvested below the city to express their gratitude for his treating them. They'd bring him things like monster meat unsuited for a nobleman, unfamiliar fruit, or medicinal herbs that he couldn't use because he wasn't an alchemist.

Even though I tell them it's unnecessary... Nevertheless, it's still less objectionable to see people in perfectly good health.

Despite Robert's painstaking efforts to heal them, some returned with new wounds. There were even a few who never came back from the Labyrinth at all.

"Are you going to enter the Labyrinth again?" Robert asked an adventurer whose injuries he'd healed more than once.

"Darn right I am," the adventurer replied, as if it were a matter of course. "No need to worry; I won't die before I've paid off my whole bill."

"That is…not what I'm saying."

No matter how expensive the cost of treatment at this clinic, the agreement was for patients to pay twenty percent of their earnings toward their bill until it was paid in full. Even if they had families, however, those families were under no obligation to pay. In other words, if they died, the debt was forgiven.

The clinic's operating costs were covered by the profits from the sale of potions, so even an unpaid bill wasn't cause for concern. So then why was the return of adventurers to the Labyrinth so frustrating? Robert bit his thin lower lip as he wondered.

All of these people had suffered terrible injuries, wound up in the slums living in squalor, and yet all of them returned to the Labyrinth once they'd been healed. It was probably dreadful to face monsters and painful to suffer injuries, yet they dared to descend regardless.

"It's 'cause I got no other options. I'm a bit of a blockhead."

They all gave excuses: "It's 'cause I got no other options. I'm a bit of a fool, y'see."

I understand...

A wish born from alchemists had been passed down through the generations over the two hundred years since the Stampede. That meager wish, one that the lineage of the Aguinas family had sought over many years to grant, was no different from the wish of those of the people he was treating.

I knew this...

Although the people Robert made into "materials" and murdered had committed crimes in the past, they too were human beings. Those people had been no different from the ones Robert now treated.

The *smell* of the people Robert administered treatment to today was indelibly ingrained in his body. The *stench* of the blood of those Robert had killed over many years, and the stink of the liquid medicine, it had all seeped into his pores, never to be washed out.

People he healed continued to challenge the Labyrinth. Their eyes were full of hope at the chance to fulfill once unattainable dreams. Having gotten their lives back, those people shone with a new determination. Robert was sure that was what kept them fighting in the Labyrinth, that drive to achieve their dreams of winning fortune and happiness. They descended into the depths even when it was that very same Labyrinth that had taken everything from them in the first place.

Robert continued to heal those intrepid people. Day in and day out, he was surrounded by the scent of humans, and his heart could never quite settle down amid all the hustle and bustle. With so much work to be done, Robert wasn't afforded the leisure of either thinking back on the past or looking to the future.

It was like a multistory sand castle, built only to collapse. Higher and higher.

It was impossible for it to reach the sky. Robert would build it, it would fall, and a wave would sweep the sand away. Right from under his feet.

It's fine if you're not in perfect health. I'll heal you, no problem. Just come back alive...

If they didn't return to see him in the clinic, then there was nothing he could do for them. He knew it, and though he didn't recognize the feeling as such, he regretted it. At the time, the number of adventurers venturing into the Labyrinth far exceeded the number of soldiers in the Labyrinth Suppression Forces. It could have very well been the highest numbers since the Stampede.

Those adventurers who sustained injuries and survived many times over, who learned through painful experience, were all cautious. They battled monsters without overstepping their own limitations and began to find the means they needed to accumulate wealth.

06

"Can't believe they decided to bring the young lady to this stratum…" Old Man Ghark looked at Mariela. He spoke like a grandfather might to a child taking their first wobbly steps.

This was the fifty-sixth stratum of the Labyrinth. A stratum of lava where the Walking Mountain of Fire and the red dragon had once held dominion. Only those two monsters had lived here. With them gone, this level of the Labyrinth was free of harmful creatures. The stratum itself remained dangerous, however. It was still hot; scattered lava pools dotted the place, and rocks scattered about from the Walking Mountain of Fire's explosion made it difficult to travel on foot. Ice Spirit's Protection potions kept the group protected from the high temperature, but if anyone carelessly fell into a pool of lava, that would be it.

"Waugh!"

Mariela, who'd been walking along the unstable rocks, tripped on one and almost tumbled over. Sieg was at her side supporting her, but the unsteady way she walked was very dangerous.

"Wouldn't it be better if ye rode piggyback?" Ghark suggested, although that would be fairly embarrassing.

"If I don't see it up close, I won't be able to find it," Mariela replied without looking back at the old man. She kept her eyes forward, watching cracks in the hardened lava. "Ah, that rock. Please break that one, Mr. Ghark."

"Right. Stand back a bit so ye don't get hit with any debris."

With a powerful motion that belied his age, Ghark swung a pickax down at the lump of hardened lava Mariela had indicated. Their goal today was to break rocks, so he was using a custom-made pickax instead of his usual double ax. It was hard to tell because of its black color and rough shape, but this rock, the result of lava rapidly cooling, had a great many cracks running along it due to the coagulation and shrinking caused by drop in temperature. Parts of the stone that contained heavy amounts of metal proved difficult to break open. However, cracking open such rocks was doable if one aimed for spots with less sturdy metal. Aiming for the spots where different materials mixed in the same lump of stone also made the hard masses easier to split.

"Ah, this really was it. With this... Yeah, this will be a secondary material."

"Lemme see... This is harsh for my old eyes."

Mariela and Ghark carefully observed the cross section of the broken lava-stone.

"Is it...alive?" Sieg asked dubiously as he peered over Mariela's head.

Freyja, who had been poking around the lava pools by herself with a metal pole, suddenly deigned to join the group. "It'd be faster to get it out of the rock if that was the case."

Cooled molten rock stuck to the end of the long pole Freyja carried, but around it was something resembling creeping ivy or the roots of a plant. Upon closer inspection, it was moving, too, albeit extremely slowly. The same plantlike thing was in the cross section of the rock Mariela and the others were looking at, but since it had crawled into the rock and only a bit of it appeared in the cross section, it was difficult to spot without close observation.

Since they each had special means of recognition—Ghark with Appraisal, Mariela with alchemy, and Sieg with the Spirit Eye—they'd each been able to spot it: a rootlike lava-dwelling creature with thin feelers.

Mariela had read about something matching this description, called *fibrous lava*, molten rock with a particular mineral composition. Yet when she and the others observed it using their special skills or divine protection, the thing was unmistakably a living creature.

The reason such a thing hadn't been decisively classified as an organism was due to its makeup. Unlike people, animals, and plants, the foundation of this creature's composition was closer to something like sand. It could move around freely in high temperatures like lava, but when the lava hardened like this, it apparently died from the cold. The group cautiously observed the fibrous lava Freyja had caught with her pole and found that the tips of the thin feelers split into five or six branches like a starfish, and it seemed to be budding even further.

If a scholar well acquainted with oceanography took a look, they would probably say it resembled a basket star. This strange creature was harder than steel right now, yet it was so brittle it would crumble if you tapped it with an adamantite needle.

"I think it'd be best if I take the whole rock to the Labyrinth Suppression Forces' base."

"Yes, please, Mr. Ghark."

Ghark waved his hand in a dismissive "don't worry about it" kind of gesture. Mariela and Sieg bowed their heads to him. The old man was still unaware that Mariela was an alchemist, but he seemed perfectly happy to take charge of harvesting activities, even in such a hot stratum.

"Young lady, ye've got other things to do, don't ye? Leave this place to me, and hurry on up the stairs. It's dangerous here, and just watchin' ye makes me nervous," he told Mariela.

When she thanked him and turned in Freyja's direction, Mariela saw her master once again plunging her pole into a pool of lava and industriously collecting fibrous lava.

"Master is actually harvesting..."

This was unheard of. Mariela half expected there to be rain on the fifty-sixth stratum tomorrow. A downpour that would harden everything here to steaming rock. What other reason could there have been for her master to work so hard?

"Marielaaa, these lava starfish are so funny! If I poke them with the pole, they wrap around it right away! I've got a big catch! They're biting at every cast! Whoo-hoo!!!"

Somehow, Freyja had gotten hooked on those mysterious creatures, even giving them the name *lava starfish*. After they twined around the tip of her pole, Freyja hauled them up, and they cooled and hardened. After several repetitions of this, Freyja had built up a huge ball of them on the tip of the pole. The sage seemed quite engrossed as she industriously poked the lava. Her eyes shone far brighter than they usually did as she moved about excitedly.

A high density of fibrous lava was wrapped around the tip of Freyja's pole. As alchemical reagents, there could've been no better state for them to be in. However, lava pools were not transparent. Above all, the luminescence caused by the high temperature meant one couldn't even stare at the puddles directly. They knew the fibrous lava didn't stick to a pole thrust into the lava at random. So perhaps Freyja's eyes could somehow spot the fibrous lava, and that directed where she poked the long metal rod.

"I wonder what's going on with my master's eyes. Sieg, can you tell?"

"No, the light the lava emits is too strong, and even if I stare with my Spirit Eye, it starts to burn."

Freyja seemed to be having so much fun that Mariela and Sieg were content to leave her. The two quietly went up the stratum stairs together. At this rate, Freyja would probably collect however much needed to adequately explore how to process the unusual creatures all on her own.

Mariela's group had a good reason for coming to gather these things that previously weren't even known to be alive. They were looking for a secondary material to use in a special potion that incorporated all four types of dragon blood.

Mariela had reached a sufficient level of proficiency to make the concoction. Usually the Library disclosed all the main and secondary materials, telling the young alchemist everything she needed. However, in this particular case, the letters naming the secondary materials were hazy, as if they were behind frosted glass. Despite great effort, Mariela couldn't decipher them.

"This potion unifies the four elements, which by all rights should be impossible to assimilate. The reason differing and incompatible things can exist close to each other in this world is because they have forms as individuals or as races. What I mean is, even with the same fire-type dragon blood, you have this red dragon that was born and raised in the Labyrinth, and then there are black fire dragons that live in a red-hot area known as the Earth's Navel. Each requires a different secondary material in order to intermingle with the blood of other dragons."

Freyja had given actual masterly guidance for once. Since that was the case, Mariela expected her teacher to tell her what was needed for this combination. But Freyja refused, only saying, "The refining process starts with discovery. You haven't crystallized the red dragon blood or the earth dragon blood yet. You should try looking at them and thinking carefully about what makes them what they are."

When Mariela heeded the advice and looked for anything in common between the red dragon and earth dragon, she got a hunch that a hint lay in this stratum of fire and stone, the very place where the red dragon had dwelled. From there, she perused books from the Aguinas and Schutzenwald estates, all relating to lava zones. Mariela gathered specimens and finally hit upon the idea of the fibrous lava. Although the young alchemist had previously learned about materials and processing methods from the Library, she was now searching for it on her own in the wild, just as the predecessors who'd left all that knowledge in the Library once had.

The fibrous lava Mariela's group found probably hadn't been recorded in the Library as a secondary material because it lacked versatility, but Mariela had the feeling she'd grown a little more as an alchemist by finding the material like this.

Dragon blood contained toxins. It was said that the blood of earth dragons melted rocks and the blood of red dragons burned all living things it touched to ashes.

One would shake up dragon blood with several types of oil with different melting temperatures and then separate them. The toxins were removed by repeating this process many times over. In the case of earth dragon blood, three types of oil were needed.

Red dragon blood required even more kinds, as well as a higher temperature, to process.

Even after the toxins were removed, the boiling trait of the red dragon blood and the ability of the earth dragon blood to easily dissolve the ground didn't disappear. The fibrous lava Mariela somehow managed to find was the optimum material for blending these two blood types.

It was to be cooled at a temperature so low it would turn the alchemist's very breath to liquid. Then the material was finely crushed and finally sifted from the ordinary lava with swirling wind. When medicinal crystals of earth dragon blood were added to fibrous lava that had been reduced to a fine black powder, the powder immediately became a liquid.

If one added plenty of Drops of Life to it in this state, it formed air bubbles, as if it was boiling, despite the low temperature. It would continue to bubble and swell until it reached around double its previous volume. Adding red dragon blood medicinal crystals at this point caused the bubbles to multiply tremendously, taking the form of a fine froth.

Manipulating the Transmutation Vessel to make sure the temperature stayed the same was crucial. Otherwise, all the Drops of Life would be lost. Great caution was required. Keeping up with the rapid change was the part that worried the slightly clumsy Mariela the most.

"Phew, I did it."

The reddish-brown liquid resulting from the procedure had a muddy color by nature yet gave off an intense light, as lava did. It looked like the exact opposite of the verdigris liquid medicine created by blending the water-type philoroilcus and the wind-type wigglertrill. That brew had used frost tree flowers, a material obtained in the stratum of ice and snow.

As its name suggested, a frost tree flower was a bloom that grew on the tip of a frost-covered tree. Such trees were a natural phenomenon in which ice clung to plants in below-freezing environments and made them look like ice sculptures. If it was just ordinary ice, it didn't cause flowers to bloom. However, if the ice came from fragments blown off ice-type monsters by the wind and then fallen to rest on frozen trees, ice flowers would bloom, though only after a long period of time.

Such flowers were wondrous and beautiful, shining faintly and swaying in snowy gales. Unfortunately, they had the tendency to attract ice and wind monsters, making them very difficult to harvest. Unsurprisingly, Edgan was the one who undertook the task, facing down monsters and suffering through the bitter cold.

"Ah, Edgan, yeah? Perfect timing! There's some flowers I want."

"How very, very modest of you to want flowers! Certainly, any flower would fade and wilt before your beauty. But if it's flowers you want, I will go to the ends of the earth to pick them, or my name isn't Edgan!"

Such a situation had become fairly common, right down to Sieg being dragged along for the ride. It had become so commonplace Mariela had even forgotten about it. Regardless, thanks to the frost tree flowers, she was able to blend the water- and wind-type dragon blood.

"Next, I need to combine these two, but..."

Mariela took out the last material she'd stored. They were lovely flowers made of blue, green, and yellow crystals. They made a light sound, like pieces of thin glass clinking together, as she took them from the box.

These were plants that bloomed in a zone called the Sacred Tree Cemetery, said to be in an interval between strata somewhere in the Labyrinth.

The cemetery was a place where many sacred trees swallowed by the Stampede had come to rest.

Submerged in what looked like a shallow underground lake, the great trees had petrified and turned white. Despite how withered they'd become, the effects of the plants were still quite potent. Their resting place was one free of monsters, despite being in the middle of the Labyrinth. The Labyrinth supplied magical power even to this haven, and while that should have created monsters, the energy instead inhabited crystals, which then budded, grew, and bloomed like plants. The blossoms transformed into butterflies that danced and flitted through the Sacred Tree Cemetery, making it quite a beautiful setting. The crystal-born things flew around until they used up all their strength, and when the magical power ran out, they turned back into crystal fragments and fell. Fallen crystals melted into the water or the earth in the cemetery and disappeared. When enough magical power was stored again, the crystals would bloom and become butterflies once more.

The unusual flowers of the Sacred Tree Cemetery couldn't be harvested as they were. Here, the conflicting energies of the sacred trees and the Labyrinth coexisted; when the flowers were removed, they crumbled and vanished in an instant.

However, if a person poured their magical power into them to make them bloom, for some reason they remained flowers instead of becoming butterflies. This made it possible to gather the blossoms. Ghark had previously taken Mariela, Freyja, Sieg, Emily, Pallois, and Elio to harvest this material together.

Due to Nierenberg's unexpected situation, Sherry had been unable to attend and had seemed extremely disappointed, so Elio gave her the crystal flowers he'd collected as a present. As a result, Mariela didn't get his portion of the harvest, but she still had plenty from gathering her own, as well as what Sieg and her master had contributed. Curiously, the flowers bloomed with the color of the eyes of whoever poured their magical power into them, so it was obvious who'd made each flower blossom.

Coexistence of the energies of the sacred trees and the Labyrinth should have been impossible by all accounts. What allowed them to be fixed in a form that could exist even within the Labyrinth was the magical power of humans—was this mere irony? Human magic was the very thing that had severed the relationship between Endalsia and the monsters. Or did the magical power of Mariela and the others instead take away the ability of these flowers to fly through the air as butterflies?

When those fragile, ephemeral petals, which seemed likely to break from the slightest touch, absorbed the liquid medicine made from water and wind dragon blood, the leaves and stems became transparent, like sculpted water. When the liquid medicine made from fire and earth dragon blood was applied, the petals turned a color resembling blazing, fiery magma.

"Should I *Dehydrate* them…? No, what they probably need is *Transposition*."

As flowers, stems, and leaves, they needed a deeper connection. Mariela felt the flowers' current shape was probably a concept to build on. In order to spread the few junction points over a wider area, the young alchemist shifted the places where they were joined and changed their skeletal structure.

Mariela altered the shape of the flowers little by little in a Transmutation Vessel filled with Drops of Life until they became small lumps with marble patterns.

"This is still no good. They're just finely dispersed, not combined into one."

Mariela heated the dragon blood within the Transmutation Vessel to nearly a thousand degrees. Neither iron nor stone melted at that temperature. But the colossal amount of energy stabilized the fire and earth dragon blood and withstood the power of water and wind.

The instant everything melted together uniformly, Mariela lowered the temperature to below freezing as fast as she possibly could so that she could secure the mixture in its blended state.

"Looks like I managed to do it. But it's still a little too forced and distorted. I need to raise the temperature a bit and stabilize it…"

After she repeated the temperature-raising and preservation process several times, the murky dragon energy finally adapted, unified, and changed into a transparent sphere.

"Now, if I soak it for three days and three nights in ley-line shards dissolved in Drops of Life until it cleanly dissolves…that should complete it, I think. Though it'd be better if they never needed to use this kind of potion at all…"

Mariela had finally uniformly blended the ingredients of the mixture. Sensing its immense power, she averted her eyes from the potion's radiance, just a little.

Dragon blood contained toxins.

It had tremendous energy and magical power completely

incomparable to those of ordinary humans. Contained within was the vitality to live for an eternity if the dragon was fortunate enough to survive trillions of struggles for survival. All of it was beyond human understanding.

This was what drove dragons to live as they did: the tremendous power of their blood.

What kind of miracle lay within this blend of all four conflicting elements? Was such a power—incorporating not just the power of the ley line, but also the power of dragons—something that could be granted to people without a price?

"No matter what…we'll all survive together."

Mariela reached for the dragon blood medicinal crystals to create the next potion.

CHAPTER 3
March of the Ants

01

When Malraux and the scout unit descended to the fifty-seventh stratum and saw it for the first time, they believed they'd found some set of huge metal posts.

Looking toward the sky to see how far it stretched, some commented, "It's like a horse without a neck or tail," while others said, "It's like a crab walking forward," or "Looks like a spider with its legs stretched downward."

In the end, they settled on referring to the monster as a "beast." Probably because crab and spider legs remained bent, whereas this monster's legs stretched straight down from its torso.

The creature's legs had black steel hair that grew like tangled wires, and the skin that peeked out here and there was dark green or purple, with a luster that made it seem like metal that had been burned or discolored—though it had just as likely been that color from the start. None of the members of the unit were brave enough to wrap their arms around one of the creature's many legs to measure its thickness. Each slightly curved leg came to a point resembling the sharpened blade of a giant sickle. The monster moved fast for its enormous size and was probably capable of immediately slicing a human clean in half.

The body of this monster, which quickly came to be known as the blade-legged beast, had four of these deadly legs on either side. However, there was no clearly visible head or tail.

Stormy gray clouds hung low over the fifty-seventh stratum of the Labyrinth. In this atmosphere, shrouded in a thin mist, the boundary between air and cloud was difficult to determine. Distant landmarks seemed dim and at times vanished completely. Just the legs of the blade-legged beast put it well over ten meters tall. If one retreated to a distance that would allow them to see the creature's entire profile at once, the mists obscured too much for such a sight to be of any use. When the more adventurous drew closer and looked up at it, they discovered that the only appendages attached to the oblong, horselike torso were the bladed legs.

No one had ever seen nor heard of a monster like this. Thus, the need for a convenient name like "blade-legged beast." To make matters worse, this stratum was swarming with the bizarre monsters.

Stab, whoosh, stab, whoosh.

The bladed legs of the beast moved with the deftness of a proper horse. As it walked, the creature tore through the mix of sand and pebbles that formed the ground of the stratum. It might have been a rocky area originally, but the ground had been pounded into sand and pebbles from all the crushing and slashing of the knifelike legs. The loose sediment made it easy to trip, and walking was exhausting.

"The previous stratum had a walking volcano, but to think there would be a monster with strange legs in this stratum, too... Could the boss of the Labyrinth have some sort of fascination with legs?"

Leonhardt, who had led the Labyrinth Suppression Forces down to the fifty-seventh stratum, was likely just talking to himself. Even so, the sage accompanying him was eager to reply.

"I suspect because it has two legs," she said. "Just like humans.

No idea if it's the right or the left, but the boss most likely *used* each leg."

"That's rather disgusting. Well, maybe I should just be happy we're getting close."

Guessing at the meaning of Freyja's strange statement, Leonhardt shrugged lightly. He'd certainly experienced a considerable feeling of discomfort with the Walking Mountain of Fire.

Until that point, the forms of all the stratum bosses had been within the realm of comprehension, if a bit abnormal. However, although the Walking Mountain of Fire was the spitting image of a volcano, the legs awkwardly attached to it made the picture grotesque. The alien creature also bore no visible mouth or eyes.

If the legs of the Labyrinth's boss had created the Walking Mountain of Fire and the boss of this stratum, which had in turn created the blade-legged beasts, what on earth awaited Leonhardt's group once they'd passed both?

The group had neither the time to shudder at this repulsive thought nor the choice not to fight these monsters. Rather, if these were both "legs," the thought that they'd be able to confront the "body" in a stratum not far from this one should have encouraged the soldiers.

That aside, where in the world were the eyes and mouths of these blade-legged creatures? Leonhardt couldn't understand how a beast constructed simply of sharpened appendages attached to a torso like an oblong mass of rock could perceive anything around it. Yet more than a few of the monsters had noticed the Labyrinth Suppression Forces and were scurrying toward them.

"Second and third units, forward!"

The two units comprised of soldiers who specialized in long-handled weapons headed for the blade-legged beasts, with the captain of the second unit, wielding his halberd equipped with an enormous ax, and the captain of the third unit, Dick, at the head of the formation.

Unsurprisingly, long-handled weapons had great utility when facing giant monsters like these.

"Take this!"

With the captain's speed and skill, the tip of the halberd could slice through a common sword, and this weapon was made of adamantite, forged by the Rock Wheel dwarves. No matter how big a lump of metal might be, this weapon would cut through it. With a resounding *shing* that vibrated all the way into his skull, the strike from the captain of the second unit sliced beautifully through the leg of one of the creatures.

It was the same for Dick. His black spear had also been remade with adamantite, and his thrusting blow became a destructive focal point that broke the beast's leg.

However, that was all it did.

The ten-meter leg had simply been shortened by about a meter.

And that was only one leg out of eight.

The blade-legged beast didn't seem to feel pain. It bent its multiple joints just a little to adjust the length of its legs and swung one downward to stab at the units of soldiers of who'd swarmed around it to attack.

"Watch out!"

The soldiers slashed at the beast's legs sticking in the sand as they dodged the sharp points coming at them from above. Those who could lop off the lumplike steel appendages in one hit boasted A-Rank strength, like the two captains. The metallic hair on the bladed legs absorbed the hits from the rest of the soldiers' halberds without issue. It took at least several hits to cut through the legs.

"Are we shortening the legs bit by bit like this?!" Dick asked.

The captain of the second unit replied. "Dick, did you forget the plan? Focus!"

The ground, which consisted of pebbles and sand, was all give, making it easy for the strange monsters to maneuver. Comparatively, it was awful for the soldiers, as they had no proper footholds to push off of. Since the battle had just begun, they had plenty of stamina to spare, but clearly, the longer it went on, the more unfavorable the situation would become for the humans.

More than anything, there were just too many of the monsters for the incursion to focus their efforts.

Although the Labyrinth Suppression Forces had only just arrived at this stratum, the silhouettes of ten or more blade-legged beasts, in addition to the one they were already fighting, could be seen heading their way, and that was just what they saw through the haze.

"The legs are exactly like the report said. What about the body?" the second unit's captain muttered.

"Body? There's no time to think about attractive women!" Dick joked back this time.

He was the one who seemed to have a lot of time to spare.

"There's always time for that, but I meant it! **Battle-ax Annihilation!**"

"Heh, right. **Rising Spear Annihilation!**"

Each of them launched ranged attacks toward the torso of the blade-legged beast they were fighting. Both attacks were techniques that fired magical power from their weapons. Since they weren't hurling their actual armaments, the strength of their attacks was lowered slightly and required no small amount of magic from either. For this pair, who specialized in hand-to-hand combat, these were usually the kind of techniques they wanted to avoid.

Ker-thud.

The combined attacks of Dick and the others sounded like blunt weapons crashing against a rock when they made impact. The strikes succeeded in gouging out about a third of the blade-legged beast's torso, seemingly choking the life out of it.

Although, that might not have been entirely accurate. The blade-legged beast stopped moving because it fell to pieces, as if its joints had come loose. It didn't look like the final moments of something that had once been alive.

Both the fallen torso and the legs that had resembled giant metal blades changed to a rocky color and shattered into several pieces from the impact of their collapse.

"The weak point is the torso. Long-range attacks are effective. Two or three people need to hit it at once. Watch out for attacks from above and for falling objects after defeating them."

"What he said. Engage!"

The captain of the second unit barked precise instructions, and Dick, the captain of the third, gave only a vague affirmation. The members of the respective units were accustomed to this, and they efficiently divided into groups to fell the monsters and began their attacks.

"Have you learned the location of the stratum boss?" Amid the main force behind the advance troops, Weishardt awaited the intelligence unit's report.

Perhaps the haze covering this stratum concealed the boss's magical power. It certainly bewildered the insect summoner and obstructed the sound the sonar user needed, rendering it impossible to probe distant areas. Thus, someone agile and possessing outstanding evasion abilities had to find the stratum boss with their own eyes, running around the stratum while avoiding the blade-legged beasts' attacks.

Complicating matters was the apparent fact that the boss seemed content to stay hidden, opting not to attack like the blade-legged beasts did. Instead, it continued to move slowly and randomly. If the intelligence unit didn't stay near it and continue to inform the main force of its changing location, it would soon disappear into the haze, and the unit would lose sight of it.

"Identified. Ahead at two o'clock. The Telepathy was from far away, maybe two or three kilometers."

"We have to maintain pursuit. All troops, move out!"

After hearing Malraux's report, Leonhardt signaled the army to advance.

The group consisted of the main force and the backup mage unit, adding up to two hundred people in all. Within the main force, comprised of eight units, two units clashed with the blade-legged beasts to open a path, then advanced in a battle formation that protected the center bulk of the army.

If the elite captains charged ahead, they could cover a distance of two or three kilometers in less than ten minutes, but they alone wouldn't be enough against the boss of the stratum. They would run dry of magical power, simply taking out the lesser monsters that blocked the path. There was such a great number of the abnormal creatures in this stratum that no matter how many were defeated, they seemed to issue forth from the ashen mists without end.

They appeared from within the haze on both sides, flanking the main bulk of the army. The Labyrinth Suppression Forces group of two hundred was a large-scale force compared to the numbers needed to subjugate the King of Cursed Serpents, but since these beasts had ten-meter-long legs, the soldiers could easily focus on the midsections of the monsters.

Shield knights in the main force protected the concentrated group from the giant blade tips, and mages pierced the beasts' weak torsos with magic.

"Those who are injured or out of magical power, head to the medical team in the center! The second and third units' magic will run out very soon. Units four and five, prepare to sortie! You'll be relieving them!"

Under Weishardt's command, the force advanced toward its destination undeterred. The second and third units, replaced by the relief group before they ran out of magical power and became a liability, returned to the center as if they'd been sucked in.

"Gaaah, I'm dizzy..."

Running out of magic was probably painful for the soldiers of the advance guard, who normally only fought hand to hand. In a contest of magical power and long-range offensive ability, the mage unit would clearly have come out on top. However, the unit was more suited for assisting with offense and defense rather than opening the way forward on the front lines.

That said, this was a battlefield, and this incursive force was made from the best of the best. Fortunately, there had been no serious injuries since the fighting started, so the exhausted soldiers' complaints seemed a bit dramatic.

A girl offered potions to those soldiers.

"Good work. Here, have a mana potion."

"Thanks, Mariela."

"I need one, too; I need one, too. Hey, Sieg, go back to your escort duties. I wanted to get a potion from heeer."

"Mariela is busy making potions. Don't approach her, don't touch her, and if you look at the potions, they'll disappear!"

"They will not!"

Mariela puffed up her cheeks in protest, but she continued her work on the mana potions with both hands, dissolving ley-line shards and the magical power of the moon into Drops of Life.

She was doing both simultaneously, a rather impressive accomplishment. It wasn't like Mariela to do such clever work. If she pushed herself too hard at it, she might soon fall flat on her face.

Regardless of such limitations, Mariela completed mana potions one after another, and Sieg warded off the hands reaching for her as he distributed the concoctions.

The process of making a mana potion was simple. All one had to do was mix magical power from the moon with a ley-line shard dissolved in Drops of Life. When done, the moon's magical power and the power of the ley-line shard became intertwined, creating a mana potion that adapted to and healed the body of the person who imbibed of the moon's magical power.

It was a truly rare specimen of potions that restored magical power just by drinking it. As long as the soldiers had them, they'd be able to fight at their utmost ability. Whether with magic or skills, they could strike as many times as you wanted at maximum power. As one might have suspected, however, such a miraculous item was not without its drawbacks.

First, the materials were rare. It required magical power from the moon. Power that didn't belong to anyone. If magical power belonging to a monster or a person was used, the potion wouldn't bring any energy to the drinker.

Even in the case of the moon's power, which was the easiest to get to adapt to someone's body, only by using the highly concentrated energy of ley-line shards and Drops of Life as an intermediary would it finally turn into a form the human body could absorb. Any extra ingredients or steps to the process caused the moon's magical power to deteriorate, making it worthless. In short, even Anchor Essence was out of the question for a mana potion.

The magical power of the moon started to fade the instant it was taken from the special crystals it accumulated in. That was also the case even after it was made into a potion.

Mana potions were powerful, but they were worthless if they hadn't just been made.

A battlefield requiring mana potions was said to be the fiercest place in the world, and a young alchemist who couldn't fight had come to such a place. What was more, crafting these wondrous concoctions required one of the few high-ranking alchemists who could make special-grade potions. Most alchemists couldn't process ley-line shards with skills alone, like Mariela could. In their case, a carriage or the like containing a simple atelier would've been necessary for them to be on the front lines. Naturally, such a person would have been a prime target for the enemy.

Even knowing they would be exposed to danger, alchemists chose to venture onto the battlefield to supply mana potions. They had to. Even they had things so important to them that they'd put their lives on the line to protect them.

Since time immemorial, battles involving mana potions had

always determined the fate of a city or country, and the life or death of the people living there. Such struggles would leave their mark on history.

02

Have you ever stabbed an insect crawling on the ground with a tree branch?

It's easy to do if the insect is simple-minded and large, like a caterpillar, but what if it's an ant?

It's easy to throw a marching line of ants into disarray, but it's surprisingly difficult to kill them one by one with a pointed tree branch. Contrary to expectations, ants move rather skillfully, so even when you intend to aim for the center of their bodies, you might only pluck off a leg.

The march of the Labyrinth Suppression Forces might've looked exactly like ants to the blade-legged beasts who were gathering to crush them. Despite the immense difference in size between the opposed troops, it was similar to crushing large ants with a sharp point.

Did these sharp-tipped spears crushing the ants experience the joy of exerting power over a smaller creature? The beasts sprang forth one after another beyond the hazy veil to swarm the ever-advancing Labyrinth Suppression Forces.

The claws of the monsters plunged deep into the damp and softened earth with a crunch, plowing, tilling, and loosening it to hinder the Forces.

Even if those under attack were just ants, it did not mean they were unable or unwilling to fight back. Not to mention this group consisted not of ants, but of elite units of people. Sometimes the blade-legged beasts' claws, which seemed to descend from heaven itself, pierced the soldiers of the Labyrinth Suppression Forces and tore off their limbs. Still, the warriors continued to launch long-range attacks—whether by magic or weapon—at the comparatively softer torsos of the beasts.

Some among the army felt that if the positions were reversed, being overpowered by the attacks of what must have seemed like insects as small as the tips of one's fingernails would've been a painful humiliation.

No one knew whether the beasts, with their oblong, eight-legged bodies and their vague appearance of life, were even capable of such thoughts. However, they certainly proved relentless, rushing at the marching Labyrinth Suppression Forces to try to crush every last one of them, no matter how many of their kin were slain.

Countless swarming beasts were left crumbling and crushed in the wake of the Labyrinth Suppression Forces' ranged attacks. At the same time, the Forces, too, suffered injuries. Neither side's strength seemed to diminish, though. The injured Labyrinth Suppression Forces were immediately healed and returned to the front lines. Meanwhile, new blade-legged beasts appeared as soon as the previous ones were defeated.

The Forces cleared the way while advancing at a surprisingly quick pace considering they were on human legs. However, when seen from above as a line of ants, their march to close the distance between themselves and the boss of this stratum was a slow one.

If one was aiming from above at a group of creatures continually moving around, where would the easiest target be? Doubtless, a blade-legged beast able to get close to the Labyrinth Suppression Forces would aim for the army's center.

"Shield Bash!"

There were few in the Labyrinth City powerful enough to entirely repel a crushing blow speeding downward from above. An A-Rank shield knight named Wolfgang, who was often hired to protect Weishardt, had been appointed as Mariela's guardian for the attack.

"Th… thank you very much…" Mariela expressed her gratitude while looking like she was about to collapse from the shock of the battle. The young alchemist lacked leg strength and all-around muscle. She didn't have the speed or stamina to keep up with the Labyrinth Suppression Forces. As such, she was the only one atop a raptor, swaying this way and that as the group marched ever forward. The raptor Mariela sat upon was the one that had once protected her from a death lizard's attacks and lost its tail for its efforts.

This raptor, which had protected Mariela of its own free will, was selected as the optimal creature for her to ride, since Mariela lacked riding skills. Sieg had wisely chosen to hide the fact the raptor's suitability had been evaluated based on Mariela's limited ability. She would likely sulk if she knew the truth.

The raptor's tail had been regrown via a special-grade potion while the creature was being ridden, so as to demonstrate the potion's performance. This raptor, named Koo, didn't seem to be rattled at all by the blade-legged beasts' attacks. Deftly, it avoided the strikes of the razor-sharp legs and advanced at a constant pace. The only frightened one was Mariela.

"Oh, it's no problem. I bet you were quite frightened, young lady. I'll protect you so you can relax and make your potions," Wolfgang said amiably after she thanked him for protecting her.

It was quite the manly speech. He wasn't all talk, either; this shield knight had successfully repelled a bladed leg that came hurtling down from the heavens right before Mariela's eyes. Between that and his gallant promise to protect her, Mariela might have grown a bit bashful had he been a bachelor around her age.

In actuality, Mariela's cheeks reddened a little, and she nodded with the kind of starry-eyed fascination usually reserved for meeting a legendary hero. Grandel—the stylish shield knight of the Labyrinth Suppression Forces—was also a "legendary hero," but Wolfgang better lived up to that title. He was one of the strongest warriors there was. It was inevitable for Mariela to want to talk to such a man.

"Even so, weren't you surprised to know someone like me was an alchemist?"

"Everyone had an idea that might've been the case back when Dr. Nierenberg established a clinic at a mere apothecary."

"Right, usually a doctor calls for an apothecary, not the other way around."

"Aw, man, I thought we were protecting her from the Aguinas family."

"Who cares? I prefer an innocent sweetheart like Mariela."

"She didn't ask you about your tastes."

Other members of the Labyrinth Suppression Forces keeping the area around Mariela secure offered their own opinions and helped to relax the atmosphere. Whether intentional or not, it did ease some of her tension.

Injured soldiers were treated where Mariela would not see, out of consideration for her. She was unused to battle, and the gruesome sights would have disturbed her. Even so, Mariela still caught sight of both the blade-legged monsters coming to attack and the long-distance attacks used against the monsters. One of the horrid legs had just come rather close to her, after all. Mariela, no different from any city girl apart from her alchemical abilities, seemed ill at ease on the unfamiliar battlefield.

Apparently, Mariela's escorts had been chosen from among acquaintances who had received medical treatment at Sunlight's Canopy, particularly those well suited to defense. They all also seemed to have accepted relatively easily that Mariela was an alchemist.

These soldiers, who fought with the main thrust of the Labyrinth Suppression Forces, understood full well both the scarcity of potions and the importance of the one who made them. They had been chosen to protect Mariela even at the risk of their own lives. All were blessed with fighting skills, and they had all spent much of their lives in battle. They had never experienced this "alchemy" before and had almost no knowledge of it.

That was why, although they saw Mariela make mana potions one after another with no tools whatsoever, they weren't particularly startled by the advanced techniques that were even beyond alchemists of the imperial capital.

People tended to judge another's character by their appearance, including their behavior and speech. In many cases, especially in short-term relationships, those who appear important through their speech and conduct are judged to be admirable people rather than those with true bravery and skill.

Mariela was a prime example. The potions she made and the techniques she had more or less mastered were rare, but as far as difficulty levels went, she was perceived as an average, ordinary girl and treated as a young lady who had simply been dragged into this because of those rare abilities. In short, the collective feeling of those guarding Mariela was that they were protecting their friendly young female neighbor.

As for the alchemist herself, she was grateful for that kind of treatment. She gave her best effort, industriously crafting potions. The conversation with the strong, kind soldiers helped to greatly loosen her tension.

However, there was one man who didn't find the situation relaxing at all.

Grind-grind-grind.

He wasn't grinding his teeth. Though he was overflowing with jealousy, it was Sieg's taut bow, not his teeth, that made the grinding sound. With a trembling vibration, Sieg's arrow flew through the haze and pierced the torso of a blade-legged beast.

The precision and distance were exactly as one would've expected from the hunter with the Spirit Eye. Unfortunately, the torso he targeted was like a mass of rock; there were no vital organs or other such weak points to be found. Since the only way to defeat such creatures was to whittle away at them, creating a few holes wasn't going to be enough, and although Sieg had put magical power into the slender arrows, he knew how little damage they could do to the abominations.

Sieg used a sword for melee attacks and a bow for long-range attacks, but he had no shield skills. Even his deadly bow quickly proved inadequate against this new enemy, failing to demonstrate the power it'd held during the battle against the red dragon. Sieg looked disquieted as he glanced at Mariela while relentlessly firing his bow, and Freyja called out to him.

"Siiieg, don't be so jealous. I bet you're thinking, 'I can't believe those other men were chosen to protect Mariela!' But then the Spirit Eye couldn't demonstrate its true value."

"Lady Frey, I..."

"This isn't a fight for you alone, remember? You have your own role to play."

"I...understand."

Sieg had known that ever since he'd participated in the red dragon battle. No, perhaps he'd even felt it every time he operated with the Black Iron Freight Corps or the Labyrinth Suppression Forces, like when they'd hunted the wyverns and the earth dragons.

There were many strong people in this Labyrinth City. Even A-Rankers like Sieg numbered more than ten these days. The city was threatened by a danger of the highest order, a labyrinth that had grown too great and too deep. Nearly half of the Empire's high-ranking military forces had gathered to combat that danger.

Although those people were also A-Rankers, it was difficult to simply ascribe quality to them since their abilities differed so much. Sieg was peerless when it came to the bow, but he was less accomplished with a sword than Leonhardt or Haage. No one could match Weishardt or Elmera in magic, or Dick with the spear, or even Wolfgang in defense.

It was natural for people to differ in their strengths and weaknesses, and the Labyrinth Suppression Forces not only recognized each person's special qualities but also formed strategies that would allow different ones to complement each other when challenging a stratum boss. However, for Sieg, who had only acted solo or in small groups since childhood, the reality that many people had abilities he would never achieve filled him with a frustrating sense of uselessness and weakness. Of course, he understood in his mind that he was doing the best he could and that his own abilities had plenty of merit. However, his heart refused to listen to reason.

"You *don't* understand. That worry of yours isn't because someone is more able than you. Well, I suppose just saying that won't really help you, though. It's a bit premature, but this is perfect. C'mere, I'll teach you how to use the Spirit Eye. It won't take much time."

Saying this, Mariela's master, Freyja, the Sage of Calamity grinned broadly and beckoned Siegmund to her.

"So, you use the Spirit Eye like this."

Freyja grabbed the right side of Sieg's face with her left hand. His Spirit Eye peeked through a gap between her fingers, so the field of view in both his right eye and his left was unobstructed.

"I can be heavy-handed with my magical power, so this'll hurt a bit."

No sooner had Freyja said this than…

"Gaaahhh!"

…a burning pain assaulted Sieg's eye.

He grabbed her arm to tear it off him, but it was like a steel beam, refusing to budge an inch.

Sieg struggled harder and harder as the sensation of scorching heat crept all the way to the line connecting his eye and brain. Freyja continued to address him in a calm tone.

"Calm down. I'm just connecting slightly to its original owner. You feel like you're burning because my magical power has a different quality from yours. Your body isn't actually on fire. Look, you should be able to see the world Mariela sensed a while back, right?"

Sieg regained a bit of his composure when Freyja mentioned Mariela, and he focused his awareness on his Spirit Eye's field of vision rather than on the pain attacking it. In his left eye, the surroundings seemed the same. The march continued; none of the soldiers clashing with the blade-legged beasts noticed that Sieg had stopped moving for a moment.

However, the Spirit Eye showed the light of life and overlaid that image with the world his other eye saw. He could see a light of life dwelling in each person that seemed to be a reflection of each's individual nature. Sieg realized that this glimmer dwelled not just in people, but in the strange attacking monsters as well. It even existed in the haze of this stratum and in a very thin layer on the ground beneath his feet. This light had flowed from the ley line and filled the world above. The Drops of Life Mariela had drawn up were emitting a particularly strong amount of the light.

The luminous drops emitted pure energy that neither favored nor belonged to anyone. Potions containing this power healed whoever drank them, regardless of whether they were people or monsters.

"You get it, right, Sieg? The spirits pour out of the ley line and exist using the power filling the world as nourishment. In ley lines ruled by someone who loves people, the spirits speak the people's language. Conversely, they speak the language of monsters in monsters' territories because the power of the ley line's warden extends to the energy spilling across the land. Alchemists who've made a Pact with the ley line can circumvent the warden and draw Drops of Life from their Nexus. Drops of Life are a pure power that none can rival."

When Mariela dismissed a Transmutation Vessel, the excess Drops of Life became a light invisible to the normal human eye that sank back down toward the ley line. Weak spirits gathered in droves at the source of that glow.

"Spirits with no physical body are unreliable, and they can't draw power directly from the ley line. They subsist on the power that overflows and spreads throughout the world. In that sense, the Labyrinth is similar. It consumes the power of the ley line and makes monsters. There are hardly any spirits in the Labyrinth City, right? Even the spirit Illuminaria of the sacred tree by Sunlight's Canopy was barely able to take shape, even after accumulating the Drops of Life and magical power the two of you gave her. There's little power the spirits can eat because the Labyrinth is consuming it all. It's especially bad in the Labyrinth itself. It's under the control of the boss monster, so all the power obtainable from the ley line is used for the monsters. It's difficult for the spirits to even exist here."

What Sieg was seeing served as proof enough to verify Freyja's words, but there was something else as well.

"My eye's Spirit Sight ability isn't just the power to see spirits…"

"Right you are. That's the eye of Endalsia, who even now is just barely keeping control of the ley line. Hers is an eye of compassion that provides the power of the ley line to the spirits. It's not that you've become able to see weak spirits. The spirits her eye shows you have received energy from Endalsia that gave them the strength to manifest," Freyja explained with a smile. Her golden eyes glittered like bursting sparks.

Sieg could see a great number of fire spirits floating around Freyja.

Concepts like life and death were likely alien to spirits. If they had the power of life from the ley line, they would appear from seemingly nowhere. Likewise, if they lost that power, they'd simply disappear. After seeing the salamander Mariela had summoned, Sieg wondered if perhaps spirits dwelled in a world that was both here and not here.

"Now, Sieg. Give more power to my kin. Bestow blessings upon the brethren who help you."

There was a stabbing pain in Sieg's Spirit Eye. What Freyja was doing was like teaching him how to swing a sword by using her hand to guide his arm. However, the eye of the forest spirit Endalsia was very likely incompatible to some extent with Freyja's fiery magical power. This kind of pain was wholly new to Sieg. It felt like a dagger slowly working its way behind his eye. The sensation was so intense he wanted to clutch his head and writhe in pain, but Freyja's hand refused to budge from his face. Sieg found he was unable to even close his eye.

Fire spirits too small and weak to be visible to other humans gathered in such large numbers that there was hardly an empty space near Freyja. To Sieg they looked like a sea of fire.

Perhaps because they were all the same type of spirit, they all acted very much like physical flames. They converged, split apart, and generally moved as if there was no notion of individuals among them. Sieg wondered if that was what it was like not to have a physical body. What free beings they must be! Human bodies seemed so cumbersome in comparison.

Paying no mind to Sieg, whose consciousness was growing dim from the pain, Freja began a songlike chant.

"O flames, my kin, let us sing and dance together. **Summon Fire Dance.**"

It was fortunate that the torsos of the blade-legged beasts were ten meters above the ground. If they hadn't been, even the Labyrinth Suppression Forces might've been reduced to ash. The blaze Freyja summoned ran wild and swallowed the blade-legged beasts surrounding the Labyrinth Suppression Forces like a tornado, and in only a few moments, the beasts collapsed. The firepower was so great that members of the Forces simply stopped their attacks. Every eye fell on the red-haired woman.

"Lady Sage! What on earth was that?!"

Mitchell, the man charged with looking after Freyja, came running up in a great hurry. The woman's cheeks were flushed, despite her being sober, and her eyes gleamed as she laughed. Her hand remained tight around Sieg's face.

"Aha… Such terrific firepower."

Freyja's expression was frightful. She looked to be in a trance from the immense power that exceeded even the *Summon Fire Dance* she'd used back in the Fell Forest against the earth dragons. The sage turned in the direction the Labyrinth Suppression Forces were moving, and she smiled happily as she spoke.

"Heh-heh-heh, found you, stratum boss. I bet it'll take one more shot, don't you? Sieg?"

The corners of her mouth curled in a smile. The golden-eyed woman truly seemed to be enjoying herself. The many fire spirits assembled had probably received strength from the power forcibly drawn out of Sieg's Spirit Eye, enabling Freyja to unleash a tremendous show of spirit magic.

As if responding that one shot wouldn't be enough, a colossal shadow about twice the size of the blade-legged beasts Freyja had scorched emerged from the mists ahead of them.

"The stratum boss, the Bladed Beast of Many Legs, has made

its appearance! Mage unit, to the front!" Leonhardt ordered as he crossed the vanguard. His voice was audible even to Freyja and the others all the way in the center the marching force.

A decisive battle was nearing: an attack on the stratum boss with the full might of the Labyrinth City behind it. This time, the army had not only special-grade heal potions at their disposal, but mana potions as well. They could not have been more prepared to challenge such a tremendous foe.

Freyja's hand still tightly held Sieg's head, even as his eyes rolled back and he lost consciousness. Mitchell and a few other soldiers from the Forces surrounded Freyja at a distance and exchanged bewildered glances, unsure what to do.

"Haaah..." Freyja lifted her chin slightly and exhaled. Her body was scorching, her blood boiling. Perhaps such a description was less metaphorical than one might have first thought, too. Freyja's breath quivered like heat shimmer, and her long crimson hair swayed and danced, despite the lack of wind to carry it. The red strands looked as though they could burst into actual fire at any moment. She was clearly in a wild state—the others around her could see that, if nothing else.

Certainly, the title Sage of Calamity seemed fitting now. Freyja was supposed to be an ally, but onlookers wondered if perhaps helping Sieg was the smarter decision. Even if Freyja unleashed another attack on par with the first, she might not even hit the boss in her current state of mind.

As Mitchell and the others began to feel a sense of danger emanating from Freyja that rivaled the stratum boss's own, a merciful rain doused the woman.

"**Water!!!** Masterrr! What are you doing?!"

Mariela had leaped from her raptor mount and came running to scold Freyja, dumping water on her head and extinguishing her.

"M-Mariela?!"

Freyja, who had quite suddenly—and very thankfully—returned to her senses, turned pale the instant she saw Mariela's face.

"You are...very angry..."

There was nothing rarer than seeing Freyja nervous, but it was understandable. Her student was furious. Mariela's eyebrows, usually low and flat, were harshly slanted like the cut of a blade, and her mouth stretched into a disapproving frown.

"I told you! I said don't cause trouble! I said you cannot, *cannot* play tricks on people!"

"S-s-s...sorry, Mariela. It was a mistake. I didn't mean—"

"You really, really never learn, ever! Ahhh! Look at what happened to Sieg!!"

It was a curious scene. One had to wonder which of them was the master.

After she tore her teacher's hand away from Sieg to free him, a panicked Mariela crammed a high-grade heal potion into his mouth. Perhaps because Mariela was so angry, her methods of helping Sieg were rather rough. It didn't resemble the kind of nursing one might expect from such a gentle young girl, but this was a battlefield, and they were preparing to fight. It was a very appropriate method for the circumstances.

"*Cough...* Ugh..."

"Sieg, you're awake?! Are you okay? Do you feel strange anywhere?"

"Ma...riela?"

Whether it was due to the effects of the potion or whether he'd simply choked on the liquid, Sieg woke up and brought a hand to his Spirit Eye. Although he was fatigued and felt a dull pain, as though his eye had been severely abused, everything seemed to be more or less normal. He could see the worry on Mariela's face, and he could also see the raptor who had run after her tilting its head in the same direction as Mariela's.

Although he'd suffered a fairly intense experience, Sieg had learned how to use his Spirit Eye because of it: a reasonable fee for the lesson.

"Yeah, Mariela, I'm all right. I can fight." Sieg smiled so as to not make Mariela worry any further. Seeing this, her master began to make excuses.

"Hey, he said he's all right. It was just a little tutoring. I didn't cause any trouble, see?"

"Master? Do you think that kind of excuse will be enough?! If you've got that much energy, go beat some monsters, and don't cause any more trouble for anyone! If you can do that, maybe I'll forgive you after you go to bed without dinner!"

"Ehh...but I already used up all the spirit power. Maybe if Sieg lets me..."

"Maaasterrr!"

"I—I know..."

Mariela's eyebrows strongly arched in anger again the instant she turned around, and Freyja, looking like a scolded child, dejectedly began walking toward the vanguard group, readying to engage with the stratum boss.

"Mariela's really something," Sieg muttered as he watched the pair.

He hadn't said it because Mariela had thrown water on Freyja and told her off, and now she looked too meek to speak with the Labyrinth Suppression Forces. Even among humans, Mariela was exceptionally physically weak. Her alchemy skills stood out, but she didn't have a trace of any qualities one could call powerful. There was a large gap between her strengths and weaknesses. No one embodied the imperfection of flesh like she did. To Sieg, she was irreplaceable. A very precious human being.

Freyja probably felt the same way about Mariela. That was why she tolerated insults like being splashed with water and why she was able to return to her senses from that wild state she'd been in.

Mariela's strength was her charm. Sieg recalled being driven by jealousy to fire arrows at the blade-legged beasts, and he now understood what Freyja had said about him worrying.

I was unknowingly worried that I couldn't become Mariela's number one. Surely this was what the sage had meant in reminding Sieg that he wasn't fighting alone. If someone else had simply told him what he was doing was wrong, he wouldn't have listened. It would have only pushed him to be more self-defeating.

After lifting Mariela onto the raptor's back again, Sieg bowed his head to Wolfgang and said, "Please keep Mariela safe."

"Leave it to me. I'll protect your princess. I'm looking forward to seeing your arrows do great things," Wolfgang replied with a trustworthy smile.

"Mariela, I'll shoot down any attacks aimed at you."

"Okay, but be careful, Sieg."

What had Sieg been worried about? Even in the middle of this battlefield, hadn't Mariela come running when he was in danger and helped him? Even if Sieg couldn't use a shield, even if he lagged behind others when it came to magic or swordsmanship, there were things only he could do for Mariela.

"Rar!"

"Ahaha, what is it, Koo? Are you saying you can protect me as well? Then I'll do my best to stick to you."

The raptor giving Mariela a ride was very similar to the salamander she'd summoned with the magic circle. Most likely, the image of this raptor had served as a base for that salamander. If there was even the faintest connection between this raptor and the spirit who'd saved Sieg countless times in the battle with the red dragon, then there was no partner Mariela could've depended on more.

Sieg vowed to do his utmost and focus on what he was capable of doing. He tightened the grip on his bow. As he did, he could see the lights of the spirits who gathered to help him flickering about.

Soldiers did little to hide their whispers about the pair.

Perhaps the guardsmen assigned to Mariela—who had astoundingly managed to stop the Sage of Calamity's recklessness—had found a new appreciation for the girl. They appeared to be praising her.

"Wow. She stopped the Sage of Calamity. A fantastic Fire Extinguisher."

"Nah, wouldn't Calamity Charmer be more exact?"

"That makes it sound as if she can speak to hurricanes. What about Water Bucket?"

"That's sounds too mundane. I like Fire Extinguisher better."

The guards seemed to be discussing an alias for the young alchemist. Surprisingly, none of their suggestions was all that impressive. The most popular suggestion seemed to be Mariela the Fire Extinguisher. Mariela herself wondered why they hadn't proposed something like Firefighting Princess. Why had none of them bothered to suggest a title that sounded good? None of the nicknames even touched on her abilities with alchemy!

I'm an alchemist! The only one in the Labyrinth City other than my master! I can make special-grade potions—I'm even better than a regular alchemist! So why don't the names have anything to do with alchemy?!

Though she'd shown such strength when confronting her master, Mariela said nothing to the soldiers of the Labyrinth Suppression Forces around her, instead merely shouting into the void of her own mind.

This is all Master's faaaaault!

Mariela made mana potions while Sieg and the raptor protected her. About ten meters ahead of the members of the Forces who were debating the Fire Extinguisher nickname, the subjugation of the boss of the Labyrinth's fifty-seventh stratum was about to begin.

03

"They're swarming."

"Oh, Lady Sage."

Freyja arrived just as Leonhardt and Weishardt were about to give the signal to attack. She had a complacent expression on her face that seemed to suggest she thought herself capable of handling all the enemies herself. Mitchell, who knew Mariela had scolded and shooed Freyja all the way to the front lines, followed her in silence with a solemn expression.

"Shall I help you as your opening act?"

At Freyja's proposal, Leonhardt and Weishardt exchanged glances and nodded.

The blow that had utterly destroyed the blade-legged beasts swarming the Labyrinth Suppression Forces had been easily visible from the front lines. It was thanks to that blow against the enemy that the brothers had been able to arrange the Forces in a superior, more dynamic battle formation. Their new troop orientation had helped to push toward the stratum boss more quickly, if only a little.

It was likely they'd have to face the master of this stratum soon. Though the creature was still little more than a vague silhouette through the haze, it was clearly heading their way with a large escort of blade-legged beasts. Freyja's offer was sure to prove most helpful, even if she only succeeded in picking off a few.

"Right, if you could use that attack from before to..."

"Oh, sorry, that one's out. I guess I'll use have to use *normal* fire magic...," Freyja said as she turned away from the brothers.

Mitchell quickly approached Leonhardt and Weishardt and discreetly informed them of what had transpired. Ever the mature gentlemen, the brothers responded to Freyja by saying, "We're grateful for your assistance."

"All right, then I'll cut to the chase: **Firestorm.**" The red-haired sage abruptly launched more standard fire magic at the blade-legged beasts blurry in the haze.

"Ooh..." The stir from Leonhardt and the Labyrinth Suppression

Forces wasn't empty flattery. There was no such thing as "subjugation for entertainment" in the Labyrinth, where every second was a fight for one's life.

Freyja's fire magic was worthy of admiration and indeed of the word "firestorm." The blaze whipped violently over the battlefield like turbid waters overflowing from a breached river. The crimson sea engulfed the front row of blade-legged beasts. None would've claimed it was on the same level as the incredible spirit magic from earlier, but even the thought that standard fire magic could be so powerful was astounding. Weishardt wasn't sure he could match it, even if he put all his magical strength into a single spell.

Gulp gulp gulp.

The flames had completely swallowed the monsters. Freyja, too, drank up a fresh mana potion she'd brought from Mariela. And then another.

"Aaah. If these were booze, I could drink them forever, but potions make me fuuull."

The woman put her left hand on her hip as she guzzled.

"Did she imbue the entirety of her magical power into one strike…?"

"When she's full on mana potions, that's it for her. She may have three…no, two shots left?"

Leonhardt and Weishardt whispered to each other as they calmly analyzed the results of their Sage of Calamity observation. Determining fighting power was important, but it was a bit complacent of them to forgo focus on the stratum boss.

In front of the army, Freyja's conjured fires dried the ground, which had been moist from the haze. Steam rapidly issued from the scorched earth, carrying the obscuring fog of the stratum away with it. With the path ahead now clear and visible, they at last saw the enormous monster that was to be their opponent: the Bladed Beast of Many Legs.

The name had been chosen by the reconnaissance unit, and it was an appropriate one. The monster's gigantic body was crowded with so many legs it was difficult to know just how many the creature had.

This may be a problem... Weishardt frowned ever so slightly. He'd realized upon seeing the Bladed Beast of Many Legs that his strategy was no longer optimal.

The foe across the battlefield was about 20 percent taller than the blade-legged beasts, and this matched the previously received reports. However, as if to see things from a better vantage point, the Bladed Beast of Many Legs straightened its legs, climbing to a height of over twenty meters.

At this rate, it will get to the alchemist...!

The current ranks had been arranged to confront monsters with ten-meter legs by making ranged attacks and eluding the blades. They had the advantage of sheer numbers, and this strategy made use of that fact. However, there were few fighters capable of striking a foe twenty meters above them, to say nothing of the number that had the strength to even injure the stratum boss.

The original strategy had been to limit the boss's movement with a constant barrage and whittle it down while the soldiers took turns recovering, but with fewer shots, not only would the monster be far more time-consuming to defeat, but they wouldn't be able to adequately pin it down, either.

If even one of the appendages of the Bladed Beast of Many Legs reached the alchemist, not just this mission but their battles in any future stratums of the Labyrinth would be in dire jeopardy.

Weishardt quickly altered his strategy on the spot and gave orders in rapid succession.

"First, second, and third units forward. Lure the boss and attack. Fourth and fifth units, perform hit-and-run attacks while keeping the nearby blade-legged beasts in check. Seventh mage unit, attack the boss from in front of the stronghold. Do not approach it. Sixth and eighth units, keep your distance while protecting the stronghold."

The Labyrinth Suppression Forces tensed in response to his commands. This wasn't one of the strategies that had been communicated to them in advance.

Members of the Forces learned many army formations to be used in different situations, and this one was similar to one for the worst-case scenario. It was used in anticipation of desperately defending the stronghold—the alchemist—while retreating.

To announce that strategy as soon as they met the stratum boss was hardly encouraging...

Would their attacks even be able to reach the towering monster? And what did that say about their chances of taking on the master of the Labyrinth? Defeatist feelings spread through the vanguard. Dick, in an attempt to dispel such pessimistic thoughts, bellowed his words like a peal of thunder.

"Chin up! Yes, it's big, yes, it's disgusting, and yes, it has a lot of legs, but we're aiming for the torso. It's a huge target; you can hardly miss! Hiyah! **Rising Spear Annihilation!**"

"Follow Captain Dick!" Perhaps the man had found inspiration in Freyja's all-out attack.

Dick had shouted to inspire his comrades—and perhaps himself—into challenging the Bladed Beast of Many Legs. His comrades in the third unit followed him. They launched attacks focusing on range and power, giving no consideration to pacing themselves. The unit fought with all their might and did indeed strike the torso of the monster far above them.

Unfortunately, resistance from the damp air and gravity greatly reduced the strength of their projectiles. Though the group's attacks struck true, the damage they accomplished was like that of a needle scratching a stone.

"It's fine! We're whittling it down! We'll defeat it in due time!"

It should be noted, however, that the mentality of the Labyrinth Suppression Forces wasn't easily broken. How many defeats had they suffered, and how many times had they escaped nearly certain death just to be here? Winning this battle was still possible in their minds.

Three units encircled the Bladed Beast of Many Legs, hoping to lure the titanic monster away while weakening it more and more. The mage unit waited in front of the stronghold, and as soon as the beast entered their range, they hurled closely concentrated attacks at it to both damage it and nudge it where they wanted it to go. The hit-and-run unit kept the blade-legged beasts that surged from the distance one after another in check. If the number of comparatively smaller monsters grew too large for the unit to handle, Freyja, Weishardt, or the A-Rank mage who was captain of the seventh unit handled them with powerful magic. If one unit became exhausted, an ad hoc unit would trade places with them while they healed and recovered in the stronghold.

With every squad rotation, those who came in from the front lines for recovery were utterly spent. It was a risky situation to be in; the front was now much farther from the stronghold than originally planned. However, even such dire circumstances were familiar to the Labyrinth Suppression Forces. As long as they were still alive, wounds would heal and magical power would return. Above all, an alchemist accompanied them this time, and she could make not only special-grade heal potions, but mana potions. Even though the enemy towered above them, the soldiers of the Labyrinth Suppression Forces watched one another's backs, supported each other's spirits, and never broke their lines.

Attacks both magical and physical colored the air above. If one had been watching this battle from a distance, it might have looked like a beautiful dance of lights, like fireworks that went on forever.

From above, one might have noticed the uniform regularity of the people streaming to the back, recovering their strength, and surging forward again in intermittent waves of attacks that whittled away at the giant enemy of the little ants. And the ants were all coming and going from a single point.

Joints bent with a creaking metallic sound, and the great beast raised several of its legs at once on the side where the Labyrinth Suppression Forces were fighting it. The creature was preparing to attack.

Most of the long-distance attacks and magic launched to hinder the monster from taking any such offensive action were blocked by its bladelike metal legs, though some managed to slip through and strike the monster's belly.

With its legs lifted high, the stratum boss paid no heed to the attacks. It turned toward the central stronghold of the army and swung down its legs as it charged ahead in a huge cloud of dust.

"Not good! Mage unit, hit it with all your power! Stronghold, fall back!" Leonhardt shouted. The mage unit obeyed, loosing bolts of powerful magic, but the Bladed Beast of Many Legs plunged into the middle of the bombardment with no regard for any blow that might've struck its body.

The myriad of razorlike legs pierced the earth, tilling the blackened soil. *Stab-stab, stab-stab.* Its blades punctured both dirt and soldiers, driving toward the group who protected the alchemist.

The monster was like a rock with legs growing in clusters from its nucleus. It might have had the ability to see, though there was no evidence. And if it did, then it knew. It had seen how the ants were moving. Those sharp points were about to swing down from on high and skewer poor Mariela.

All the shield knights entrusted with guarding the alchemist assumed a stance with their shields. Their captain, Wolfgang, was at the center of the formation. They wouldn't let the deadly sword-legs get beyond them, even if that meant guarding the young alchemist with their own bodies.

Siegmund sprang out in front of that group and drew his bow as far back as it would go. He trained an arrow on the Bladed Beast of Many Legs.

"Spirits, grant me power!"

An arrow parted the air. Encircled by spiraling, mysterious light, the missile sped toward its target like a meteor in reverse. Higher and higher it climbed into the air. Sieg's shot, loosed with as much power as he could give it, traveled in a definite trajectory as though guided along some unseen pathway. The projectile found purchase, striking a joint in one of the beast's legs.

Claaang.

With a sound like stone against steel, the hunter's arrow completely destroyed the joint in the leg that had been aiming for Mariela. The injured appendage fell, severed at that point.

Two arrows, three arrows. Every time the Bladed Beast of Many Legs made an attack on the girl, an arrow from Sieg's bow precisely plucked off another leg. Even with several legs excised from its body, the creature still had seemingly innumerable to spare.

However, Sieg's efforts had created a gap in the legs the gigantic creature was using to attack, like a comb missing teeth. That alone proved useful, affording members of the Labyrinth Suppression Forces more room to maneuver and dodge. With the great beast less able to aim for the alchemist, it would be much easier for the army to continue its attack.

"Nice goin'!"

The figure of a hunter confronting the beast undaunted as he continued to nock his bow was quite an attractive one. Even Wolfgang, who had stood ready to meet the enemy with his greatest shield skill, smiled broadly and praised him. There was no doubt that any woman who saw such gallantry up close would've felt an arrow piercing her heart.

The old Sieg used to evoke the excited screams of fair women with easy shots that brought down birds. He turned his head just a little to glance behind him, hoping for such a sound from Mariela.

"Combine a ley-line shard and moon magical power in a Transmutation Vessel with Drops of Life and various controls… Okay, done! Next, next!"

"Raaar?"

Not aware that she was the target of such a deadly monster, Mariela was making mana potions three at a time to fulfill the endless line of orders. Naturally, Sieg's heroism was the last thing on her mind.

Seeing the stalwart figure of a young alchemist making

potions with such speed, Sieg commented, "This whole time, she was much less clumsy than she seemed..." He recalled the days when Mariela had only had a three in dexterity. Wolfgang looked at the clearly disappointed man and roared with laughter.

"She's quite a tough little lady, isn't she?" the shield knight asked.

"The stronghold is fine! They requested we continue attacking!" a messenger reported to Leonhardt.

The battle raged. How many casualties had the Bladed Beast of Many Legs just inflicted? How many soldiers had died? How much bloodletting remained ahead of them?

Nierenberg and the medical team healed the injured, and Leonhardt gathered those able to fight to challenge the boss of the stratum. Their efforts had certainly not been in vain up till now: the horrid creature's life was being worn away with each arrow and spell. The Labyrinth subjugation was moving ever forward. This was the combined strength of the small. A united attack.

"Follow me!" Leonhardt bellowed with the voice of a lion. His Lion's Roar transformed the Labyrinth Suppression Forces from an army into a beast. His cry rallied them into a single fighting force. No, perhaps what was truly strong, what truly couldn't be uprooted, was the spirit of those who chose to fight.

The Bladed Beast of Many Legs continued to attack the soldiers of the Labyrinth Suppression Forces, raking the earth. Even the lesser monsters that were its allies were not spared the incensed titan's wrath. With each sweep of metal legs, the Forces suffered injuries. Some even lost their lives, yet the attack didn't let up. Honed techniques, magic, and spirit arrows rose from below like a shower of stars and struck the Bladed Beast of Many Legs in a flurry.

Did the march of the small people seen from far above still resemble ants? How many volleys did it take for that image to change?

After what felt like an anxious eternity—during which none dared to lower their guard— the Bladed Beast of Many Legs was at last reduced to nothing but a giant rock and fell to the earth of the Labyrinth's fifty-seventh stratum.

The stratum boss was defeated; the battle was over at last.

Subjugating a stratum boss was regarded by society as extremely honorable for people like soldiers and adventurers, those who battled for a living. Many among the Labyrinth Suppression Forces had accomplished this feat on more than one occasion. Their efforts were a great achievement that merited honor and praise. But did those assembled on the fifty-seventh stratum really feel that was the case right now?

Leonhardt watched the soldiers gathering around their established stronghold, the center of their company's forces. There were people who'd lost arms. Some were lending their shoulders to comrades who'd lost legs. Even so, dismemberment was preferable to the alternative. Against seemingly impossible odds, they had grasped victory, and on such a deep stratum, no less. Their kill, a giant among the largest of monsters, lay defeated on the ground.

Likely, the Forces owed their victory to each soldier having reached the highest proficiency in their individual specialty. Each unit had been able to link together; they'd fought as a single entity. Of course, the fact that they'd been able to distribute enough potions to all soldiers participating in the subjugation wasn't an element to be overlooked. So long as a man wasn't struck dead on the spot, he could receive easy treatment via potions or healing magic if he suffered serious injuries or even lost body parts.

Such knowledge did little to comfort the wounded, however. Folk rushed to Nierenberg's team, carrying their comrades. "Please help him," they begged with great tears in their eyes. Yet no matter how skilled the medical team, no matter how many potions they had, the dead could never be brought back to life. When Leonhardt listened carefully, he could hear people sobbing, mourning their lost comrades.

The alchemist was surrounded by a hanging screen. Other than those who were appointed, none were permitted to show themselves to Mariela. Even the Labyrinth Suppression Forces soldiers were ordered not to go beyond the curtain. This was to keep the young alchemist from witnessing the terrible scene and to ward off those who would implore her for a miracle.

Potions weren't an almighty medicine. Even such powerful concoctions could never do something like resurrect the dead. Everyone present knew this, even those completely unfamiliar with the nature of potions. But though they understood with their minds, their hearts were not so easily convinced. The human heart was not easily shackled by logic. Many already thought the mere presence of an alchemist in the Labyrinth City was a miracle. It was little wonder that they held on to some impossible hope because of her presence on the stratum. Truthfully, even Leonhardt had wondered if the soldiers he'd lost could be brought back by the young girl.

Hweeeee. A high-pitched whistle notified the scattered Labyrinth Suppression Forces soldiers to withdraw. The arrangement was for those who could move to take it as a sign to gather, while those who couldn't move would use a whistle to send a signal. It was unknown how the blade-legged beasts of this stratum figured out the position of the Forces. However, it had been confirmed that they could not hear—or at least did not respond to—the whistles. Perhaps the haze itself enveloping this stratum was their sensory organ.

After the stratum boss was defeated, the blade-legged beasts wandered aimlessly. They didn't attack unless someone happened to draw especially near them. The boss might have served as some kind of brain or control tower for the whole stratum.

Even if that was the case, there were still many of the beasts crawling in this stratum beyond the portion of mist Freyja had blown away. It was best for everyone to exit this stratum as quickly as possible, but the injured soldiers would first need to be restored to a state where they could fight if it came to that.

At the center of the Labyrinth Suppression Forces' assembled ranks, Nierenberg and the rest of the medical team treated the soldiers by temporarily reattaching torn-off limbs, connecting bones, and regenerating muscles and organs enough so that the wounded could at least move on their own. The Forces had brought as many potions as they could without slowing the march. They'd also been supplied with mana potions so the medical team could perform treatment without worrying about running out of magical power. Even if the healers found themselves lacking a particular potion they needed, an alchemist behind the hanging screen could make it on the spot, in most cases.

Hmmm, that appears to be Crystallize Medicine, *if I'm not mistaken... I must make the soldiers vow not to disclose this.*

Weishardt, who busied himself by taking stock of the situation, watched Mariela going about her work. As she continued to synthesize a variety of potions, the lord was suddenly struck with the thought that he should strengthen their precautions about the alchemist's identity.

The strategic superiority of transforming materials into small sandlike grains known as crystals was beyond comprehension. Ley-line shards were the bulkiest material—each one was the size of the tip of a pinky finger once crystallized—but even hundreds of potions' worth could easily be loaded into a bag small enough to carry. So long as she reused vials without breaking them, Mariela could carry all the crystalized materials around instead of hundreds of potions.

How frail Mariela seemed in contrast to her own abilities, her own usefulness! She would fall from a single arrow. She still had the heard of the ordinary girl she appeared to be.

Weishardt believed they should give her ample consideration and work to never forget that frailty. This was to protect the person known as Mariela, but also to ensure the well-being of both the Labyrinth subjugation and Labyrinth City.

Around the time Nierenberg and the medical team had almost finished treating the wounded, the majority of scattered soldiers had reunited with the main force. They'd finished distributing and replenishing the transported potions.

"Retreat." Leonhardt gave the order. Their victory in this stratum had cost around 20 percent of his fighting force. It was cause for celebration that the victims were few compared to the number of people they'd lost in battle with the King of Cursed Serpents. Leonhardt thought how best to praise the surviving soldiers for how admirably they'd maintained their numbers against such a strong enemy and how to properly extol the struggle of those who'd sacrificed themselves. But he didn't have the courage to make such a speech here.

I hadn't lost any soldiers recently...until now... Even if they'd suffered fewer casualties than in the battle with the King of Cursed Serpents, the heartbreak never got easier. Other survivors of the battle probably felt the same way.

Having somehow recovered from the chaos of losing brothers-in-arms, everyone quietly made the mournful march home. It had been ruled that, for now, no one would badger the alchemist for the impossible. Mariela had emerged from the hanging screen and was also quietly heading home, accompanied by the sixth unit and Sieg. Although they'd defeated the stratum boss, the march of the Labyrinth Suppression Forces had the air of a funeral procession. Its men and women seemed content to sink into the heavy gloom of the stratum.

Ahead of the less-than-triumphant return, the curiously humanoid shapes took form in the mist.

"Were there survivors?"

It wasn't just one or two figures that were shambling forward. With hope in their eyes, everyone wondered if these survivors had miraculously managed to find the bulk of what remained of the army.

Hweeeee, hwee-hwee-hweeee.

Although they signaled to inform these mysterious people that they were allies, no reaction was visible from the bodies in the fog. Could that many people have lost their whistles?

"Reporting in! Large numbers of enemies are approaching ahead! The enemies are walking corpses! Malraux and the other lieutenants have already engaged. They've requested we prepare to return fire at once!"

"Did you say corpses?! There shouldn't be monsters like that in this stratum. The boss was defeated. It shouldn't be possible for a new type of monster to generate. Where in the world did they come from...?"

"From the staircase connecting to the floor below, the fifty-eighth stratum! They're flooding up from below!"

The scout's answer to Leonhardt's question keyed him in to something incredibly important and equally dire. "Wha— You're saying monsters are moving through strata?! Isn't that...!!!" Leonhardt couldn't bring himself to say it, but everyone knew. Monsters moving up the strata could only mean one thing.

A stampede.

"Sixth, seventh, and eighth units, medical team, prioritize defense! Everyone else, follow me! Our objective is the swarm of corpses ahead! Number unknown! Under no circumstances do we allow them to reach the surface!!!"

Leonhardt pulled his sword free of its scabbard. New, desperate purpose dispelled the Labyrinth Suppression Forces' sadness. If they had held any doubts as to the significance of their sacrifice and the meaning of their existence, the members of the Forces were now free of such hesitations.

Strength and fighting spirit once again flowed through minds and bodies that had been so beaten and exhausted from the previous encounter. The power of these stalwart warriors' determination surpassed even the limits of their own flesh.

"Protect our town! Now is the time for glory!" A rallying battle cry erupted from the ranks.

With weapons in hand, the Labyrinth Suppression Forces faced the swarm of corpses descending like an avalanche from beyond the veil of mist. The fierce appearance of the soldiers and adventurers made Mariela, who watched from behind, remember the Stampede of two hundred years ago.

It's the same as back then... Mariela felt the chill hand of fear at her back.

The day of the Stampede, she hadn't been able to do anything but flee. Even now, though she made the potions they asked for, people still got hurt, even died. Though the soldiers were careful not to let her catch sight of the carnage, Mariela still knew many had returned to the ley line.

On that day two centuries ago, many had urged her to flee. They'd pushed her not to delay, to make her escape. Now the young alchemist understood that they'd been trying to save her. Kindness had been disguised by acidic words and sharp tongues; they had been concerned for Mariela's safety. Her heart suddenly overflowed with gratitude.

So when she saw the figures looming through a clear patch of air, Mariela opened her mouth in a soundless cry. Not just because the corpses had humanoid shapes. Nor because the monsters about to clash with the Labyrinth Suppression had such wretched and unsightly forms, though that hardly helped. Mariela could see an arm that clearly belonged to someone else stuck in the place where a leg should've been. Another corpse had a monster's torso stuck below its own shredded midsection.

"Take up your swords! Let loose your magic. Protect our city!"

It was a cry nearly identical to the call for battle that Mariela had heard on the day of the Stampede.

"Protect our town! Now is the time for glory!"

The alchemist couldn't help but wonder which group's voice she was hearing right now.

The lifeless people flooded ceaselessly from the Labyrinth's fifty-eighth stratum. The surge of corpses didn't know they'd lost their lives—or that they'd been lost to history. Ignorant of their own deaths, they had taken up swords and were coming this way. They marched just as they had two hundred years ago.

Yes. What truly frightened Mariela the most was that the advancing corpses were unmistakably the people of the Citadel City and the Kingdom of Endalsia—those who had once fought the Stampede and lost everything for it.

CHAPTER 4
Onward, Brethren

01

"How is this happening?! They've fused with monsters!" cried the soldiers in disbelief at the corpses surging forth.

Perhaps the dead weren't used to their haphazardly pieced-together bodies, as they moved somewhat stiffly. Some of them carried themselves in ways that suggested they had probably been high-ranking adventurers in life. Only their original body parts showed such refined movement, however. The way the monstrosities had been pieced together offset their centers of gravity, and differences in leg lengths hindered them from showing their true abilities. Nothing resembling reason could be found in the vacant expressions of the creatures; hopefully, they did not realize what a terrible thing had befallen them. Whether that was fortunate for the walking corpses or for the Labyrinth Suppression Forces who would have to face them was up for debate.

At the very least, the clumsy bodies of the seemingly endless supply of enemies proved a boon to the Forces, whose fighting-ready members had dropped below two hundred.

Swords were swung, lopping off heads and limbs. Spears punctured holes in torsos. Halberds sliced bodies clean in half. Great showers of arrows rained down. Magic swallowed and engulfed the rotting bodies. It was an overwhelming march that resembled a massacre.

As a group, with Leonhardt in command, the Labyrinth

Suppression Forces clearly boasted higher strength. So why didn't the corpses falter?

Death had taken from them fear and pain, and none of them seemed to care if they had holes in their chests. If one didn't have legs, it crawled with its arms, and if a corpse didn't have arms, it gripped a weapon in its mouth. Over and over, the creatures would fall to the Forces, but the army of the dead continued its offensive. There was a palpable sense of preparedness for death, a conviction that emanated from the lurching army of deceased men. In truth, such a preparedness for the end was no different from the feelings of their living brethren, who willingly entered the Labyrinth and delved into such perilous places.

"Protect our city! Now is the time for glory!" Mariela could hear those words emanating from the battle, but *which side* did the cries belong to?

From Mariela's point of view, that first disaster was only around a year ago. The hopes the people of the Citadel City had carried in the middle of the chaotic Stampede hadn't yet faded. The will of the Kingdom of Endalsia had persisted for two hundred years and now filled this stratum.

As a mere alchemist, Mariela had no way to grant those ancient desires. The young woman simply clung to the back of her raptor and ran through a time that should have been long past, charging forward with the army that fought back against the wave of death.

"Protect our city! Now is the time for glory!"

"Even if I fall in battle, as long as someone important is able to survive…"

Such feelings were expressed in the clash of blades. With each foe his weapon met, Leonhardt could feel it, too.

"These things still hold on to the dreams they once had. It's an endless nightmare that's lasted for two centuries," Freyja said to Leonhardt as the two finally reached the stairs leading to the fifty-eighth stratum. Her voice was unusually quiet, as though she were offering words of condolence.

"So they're the victims of the Stampede from two hundred years ago?"

Freyja nodded in response to Leonhardt's question. To the walking dead, the tragedy of so many lifetimes ago had never ended; they probably saw Leonhardt and the others as the monsters that were attacking. That was what drove them to fight eternally, even in such a state.

"In other words, an entire kingdom's worth of corpses from Endalsia awaits us below."

"That and all the monsters that perished."

"Why *are* they fused with the monsters?"

As she listened vaguely to Weishardt and Freyja's exchange, Mariela recalled what Sieg had related to her about how Endalsia came to ruin. The story of the Stampede two hundred years ago had been passed down like a fairy tale. It was said that the swarm of monsters that closed in on the Citadel City consumed both the heroes who opposed them and the people of the kingdom. Then they ate their fellow monsters. The last one remaining swallowed the spirit of the ley line, and subsequently, the Labyrinth was born.

Freyja's response to Weishardt was both straightforward and repulsive. "This stratum and the one above us were the Labyrinth boss's 'legs,' right? What lies above the legs?"

"The stomach...?"

In other words, those who had been eaten in the battle two hundred years ago and settled into the stomach of the last remaining monster were gathered in the stratum below as remnants of their former selves.

Most likely, only a small portion of the true horde was overflowing into this stratum—the corpses storming up from the newly opened stairs. However, the number that could reach the stratum was limited by the actual physical dimensions of the path. Elite soldiers positioned in front of the stairs kept the swarm of the dead at bay, using skills to burn them or reduce them to chunks of flesh to keep them from moving farther upward.

"Lady Sage, why do you think the corpses are able to cross through strata?"

This time, it was Leonhardt who sought Freyja's opinion. Admittedly, his question might have been meaningless in and of itself; the knowledge would've made little difference. It was more for the man's own reassurance than anything else.

Freyja's answer was quick to cut down any hope Leonhardt may have been holding on to.

"You think it's just the corpses that can?"

It wasn't that these shambling dead things had some unusual ability to move between strata; rather, whatever prevented *all* monsters from moving up the levels had been removed when the fifty-eighth stratum opened. Just as Leonhardt had feared, a stampede had begun.

Realizing this, Leonhardt looked to the heavens and closed his eyes. He wanted to remind himself not of the dark ceiling of the Labyrinth, but of the blue sky stretching over the Labyrinth City and the future that awaited them all at the end of this battle. After this quiet contemplation, Leonhardt issued an order to his younger brother without a hint of hesitation.

"Weis, take the scouts, the fourth and fifth units; return to the surface."

"But, Brother!"

"Don't worry. The boss of the Labyrinth has lost its legs; it's squirming and struggling. We can't afford to miss this opportunity. I have long desired to kill the Labyrinth and give this city, and our territory, a future. But the future of this city, and of our territory, is nothing without its people. What is a lord without the masses? Protecting them is our duty as well. That is why I entrust you with this duty. Go, Weishardt! I leave them all in your hands!" Leonhardt placed a hand on his younger brother's shoulder. As the brothers passed each other, he added, "Go, protect your princess."

Weishardt clenched his teeth and firmly grasped his brother's hand in his own. Taking command of his new charges, Weis issued orders with resolve and speed. "We're running through! Follow me, and don't fall behind! Scouts, order the adventurers within the Labyrinth to return home! Gather as much information as possible about the migration of the monsters through the strata!"

Since the second stratum connected to the underground Aqueduct, the situation could deteriorate quickly if monsters reached it. An immediate blockade would be required. The Forces needed to guard the protective wall around the Labyrinth and prepare to meet the monsters that were no doubt going to charge forward from its depths. At the same time, those who couldn't fight needed to be given evacuation instructions. Weishardt's troops had to return to the surface before the monsters in order to minimize the number of victims.

Dick, I'm heading for the surface. Stay alive so we may meet again.

Malraux joined those returning to the City and sent a parting telepathic message to Dick. The man's mental communication wouldn't function over distances as far as the deepest part of the Labyrinth to the surface. However, it would undoubtedly be helpful in the extreme chaos that was to come topside.

Yeah, they need your telepathy. Make sure you get out of there in one piece. Dick replied with a short message.

As a constant precaution against the worst-case scenario in subjugating a stratum boss, soldier slaves accompanied the Forces and served as a supply train for consumable goods such as spare weapons, arrows, food, and potions, among other things. Now was no different, and they still had goods to spare. However, with the stratum stairs no longer safe, the supply line was severed. Proceeding from here to the lower stratum meant confronting an unknown enemy with scant information and no hope of reinforcements or supplies. How likely was it that they'd actually be able to return alive?

While you're at it, make arrangements for the celebratory party. Despite such grim circumstances, Dick's mental reply was very characteristic of him. It carried neither excitement nor fear and made it sound like he was merely heading to the Fell Forest as he had during his time with the Black Iron Freight Corps.

"Mariela, you're probably a little frightened, so close your eyes and hold the raptor tight. Salamander, Come Forth. Light Mariela's path." Freyja spoke wearing her serious "master" expression. She gently stroked Mariela's head, took her hand, and placed the reins into it.

The young alchemist's hands were as cold as ice and violently shaking at the swarm of grotesque and unpleasantly familiar bodies. After wrapping Mariela's right hand tightly in both of her own, Freyja touched the ring on the girl's middle finger, summoned a small salamander about the size of one's open palm, placed it on the raptor's head, and smiled.

"Rawr!"

"Rar?! Raaar!!!"

The little salamander communicated something, and Koo replied as though saying "Leave it to me!"

"Well then, Sieg. I'm counting on you," said Freyja. The Sage of Calamity then departed no more dramatically than if she was simply going to get a bottle of alcohol and began walking toward the front lines to join Leonhardt.

"M-Master…"

Freyja looked over her shoulder at the voice calling to her and waved in response. Mariela had a terrible feeling she'd never see Freyja again.

Mariela wanted to tell her to stop, but she felt that was almost certainly the wrong thing to do. She believed her master had awoken in this era because there was something she needed to do. Freyja had probably left to go do just that.

If her master told her to, Mariela would fulfill her duty as well. Even if that responsibility lay beyond the great hordes of the walking corpses. Resolving not to simply be a burden, like she had been when they'd lost Lynx, Mariela gripped the raptor's reins tightly in her hands.

"Well, Your Excellency. Shall we go?"

"Oh, Lady Sage. It's heartening to have your support. I don't suppose there's a good strategy you know of?" Leonhardt asked. Freyja had previously demonstrated unparalleled understanding of the situation, after all. Even facing an army of the dead, Leonhardt showed no fear; his majestic appearance made him worthy of the nickname the Gold Lion General.

"This isn't a 'strategy' per se, but those corpses were slapped together; their individual attack power is low. Trouble is, there are a lot of them, and they're extremely hardy. In this stratum, they'll stop moving if you *chop them up*, but since the belly of the Labyrinth's boss is right beneath us, they'll probably be remade right away if you just slice them without a plan. If everyone cut down a hundred of them, that still wouldn't be enough to keep up. Instead, just charge through without worrying about them. No more limit on stratum movement, remember? The way down should already be open. Luckily, the inside of the belly is a straight shot, no forks. If you plow your way through the corpses, you'll definitely get there."

"If we do that, the corpses will flood up the stratums."

"I'll stay to make sure that doesn't happen."

"Lady Sage..."

"No need to worry. This'll be a piece of cake compared to culling earth dragons in the Fell Forest two hundred years ago. Besides, these people are from my time. It's only fitting that I be the one to send them home, don't you think? It's fine; no need to worry about me. Living a long time gives you a sense of when you're nearing the end. And I won't meet my end in a place like this." Freyja's big grin brought the conversation between the pair to a close.

There was no time left for deliberation. The strategy had been established. After directing the entire army to use the monster-warding potions they carried, Leonhardt ordered the start of the operation. "Mage unit to the front! Unleash your magic at maximum firepower! Everyone, follow me! We're running through at full speed!"

"Huuuooooooh!"

The war cry was intense enough to shake the Labyrinth, but to whom did it belong? Like the high-powered flames the mages unleashed, Leonhardt plunged into the enemy vanguard and cut through them, his soldiers close behind.

People and monsters alike burned as the swallowed city turned to ash, and every single person shouted as if a war cry could keep the stench at bay. They all charged forward with weapons in hand and unleashed magic and techniques to open the way down.

Just like a charging beast.

Just like a monster closing in.

Just like the day of the Stampede.

The Labyrinth's fifty-eighth stratum was a cavern resembling an intestinal tract smeared with blood. Although there was no visible sky, the reddish-brown walls made it look like a city in flames, and the wet red floor gave the impression of a ruined, bloodstained country.

The Labyrinth Suppression Forces shook off the clinging corpses as they might shake off past nightmares, literally cutting through them, and crossed the ceaseless vision of horror, leaving the corpses behind.

Take up your swords! Ready your bows. You damn monsters. How dare you! How dare you—

Which side harbored such thoughts?

"It's all over." Freyja calmly stood at the entrance to the Labyrinth's fifty-eighth stratum—the unending nightmare—far behind Leonhardt and the others. Multiple layers of flaming walls surrounded her to prevent the corpses from surging into the upper stratum.

"It's your turn, my kin. Your first big stage in two hundred years. The job is to lead home those poor lost children who are trapped in the past. You've received plenty of offerings, so how about you show me what you can do?"

Despite the fact that they'd be burned to charcoal by the flames, the corpses accumulated and closed in, and the blazing walls surrounding Freyja began to narrow, bit by bit. She smoothly dodged the spears and magic that flew her way while desperately defending the stairs to the upper floor in a beautiful dance of flame, and she wasn't performing alone. A group of fire spirits was emerging one by one around her.

A lone corpse stepped in front of Freyja, as if lured by her steps. Perhaps as a result of the crimson dance, a trace of reason could be seen in his eyes. "Say, have you seen a girl? I wonder if that alchemist made it home safely?"

The corpse had severe injuries, and more than half of his body had been blended with a monster's. The little bit of clothing remaining suggested he had once been a guard. In fact, it was the same guard who had given Mariela his own monster-warding potion on that day two hundred years ago.

"Yeah, she made it. So you can rest easy and go home, too." Freyja began to sing while she danced. It was a song she offered to the spirits, one with which she commanded her kin. No, perhaps it was more appropriate to call it a requiem for the dead.

"Come, great flames. Come, great flames. True fire, deep fire, you are primordial blood. Ignite, destroy, burst, barrage. **Summon Fire Blast!**"

In that instant, the stratum of the ancient dead was engulfed in a thunderous roar and a blast of overwhelming heat. The inferno purified the hellish scene, reducing it to ash and scattering the remnants to the wind.

A great many corpses had awoken from their two-hundred-year nightmare. As properly deceased people, as they were meant to be, the dead at last embarked on a journey to the one place they were meant to go.

Weishardt was dashing up the stratum stairs that ran through the Labyrinth when he felt a blast rock the foundation of the entire underground.

The fifty-sixth stratum's red dragon hadn't yet revived, and Weishardt continued through to the fifty-fifth and then the fifty-fourth. Thankfully, the only monsters here had been each floor's respective bosses: the Black Fiends and the Sea-Floating Pillar. Weishardt ran all the way up to the fifty-third stratum, where he at last saw with his own eyes that monsters were moving between different strata.

...Are they eating each other?

Basilisks had left their habitat on the fifty-second stratum and moved to the fifty-first, where they were attacking and greedily devouring the beasts that lived there. In such a state, they resembled the monsters inhabiting the Fell Forest.

Monsters of the Labyrinth ate people. However, Weishardt had never heard of monsters here eating their own kind or dying of starvation from lack of people to consume. The purported reason for this was that monster bodies were maintained by the magical power filling the Labyrinth. However, when different species met, did one species naturally become prey?

"At any rate, they do not seem to be heading for the surface en masse. If that's the case... Let's hurry to the surface while we have the chance!"

Without a moment to lose, Weishardt and the others ran up to the fiftieth stratum and used the Teleportation Circle to return to the second stratum.

"I don't believe monsters can activate a Teleportation Circle, but keep watch over it for caution's sake. If you confirm a suspicious transition, destroy it immediately!" said Weishardt.

Considering that this magic circle was a way back for Leonhardt's group, Weishardt wanted to leave it the way it was. However, he couldn't overlook the danger of powerful monsters from around the fiftieth stratum suddenly appearing in the second.

"Blockade the Aqueduct entrance on the second stratum! Don't allow monsters to invade from underground! Fifth unit, establish a defense on the tenth stratum, and sixth unit is to be stationed at the Labyrinth entrance! If you encounter any adventurers, immediately have them return to the surface for the time being. Malraux, take command of half of the scout unit and get me some intel on the situation from the tenth stratum up. The rest of you, get in touch with every location! This is an emergency summons!"

"Sir!" The soldiers immediately took action under Weishardt's orders. During the brief time when the monsters moving between strata were eating those in the earlier levels, the protectors of the Labyrinth City had to get ready. This was a race against time, and no one was about to let the tragedy that had befallen them two centuries ago repeat itself.

03

A handful of goblins were the first monsters to reach the surface. They were a hideous sight to youths aspiring to be adventurers, but they made for an easy battle.

Goblin skin was a dark, greenish-brown hue, a pigmentation never found in humans, and they had small, childlike bodies. However, the fact that goblins walked on two feet and were similar to humans in a few ways helped to inspire a type of readiness in those considering the life of an adventurer, a person who continually fought and slaughtered monsters. The sight of a slain goblin brought many to consider that it just as easily could have been them. Such monsters had a certain unsettling familiarity about them. However, the ones that crawled from the Labyrinth for the first time were noticeably different.

Their skin was darker and duller than that of normal goblins, and they had bloodshot eyes. Blood mixed with saliva dripped from their mouths, staining their chests. Each held a low-quality sword covered with blood and fat. Whether the creatures had picked up the weapons in the Labyrinth or had taken them from some unfortunate victims was unclear. Unusual monsters like these had previously only been encountered in the Fell Forest: for example, the black death wolves and werewolves that the Black Iron Freight Corps had once come across.

Those wolves would eat people, go mad from magical power, eat their fellow monsters, and become more ferocious individuals. Any living thing that ate of its own species could hardly have been considered acceptable, but perhaps it was a fitting evolution for creatures that originally arose from corrupted magical power.

The goblins, felled by soldiers who were keeping watch, had been stronger than the average specimen of their kind. Strangely, despite having been generated within the Labyrinth, their corpses didn't vanish.

"Were their bodies fully incarnated?" Weishardt received a report regarding the goblins in a council room of the Adventurers Guild, and that was when he hit on the reason for the monster cannibalism he'd witnessed. "Are they eating each other to acquire physical bodies? What is the status of monster generation within the Labyrinth?"

The magical power of the Labyrinth's boss hung thick in the air of the deep strata. Among the monsters generated from the stagnant magical power, individuals whose bodies hadn't incarnated much probably couldn't exist without a constant supply of magical energy. So they would eat one another to replenish their magical power and achieve full incarnation.

If monsters ate each other and evolved into stronger forms, their numbers would decrease. As long as those creatures of the Labyrinth didn't come thundering through like an avalanche, it was possible to hold them back and buy more time.

"According to a report from the fifth unit defending the tenth stratum, the number of monsters being generated in the shallow strata has doubled, and about ten percent of those are one rank higher than the rest. Higher-rank ones are eating the other monsters in the area and moving toward the surface. The fifth unit is blocking the progress of the monsters from the tenth stratum upward, but the report says that the strength of the fiends is increasing slowly over time."

New monsters were appearing one after another and moving to reach the surface. It seemed like a desperate situation for sure. However, Weishardt had noticed a silver lining in that report. Not even two hours had passed since they had established their headquarters in the Adventurers Guild, the place closest to the Labyrinth. If there was a time for action, it was now.

"On that note, Your Excellency, how do ya want us to welcome our guests of honor from the Labyrinth?" asked Haage, the master of the Adventurers Guild.

It wasn't just the Labyrinth Suppression Forces who had been assembled, either. Elmera, master of the Merchants Guild, and division chairs with high fighting strength had been summoned as well. The City Defense Squad, charged with guarding the Labyrinth City, was also present. It was understandable for the colonel and Captain Kyte to be there, though Adviser Teluther's presence was questionable.

However, Teluther was observing the situation not with his usual excitement at being in the presence of his admired Lightning Empress Elsee, but with a tense, extremely serious expression. Perhaps he'd hastened here believing that his long career in the City Defense Squad meant he would be able to provide something of use.

"The Labyrinth's northeastern gate is closed, so enter and exit on the southwestern side. The Labyrinth City's large southwestern gate, western gate, and southern gate are closed. City Defense Squad, continue to guard the protective wall while advising residents who can't fight to evacuate. Just like with the drills, we will use the mountain road leading from the large northeastern gate for evacuation."

Around the Labyrinth was a reconstructed, protective wall that had once been the castle ramparts for the Kingdom of Endalsia. The barricade was meant to hold back the monsters in the unlikely event they flooded out of the Labyrinth. Not one had emerged in the past two hundred years; the wall had simply served to give a sense of security to the people living in the Labyrinth City. However, thanks to how carefully it had been repaired, it would now serve as the city's final line of defense.

The barrier around the Labyrinth had two entrances, one on the northeast side and one on the southwest. The former, which many residents used, was closed. The purpose of this was also to buy time to evacuate, because if you left the Labyrinth City and headed northeast along the mountain road, you would arrive at the dwarves' autonomous region, Rock Wheel.

A route through the Fell Forest by way of monster-warding potions also existed, but there was a possibility the forest's monsters were linked to—and had been invigorated by—the Labyrinth. It was safer to use the mountain road, an already well-known evacuation route, in times of emergency.

"Adventurers Guild, organize your people to subjugate monsters in the Labyrinth. Form lines of defense on the tenth, twentieth, and thirtieth strata. Keep the monsters' progress in check while bringing down as many as possible. I would also like to request that the Merchants Guild supply and transport reinforcements and goods. I will ask Lord Royce and the Aguinas family to make potions available. The house of Margrave Schutzenwald will be responsible for all expenses." Weishardt took command just as easily as his brother would've.

"We were gonna do that from the get-go, but how long do ya plan to fight?" Haage asked as both the mediator for the adventurers and as a guildmaster.

Was the battle they were ordered to fight meant to buy time to save the residents' lives, or were they sacrifices meant to prevent damage from reaching the imperial capital?

Adventurers had far more freedom than soldiers. They had few obligations, but in exchange, there was no security. Of course, those who belonged to the guild were entitled to guild benefits in exchange for defined responsibilities, so it was possible to mobilize members by force. It was even within the power of the guild to send adventurers into an extremely dangerous place without telling them the particulars.

However, in addition to being a guildmaster, Haage held classes for young adventurers and had been teaching people how to fight for a long time. He wanted to help raise strong adventurers and see them return alive; he couldn't send them somewhere perilous without telling them anything.

"What should I say to 'em before I send 'em off?" Haage's eyes were serious. He was not about to falter, not even in the face of the house of Margrave Schutzenwald's influence.

They faced threats from the Labyrinth on the inside, the Fell Forest on the outside.

The man who had long watched over the adventurers of this isolated human land was also their protector.

"They're to remain until my brother has killed the Labyrinth, Haage." Weishardt looked the bald man straight in the eye as he answered. Leonhardt was still fighting, and Weishardt trusted that his brother would slip through the sea of the deceased and deliver the point of his sword to the boss of the Labyrinth. "New monsters are being created, eating each other, and incarnating. That means there are fewer monsters than there have been for a long time, but they're also strong enough to move to the surface. The Labyrinth Suppression Forces and adventurers entering the Labyrinth for many years and continuing to weaken its power was by no means pointless. Our time spent, our sacrifices, from drops of blood to chunks of flesh, were all worthwhile."

Weishardt stood before them and made his speech. Although they had different affiliations, the people gathered in that room all lived in the same city and fought together against the Labyrinth.

"And now, the monsters can move freely, despite the fact that without enough incarnated monsters, preparations for a stampede are not complete. There is no doubt that our accursed, longstanding enemy in the Labyrinth *has its back to the wall*. My brother, the Gold Lion General Leonhardt, will kill the Labyrinth. Of that I am certain. So in answer to your question, Haage… Until that time, we will protect the Labyrinth City and the people who live there, defeat monsters, and work to weaken the power of the Labyrinth."

Weishardt didn't have any skills like Lion's Roar to inspire the people. However, an equally powerful force existed in his words. The man continued to stare straight at Haage, and all present sensed the unwavering fighting spirit burning within him.

"Listen, everyone. This is not a battle of defense with no end in sight. This is a battle to take back our city, this region, from the monsters and return it to human hands. Understand that we are at a turning point. Will we win the right to build a happy future for ourselves and welcome each day in this land that will be truly ours? Or will those days, will our very lives, be snatched from us and devoured? I know my brother, the Gold Lion General, will defeat the Labyrinth and return this land to us. Until then, we must protect it, together."

There was no despair in Weishardt's eyes; instead, there was confidence, and the conviction that he would protect the people. Such was the duty of those born into the house of Margrave Schutzenwald. It was their dearest wish and for Weishardt, his raison d'être.

"I see. So the Gold Lion General is still fighting, is he? In that case, our blades are yours, Lieutenant General Weishardt. The Labyrinth Suppression Forces have the support of the Adventurers Guild!" *Bam!* Haage gave his answer along with a snappy thumbs-up and a radiant grin.

If the Schutzenwald brothers hadn't given up the fight, then the Labyrinth City, built so the Labyrinth could be killed, would fulfill its purpose. In this pivotal moment, adventurers would not fail to take up arms.

"Let's go, ladies and gents! Summon the adventurers! Now's the time to stand our ground! This is a once-in-a-lifetime chance. Don't forget to take care of the idiots and make sure they don't rush into danger! Let's go! It's time for Team Haage!"

Was it the destiny of an adventurer to be roused to action in exactly this sort of situation? Haage had directed his thumbs-up toward the assembled top brass of the Adventurers Guild, and they all responded at the same time: "Guildmaster, please go on your own."

"Even with all of us managing things and assigning adventurers according to their abilities, we'll be short-staffed. Honestly, you should know that much."

"Ah, but we don't need your help here, Guildmaster, so please fight to the utmost on the front lines."

"Besides, no one wants to call us 'Team Haage' except you."

"Wh-what's is wrong with all of you?!"

Even though he'd expressly gone "Bam!" when he made the decision, nothing had come of it, as per usual. Despite the state of emergency, the strong-willed staff members of the Adventurers Guild didn't budge an inch but ran things as they always did. They really exuded a sense of stability, likely thanks to Haage's daily training.

The top brass of the Adventurers Guild left the council room to summon adventurers, as Weishardt had directed. They were quite calm, even finding the time for pointless chatter.

"I've always had objections to the name Team Haage."

"I'd at least like it to be Team Limit Breaker. Something even a little less embarrassing."

"No, what about Team Hair? That way, the boss can't join. Not that he ever had to join us."

"You all know I shave this, right?"

"Mm… So you've gone out of your way to encourage hair loss? That's a very fresh interpretation. Still, it's impossible to say you're not bald."

Although they cracked jokes with each other, the guild staff members were hastily dividing up their work. Watching, Weishardt peered curiously at the adventurers, tilting his head, his beautiful blond hair bouncing slightly.

"He shaves it… So pure!" Telluther seemed to have been deeply moved by something.

04

The stairway heading into the abyss of the Labyrinth began at the end of the corridor creating the nightmare, just as the Sage of Calamity had said.

They'd managed to shake off the corpses, flying down the stairs as if an explosion were propelling them forward. The Labyrinth's fifty-ninth stratum was pitch-black, keeping Leonhardt from seeing what awaited him.

The corpses on the fifty-eighth stratum had lost interest in the Labyrinth Suppression Forces that had charged through. Instead, the walking corpses appeared more interested in heading toward the upper strata. Would they reach the surface, or was Freyja still going strong even after the explosion powerful enough to devastate the entire fifty-eight stratum? There was no way for Leonhardt and the others who walked among the abyss to know for sure.

The stairs connecting the strata of the Labyrinth up to this point were aptly called "stratum stairs"; they had been constructed with uniform steps. Here, however, the way down was a slope of accumulated rocks and dirt. No longer was there a structure one would call a "staircase." The stratum's ceiling was high, likely dozens of meters above, making the path down seem even steeper.

Not a single blade of grass had sprouted in the soil, giving the impression the place was a newly excavated cave. The dirt appeared to be claylike rather than coarse and sandy, and there was enough water underground to dampen the chill earth. Although soft, the soil wasn't loose and posed no threat to anyone's footing; rather, it had the texture of something like soft rock made of densely packed particles.

"**Light**. I can't see anything. Light the lamps and confirm the damage." At Leonhardt's order, the soldiers lit their lamps one after another and filed into ranks.

Normally, the walls and ceilings of the Labyrinth contained shining rocks called luminous stones or another material called moonstone. Both made the strata as bright as day. Even in gloomy strata, you could use night-vision magic to ensure a sufficient view. However, there were neither luminous stones nor moonstones in this stratum. This was truly the bottom of a dark hole that any would have rightly dubbed an abyss.

In this level, devoid of light and as silent as the grave, the signs of life were the roll calls taken and the lamps lit by the Labyrinth Suppression Forces. The damage check was surprisingly quick, but both the reports and the roll call were done in near whispers. No one believed the stratum was free of monsters.

The Forces had lowered their voices so as to listen carefully for the sound of monsters approaching. Monsters in this stratum could have been heading right for them, guided by the light from magic or lamps.

Shining lanterns in this darkness would mean telling the

fiends their position, but the soldiers wouldn't have been able to sense monsters approaching otherwise. More than anything else, however, it was fear that caused Leonhardt and the others to use illumination magic.

It's hard to believe that this is what came after a nightmare like the Stampede two hundred years ago...

Mariela recalled the cellar of her cottage in the Fell Forest, where, terrified of dying, she'd used the Magic Circle of Suspended Animation.

Back then, I was so, so scared... I just didn't want to die there all alone...

Perhaps sensing Mariela's uneasiness, the salamander riding on the raptor's head looked back at her with a "Rawr?" and tilted its own head a bit. The little spirit had been given form with her master's magical power and so had a physical existence. Despite its having been born of fire, the salamander wasn't too hot for the raptor's head. The flickering flame reminded Mariela of the lantern's light back when the Kingdom of Endalsia had fallen.

On the day of the Stampede, the flame of the lantern she'd carelessly forgotten to extinguish had led her to the world of two centuries later. The young alchemist wondered where the salamander's light was leading her now.

"It's all right, Mariela, I'll protect you." Sieg, who was holding the raptor's reins, tried to reassure her. The alchemist's worries must have shown on her face.

"Yeah, thank you. It was scary, and I'm still worried, but I'll manage." Mariela put on a smile as she answered Sieg.

She'd run through the Fell Forest to escape alone on that day two hundred years ago, but she wasn't by herself now. This time, the Forces and, most importantly, Sieg were at her side. She would be all right. Mariela wasn't taking refuge in a cellar alone; she was in a place everyone had worked together to reach.

When the young alchemist took a fresh look around, she saw that the stratum was extremely large. However, the darkness kept her from taking it all in. This lack of vision might have made the place feel more expansive and more mysterious to her than it actually was.

Within the illuminated area, enormous lumps of earth stood in a row. They varied greatly in size, ranging from only a few meters to over ten, but all of them towered over the average human. Their irregular shapes, as if a child had made them out of dirt, made it difficult to call them rocks. They looked like they'd been carelessly molded from clay.

The damage report seemed to have wrapped up while Mariela was surveying the place.

A short distance beyond the entrance to the stratum, each unit formed a line in front of Leonhardt and the captains, who themselves were standing as though to guard the general. Nierenberg, his medical team, Mariela, and the sixth unit in charge of protecting them were in the center line.

The Labyrinth Suppression Forces, which had numbered over two hundred people when they'd first entered the Labyrinth that day, had suffered losses during the battle with the Bladed Beast of Many Legs. After some had split off and made for the surface with Weishardt, the group that remained had steadily lost more of their men while pushing through the stratum with all the walking dead bodies. Only about a hundred of them remained. Roughly half of those lost had returned alive to the surface, but the Forces had clearly suffered some heavy casualties.

Most likely, everyone felt the same. They'd given their all in the battle with the Bladed Beast of Many Legs; neither fighting power nor resources had been spared. Crossing the sea of corpses had been no easy task, either. The alchemist was still going strong, and the army hadn't yet run out of potions, but was it really possible to make it through this stratum with only half of their original fighting force and without adequate preparation?

Like this floor of the Labyrinth, a darkness seemed to swallow the hearts of the remaining members of the Labyrinth Suppression Forces. The gigantic clumps of earth might as well have been a high wall that barred the way.

"Rawr!"

A sharp cry from the salamander broke the silence. As if in response, the raptor leaped to the left to pull Sieg, who was holding the reins, and the nearby soldiers away.

"Eek, Koo?!"

"Whoa, hey!"

Mariela and Sieg cried out in surprise at the sudden movement of the raptor. The soldiers whose ranks had been thrown into disorder all stared, equally startled.

"What's going on?"

Before the words even left his mouth, some kind of enormous explosion blew away the soldiers to the right of Mariela's group like a pile of wooden splinters.

05

The city was in an uproar.

The news that monsters from the Labyrinth were heading to the surface was sweeping the streets, so such a reaction was understandable.

The Adventurers Guild was near the Labyrinth, and adventurers gathered there one after another, each fired up. A person who would flee upon hearing that monsters were attacking would never have been among their ranks. Every person there jumped at the chance to make a good profit and earn a reputation for themselves.

Of course, in order to survive and be able to earn money and prestige, information was needed more than anything else. People packed the Adventurers Guild because they understood that rashly storming the Labyrinth was not a good plan. Staff members more than had their hands full with distributing information on the status of the monster outbreak, suitable ranks for each stratum, and deployment locations of support items such as potions.

Running against the stream, Elmera hurried toward Sunlight's Canopy. Of the work entrusted to the Merchants Guild, the duties of transporting and supplying goods were things Leandro was qualified to handle. Elmera trusted that he would skillfully allocate work to the staff and that everything would proceed without issue.

What Elmera was better suited for in an emergency situation like this was fighting on the Labyrinth's thirtieth stratum and below as the Lightning Empress. There she would cull the monsters, even if only a little. A single monster's death weakened the Labyrinth, and delaying the progress of powerful monsters meant buying more time for the people who couldn't fight to escape.

And to that end, Elmera was heading for Sunlight's Canopy to prepare. She fought for the sake of her children and faced the battlefield to ensure that they would not come to harm. That was why she had to make arrangements to ensure that they got away.

Elmera's precious children awaited their mother at the entrance to Sunlight's Canopy, along with Voyd and Ghark.

"Hello, Elmera. I thought I'd run into you if I waited here for a bit." Elmera's husband, Voyd, smiled and called to her as if he'd been waiting for a lost child. Next to him stood their two sons, Pallois and Elio, as well as the woman's grandfather, Ghark.

"Darling, Pallois, Elio, Grandpappy..."

Elmera's two children were wearing some unusual outfits. Both had donned the armor they normally used during combat training at school, and they carried no luggage for evacuation.

Elio was the type who fought with magic, so he had no weapons to begin with. Pallois, on the other hand, was holding a real sword and shield. Ghark, who accompanied them, had brought his customary double ax and was brimming with an amount of vigor one wouldn't have expected from such an old man.

"Mama! I'm going to the Labyrinth, too!" Elio embraced Elmera in a cute gesture appropriate for his age while saying something rather troubling.

"My, what are you talking about, Elio? You will leave the monsters to your mother and evacuate with Grandpappy."

Elmera responded as any mother would have. In truth, she wanted to take her children and evacuate, but she knew where she was needed.

"Mother, the guards told us 'Those who can fight go to the Labyrinth; those who can't fight evacuate.' That's why we have to go. We learned how to fight in school."

Pallois's assertion that they were ready for battle put Elmera in a bind. Certainly, two children with the blood of Elmera and Voyd possessed plenty of the qualities needed in warriors. However, they were still children.

"'Don't go in too deep. If it becomes dangerous, run away, no questions asked. That's the hardest part.' That's what we learned from Miss Master. We don't want to go with everyone out of selfishness, Mother. We'll make sure to fight in a place that's appropriate for us. We can do it. Believe in us."

The "Miss Master" Pallois referred to was Freyja. The red-haired woman had always seemed to be just playing with the children, but apparently, the sage had been teaching them important lessons.

Even so, Elmera was dumbstruck. Voyd gently nestled up to her and spoke. "Let's let them go. It's all right—they're our children, after all. Your grandfather will be with them the whole time, and I want to respect their desire to stand and fight."

"Darling... I understand."

Elmera nodded, and Voyd smiled tenderly at his wife.

The family was soon joined by Sherry and Emily, who had met them there, as well as Amber, who had finished closing up Sunlight's Canopy. Although they weren't very well equipped, they wore armor that covered their vital spots. Amber had a pole about the length of a broomstick, Sherry wore two cooking

knives at her waist, and Emily carried monster-warding potions, as well as smoke bombs with a variety of effects, such as sleep and concealment.

Evidently, they also intended to go to the Labyrinth. Amber dealt with drunken adventurers all the time, so she was likely fairly capable, and schools in the city taught children how to fight, so the girls would know enough to handle goblins.

Even Emily, the girl of the inn, was ready to head to the Labyrinth as if it was the obvious thing to do. Likely more than half of the Labyrinth City's children were adhering to the orders for those capable of fighting to make for the Labyrinth.

Seeing this, Voyd crouched so that his eyes were level with Pallois and took his son's hand. "Pallois, you must protect everyone."

"Yeah, leave it to me, Father. Miss Master taught me how to use my power. You heal wounds by absorbing attacks, but I don't have a special recovery ability. She said I could make the 'Hollow World' swallow stuff, and that I could just 'isolate' the energy that hurts the ones I love."

Voyd's eyes widened a bit at Pallois's encouraging answer. "Is that so? Very well." Voyd nodded as if to say he understood the truth of the secret Freyja had imparted to the boy.

"I learned from Miss Freyja, too. She said if I train my dismantling skill, I can 'Dismantle' living monsters, too. My teachers at school didn't tell me that. They said I shouldn't talk about it or use it unless I was in danger. But I don't think I'll get in trouble if I use it now."

"I learned things toooo!"

"Meee too!"

Master Freyja seemed to have been busy teaching a variety of things to the children while playing around with them at Sunlight's

Canopy. Sherry's remark in particular was frightening. What had she meant by dismantling something while it was still alive? Despite Sherry being such an adorable girl, one had to wonder if inheriting not only Nierenberg's blood but also his disposition was having an effect on her development.

In any other town, Freyja might have received a litany of complaints from parents, but this was the Labyrinth City, where the sort of knowledge she taught was useful. Even Nierenberg and the owner of the Yagu Drawbridge Pavilion, neither of whom were aware of the sage's lessons, would probably have given their blessing to this Youngster Bloodbath Squadron. Though, like Elmera, they would have done so with rather complicated expressions.

"Just leave the brats ta me. I may be gettin' on in years, but I was once an A-Ranker. I'll make sure ta take care of 'em," Ghark assured his granddaughter. The man was not one to be doubted, but since when was the Labyrinth City a place where people were on active duty well into their golden years?

"Grandpappy, remember your age. Don't overdo it."

"I'm counting on you, Grandfather."

Elmera and Voyd bowed their heads while they spoke.

"Hey, Old Man Ghark, we're gonna get a head start!" Gordon and Ludan, who were nearing elderly status themselves, ran past, brimming with energy and weapons in hand. Gordon's son Johan appeared to be falling behind as he chased after the two.

"Shall we go, too, Elmera?"

"My, you're coming, darling?"

The S-Ranker Voyd, master of the Hollow Rift, had chosen to go to the Labyrinth with his wife, Elmera, yet again. Choosing to trust their children, the couple had changed their minds completely. The powerful pair was already making their way toward the deepest levels of the Labyrinth.

"I'm the only one who can keep up with you at your full power. You're quite the stubborn young lady."

"The last time we were alone together in the Labyrinth must have been when we first met, darling. It's been a long time since we had a Labyrinth date."

The fate they were burdened with and the place they were heading for both promised tremendous danger, yet Elmera and Voyd began to walk with their arms linked, a show of their affection.

Watching his parents head to the Labyrinth, off in their own little world, the precocious Pallois wondered if perhaps he might find himself with a new sibling soon. He hoped for a sister.

A towering lump of earth exploded, sending the Labyrinth Suppression Forces reeling right before Mariela's eyes. Referring to it as a "lump of earth" didn't exactly speak to its actual nature, but rather to what it first appeared to be.

What was once an enormous clump of dirt had become something else, a thing that imitated the form of a powerful monster. After seeing his soldiers get blown away, Leonhardt at last understood the true nature of the mound-turned-monster.

"You again? How many times will you stand in our way?" Anger was boiling from the depths of the man's heart.

Leonhardt's men had been knocked back by a powerful tail, and following the attack had been a boastful roar—their foe was a dragon. It was a monster that had once defeated Leonhardt's group on the fifty-sixth stratum of the Labyrinth. Although they'd felled the creature on a second attempt, the follow-up battle hadn't been an easy one.

The transformation wasn't limited to the single earthen mound. Spiral cracks formed on the surfaces of all the visible lumps. Fractures spread across them in a way suggesting that perhaps the strange piles were of deliberate design, that their purpose from the very start had been to transform. Each then took on the countenance of a monster.

One became a dragon, another a basilisk; there was a manticore and even a one-eyed giant. Every one of them was an enormous and fearsome foe.

"Sieg! Aim for the wings! All of you, follow me!"

Not a moment after Leonhardt gave his instructions, Sieg fired an arrow. Thanks to Freyja's guidance in revealing the true strength of the Spirit Eye, a great number of frail and formless spirits gathered and surrounded the Sieg's projectile, making it look just like a comet. The arrow, with light swirling around it like powerful magic, pierced and tore the dragon's wing membrane as easily as it would have torn a piece of cloth.

"Rrrrrroooar!"

Its wing damaged and no longer able to fly, the monster opened its jaws in furious anger.

"Oh no you don't! **Rising Dragon Spear!**"

The deadly flame would have left the dragon's maw before

Leonhardt and the others could do anything, but Dick's spear crashed into the monster with enough force to leave a crater in the stratum floor. Leonhardt and his soldiers charged at the dragon, attacking mercilessly.

"These are young monsters, just formed! They're nothing to be feared!"

Leonhardt's cry as he brought his sword to bear wasn't made of empty, encouraging words. This wasn't a stratum of lava, so the Labyrinth Suppression Forces could move as they pleased. The ceiling here was also much lower than that of the fifty-sixth stratum. What was more, this dragon, generated from a lump of earth, was clearly far weaker than the red one that had given them so much trouble.

Although the soldiers had suffered serious injury for their moment of carelessness, they'd avoided death. As soon as the wounded drank the potions they'd kept on hand, they rejoined the ranks to challenge the dragon. It was as Leonhardt had said: There was nothing for them to be afraid of here.

A lone dragon of this caliber was something they could most definitely handle. Things would swiftly change, however, if all the many lumps of earth in this stratum suddenly turned into monsters and headed their way. While the dragon was unlikely to be difficult to defeat, it was also a matter of how long it would take to bring the creature down.

If they weren't quick, the Forces would soon find themselves surrounded by a multitude of monsters while they'd wasted time felling this one individual. Speed was essential if the Labyrinth Suppression Forces were to escape becoming prey themselves. None of them had descended this deep into the Labyrinth to dig their own graves. That was precisely why Leonhardt announced a decision to all those in his command.

"I permit the use of regenerative medicine! Now is the time to carry the power of dragons in your bodies! Warriors who have traveled to this most dangerous place! My proud brethren! Let your names be forever remembered as heroes of history and the Labyrinth City!" Leonhardt took out a potion of shimmering red and downed it in front of the assembled soldiers.

All at once, the general's entire body began to exude light and the man's wounds healed before their eyes. Leonhardt's offensive and defensive powers—indeed, every one of his physical faculties—seemed to greatly increase. He appeared to have instantly gone up an entire rank.

This was one more miracle the alchemist had brought along with the mana potions; it was the effect of the special-grade version of Regen.

Earth-element earth dragon, fire-element red dragon, water-element philoroilcus, and wind-element wigglertrill. Crafted from the four elemental types of dragon blood, this potion was further enhanced with Drops of Life and ley-line shards such that it manifested a miraculous power that not only rapidly increased recovery ability but also boosted every skill of the person who drank it, though only for a fixed period of time.

Dragon blood dwelled in individuals who had acquired abilities worthy of dragonkind. Such a creature didn't gain power from its blood. Rather, possessing power worthy of a dragon was made its blood worthy of the title.

Despite engendering such incredible effects, the potion could cause harm to the bodies of those unable to handle the power.

This was a medicine that was overly potent while simultaneously being very poisonous.

Still, the miracles of this concoction came at a cost: the deterioration of their honed physical strength and magical power, the dulling of their reflexes and sensory organs, and sometimes even the shortening of their lifespan. It was said that so long as you drank of it only once, anything lost from the effects of the potion could be regained later in life. Negative effects differed from one person to the next, though, so that was hardly a proven fact. An overreliance on this potion could even rob someone of their life.

The price for achieving tremendous military gains and carving their names into history as heroes was heavy: possibly even their futures. And yet not a single soldier had any doubts.

"If I can protect those I love, if I can cut a path to a peaceful and happy future for them, I will not hesitate for a second. Even if I lose my arms and can never take up the sword again, even if I lose my legs and never walk again!" The golden-maned general worthy of his name continued his valiant speech. What was a dragon before a lion such as him?

"My sword, my body, my life, are for my people!" Perhaps most of all, Leonhardt fought for the children who would inherit his will and carry the future.

The soldiers of the Labyrinth Suppression Forces gulped down the potion one after another and faced the dragon and, beyond it, all other monsters that came their way. The bodies, techniques, and hearts of the soldiers of the Forces had grown strong through years spent battling monsters more powerful than they were. Each of the brave warriors was deemed worthy and received the power of the dragon, pushing their abilities to new heights. Blows crushed dragon scales; magic pierced the eyes of the enormous monsters. Fiendish enemies who before required hundreds of hits to whittle down their stamina and finally defeat could now be felled in only a few dozen strikes. But no matter how many they defeated, there was no end in sight to the waves of monsters or the enormous, dark stratum.

The war, it seemed, was only just beginning.

07

The united front of the Labyrinth Suppression Forces and the adventurers holding back the monsters' advance functioned via a certain kind of paradigm. The soldiers of the Labyrinth Suppression Forces, who were trained and accustomed to group operations, but adventurers were not. They were more of a mob, so one might've expected there to have been a great many of them running to try and get ahead of the others.

The reason Weishardt made the Adventurers Guild participate in the defense of the city was because he trusted that its staff members would have a crystal-clear understanding of those idiosyncrasies, meaning they'd be able to deploy adventurers effectively.

The current state of the Labyrinth differed from what anyone was used to. Far more monsters than usual were appearing, and in every group, there were a few that were clearly stronger than the rest. Since each adventurer had a hunting ground they were accustomed to, it normally would've been more efficient to deploy adventurers in corresponding places where the monsters were springing up the quickest. However, such a strategy would leave those adventurers unprepared for the occasional foes a rank higher than the others.

To help combat this issue, battle-ready staff members of the Adventurers Guild and the Merchants Guild patrolled the strata, defeating the higher-ranked monsters. They moved from one stratum to the next, supporting those groups of adventurers who were beginning to falter, making sure such parties would be able to continue fighting.

In particular, the shallow strata up to the tenth were packed with crowds of children, the elderly, and city residents who ran shops—all people who, up to a short time ago, wouldn't have been considered fit for combat. They'd formed small squads of only a few people each and engaged monsters like goblins, orcs, and lizardmen, using teamwork to their advantage.

Elba, the owner of Elba's Shoe Shop, and other shopkeepers who dealt in leather products commented on the condition of monster hides as they beat them to a pulp, while butchers from the wholesale market cleaved their enemies with carving knives. It was quite the bloody spectacle.

In particular, the groups made up of children fought surprisingly effectively, employing what they'd learned in school so they wouldn't be surrounded. The adults and elderly who saw this wanted to stay strong for the younger generation, so they kept calm in this truly urgent situation and fought all the better for it.

The Youngster Bloodbath Squadron, the pride of Sunlight's Canopy, played a very active role in the fighting. Pallois used his shield to parry any monsters that leaped at him, Emily used magic and smoke bombs in accordance with monsters' weaknesses to create openings, and Elio and Sherry worked marvelously in sync to defeat even the higher-ranked lizard monsters that otherwise rarely appeared around the tenth stratum. First Elio paralyzed them with electric shocks, then Sherry dismantled and killed them.

Having evolved from the common lizardmen, these more fearsome creatures were, under normal circumstances, found only on the nineteenth stratum. Such a feat seemed to impress Ghark. "Kids sure do grow up fast," he commented in a brief spell of sentimentality. Not to be outdone, however, he continued to cut down monsters with his ax with a strength and speed that was truly shocking for his age.

At Ghark's side was Amber, who was kicking down monsters with magnificent footwork and beating them with her pole. "These children are special, but it's because of that Lady Sage's guidance," she said in reply to Ghark's comment.

"Eek!"

"Are you okay, Sherry?!"

"Sherry!"

"Don't pick on heeer!"

Although the children fought magnificently, there was no way for them to make it through unscathed.

"Here, have a potion. We only have a few left. Why don't we take a break and go get some more?"

At Amber's suggestion, the group headed for a potion distribution location. The stations had been set up next to the Teleportation Circles at the entrance to the Labyrinth and on every tenth stratum. The one on the tenth was the closest for them. Defense of this key stratum and the managing of its potion distribution had been entrusted to the City Defense Squad. Curiously, Teluther was also encamped at the distribution center.

The City Defense Squad was originally supposed to help evacuate any citizens who weren't able to fight, but there were surprisingly few residents who wanted to leave. Excluding the guards leading the evacuation and keeping looters in check, most City Defense Squad members had announced themselves as the escorts for the tenth stratum.

Even before this development, Teluther had always enjoyed generously distributing goods, but the items he was handing out now had been, until just a short time ago, extremely rare. Teluther himself, who handed out the concoctions fully conscious of that fact, and the people he gave them to seemed in extremely high spirits. Perhaps they all recognized that they were collectively writing a new page in the annals of history.

Teluther offered encouraging words like "Keep at it!" and "I respect your efforts and courage!" as he watched over the potion sharing.

People of the Labyrinth City who weren't used to being praised or receiving exceptional respect were suddenly brimming with motivation. Curiously, Teluther's words also caused those folks who'd planned on stealing the vials to be filled with feelings of guilt, inciting them to fight for the cause to atone for their lawless intentions. Teluther's work was really something.

Seeing a man who was usually nothing but a nuisance playing such an active role nettled both Captain Kyte and the soldiers of the City Defense Squad. None of them wanted to be outdone by Teluther, so they grouped up and challenged the powerful monsters that had eluded subjugation and were going up the stratum stairs.

The Labyrinth Suppression Forces' backup troops had taken upon themselves the responsibility of defending the twentieth stratum, where more powerful monsters appeared. They also worked to bring down monsters from the twentieth to the thirtieth strata. The Forces' fourth and fifth units, along with Haage's group, dealt with things from the thirtieth stratum onward.

Since Voyd and Elmera Seele had strolled by not long ago on their date, no monsters had made it to the thirtieth stratum. Floors below had probably become a veritable nest of lightning strikes. A rather intense date, to say the least. Only someone like the Isolated Hollow—a man with superhuman defense and regenerative power—would've dared describe it as merely "stimulating." Doubtless, the couple had the entire place to themselves.

Unsatisfied by the weaker caliber of monsters springing up in the thirtieth stratum, Haage had been keeping track of time and wondering if it would be best for him to follow the two and hunt for monsters deeper in the Labyrinth. However, he feared he'd get in the way of Elmera and Voyd's date if he went now. It was a thoughtful gesture to show a married people, but the pair had gone to battle monsters. It was not a romantic getaway. Really, Haage had no need for such strange concerns.

"This is the first time I have been to such a deep stratum. Its surprisingly calm."

When Haage looked back toward the sweet if out-of-place voice that had come from Teleportation Circle, he saw Caroline. The young lady of the Aguinas family had tagged along with the potion transportation unit. At her side stood Weishardt, assessing the situation, while likely also serving as her guard.

"Oh, it's Miss Aguinas. I know you're with Lieutenant

General Weishardt, but do ya really need to come here when it's so dangerous?"

"That danger is the very reason I deemed it necessary to see the battle with my own eyes," Caroline answered.

How was the battle progressing? How many potions should they transport? Were any other goods needed? The young head of the Aguinas estate had come to the thirtieth stratum to check such things firsthand.

"Help! First-aid treatment didn't do anything!" At that exact moment, an adventurer rushed in carrying a wounded comrade.

"This way!" called Caroline.

Though a young woman of noble birth, Caroline Aguinas was also a resident of the Labyrinth City, born and raised. She'd never tended to living things, and it was probably incorrect to say she was accustomed to the sight of blood. However, Caroline had learned the basics from Nierenberg, as well as the fact that knowledge alone was useless. In recent days, she'd visited the clinic where her older brother worked. Even if Caroline didn't perform the medical treatments herself, she refused to succumb to fear and avert her eyes from the terrible sight of one who'd suffered gruesome injury. Watching a doctor who'd come with her tend to the wounded adventurer, Caroline got to work taking orders for potions.

"She's quite the impressive young lady," muttered Haage.

"Indeed. Carol refused to evacuate and came all the way here," Weishardt responded as he watched his bride-to-be. He looked both troubled and proud.

"Carol, I must protect this city. However, I want you to go somewhere safe," Weishardt had told her.

But Caroline had turned down his plea with a smile.

"During the Stampede of two hundred years ago, the Aguinases were the ones who rushed in with soldiers before anyone else. I take pride in having come from that bloodline. There's not much I can do, but I at least want to deliver potions to those fighting for our future."

Even against her impassioned reasoning, Weishardt again begged Caroline to leave. "Please, evacuate for me."

Caroline faced the man and delivered the finishing blow. "Lord Weis, you will be protecting this city, correct? If so, this is the safest place to be!"

"After she put it that way, I had no choice but to stay with her."

Although Weishardt looked troubled as he explained what had happened to Haage, he was obviously proud of the woman he loved.

If anyone, the lieutenant general's aide was more likely to be worried. With Weishardt's older brother currently engaged in a life-or-death struggle, Haage had been hoping the younger sibling would be stricter.

Caroline finished gathering all necessary information and promptly returned to Weishardt's side. "Lord Weis. Thank you very much for bringing me here. I now have a general grasp of the situation. From here, I will return and begin to expand the transportation and preparation of potions, as well as the readiness of my brother's clinic to accept patients. Please, continue as you were, Lord Weis."

Caroline seemed to have her act together far more than Weishardt did. Thanking everyone for their time and giving a beautiful if tremendously out-of-place curtsy, the young lady left Weishardt and vanished into the Transportation Circle, accompanied by the transportation unit.

"...Well, I'm off to subjugate some monsters!" Haage seemed to be suggesting that despite how critical the situation was, he would lose his mind if he remained in such a boring stratum any longer, so he too left Weishardt and descended the stratum stairs.

08

Having left her fiancé and returned to the surface, Caroline reported to her father, Royce, and the family steward on the situation and the estimated potion consumption.

Considering the monsters moving between strata and the unusually ferocious variants prowling around, the fights on each stratum remained relatively contained. Of course, the conflict was still highly unpredictable, but it was doubtful that monsters would surge to the surface in great enough numbers to pack the streets and leave a mountain of death in their wake. Caroline anticipated a lengthy fight, however, so a large delivery of potions was going to be needed to handle the accumulating fatigue.

"Hrm, in that case, let's take a break and make preparations so our transportation unit can move when it's needed. Carol, you should rest a bit, too."

"I can keep going. I will rest after I check on my dear brother."

Royce was clearly concerned for his daughter, and she

responded with as much of a smile as she could muster before going out into the city again. Robert's clinic was already packed with the injured and the maimed.

"Brother, do you have enough potions?"

"Carol? It was by your orders, wasn't it? Plenty of potions are being delivered not just to the Labyrinth but here as well. What we lack is hands to administer the actual treatment." Even as he spoke, Robert continued to tend to the injured.

The former prisoner went about his duties, shouting things like "This is what happens when you to close a wound with a potion while a monster's fang is still stuck in it!" as he opened a patient's abdomen and removed a foreign object from it.

Compared to his once-gloomy demeanor, Robert now brimmed with vitality. Although her brother had been ousted from his previous position as the head of the Aguinas family, it seemed to Caroline when she looked at him now that everything had turned out for the best.

Nevertheless, it would have been unthinkable a short time ago in the Labyrinth City for there to be a place like this where adventurers received surgical incisions while their bodies were still dirty. Thankfully, a potion after such rough medical treatment allowed those operated on to heal themselves without any problems. Truly, the little concoctions were extremely useful.

"Honestly! This is what happens when benighted cretins depend too much on potions! It creates double the work! Right, you're healed. Next!" Robert insulted the adventurers as he treated them, but being of a lower social standard, they didn't understand difficult words like "benighted" anyway.

Even if they had, Robert was awfully polite for his insults. Most would have found such anger amusing, though they probably would've hidden such feelings from the man himself. However, likely because of the day's pressures, an adventurer unintentionally blurted out what he really thought: a complaint.

"Then why don't *you* go to the Labyrinth, Doc?"

Currently, people could still come up from the Labyrinth and get to this clinic to receive treatment, but if things worsened, there would probably be some who couldn't make it all the way back to get medical assistance.

One could tell just by looking at this aristocratic youth that he was a man who had no strength to lend to battle against the Labyrinth. However, Robert had healed every last one of the injured who had come to him. Adventurers Robert treated believed that so long as they could reach the man, he would surely help them, no matter how seriously wounded they were. Perhaps that confidence was why the adventurer had made his comment born from the unease of risking his life in battle with monsters.

"Hrm, yes, it does seem that would be more efficient. I will do so."

"Huh? Doc?!"

With a side glance at the now-dumbfounded adventurer, Robert began stuffing medical devices into a bag, cursing himself for not having thought of that himself.

"Brother, if you are going, I believe the twentieth stratum would be best. It is the one with the most wounded. I will make arrangements for the transport of additional potions as well as for someone to take your place here."

"I'm sorry to create extra work for you, Carol."

Robert hastily departed, with soldier escorts in tow. Even the adventurer who'd just been treated followed him, perhaps feeling as though he'd said too much. As she saw them off, Caroline headed for the command room in the Adventurers Guild. She would need to set some things in order to ensure her brother could administer treatment as freely as he wished.

09

Leonhardt and his forces charged through the seemingly eternal darkness. How much time had passed since they began fighting in this dark stratum? How many special-grade Regens had this latest vial made?

No matter how many powerful enemies fell to his blade, they kept coming. Still the Labyrinth Suppression Forces continued their advance, regardless of the grave injuries they suffered or the number of times their magical power ran dry. The hundreds of potions created by the alchemist in their ranks would heal them, and the soldiers would return to the front lines.

In this endless world of shadow, it was hard to even tell what direction they'd originally come from, but there did begin to be some evidence of change. The ground grew uneven, like parts of it had been gouged out, and the earth at the jagged edges of the shallow pits was soft. When the Forces advanced farther, a more distinct landmark came into view: a pair of identical trees.

Though still at a distance, Leonhardt was certain the things resembled great weathered trees. Or they would have, *if they hadn't been moving.*

Despite having nothing you could call a trunk, the bizarre growths had many branches. They looked something like trees that had been planted upside down, with their roots visible above ground. Of course, there did exist proper plants without trunks that had many branches sprouting from the earth. But the way these curious things spread in such a complex manner, coupled with the densely growing "leaves" comprised solely of veins, gave them the countenance of withered trees.

However, the definitive difference from the plants Leonhardt and the others knew was that these twin things squirmed sinuously, grabbing things. This was far more than just the tips of branches that quivered like the wind was blowing through them. Each bough that protruded from the earth moved as an independent appendage. If the Forces had managed to get close enough, they likely would have noticed that even the veiny leaves were squirming.

"So these are the 'hands,' then?"

There was one tree for each hand. The boss of the Labyrinth had left behind its legs and torn open its stomach; now it seemed to have left its hands behind in this stratum.

The concept of walking on legs had transformed into the Walking Mountain of Fire and the Bladed Beast of Many Legs, and the people and monsters the boss had devoured in the Stampede had overflowed from its stomach. So then what sort of things were these "hands"?

The answer to that question was evident almost immediately. The twin things bent low, motioning like they were grasping and kneading something. They tore up chunks of the ground. When they were finished, the "hands" had produced a single lump of earth.

"'Hands of Creation' is far too good a name for such repulsive things. Why don't we call them the Wicked Hands of Creation. Everyone! They are the boss of this stratum! Those abominable hands create monsters from clods of earth and defy the laws of nature! If we defeat them, these monsters will no longer be reborn." Leonhardt's call to encourage the Forces cut through the dark of the stratum.

"Take heart! The boss of the Labyrinth is near! Take heart! Soon they will know the points of our swords!"

"Take heart, take heart," Leonhardt told the soldiers—and himself. "Take heart, take heart."

"Take heart!" "Take heart!"

Dick, Nierenberg, and the soldiers following Leonhardt all raised their voices.

"Take heart!" "Take heart!" "Take heart!"

It didn't matter how many times they fell. The lights of lives that had been on the verge of disappearing, the torn-off limbs that had been reattached, all had been healed with potions. It was because of them that the Labyrinth Suppression Forces had made it this far.

"Take heart!" "Take heart!" "Take heart!" "Take heart!"

Stamina, magical power, and even willpower had long ago been pushed past their limits. The soldiers had reached this place by gambling their lives on the special-grade Regen potions. Even now, their bodies swayed amid the cries of encouragement. Leonhardt's field of vision blurred, and even breathing was unpleasant. The man tasted blood when he exhaled.

It was agonizing, difficult, and painful.

Leonhardt's body and soul had been so whittled away that nothing remained. The temptation to stop and rest was overwhelming. Yet, if they quit here, resigning themselves to dwindling away in this place, what would remain as proof of the lives they had all lived?

That was why they shouted. To drive away despair, to encourage themselves and their comrades.

"Take heart!" "Take heart!" "Take heart!" "Take heart!"

Leonhardt brandished his sword. The blade, which had brought low so many monsters, had grown damaged and weak. It was unlikely to last much longer, much like its wielder. Still, Leonhardt's gold lion roar reached the hearts of those who followed him, even if his throat was crushed and his voice was dry and hoarse.

Dick and the captains of each unit inspired and encouraged their subordinates, and attacked over and over with the weapons they had grown so accustomed to. Each body was pushed past its limits; muscles tore with every swing, and the Regen healed their bodies every time.

Even if the monsters' claws and fangs wounded and sent them all reeling again and again, though blood poured from their bodies, these brave people weren't ready to quit. Having slain monsters many times over, their bodies were coated with both their own blood and that of the enemy. If anyone had seen the Forces in such a state, they might not have recognized them as human anymore.

Nierenberg continued to heal. He would never force those with the will to stand and fight, and the will to move forward, to stop. Nierenberg knew they had the determination not to lose heart, no matter how stained with blood their armor became, no matter how much pain racked their bodies.

"I could not be more grateful to have all of you beside me." Siegmund drew his bow. To him, this place at the bottom of the world was like some kind of hell. Even here, however, the darkness was brimming with a radiant determination.

The pain and suffering he'd gone through up to this point felt like child's play compared with the agony he was experiencing right now. The beauty of the Labyrinth Suppression Forces overcoming such incredible torment, and moving forward in spite of it, left a deep impression on the hunter. What strength these men and women had! How weak Sieg had been before!

It was in this place that Siegmund found he was deeply grateful for his fate. It had allowed him to fight alongside these people to create a better future. He offered an earnest prayer for a time to come when he could keep Mariela completely safe with his own two hands. Charged with with Sieg's prayers and gratitude, the Spirit Eye boosted his arrows, and many spirits gathered to them. The blood he lost after using his eye so heavily was restored by Regen potions.

Flesh was regenerated and destroyed, monsters were born and annihilated repeatedly...

And Siegmund loosed his arrows at the Wicked Hands of Creation to put an end to the cycle.

"Potions are meant to heal people. They're meant to get rid of pain and suffering...," Mariela muttered.

Even with their arms missing and their legs torn, no one was about to stop walking. No matter how much agony they were in, their wounds would heal and they would return to the battlefield as long as they had potions. Blood flowed in rivers, and Mariela had walked along the trail of that blood to make it this far.

"Young lady, I found a ley-line shard. Use it to make potions." A soldier stained with crimson handed a ley-line shard he'd obtained in this stratum to Mariela. She still had crystallized medicinal herbs and magical power of the moon left, but the shards she'd brought had already been used up. It was only the continuous recovery effect of the Regen potions that had enabled everyone to hold on.

"Mariela, you make potions. Because of everything you create for us, because we can recover, everyone can stand against the monsters. That's why everyone's able to show such courage!" Through it all, Sieg had constantly been at Mariela's side, protecting and encouraging the young alchemist.

"But…" The ley-line shard in Mariela's hands began to tremble.

"Guh, look out!"

It was then that a small dragon at low altitude unleashed its breath at the young woman. Sieg leaped in front of her and fired several arrows that managed to alter the breath's trajectory and even brought the dragon to the ground. A shield knight further repelled the attack and kept Mariela safe. The attack had grazed and scorched the left half of Sieg's body, however, and smoke rose from his skin.

"Sieg!!!" Mariela cried.

"I'm fine. The Regen is working. This kind of injury will heal immediately. Don't stop, Mariela. Keep at your work. Lynx didn't give up, and neither will we. Lynx's dying wish now lives on in me, in us. Keep working; make sure our hopes aren't extinguished."

Sieg spoke to Mariela, but his eyes remained locked on the fallen dragon as he drew his bow.

"But, but, Sieg…the blood… There's even smoke…"

Mariela sounded like she was about to cry. Siegmund looked back at her and cracked a smile. "Mariela, this is the part where you tell me to give it my all."

"…Sieg… I understand. You can do it, Sieg! Give it your all!!!" Mariela tightened her grip around the ley-line shard.

Everyone is doing everything they can! What am I doing getting disheartened when all I've done is hide behind them?!

Both the raptor and salamander roared encouragingly at the young alchemist.

"Transmutation Vessel."

All she could do was make potions. There was little else she was capable of here, but still, Mariela was glad she'd continued as an alchemist. She was glad to keep at her work.

This is something I can do that helps them all!

The only ley-line shards she had now were those she'd obtained from felled monsters in this stratum, and few remained. She couldn't waste a single one. As she made potions, she put a prayer, a wish, and as much Drops of Life as she could into each.

Keep at it! You can do it, everyone!

Surely the hope she put into the potions would reach them.

The concoctions charged with Mariela's feelings would heal the wounds and restore the magical power of Sieg and the soldiers of the Labyrinth Suppression Forces. Her hope would warm and permeate the spirits strained by the battle with no end and the bodies withering from pain. Those who imbibed her works would remember who they had been before they headed into the Labyrinth.

The relentless attacks from Sieg and the Labyrinth Suppression Forces buffeted the Wicked Hands of Creation. Trembling and spasming, the things grasped at air and earth.

When the hands clawed at the seemingly empty air, they were most likely reaching after the magical power that filled that stratum. New monsters were still being born from the earthen clods, but their shapes had clearly become sloppy, as their necks were longer and thinner, and the number and length of their limbs differed from those of normal monsters.

"Just a little longer!"

Leonhardt and the others pushed harder, charging ever forward. Just a little longer and they could put an end to the creation of the deformed monsters that boasted no strength but that of numbers. Soon they would strike down the stratum boss molding those misshapen things to desperately defend this place. Just a few moments more and their attacks would finally strike home, ending the life of the stratum boss. Surely the soldiers had felt Mariela's wish for them to keep fighting.

Leonhardt led the Labyrinth Suppression Forces in a charge through the monsters protecting the stratum's boss.

10

"The number of injured has suddenly increased. What caused this?" Robert, who'd been administering medical treatment on the Labyrinth's twentieth stratum, posed his question calmly.

"A bunch of weird monsters suddenly started appear—Owwww!"

"Does it hurt? Hrm, that's good. It's proof you're alive. There, you're healed."

Robert was certainly healing his patients, but he did so quickly and with a physical roughness that was difficult to describe as courteous. It was probably unavoidable that he'd get angry over a sudden increase in the number of injured, but Robert's words had called to mind a certain medical engineer. Did he resemble that man now because they'd been providing medical treatment together for a long time, or was such bluntness a common trait among those of this occupation?

"H-heeelp!"

Robert was currently in a provisional clinic established in the twentieth stratum of the Labyrinth. Although he had been afforded several adventurers who knew how to use healing magic—they'd all offered to help administer treatment—the place had originally been a potion distribution location. As such, soldiers and adventurers who'd used up their potions and suffered wounds were already gathering there, making things fairly convenient for Robert. Among those warriors were those fleeing from monsters. Normally, the act would have been an utter breach of conduct.

"Gh, again?! And it's a wyvern?!"

The second-string soldiers of the Labyrinth Suppression Forces protecting the twentieth stratum dashed toward the monster chasing the adventurer who'd rushed in. More than half of the second-string soldiers were C Rank. A wyvern was a monster of around B Rank, a powerful enemy that was troublesome even for a group of fighters.

Now that the areas around stratum stairs were no longer safe, this potion distribution location was one of the few safe zones in the Labyrinth and had to be protected. Especially since it was the main source of medical treatment. The strategic placement of the clinic on the twentieth stratum also allowed others to reach it via Teleportation Circle. As such a crucial bastion in their fight, the place needed to be defended no matter what.

In the twentieth stratum, adventurers ranging from D-Rank youths to more intermediate-level combatants had gathered. Excluding those not combat ready, such as children and the elderly, these types of people made up the largest portion of the Labyrinth City's population. If more powerful monsters flooded the twentieth stratum, there would probably be a great many casualties.

"Grakakakakar!"

Even a single wyvern was a challenge for the soldiers defending this place, but it summoned another two with a birdlike call. They came flying in, weaving their way between closely packed pillars. To make matters worse, one of the newly appeared wyverns had most likely eaten another monster or a person. The surface of its body had obviously blackened, and bloody saliva dribbled from its mouth. It was clearly an anomaly, more brutal and powerful than others of its kind.

"Lord Robert, this place is dangerous. Please evacuate." Robert's guard concluded that the situation had worsened and urged him to evacuate in a voice low enough that the surrounding people wouldn't hear. Robert quietly shook his head, however, and answered his guard without pausing his treatments.

"I promised them, these adventurers, that I'd help them as long as they were still alive. No, this is a promise I made to myself. I won't abide failure to save anyone anymore. This is clearly some kind of counterattack, or perhaps the Labyrinth is truly growing desperate. Truthfully, I suppose the reason doesn't much matter. I want to see this with my own eyes. All of you should go on and evacuate yourselves."

It wasn't that Robert had given in to despair or that he wanted to die. The doctor simply wanted to help. That was all he had. Seeing Robert continue his medical treatment, the soldiers at his side exchanged glances, then drew their swords and turned to face the wyverns that were mowing down adventurers.

"If we live through this, please help us, too."

"We'll be in your hands, Dr. Robert."

"You..." Robert lifted his head and looked at his guardsmen. He surveyed the adventurers in the vicinity.

All around, an extremely disastrous scene was unfolding. A mere three wyverns were routing adventurers left and right; many among them were faces Robert knew. They were people who'd broken free of the slums and returned to being adventurers thanks to potions and Robert's medical treatments. Every one of them was covered in blood, but not a single one fled.

They knew this was an important place that needed defending to the last.

A blow from a wyvern sent an adventurer flying into a wall. Robert recognized him as the man whose leg he'd healed. The leg he'd gone to such lengths to fix was bent in an unnatural direction, and the adventurer appeared to have lost consciousness as he fell into a puddle of his own blood. The occasional twitch meant the man was likely still alive, but the presence of the wyverns prevented Robert from rushing over. If the adventurer couldn't return to him, Robert could do nothing to save him.

Don't die. Please, don't die. Someone help them...

Was there anyone to hear such a prayer?

"My left arm is a pedestal for flames; my right arm a pedestal for thunder. Abide in me! Dual Sword Elements!"

Fire surged and wind danced. Flames, undulating as if they were a living creature, engulfed the wyverns. Their wing membranes burned to nothing in an instant, and the wyverns fell to the ground. On the way down, they tried to attack using their powerful legs, but before they could, blades of wind whirled around them and cut into their necks one after another. That frenzy of flames and wind was more than enough to overpower both the normal and evolved wyverns. The fearsome monsters were rendered little more than hunks of meat.

"Incredible...," muttered one young adventurer after witnessing the power of an A-Ranker. As if in response, the man who'd appeared in this hour of crisis looked back at the adventurers and gave them a dauntless smile, because that was simply who he was. His dramatic entrance seemed to say "The hero always arrives late!"

"The hero always arrives late!" Then Edgan went and ruined it by *actually* saying it.

"Uh...say, who is that guy? He's kinda pathetic, isn't he?"

"Yeah. He's kinda... Well, maybe not entirely pathetic. Who is he?"

Edgan, the young A-Ranker who'd made such a gallant appearance at a pivotal moment, cut quite an attractive figure, though likely only because of the heat of the moment. Many of the adventurers in the twentieth stratum were young women. Edgan ought to have been grateful to the wyverns he had so thoroughly defeated.

"Hey? Didn't you get too far ahead of us, Edgan?"

"That's right. It's important to act as a group."

Yuric, Grandel, and the other members of the Black Iron Freight Corps appeared in succession after him.

"Whoa, Edgan's nostrils are flaring?! Gross!"

"Yuric! As much as I hate to say it, it's improper to call the captain 'gross'!"

Evidently, Edgan was fairly full of himself after receiving the adulation of female adventurers, and his nose was twitching. His fellows in the Black Iron Freight Corps likened him to a monkey.

The raptors Yuric brought along were practically stacked with the wounded, and the beasts hastened to retrieve the adventurers that fallen prey to the wyverns.

Edgan was standing arms folded, with one foot atop a wyvern in a contrived pose. The rest of the Black Iron Freight Corps seemed perfectly content to ignore him and instead dropped off the many wounded at Robert's clinic.

"Good, they're still breathing... I'm grateful for your aid with the wounded." Quickly assessing the status of those injured the

Corps had transported, Robert expressed his thanks to the members of the Black Iron Freight Corps, save Edgan.

"We gave them all basic first aid, but that's all we could do for them. We need to keep moving, so we'll entrust them to you," said Franz, the healing magic user. The Black Iron Freight Corps took their raptors and headed for the stairs leading to the lower strata.

"Onward to the next stratum."

Despite the seriousness of his surroundings, Grandel used his umbrella as a walking stick as he sauntered along in his usual lightweight equipment. He struck a sharp contrast to Donnino, who walked with a heavy hammer over his shoulder. Behind them, Newie and Nick carried so many umbrellas they looked like umbrella peddlers. As Grandel was unable to carry a proper shield, his strategy likely consisted of cycling through disposable umbrellas, discarding one when it broke and picking up a fresh one.

A magic-wielding swordsman, a heavily armed warrior, a healing magic user, and an animal tamer. The group was a bit lacking in long-range skills, but Grandel, the "legendary hero," had fashioned himself a fairly balanced party overall. Though the four were just members of the Black Iron Freight Corps, in that moment, they truly appeared to be the companions of a legendary hero. Perhaps because their *real* leader was a captain who defied all meaning of the word.

"I didn't know the Black Iron Freight Corps were in the City…"

"Isn't that Edgan?"

"Is he the new captain?"

Female adventurers whispered to one another as they assessed Edgan. The man himself turned his back to them in an affected manner, as though to suggest he had no interest in the likes of them. He was, in fact, listening with keen interest to their conversation, however. As evidence of this, his ears twitched, and his face was plastered with an idiotic grin.

Again, Edgan's subordinates commented on his monkey-like behavior. Whether or not the female adventurers noticed Edgan's unflattering expression, they didn't seem to mind. After all, Edgan had demonstrated considerable strength, far beyond that of the other adventurers fighting in the stratum. Plus, he was good-looking—so long as he kept his mouth shut—and managed a successful business.

"Umm, thank you very much for your help."

"I'm Anja. How about I give you a little token of my appreciation later?"

"Hey, no fair butting in. I'm Mirke."

Though they were still in the monster-filled Labyrinth, a few female adventurers ran to Edgan to express their gratitude. They even took his hands in theirs, hoping to leave a more lasting impression. Perhaps Edgan's true golden days were yet to come. Who could've said what sort of life awaited him after defeating the monsters overflowing from the Labyrinth?

"Hey, Edgan? Come on!"

"Rar! Grr!"

"Wah! Hey, raptor, don't bite me. Leggo, leggo of my ass…!!!"

If he managed to make it back to the surface, of course.

Ridiculous…, Robert thought. He'd been on the cusp of expressing his own wish for the safety of those who'd been fighting so bravely when Edgan had butted in. *What an absurd charade.*

Although situated in the middle of a deadly battlefield, Robert continued to conduct himself with an air of nobility as he treated the wounded. In truth, he was getting more acclaim from the adventurers than Edgan was, but Robert wasn't taking notice. All he wanted was for everyone to make it through this alive. Conversations about the future could wait until everyone had safely made it back to the surface. Their tomorrow still lay just beyond the defeat of the Labyrinth.

"So they really are here."

"These sorts of abnormalities have a pattern to them. They seem to be few in number because they're high-ranking monsters. Nick, Newie, an umbrella, if you please. Take care not to leave my side."

The Black Iron Freight Corps hadn't gone into the Labyrinth after Edgan, the man willing to do anything to meet someone, anyone, for a date. Even Edgan himself hadn't come to the fight merely looking for a chance romantic encounter. The Black Iron Freight Corps's destination was the Labyrinth's twenty-third stratum, the Shores of Eternal Night.

This stratum was one normally enjoyed the gentle glow of moonlight and the sounds of babbling streams. Today, however, all anyone could hear were the echoing cries of armored lizardmen.

One had to wonder if the lizardmen had gone mad, as they struggled against a single paler creature despite some truly gruesome wounds. The monsters were trying to eat their comrades-in-arms.

The alabaster monster, a death lizard, was gobbling down the torso of an armored lizardman with no regard for the other lizardmen snapping at it. Perhaps it was because the magical gems of armored lizardmen lay somewhere in their intestines.

"Those're some really disgusting monsters, aren't they?" Yuric spat.

In most of the strata, there were a few monsters one rank higher mixed in with the ones that normally appeared. However, death lizards were actually two ranks higher than armored lizardmen. The death lizard continued to tear through the armor-like scales of the lesser monsters as though they were butter. It consumed one lizardman's intestines while seemingly paying no heed to the many other armored lizardmen trying to eat it—a clear demonstration of how much stronger a death lizard was.

The A-Rank death lizard was probably still far from achieving a full incarnation, no matter how many C-Rank armored lizardmen it consumed. Still, it continued to eat mindlessly, as if it had been starved for months.

Without warning, the death lizard suddenly turned its neck halfway around to look directly behind where it was standing. The monster's mouth split into what appeared to be a smile. It had spotted prey of much finer quality.

There were seven humans and eight raptors. Although the strength of humans clearly varied, to the death lizard, the Corps were first-rate food when compared with the C-Rank lizardmen.

The monster barreled toward the Black Iron Freight Corps with the armored lizardmen still chomping at its body. The creature's strange gait—four long, thin limbs carrying an undulating torso—called to mind a strange insect more than any reptile.

Edgan took a step toward the approaching death lizard, his eyes narrowed. "I know you're not the same monster that killed Lynx. This isn't revenge. I'm just venting a little anger."

Edgan charged his dual swords with magical power.

The Black Iron Freight Corps had made sure to exterminate the death lizard that had killed Lynx after they'd received news of his passing. This death lizard had only recently appeared; it couldn't have been the one that had attacked Lynx and the others.

However, it was because death lizards appeared on this stratum that the Black Iron Freight Corps had chosen it as their hunting ground should they ever venture into the Labyrinth.

The day they'd lost Lynx, the members of the Corps had talked until sunrise.

"We'll make sure Lynx is avenged. Let's kill the Labyrinth," they'd sworn.

Unfortunately, few among the Black Iron Freight Corps were fit to battle alongside the Labyrinth Suppression Forces. Only Dick, Malraux, and Edgan had the necessary strength. The rest had the solo fighting power of second-string soldiers at best.

Yuric specialized in handling beasts like the Corps's raptors, and Franz possessed demi-human characteristics. This had made it difficult for them to integrate with a human group, even if it was the Labyrinth Suppression Forces. Likewise, Grandel and Donnino had both transferred out of the Forces because the group's fighting style didn't cater to their specific talents. You could say it was the iron carriages that had really let them come into their own.

The Black Iron Freight Corps's frequent trips between the Labyrinth City and the imperial capital by way of the Fell Forest were vital to both the Forces and the City itself. That was why only Dick and Malraux had returned to the Forces. The remaining members of the Corps supported the subjugation of the Labyrinth in a different but no less vital way.

As it happened, Edgan had already surpassed Malraux in terms of strength. Edgan had ostensibly remained with the Black Iron Freight Corps to defeat the occasional powerful foe, but in truth, it was for a far more foolish reason: he'd cultivated too much of a reputation as a philanderer during his time in the Forces, so he couldn't return. There was no two ways about it; Edgan was reaping what he'd sowed. The promise of working with people who thought better of him, if only a little, made the decision to stay with the Black Iron Freight Corps an easy one.

The remaining members of the Corps had their own reasons for staying with the trade group. Today, however, they'd all been contacted in advance about the Labyrinth Suppression Forces' expedition and had been on standby in the Labyrinth City in case of the unlikely worst-case scenario.

While it was unfortunate that a stampede had begun, it was incredibly fortunate that the Corps, usually preferring to help only in discreet ways, chose to get involved.

"With our fighting power, around the twentieth stratum is probably the most we can handle. No matter what, if we fight, let's do it on the stratum where Lynx fell."

After someone among them had said that, the members of the trade group headed for the twentieth stratum, which, unbeknownst to them, was in need of aid.

*   *   *

With several armored lizardmen chomping on it, the death lizard's movements were more sluggish than they would have otherwise been. The members of the Black Iron Freight Corps watched its approach as bloody saliva dripped from its quartered mouth. Edgan charged his dual swords with magical power to strike down the monster.

"My left arm is a pedestal for flames; my right arm a pedestal for......"

"Now that the anchor is set, heave-ho, **Shield Bash**. It's done, Donnino."

"Right. **Mega Hammer!**"

There was a loud thud, followed by a whomping noise. Before Edgan had been able to strike down the death lizard in style, Grandel had opened his umbrella and thrust it into the ground handle-first in place of an actual anchor. Then Nick had driven the "anchor" into the ground with his hammer. With Grandel's weapon now firmly rooted in the ground, his Shield Bash sent the attacking monster flying.

Grandel's slender build meant he could never repel a death lizard on his own. Knowing this, he'd angled the umbrella he was using as a shield diagonally to deflect the impact of the attack. What was more, the handle had remained anchored against the attack. After the setup, all Grandel had to do was simply open and close the umbrella. Despite being rather gaunt and enervated, Grandel had definitely manned an attack of "legendary hero" caliber. Newie recovered the umbrella, now in tatters after sending the death lizard flying, and handed a new one to Grandel. Apparently, this was a system that had been worked out in advance;

Nick was in charge of setting the anchor, and Newie was in charge of reloading.

The Shield Bash knocked the death lizard toward the ceiling, and when it fell back down, Donnino's hammer turned its head into ground meat. Donnino boasted incredible strength, but his speed and accuracy meant he needed help to strike at opportune moments.

Apparently, the death lizard was still alive in some form after the attack, as it twitched from its spot on the ground. Perhaps that was to be expected of a high-ranking monster, but its head had been flattened. Were death lizards' brains somewhere other than their skulls?

The armored lizards attached to the death lizard had gone flying with it and fallen off partway through its soaring arc, but they were unconcerned with that. They armored lizards quickly resumed gnawing at the other monster with little regard for anything else.

"Surfeit Heal."

Franz used a peculiar type of recovery magic on both the chomping armored lizards and the death lizard to heal the bite wounds on the now-distorted head Donnino had crushed and to glue all the armored lizards to those injuries. This resulted in a single mass of monster meat. A skill that forcibly manipulated parts of creatures' bodies in such a way could hardly have been called "healing." This technique that transfigured the flesh of a living thing wasn't something humans could use. Only a demi-human like the masked Franz was capable of it. This inherent ability of Franz's went beyond mere recovery, and he had only ever dared to show it to the Black Iron Freight Corps before.

The joined mass of monsters, with both their fangs and their

claws impeded, was now little more live bait awaiting the finishing blow.

"All right, Yuric," Franz called.

Yuric looked down on the squirming lump of flesh and bone that had once been the death lizard with a frigid expression, then held out a hand and cut it open, dripping blood in some apparent pattern onto the foreheads of the raptors.

"Now it's time to dine. **Go Wild, My Children!**"

"Raaararararararaaaaaaaaaaaaaar!!!"

The power of an animal tamer was one few possessed, even in the imperial capital. It was an ability only members of the borderland tribe inherited. Although prized for its usefulness, it was the very reason the tribe was so ostracized.

It had likely been precisely because of this ability that Yuric—an orphan bearing the unique trait of his people—had survived in the slums of the imperial capital. The demi-human had prowled the streets like a beast with no land to call home. One had to wonder which defined Yuric more: his time living as a beast on the streets of the capital, or his time living as a human after Franz adopted him.

At Yuric's command, the raptors made a savage charge at what remained of the death lizard, tearing off the entirety of its tough skin, and started to eat it. Screaming as they devoured the monster-turned-meat, the raptors appeared free from the constraints of human domestication, displaying their bestial nature. It was an extremely cruel and brutal feeding, but there was a certain natural beauty to it—this was the way animals were.

The same was true for Yuric. The demi-human was all smiles while watching the scene unfold. Something about killing the species that had killed a friend felt right.

"Uh...my prey is...? Huuuh?"

Edgan had been completely left out of the combo attack, being outdone before he could show off his Dual Sword Elements. He stood at a loss, holding his half-charged blades.

"Edgan, there's a fresh death lizard over there!"

"Yes, he's right. It's waaay over there. See it? You should get after it."

"We're relying on you, Edgan."

"Yeah, we're countin' on you."

Grandel, Yuric, Franz, and Donnino treated Edgan as they ever did. Edgan may have falsely represented himself in many ways, but his strength was most certainly real. Both Nick and Newie thrust their fists into the air to cheer him on. "You can do it."

Per Grandel's theory, a leader was one who "creates an environment where his team can demonstrate their true strengths." Edgan was an A-Ranker who could defeat death lizards even by himself. He'd culled monsters whose numbers had made victory unthinkable for the other members of the Corps. Then he'd gone off to slay more-distant monsters on the twentieth stratum who hadn't noticed the group yet. The number of subjugations alone made his work worthy of an A-Ranker.

The frenzied death lizards paid no heed to the apparent difference in strength and eagerly attacked Edgan at every turn. He didn't know whether the monsters were or male or female, but it seemed that Edgan's popular phase had arrived at last.

Being popular did have its challenges.

12

Around the same time that the Black Iron Freight Corps was killing death lizards, Voyd and Elmera were strolling around the thirty-eighth stratum. It was a world of whirling clouds with the couple at its center, as if they were in a place that belonged entirely to them.

Even subjugating ferocious monsters was an activity for Elmera and Voyd to do together. Monsters struck by the Lightning Empress's thunderbolts were burning in place of romantic candlelight.

"I'll be with you come hell or high water."

In contrast to the sweet atmosphere in which the couple routed monsters as they advanced to the deepest parts of the Labyrinth, Haage was in the thirty-fifth stratum, three levels up from them. The lonely man loosed his Limit-Breaking Cleave against the grotesque creatures that were starting to appear again, giving a thumbs-up to the empty air every time he defeated a formidable monster.

Since Haage was skilled enough to teach young people how to fight in the Adventurers Guild, he was more than safe fighting solo. The way he maintained distance between himself and his enemies was flawless. Seemingly unconcerned with the strange-looking monsters that sprang up one after another, Haage dealt with them as they came. By any measure, he should have been happy with how his fight was going, but he looked somewhat dispirited.

Could the long, lonesome fight have finally started to wear him out?

Bam! There was no one to ask him, because Haage was the only human in this stratum.

"…" The smile gradually faded from Haage's face, and a deep sorrow started to make him wonder if he should stop giving the thumbs-up. He seemed to be mentally exhausted.

Haage sliced up monsters by using his Limit-Breaking Cleave, and the defeated monsters became magical power for the Labyrinth and disappeared. Even that stagnated, corrupt magical power wasn't as gloomy as the atmosphere surrounding Haage. After breathing a small sigh, Haage began to look for his next prey without flashing a snappy thumbs-up, when…

"This is nice and quiet."

"Seems even the guildmaster stops his pointless exercises when he's tired."

"I'd like to think he realized how meaningless inefficient words and deeds are."

"Wh-what?!"

The top brass of the Adventurers Guild, the members of Team Haage, came running in. Haage didn't appear to be in any actual danger, but he'd been on the verge of losing his unique affectations. That in and of itself was a kind of tough spot. After seeing his subordinates appear on the scene like a team of heroes, there was only one thing Haage could do in reply…

Bam!

He threw a snappy thumbs-up with a great big smile on his face.

"…Now I wish we'd been a bit slower in coming."

"It was absurd to finish our work in a hurry…"

"The change in mood has made him twice as annoying."

Haage's recovery speed was too fast. Evidently, a potion was not needed for the man's mental health.

The top brass of the Adventurers Guild seemed to want to say they were fed up. Still, they remained unwilling to admit defeat, and they surrounded Haage in their usual battle formation. The arrangement created an impregnable fortress around Haage while still letting him leverage his attack power against monsters. It allowed the group to search for, restrain, and defend against monsters—perfect for long battles.

"Let's go! Team Haage's battle starts now!!!"

"Please stop using that name."

"Maybe you'd rather we leave you alone?"

"You'll bring bad luck."

Haage shouted a rallying cry they'd heard somewhere before as he happily challenged swarms of monsters. Conversely, the guild's administration accompanied him in low spirits. Haage's battle was one of many dramas unfolding in the Labyrinth at that moment.

13

Everyone was challenging the Labyrinth today. There was a large number of adventurers and soldiers, of course, but many of those embroiled in the battle didn't normally fight. People like farmers, merchants, young women, the elderly, and even children all rallied to the cause.

That didn't mean everyone could defeat powerful monsters. Many could defeat only weak monsters like goblins, and only if they were in groups, but even a single slime or goblin was part of the Labyrinth's power. Monsters were created after being defeated and were defeated again after being created. The greatest strength the monsters had was their numbers.

Just as the monsters had stormed the streets of the Kingdom of Endalsia on the day of the Stampede, the people of the Labyrinth City now crowded the Labyrinth to protect their homes, their way of life, and their families.

Had anyone, even the boss of the Labyrinth, ever expected this day to come?

Even supposing the boss had the ability to think, it probably hadn't imagined that opening movement between strata and sending out monsters and corpses to crush the Labyrinth Suppression Forces underfoot would cause the people of the Labyrinth City to surge into the Labyrinth.

Two hundred years ago, considering the scale of the Kingdom of Endalsia, comparatively few adventurers had fought against the monsters. It had been easy for the monsters to chase after and devour the people who tried to escape, because perpetual peace had robbed the citizens of the kingdom of the knowledge of battle.

Such was not the case for the Labyrinth City. Even children took up arms in the fight.

Not a single person gave up hope; an indomitable light burned in each person's eyes.

Did the Labyrinth's own confidence quail, if only for a moment, at that determination?

The Wicked Hands of Creation would occasionally stretch into the air. They were probably making monsters in other strata far above. All it did was create a good opportunity to attack, as far as Leonhardt and the others still fighting in the fifty-ninth stratum were concerned.

Every time the people who'd gone into the Labyrinth defeated monsters, the Wicked Hands of Creation produced new ones to replace them. Leonhardt and the Forces seized upon those moments, advancing toward the hands. Slowly but surely, they crept closer.

Their progress was like that of the Labyrinth City, or of the Schutzenwald family's Labyrinth subjugation—slow but deliberate forward momentum over the span of two hundred years. The Schutzenwald house had been wounded and defeated countless times but had continued to pass down their wish to subjugate the Labyrinth to the next generation. Every time the noble house had fallen to its knees, comrades and people of the City had helped to lift them again and again. It was no different now.

The men and women of the Forces would never concede. They continued their march, until at last, the weapon of the Gold Lion General, Leonhardt Schutzenwald, rested just before the core of the Wicked Hands of Creation.

"This ends here!!!"

Leonhardt mustered his unshakable determination, his unstoppable wish, and thrust his sword forward. By his sword, Leonhardt would end the days of endless fighting, the bloodshed, and the centuries of lives lost. To Leonhardt, the stairs leading

to the deepest part of the Labyrinth were more than mere steps. They were a bloody path built by the hands of all his comrades who had died.

"I won't let it all be for nothing! Those following me, the time we've spent, everything! I won't!!!" There was no doubt Leonhardt was more relieved than anyone to have seen none of his own people among the lifeless warriors they'd run through in the stratum above. Even now, those fallen members of the Labyrinth Suppression Forces were with him. They held Leonhardt's sword as tightly as he did, driving it forward to kill the Labyrinth.

The tip of Leonhardt's blade, Dick's spear following behind, the weapons of the captains, and Sieg's spirit arrows struck the Wicked Hands of Creation one after another.

Their blows were techniques honed over each of their lifetimes for this very moment. The hearts of those men and women swelled with their unified purpose.

Throughout the past two centuries, innumerable people had met their end in this Labyrinth. Yet it had never extinguished the dream of its death, instead spurring them to further action. Those comrades-in-arms marched ever onward, ever deeper—to that final place.

At long last, the Wicked Hands of Creation, the limbs of the Labyrinth's boss, the strange things that created the monsters of the Labyrinth, met the steel of the City.

CHAPTER 5
Arrival at Last

01

The bizarre, treelike hands twitched and stiffened, almost trembling, as they grasped at the sky. However, whatever they sought to cling to was now beyond their reach, and they wilted to the ground, never to move again.

"Have we won?" Leonhardt asked himself as much as anyone else as he gazed at the Wicked Hands of Creation. The stratum boss had quickly blackened and collapsed, just as proper trees would have if they'd been struck by lightning.

Leonhardt had felt neither an expectation of victory nor a reaction at finally routing their enemy. The job was not yet done, and there was no choice but to keep marching forward. There was no path that led home now, other than the one that demanded he and his allies brandish their blades to cut a way through to the future.

All their weapons and armor had been strengthened for the battle with the Bladed Beast of Many Legs on the fifty-seventh stratum. No expense had been spared; they had used the strongest materials they'd possessed. Adamantite, basilisk hide, and red dragon scales had all been liberally put to use. Additionally, they'd been provided with enough spare weapons, potions, and other supplies to engage with several stratum bosses. What was thought to have been more than enough had been furnished in preparation for the worst.

After they'd felled the Bladed Beast of Many Legs, Leonhardt and the soldiers had been given no recourse but to advance because of the corpses that flooded up from the stratum below. Thanks to the Sage of Calamity covering for them in the fifty-eighth stratum, all they'd had to do was push through the army of corpses and dive deeper in to the Labyrinth. Unfortunately, the fifty-ninth stratum had depleted far more supplies than expected.

Although their preparations had seemed perfect, what remained of the army had long since used up the spare weapons. Their armor was dented, and some had damaged joints, even coming apart in some places.

The cache of arrows and throwing spears that the baggage-carrying slaves and raptors had brought had very nearly run dry. Even the store of ley-line shards, critical ingredients for potions, had been exhausted. The potions themselves had been used up as well.

Even so, Leonhardt and his men continued to draw breath.

"We won…" Leonhardt clenched his fists. "We…survived!!!"

There had been no need to announce victory with a shout, as everyone knew that true victory still lay ahead of them. Contenting themselves here would mean not seeing Leonhardt's lifelong desire made manifest.

Leonhardt looked back at his soldiers, at the comrades who'd fought alongside him.

Everyone was bone-weary and sitting on the ground. Their numbers were even lower than when they'd first arrived on this stratum, and not a single person was uninjured. All were steadily recovering, thanks to the special-grade Regen, but some were severely wounded and clearly needed further attention. Nonetheless, everyone still had hope in their eyes. They'd made it this far.

They'd secured yet another stratum. Not one among them would hesitate to take the next step.

"Nierenberg, you all right?"

"Yeah, better than the general."

Nierenberg approached, dyed in frightful colors from the blood of monsters and patients. Likely he had gotten involved in the fighting as well. The left hand he casually hid in his pocket bore a severe wound that traced its way up to his elbow, though it was currently healing, due to the effects of the special-grade Regen.

Most likely, Nierenberg had suffered other, less visible injuries as well. Although he approached Leonhardt with no small amount of difficulty, he wore the same sullen expression he would have any other day. Something about the sight elicited a feeling of gratitude from Leonhardt.

Leonhardt was the general, the leader. He was more inspiring to the troops than anyone else, and every member of the Forces counted on him to lead the way. However, Nierenberg hid his own condition from Leonhardt and feigned calmness so as not to cause the general unnecessary worry. Even the other soldiers, wounded and weary though they were, could see it. That Leonhardt was still able to stand on his own feet was a testament to those who supported him. The thought inspired a new well of energy from within Leonhardt's exhausted body.

I can still do it. I can still hold my sword. The boss of the Labyrinth still lives...

Leonhardt took a breath, clenched his weapon tight in his hand, and issued an order to Nierenberg.

"Focus treatment on the soldiers who look like they can still fight. As soon as you're done, we move onward."

"Understood."

It was a cruel order, but nobody voiced an objection. Even if they'd wanted to temporarily return to the surface, surely the stratum immediately above them was crawling with corpses. The Sage of Calamity had sacrificed herself to lure the corpses and open the way, but it was a whole kingdom's worth of walking dead fused with the monsters that had destroyed them. No matter how unintelligent and weak their cobbled-together bodies were, their numbers were likely more than a single person could have ever hoped to burn to ashes alone.

Supplies were nearly exhausted, and many soldiers of the Forces were seriously wounded. The prospects of them overcoming another battle were slim. However, if they turned back here, if they gave the Labyrinth time to recover after they'd gone to great pains to weaken it, the city above would not survive.

Under Nierenberg's direction, the Forces were able to gather some ley-line shards for Mariela, though only a few. All the shards had been recovered from monsters defeated on this stratum. Little remained of the magical power of the moon or the crystallized materials, and Mariela made sure to craft only the necessary concoctions that Nierenberg requested.

"These are the last two mana potions..."

"You two should drink those."

"What...? But..."

Mariela's colossal magical power had almost run dry from frequent potion making, as evident from her hazy grip on consciousness. Even so, she'd refused to drink a mana potion until she was at her breaking point, because once she finished making potions, there was nothing more she could provide.

Likewise, Sieg had expended nearly all his own magical power using his Spirit Eye. Although he had a few arrows remaining, he was probably unable to fire any more. He'd reasoned he could still protect Mariela with his sword, and that would be enough. That was why he hadn't bothered to drink a mana potion.

"Drink them. Your work here isn't done."

"…I understand."

"All right."

Other than Leonhardt and Nierenberg, the only ones present who knew why Mariela and Sieg had been ordered to restore their magical power were the pair themselves. The four had heard it the day Sieg's Spirit Eye had been restored. Freyja had explained it to those present in Sunlight's Canopy at the time, though the "reason" she'd given was characteristically vague: "Endalsia's about to be devoured, and those two are essential to saving her."

Originally, even Nierenberg had believed that Mariela's presence was essential because she could make the quickly deteriorating mana potions and that Sieg was needed as her escort. In other words, he'd thought the two were necessary because of what they could provide in terms of fighting power. However, now that they'd reached the deepest part of the Labyrinth, Nierenberg felt he'd been mistaken.

There was no logical basis for Nierenberg's new presumption, but this flash of intuition was similar to what he'd felt that night in Sunlight's Canopy when he was in the ley line and saw Endalsia. The sensation in his gut was the same. He understood that Endalsia had little life left and that these two were needed to save her. Nierenberg trusted that Leonhardt harbored a similar intuitive feeling.

Those few remaining soldiers gazed at the stairs that led to the stratum below. Though it would have been more accurate to say they stared down a hole leading into the abyss, as the path forward could no longer be rightly called stairs.

The seriously wounded soldiers who couldn't be healed enough via potions or healing magic to return to the front lines stayed behind, reducing the Labyrinth Suppression Forces to about fifty people.

"Let's go."

With the few remaining troops, Leonhardt, Mariela, and Siegmund quietly proceeded toward the next stratum.

02

The place below was flooded with light, as though the darkness up to this point had been merely a bad dream. The soldiers could almost feel their weary bodies being healed and comforted by that divine glow, the dawn painting over the long, dark night in an instant. The light filled their bones, which had grown chill from the dark above. In that light, there was hope.

Although they were still in the Labyrinth, this stratum had no end, and other than the spot where they stood, even the ground seemed ephemeral. It reminded Mariela of the ley line. The reason the Labyrinth had dug deeper and deeper was to reach this place.

The last remaining monster, after consuming the people of the Kingdom of Endalsia and of the Citadel City, had devoured its fellow monsters. Then it had eaten its way below the kingdom, toward this strange location, while absorbing the power of the ley line and creating monsters as it went deeper and deeper. That path had become the Labyrinth, serving to protect from invaders.

Now Mariela at last understood the reason for the Labyrinth: it was all an effort to buy time. A stall tactic to ensure that the boss of the Labyrinth would reach this place.

On its journey, it had cast off its right and left legs, discarded its stomach, and even lost both hands before finally arriving here. This was as far as the Labyrinth boss had gotten, and the Forces had caught up.

Here, the sixtieth stratum of the Labyrinth, was where the boss had finally reached the ley line, though not physically. Instead, the immense magical power gathered by the enormous Labyrinth had allowed this sixtieth stratum to transcend mere physical distance, enabling it to connect to the far-off ley line.

In front of Leonhardt and the rest who had made it to the deepest part of the Labyrinth were the figures of the Labyrinth's boss, their archenemy over the span of two hundred years, and the spirit Endalsia.

Long had it been said that only those who dared to challenge the Labyrinth would know its boss when they confronted it. When he looked upon the visage of this being, Leonhardt felt that old story was true. He sensed the will of the Labyrinth, his own hatred and that of his fellows who dared to descend deeper and deeper, from the monstrous thing before his eyes. But Leonhardt had never imagined the boss would look like this.

With no arms or legs or even a visible spine, the horrible shape possessing only a head and torso, the boss of the Labyrinth, had its teeth sunk into Endalsia.

Endalsia was a being with a silhouette so vague one could

only barely recognize it as humanoid, though warm light still emanated from her. Mariela understood by way of her own Nexus that Endalsia was a part of the power of the vast ley line, the depth of which couldn't be measured through mortal means.

Mariela and all other people, spirits, magical power, and life forces that couldn't be seen or touched existed in the same world. The ley line connected all of it, and it was the very reason seemingly different substances and energy could exist together and change each other.

Endalsia, being unified with the ley line, most likely arranged and controlled the flow of Drops of Life and the energy that circulated through the ley line and the world. She used that power to continue protecting both the humans she loved and the kingdom they lived in.

This had been done through her eye, the Spirit Eye.

Unfortunately, Endalsia was now so frail that she seemed like she could vanish at any moment. To the naked eye, the Labyrinth boss seemed to be "eating" her, but what Mariela felt through her Nexus and what Sieg saw with his Spirit Eye was that even if the boss decided to open its mouth, Endalsia wouldn't be set free. Her power as the warden of the ley line, and her very existence, were being absorbed by the boss of the Labyrinth.

Endalsia loved people and had chosen to live with them. She had refused to accept the Labyrinth boss's desire to destroy humans and remake the land as a place only for monsters, even if that refusal came at the cost of her own existence. What remained of the Labyrinth's boss as it slowly consumed Endalsia and grew ever closer to unifying with the ley line was being burned and destroyed. Perhaps that was Endalsia's way of resisting.

The monster was already a pitiable sight without its limbs,

but its blood was boiling, and its body was burned and blackened like coal. What skin there was looked lumpy and swollen, possibly from the boiling body fluids. The horrible creature's internal pressure must have been fluctuating, as its eyes had protruded and ruptured, and bloody foam bubbled from its mouth.

No one dared to even hazard a guess as to what kind of monster the boss of the Labyrinth had been originally. This transformation had rendered it unrecognizable.

However, great power also streamed into the boss of the Labyrinth from its partial unity with the ley line. The ley line's power was now the boss's own, immediately healing any injury, and then the energy from the conflict immediately destroyed its body again. It was an endlessly repeating cycle of destruction and regeneration. What could the boss of the Labyrinth hope to achieve from such hellish suffering?

—I must get it back.—

Mariela had the feeling she'd heard the thoughts of the Labyrinth boss through her Nexus.

It's just like that story Emily and the others were reading... Mariela recalled the story she'd overheard children reading in Sunlight's Canopy, "The Legend of Endalsia."

The poor monsters had been living peacefully with the animals and the spirit Endalsia, but then they were driven to another part of the forest because of the arrival of the human hunters. The monsters attacked the village of humans to try to take back their home, but Endalsia's grief over losing her love, coupled with her powerful determination to protect her child, drove the monsters into the Fell Forest, and they were unable to return to their former home.

The Fell Forest was far, far larger than what eventually became the humans' territory. It had plenty of places for the monsters to live. They could have easily found free and happy lives. At least, that was how Mariela had felt after she'd first heard that story. Now that she saw the state of the Labyrinth's boss, however... Mariela realized that what the monsters wanted wasn't the land itself, but rather the place where they could be with Endalsia.

It was said that the magical gems inside the bodies of monsters determined their form. Corruption in the world mixed with magical power to form those gems, and the corrupted magical power they exuded would gather to form monsters. Though monsters produced magical gems when killed, their source was the evil that people produced: malice, hatred, jealousy, terror, anger, and lust.

Hungry, thirsty, and unfulfilled, that corruption coagulated and produced monsters, so it was no wonder they hated people. If there just weren't any humans, the monsters could have lived with Endalsia and the forest animals as gentler creatures.

Monsters couldn't coexist with humans. If a monster and a human met, they'd have to be separated, or one would destroy the other. Endalsia loved a hunter and had chosen the humans. That was why she couldn't be with the monsters anymore. Still, she didn't have it in her to destroy the monsters, her former friends. So instead, she chose to stay sequestered from them. From the Kingdom of Endalsia. Even that decision had likely been born of Endalsia's compassion. However, the poor monsters hadn't understood those feelings. Maybe they'd felt like they'd been cast aside, or even robbed.

—I must get it back.—

Even though they'd been shut out of the hunters' village, the monsters had probably been awaiting their chance from within the Fell Forest the whole time. The faint memories of their once-happy lives remained as the years wore on.

—I must get it back. I must get Endalsia back.—

Even now, a poor monster was consuming Endalsia and trying to absorb the entire ley line, urged to do so by those very same feelings as when the monsters had attacked the village of the hunters.

As Mariela and all the other onlookers found themselves at a loss for words at the unimaginable sight of the Labyrinth's boss, Endalsia suddenly opened her eye as though she'd awakened from slumber. It was only her left eye that opened. It shone the same brilliant verdant shade as Sieg's Spirit Eye. The color was a gentle, comforting shade to them, like new leaves sprouting on a dead tree in winter.

—I am so glad you have come. My beloved children.—

For the spirit Endalsia, who had lived for so very long, all people who dwelled in this land were her children: Sieg with his Spirit Eye, Mariela with her Nexus, Leonhardt, every single soldier in the Labyrinth Suppression Forces. She cast her affectionate smile upon all of them indiscriminately.

After Endalsia looked upon everyone like a mother delighted at the growth of her children, a terrible sadness clouded her expression, and she turned her gaze to the boss of the Labyrinth as it continued to consume her

—This child has not had a single thought ever since that day two hundred years ago.—

Had the loss of self-awareness been the price of obtaining power beyond any individual's capabilities in order to consume humans and fellow monsters? Or was it instead the result of continuous regeneration and destruction over two centuries? Regardless, in its current state, the boss of the Labyrinth no longer understood that just because it was driven by a desire to get Endalsia back, that did not mean the day would ever come when it could live with her again.

This monster, the Labyrinth boss that was the mere shadow of its former self with no arms, no legs, and no abdomen, simply continued to devour Endalsia. It could not survive unless it devoured her and become the master of the ley line in her place. Even if it did become the master of the ley line, could it even endure it, now that its senses had been worn down until not even a fragment remained?

—Please set this poor child free.—

Endalsia gazed at Siegmund, who had most markedly inherited the blood of the hunter she loved. Then she turned her eye to Leonhardt, who had led the others in the fight to this point. Leonhardt nodded in affirmation of the request and focused his attention on the boss of the Labyrinth, his longtime enemy.

"Pitiful... This is the enemy that has opposed us for so long?" Leonhardt muttered as he stood before a monster that didn't even have the strength to fight back. Perhaps, in that moment, Leonhardt felt something akin to compassion toward the monster that had tried so hard to go back to the happier days its kind had once known.

"Siegmund, release it from its fate, and save the spirit Endalsia."

"Sir," Siegmund replied in obeyance. He felt sure that it was for this very deed that he had regained his Spirit Eye.

"Sieg, take this."

"Thanks, Mariela."

Mariela handed Sieg a single arrow she'd taken from a wooden crate. Freyja had given it to her, saying, "Use this at the very end," and Mariela had fastened it to the raptor. Surely if ever there was a time to use it, it was now.

The wooden arrow, bereft of a metal arrowhead, had been carved from the sacred tree behind Sunlight's Canopy. When Freyja had spoken to the tree's spirit, Illuminaria, the tree had dropped a branch, and Sieg had personally carved the arrow from it.

Endalsia was the queen of the forest spirits. That included sacred tree spirits.

An arrow made from the branch of such a tree wouldn't hurt Endalsia. If Sieg used the arrow in conjunction with his Spirit Eye, it was possible to defeat the boss of the Labyrinth without endangering Endalsia herself.

Siegmund nocked the arrow and drew it back. The spirits, guided by Sieg's Spirit Eye, gathered to save their queen.

Endalsia, queen of spirits, did you guide me here...? Sieg wondered. Had it been due to her guidance that Mariela awakened the exact same day Sieg was being transported to the Labyrinth City? His meeting with Mariela wasn't the only happy coincidence, either. There was the time when the guidance of a forest spirit had saved his life back when he'd been taken to the Fell Forest by the son of the merchant who had been his master. Perhaps even the arrow that had defeated the wyvern by chance when the monster had crushed his Spirit Eye had been because of Endalsia. It all seemed to Sieg like some sort of mysterious guidance he'd been previously unaware of.

If that was the case...if even his meeting Mariela had been the will of Endalsia, or of the ley line...

My profoundest gratitude for your guidance, and for a destiny

that allowed me to meet Mariela... Siegmund drew his bow, imbuing it with a magical power that only he possessed, along with his deep, unwavering gratitude.

Those observing the scene thought they saw rainbow-colored light envelop Sieg's arrow.

The power of the spirits and their desire to help Endalsia, the queen of the forest spirits, amplified the Spirit Eye's power and gathered in Sieg's nocked arrow. This power was so great it surpassed the limits of Sieg's own body. Weak from his many injuries, Sieg felt his joints, his muscles, and even his bones screaming.

Please just hold out for this one shot...

Through his harsh days spent as a slave and the daily training in the City, Sieg had come to terms with himself and grown stronger. In this final hour, his body moved in harmony with his wish. Sieg's arrow flew unerringly—the shot of a true hunter.

The arrow from the sacred tree flew like a huge rainbow-colored comet. The perfect shot carried the power of the spirits and hit its mark.

And the boss of the Labyrinth...

—I must get it back.—

—It's all right now. I don't mind if you go home. Everyone is waiting for you.—

—Everyone is...—

—You were lonely for so long, weren't you? It's okay now. Go on, join them.—

The light of Sieg's arrow powerfully and gently washed over the boss of the Labyrinth as if it were wrapping the monster up. The creature crumbled in the dazzling light like piled snow melting in the warm rays of the sun, vanishing beneath that enveloping blanket.

—I…can join…them.—

The dazzling, radiant light wasn't so bright as to be blinding; rather, it was a peaceful, gentle sort of glow. When it at last subsided, no trace remained of the Labyrinth's boss. All that stood now was Endalsia, surrounded in a calm, warm light, and smiling.

03

—Thank you, my dear children… Ahh, all of you have truly grown into fine people. You went through so, so many difficult times. Oh, such strong, warm hearts you have.—

Endalsia slowly took in the faces of Sieg, Leonhardt, Mariela, Dick, Nierenberg, and every other person who had struggled to reach this place. After lovingly gazing upon all present, she shifted her gaze back to Sieg.

—Your eye is a beautiful blue, just like his was. You endured especially terrible hardships, didn't you? My beloved child, heir of my eye, the eye of the spirits. My darling children, I will entrust this to all of you, the ones who will walk into the future…—

Endalsia stretched her hand toward Sieg with her palm facing him, and a dark sphere emitting a dim light appeared before his eyes.

"What is this…?" he asked.

—That is the Core of the Labyrinth, and a manifestation of the power of the ley line's warden. I wish to watch over all of you always, but I no longer have any power left. So please give this to a spirit with strength, a sacred tree spirit who can be my successor. Right now, this power is corrupted by monster miasma, but when it is purified in due course, it will protect this land once again.—

Endalsia looked upon them as if they were her most beloved, precious people in the world. It seemed as if she was trying to etch their faces into her heart and memory as she parted from this world.

The Core of the Labyrinth was the ley line warden's power in physical form. The Labyrinth's boss had sunk its teeth in Endalsia and weakened her existence for a long time. She no longer had any strength, even to exist as a spirit. Endalsia had endured the Labyrinth's boss in expectation of this day, two hundred years after the birth of the Labyrinth.

Endalsia had watched over this land for untold generations. Now it seemed that the humans of the land she had guarded for so long would lose her without being able to repay her for such a great kindness.

With the Core of the Labyrinth in his hands, Siegmund looked back at Leonhardt. Only one way to save Endalsia existed, and it came at a tremendous cost. So heavy was this price that only Leonhardt, the successor of the house of Margrave Schutzenwald, one who had fought all his life to protect his home and its people, could make that decision. Leonhardt met Siegmund's gaze and nodded calmly.

"Mariela, alchemist granted to us from across the span of two hundred years...save the spirit Endalsia. Now is the time to create the Elixir—the greatest treasure of alchemy—by using the Core of the Labyrinth."

The Elixir was a legendary secret medicine, the ultimate miracle remedy.

The peak of alchemy, which could heal any injury or illness at once no matter how severe.

It was so difficult a potion that no one had ever made it before. Freyja, the Sage of Calamity, had informed Leonhardt, Sieg, and Mariela about it right before the expedition.

"Mariela can't make it yet, but there's no time left. So take her with you. She can't make it if she's not there, anyway. It'll just be a little longer. If she makes plenty of potions on the way, that should be enough."

The Aguinas family had stockpiled ley-line shards for over a hundred years. The majority of those had already been used to make special-grade heal potions and special-grade Regen before the expedition, but some still remained. Even in the course of this expedition, Mariela had tirelessly worked to make mana potions and other the concoctions they'd needed, using ley-line shards along with crystallized materials for each type of potion.

Even when Mariela had run out of the ley-line shards provided, she'd made more and more potions with the ones the Forces had obtained along the way. She'd made an enormous amount all by herself, an amount that would've otherwise taken a single city over a hundred years to produce. Perhaps, with her skills at such a point, she had indeed reached a summit none before her had? But even if the alchemist had indeed reached those heights, she couldn't make the Elixir without the crucial ingredient—the Core of the Labyrinth, the crystallized power of the ley line's warden.

No doubt if they gave the Elixir to a powerful spirit and its corruption was cleared away, this Labyrinth City would become a peaceful place free of monsters, just like the Kingdom of Endalsia had once been. If a person gained that power, it was unknown what would happen. No one knew if a human was even capable of wielding that much magical power.

The Elixir's key material was the Core of the Labyrinth. To use it would mean relinquishing eternal peace and tremendous power. Yet when it came time to make the decision as to whether the Elixir should be made, Leonhardt hadn't shown the slightest hesitation.

"The promise of peace will invite corruption—extreme power tempts ruin. We won't survive without diligent daily training. The Labyrinth City is the city of us humans. We will protect it to the end with our own hands." At Leonhardt's decision, Sieg handed the Core of the Labyrinth to Mariela.

The Core was stained black, yet it emitted a continual light as it sat in Mariela's hands.

It seemed to be a symbol for those who didn't give in to despair.

"The Core of the Labyrinth... Uh, um... I..." After staring fixedly at the Core resting in her palms, Mariela turned to face Sieg and Leonhardt. She had a serious expression on her face that suggested she'd made up her mind about something.

"Um, I still...can't make the Elixir!"

"What?"

"Whaaat?!"

Sieg and Leonhardt were dumbfounded.

"What should I do?" Mariela hung her head.

Leonhardt had pondered the question of what to do about the

Core of the Labyrinth from many different angles, but he hadn't expected this. What were they to do? Leonhardt, usually so calm and collected, turned to Siegmund with a bewildered expression.

Although Sieg had been dragged into his share of terrible, unfortunate developments, he, like Leonhardt, had never expected that Mariela wouldn't be able to make the Elixir at this climactic moment. He returned Leonhardt's look with one very much like it.

Though all were stunned silent, everyone's feelings on the matter were made plain by their incredulous expressions.

"Mariela should be able to make the Elixir by the time you make it to the boss of the Labyrinth. That's plenty of time, dooon't worryyy." That was what the drunkard sage had said. Perhaps it had been a mistake to trust those words. Still, although Freyja was always drunk and fooling around, she did seem to possess a tremendous understanding of the world around her, almost as though she could see the future. That was why everyone was content to trust her.

"Ugh... It was a mistake to believe what Master said... She really was a good-for-nothing after all..." If Mariela had known this was going to happen, she wouldn't have blindly trusted Freyja's words. Instead, she would have used ley-line shards with greater care from the time she first started training to make special-grade potions. Mariela hung her head in defeat beside the still-bewildered Sieg and Leonhardt.

"Ugh, it's all over. This is the end. Everything, absolutely everything, is *her* fault..." Until a moment ago, the image of Freyja in Mariela's mind had been that of a cool, gallant figure with a noble, self-sacrificing presence. A person who stayed behind alone in the Labyrinth's fifty-eighth stratum. That image was shattered, replaced with the image of a useless drunk. Mariela thought so poorly of her master that it felt to her as if all the misfortune in the world were Freyja's fault. She felt tears begin to well in her eyes.

"Master, you good-for-nothing! You're so irresponsible! I'm holding you accountable!" Mariela easily put aside her own inadequacy and began to bad-mouth her master, though it was considered improper to speak ill of the dead.

"Just whooo is a good-for-nothing? If it's anyone, it's this ridiculous pupil of mine!"

"Bwah?! Master?!"

Freyja had come running to this lowest stratum of the Labyrinth as though in response to the crisis of her favorite pupil.

"M-Master, Maaasteeer! A-are you okaaay?!" Though she was on the verge of tears from all the recent chaos, Mariela was delighted to see that her master was safe. Freyja's clothes had been scorched here and there, but she didn't seem to have suffered any major injuries.

"Ah, Lady Sage. It's wonderful to know you're unhurt after that swarm."

It was unbelievable to see that Freyja had made it through uninjured after facing down that army of corpses. Even Leonhardt was both pleased and astonished at her arrival.

"Ah, yes, yes. Mariela, calm down a bit. Well, you know, most of the corpses had saponified, so they burned up on their own after a few shots. Whoosh, whoosh. I actually started having trouble breathing. So I escaped to the stratum above for juuust a bit and wound up getting here a little late." Instantly, Freyja's explanation made her seem far less impressive.

Of course, the Sage of Calamity's fire spirit magic was incredible. So incredible that even the soldiers of the Forces had trembled at the blast that had rocked the stratum while they charged on through. Still, they'd thought Freyja was outmatched, sheerly because of numbers. In particular, Mariela had thought the swarm of corpses who didn't feel pain would take the opportunity when her master had run out of magical power to close in like an avalanche and swallow her up.

"Saponified"... I've heard that corpses that don't decompose become like wax. So the fire just spread...

Not only were there a lot of corpses, but they'd all been closing in on the narrow stratum stairs, so when an adequate portion of them got there, apparently the blaze simply spread from one to the next.

"Anyhow, this is Master we're talking about, so didn't you send wind or something from the upper stratum down through the stratum stairs?"

"Ooh, very sharp, Mariela."

Freyja loved fire magic, but she was pretty poor with anything even close to water magic. She was, however, quite skilled at using wind magic to stir up flames. Choosing magic that focused on firepower was very like Freyja. Regardless, she'd diligently supplied oxygen from the relatively safe stratum above to ensure that the corpses would keep burning until none remained. Was such a feat more befitting a "sage" or a "calamity"? Mariela and the others had to decide that for themselves. Either way, no one felt particularly inclined to praise Freyja.

"I would like to celebrate your safe return, but we have a problem." Leonhardt, ever the pragmatist, quickly returned to the real issue at hand.

"Yup. Mariela doesn't have enough experience, right?"

"Master...you knew?"

"Heh-heh, that's why I came. To transfer all my alchemy experience to you, Mariela."

"Transfer...experience?"

"Yup. When you connected to the ley line with your Nexus, I transferred experience to you to bring you back from the ley line, right? It's putting that to use. Normally, it can't be transferred while you're in your body, but y'know, we're super-close to the ley line here. I can give it all to you here, even if you're still flesh and blood." Freyja said all this with a cheerful smile.

"B-but...if you do that, you won't be able to..."

Such a thing would mean that Freyja would become unable to create potions. For someone like Mariela, who'd spent so much of her life crafting the things, even finding purpose in making them, just the idea of that was unbearable. Mariela screwed up her face, displeased. Her master, however...

"Well, I wasn't making potions to begin with. Too much work," Freyja retorted.

That's right... That's why she can only make mid-grade potions...

Since Freyja had taught Mariela so many things, Mariela thought her to be a master of alchemy as well. However, the Sage of Calamity was more of a typical teacher—skilled in many things, including alchemy, but not a master of them.

"Okay, I understand. Thank you, Master." Mariela had managed to calm down a little, but there was no time left. Even now, Endalsia's existence was steadily weakening. She looked ready to disappear at any moment.

"Sure. Well, here you go, Mariela."

Freyja wrapped both of her hands around Mariela's, still holding the Core of the Labyrinth, and bumped her forehead into her pupil's.

"My experience to my pupil. Guide her on the road ahead."

Although Mariela had assumed it would be accompanied by pain, like the Imprints she'd suffered many times over, the transfer of experience was extremely gentle. She was enveloped in a calm, warm feeling that reminded her of Freyja leading her home by the hand when she was little.

"It's done. This is all I can do for Mariela."

"Master..."

Freyja was kind at heart. She was an arrogant drunkard and a good-for-nothing who caused trouble for others, but she was also a wonderful person who lavished love on a child like Mariela with no special skills other than alchemy.

In the depths of the Labyrinth, Freyja had taken on a swarm of corpses alone and shown everyone the way forward. Even though she should have been in dire peril, she had managed to slip from the jaws of death and come running at just the right time to help Mariela out of a tough spot. However, despite seeming to know everything, Freyja refused to do any kind of housework, and she was a tactless scatterbrain. That was why, even though it seemed that the sage had managed something truly incredible, what came next wasn't a surprise to Mariela.

With an extremely clear understanding, Mariela faced her master and shouted, "Master! It's still not enough!"

04

"Whaaaaaa—?!"

The legendary Sage of Calamity had known of Mariela's lack of experience and had used it to make a cool entrance. She'd even looked the part of a noble sage in the way she'd taken it upon herself to transfer her experience to Mariela. Yet the Elixir was still just a tiny bit out of Mariela's reach.

"Uh...how? You're kidding, right?!"

"I'm not! It's all 'cause you slacked off on your alchemy! Aaargh, what do we do?!"

"Wow. So about how much more do you still need?"

"Erm...probably...one special-grade potion's worth?"

The alchemist master and her pupil were both completely flustered.

Leonhardt, Sieg, and indeed all the present members of the Labyrinth Suppression Forces had become mere spectators to this display, dumbfounded and wondering what would happen next. As for Endalsia, she had a somewhat distant look in her eyes as she quietly continued to fade.

"One more potion's worth? You've still got medicinal crystals, right? So you just need a ley-line shard! Right, all of you! Yes, you, soldiers! Everyone! Jump right now!" With an incredibly threatening look, Freyja barked out an order. Whether it was because of the presence she commanded or because her masterly ways

evoked some sort of childlike obedience in the soldiers, the Labyrinth Suppression Forces began to jump up and down. Clinking
accompanied the hops, along with flying coins.

It was chaos.

The medical staff hadn't gone to the trouble of healing the
soldiers for a charade like this. Nierenberg shoved his glasses
upward as he turned his pockets inside out to check whether he'd
forgotten about any ley-line shards. The only ones who didn't join
in the ridiculous jumps were Leonhardt, who hadn't been picking
up materials, and Sieg. Sieg had sunk to the ground next to Mariela; his grip on consciousness had grown hazy after sustaining so
many injuries and using up his magical power to kill the boss of
the Labyrinth.

Even Mariela was jumping up and down in the hope she might
have a shard. Perhaps the raptor and the salamander on its head
both thought it was some kind of game, because they jumped, too,
with little growls.

Despite the rather absurd efforts, not a single ley-line shard
fell from anyone's pockets. Before they'd come here to the deepest
stratum, though, they'd resolved to do their utmost and scraped
together everything they had to make potions, so it was no surprise that no shards remained.

Endalsia's existence continued to fade as they wasted time in
a futile effort. All Mariela needed was just a little more...just a
tiny bit more...

"Ahhh, what should we dooo?!" Mariela shouted, looking
ready to cry again. Sieg, still on the ground, hurriedly searched
his own pockets in vain.

"You reeeally are a klutz, huh?"

"...Lynx?!" Mariela could have sworn she'd heard Lynx

whispering in her ear. She whirled around to look behind herself, and the pendant Lynx had once given to her swung, and the chain broke with a snap, sending the pendant flying.

Thunk, thunk-thud.

The water droplet-shaped trick locket bounced and rolled on the Labyrinth's floor.

"Ahh, my pendant!"

Flustered, Mariela rushed over and picked it up. The trick locket, which she had never opened, now readily bore its concealed contents in her hands. A ley-line shard tumbled out.

Lynx had given Mariela this pendant around the time she'd first come to the Labyrinth City. It had a complex gimmick to it, and no matter what Mariela had tried, she'd never been able to open it. As a prank, Lynx had shut a ley-line shard within it, where it had remained until both Mariela and Sieg had forgotten what was inside. Even so, Mariela had always carried it close to her as a memento of him.

"Lynx..."

Had the voice just been a hallucination brought on by exhaustion, or, now that they were so close to the ley line, could Lynx have provided them with a miracle? The ley-line shard in Mariela's hand was unable to answer, but it gave her a more nostalgic feeling than anything she'd ever touched before. This shard was the final piece. With this, the puzzle would be complete...

"Mariela, that pendant..."

"I know, Sieg. Lynx is helping us."

Leonhardt and the Labyrinth Suppression Forces were wide-eyed at this inconceivable development. Even Sieg was surprised at Lynx's unexpected aid.

Mariela entrusted the Core of the Labyrinth to Sieg for the

time being and put power into the ley-line shard Lynx had given her. The process of refining special-grade potions was the same one she'd repeated many, many times over—quite possibly the last refining process she would ever perform.

"Transmutation Vessel."

When I'd just started making special-grade potions, I made the Transmutation Vessels too strong and wasted magical power. Mariela expanded the Transmutation Vessel as she reflected back to when her master had first arrived in the Labyrinth City.

In her peripheral vision, Mariela spotted her master wearing an expression that said "I knew it." However, Mariela chose to ignore Freyja for the moment. Turning away, Mariela decided to play back the memories of that time with a more glorified, responsible version of her master instead.

Dissolving a ley-line shard into Drops of Life required high temperature and high pressure, but that didn't mean she could just force it in. You could say a ley-line shard was the crystallization of a monster's vitality, formed inside its body. So traces of the monster's consciousness remained. Each ley-line shard held traits related to vague qualities about the monster it was once part of.

Some melted easily at high temperatures; some preferred sudden changes in pressure; some wanted greater pressure and lower temperature. If you put magical power into Drops of Life and adjusted the environment in accordance with preferences like those, the shard would melt surprisingly well.

I wonder what kind of creature this was, Mariela thought.

Lynx had said he had gotten this ley-line shard from a monster he'd defeated on the way to the Labyrinth City from the imperial capital.

What kind of monster did Lynx fight, and how did he fight it?

As she recalled Lynx with fondness, Mariela probed the ley-line shard as if she was asking it questions.

What kind of special-grade potion was she to make with this last shard? Mariela had repeated the refining process so many times she'd lost track, and she'd also gradually become better at tuning in to the individuality of ley-line shards. Moreover, now that she'd inherited her master's experience, Mariela's proficiency in alchemy had been boosted so much that it was only a hair from the highest level possible.

Recently, Mariela had fervently handling shards en masse, so she'd been unaware of their individuality. However, now that she had a moment to focus her awareness on one, she found that grasping the unique qualities of the material came surprisingly quickly. Mariela had always understood well the condition of medicinal herbs and the processing they'd gone through, but now the ley-line shard transmitted even the memories of its host from when it was alive.

Oh... This was a wolf monster. A strong force, the ley-line shard, suddenly formed in its body, and it ran wild. Its friends were the same way. Some of them went even wilder... Then they attacked Lynx and the others, who defeated them.

This ley-line shard had come from a black death wolf. Some of its comrades went on to evolve all the way to werewolves, but this individual had been the only one with a ley-line shard inside it. Since it had been a wolf, Mariela reasoned she could raise the temperature and pressure in her vessel to simulate the creature running through the forest.

Black death wolves are strong, but not so strong that they have ley-line shards in them. This is unusual. I wonder what it could've eaten? Mariela thought.

I want to run, I want to dash. Faster, faster, faster. Such were the feelings coming from the shard.

As she radically changed the temperature and pressure of the Drops of Life to fulfill the desire of the ley-line shard, Mariela further attuned her awareness to its history.

These wolves attacked a merchant caravan... This is horrible. Everyone's so thin, and they don't have decent equipment... Wha— This is...

Mariela turned an eye toward Sieg. This ley-line shard had dwelled in the black death wolf Lynx had defeated. That black death wolf had evolved from a black wolf that had attacked a certain merchant.

The memories flowing from the ley-line shard replayed the details of the attack to Mariela. A lone man climbed onto a raptor and fled while the pack of black wolves attacked the merchant caravan and devoured their poor victims. Although the fleeing man wanted desperately to escape, he stopped to save a man in heavy armor, allowing the pursuing black wolves to close the distance.

A wolf sank its teeth into the man's left leg and tore flesh from his calf before eating it. And so it consumed the flesh of a man beloved by the spirits and filled with power.

This wolf tried to eat Sieg...

When Sieg was still a debt laborer, he was taken into the Fell Forest by his then-master's son. Wolves had attacked him, and he'd survived the ordeal but suffered a grievous wound to the leg.

That flesh and blood, full of great ability and loved by the spirits because of the Spirit Eye, was what had allowed the black wolf to evolve into a black death wolf after consuming only a relatively small amount. That was why a ley-line shard had formed within the monster. Another monster had evolved all the way to a werewolf, and that one had indeed devoured many of the poor debt laborers. However, only the black death wolf who ate Sieg's flesh had absorbed enough Drops of Life into its body to produce a ley-line shard.

About a month after Sieg had been attacked, the Black Iron Freight Corps had defeated the werewolf and the black death wolves. Lynx had given the ley-line shard to Mariela, and the wolf had ended up back near Sieg again, in a way.

This was the final shard, the last piece, connecting the present to the future.

What a turn of fate. It's like it was predetermined. No, that's not right. This is more than just fate, Mariela reflected as she crafted the potion. She believed she'd survived the Stampede and woken up two hundred years later in order to be here now. However, she'd only made it here because of her own actions, her own will.

Mariela could have just as easily drawn Magic Circles of Suspended Animation and escaped with her master and Sieg. She'd been aware of that option, yet she had chosen to come here, to the deepest part of the Labyrinth. Mariela fixed her gaze on Sieg.

When Mariela looked at Sieg during her potion-making process, Sieg stared back at her, the Core of the Labyrinth still in his hands, wondering what she wanted. He had pushed himself so hard in order to defeat the Labyrinth boss that even standing was a monumental task.

"Sieg, you're always wearing yourself out, aren't you?"

"Hmm? Ah, sorry. I'm just resting a little so I can recover enough to protect you."

"That's not what I meant. Sieg, you've always given it your all. You've worked super-duper hard."

Sieg was always worrying about something, lamenting something, and yet he'd come all the way here with Mariela without even the slightest hesitation.

"Sieg, you always do your best and never give up. That's why I'm here right now."

Although it did seem like both the timing of Freyja's awakening and her teachings followed a predetermined destiny...

Surely fate alone wouldn't have been enough, Mariela reasoned. Sieg's tenacity, and this journey he and Mariela had walked together, were by no means the workings of destiny.

"Anchor Essence."

Mariela completed the final stage of the special-grade potion refining process. With the potion finished, Mariela understood that she'd finally reached the end of her training, the pinnacle of alchemy. And she'd done so by her own will.

05

At last, Mariela could refine the legendary potion, the Elixir. She understood now that she was capable of making it. First, however, Mariela had the Sieg drink her newly made special-grade heal potion to relieve his exhaustion.

Sieg had pushed his Spirit Eye to the limit and was about ready to keel over. He likely had a few torn muscles, too. Yet he suspiciously turned down the offer.

"I'm fine," he said.

So Mariela simply thrust the concoction into Sieg's mouth with a "Hup." Although he gagged on it at first, he did drink it down.

Didn't something like this happen on the day we first met? Mariela wondered.

Since the pendant had opened, all Mariela could think about was the past. As she reflected with nostalgia on her time since awakening in the world of two centuries later, Mariela accepted the Core of the Labyrinth back from Sieg.

The recipe for making the Elixir wasn't recorded in the Library, but Mariela no longer needed the likes of a recipe. She understood what to do. The Core of the Labyrinth would tell her.

"I'm going to start," Mariela announced; then she slowly expanded a Transmutation Vessel.

The Core of the Labyrinth was a mass of pure, high-density energy. The miasma of the monster that had been the boss of the Labyrinth had permeated it, turning it black and corrupted. Which meant the first thing to do was excise the corruption.

Excise? No, it's more like sending it back.

If the world's corruption, which made monsters what they were, had been created by humans, then it was a part of those humans. That being the case, Mariela reasoned that she should be able to send it back.

"Drops of Life."

When she filled the Transmutation Vessel containing the Core of the Labyrinth with Drops of Life, the Core sucked up the Drops of Life like a thirsty beast drinking water, and it began to swell gradually with the amount it took in. As she constantly drew up more Drops of Life for the Core of the Labyrinth to absorb, Mariela lowered the pressure and temperature a bit at a time, little by little.

The control was precise, exact, and advanced enough that only a person worthy of working with Core of the Labyrinth could have ever done it. She didn't deviate even slightly from the needed temperature or pressure. To others, it might have seemed incredible, but to Mariela, it was hardly anything. She'd done work like this many thousands, tens of thousands of times since she was a child.

When she lowered the pressure below what one would have found atop the highest mountain in the world and the temperature below the air of the frigid north, the Core of the Labyrinth suddenly turned jet-black. In the next instant, the black color was replaced by pure white, as if the darkness was being erased.

After that, Mariela changed the temperature, pressure, and atmosphere in accordance with what the Core of the Labyrinth, now fat on Drops of Life, wished. There were as many steps as there were stars in the sky, and Mariela dared not risk a single error among them.

Such technique combined minute, precise, and fundamental methods in limitless combination. This was a peak of alchemy that only those who had made potion after potion after potion could reach.

Searing lava leaping within the deepest reaches of a volcano's crater. The unreachable bottom of a fissure in the sea. A hot, massive, ancient site shut away in the deepest reaches of the earth. Mariela changed the Transmutation Vessel, changed her world, as if she was traveling to the most extreme places known to man. With each alteration, the Core of the Labyrinth changed color, changed size. Before

Mariela knew it, the Core had become a liquid floating within the Transmutation Vessel.

The red of blood, the red of the setting sun, and the deep, fiery red of the swaying autumn trees.

The light yellowish-green of new leaves in spring, the bright green of jade beads, the deep green of the trees in the Fell Forest. The indigo of the sky when nighttime nears, the blue of the endless seas, the blue of Sieg's eye.

No sooner had the Core of the Labyrinth taken on a large gaseous form, filling its container like a cloud, than it condensed. The vaporous form rapidly shrank, coalescing into something like a berry or nut. The mass winked out of existence and immediately began growing like a sprouting plant.

The silver of the moon, the gold of flames, the luminescence of fireflies, the lightning on a dark night. Pale, fierce, gentle, intense. Both the color and the light shifted, and the transitions themselves appeared unstable. It was as though everyone present was watching a world change at a rapid speed.

What they were seeing in the transformations of the Core of the Labyrinth—or rather, the core of the ley line—might have been its very memories.

"Ahh, how plentiful and beautiful, this ley line," Freyja murmured in wonder as she attentively watched the growth of her favorite pupil and the refining of the Elixir. And just as she spoke, the Elixir, the legendary secret medicine, suddenly reached its completion.

"It's…done." Mariela breathed a big sigh and offered the glittering liquid in the Transmutation Vessel to the spirit Endalsia.

"So this is…the Elixir."

"It's shines just as the ley line does."

As Leonhardt and Sieg watched attentively, the spirit Endalsia shifted her focus to the Elixir, then to Mariela, Leonhardt, Sieg, and each of the other humans.

—Are you truly certain? If you help me, the Elixir will disappear. Even if it extends my life, I can no longer manage the ley line in this weakened body. I am now a mere spirit. I have not the power to manifest in this world, and only a little remaining to watch over you all and illuminate your path—.

At Endalsia's question, Mariela looked back at Leonhardt, Dick, Nierenberg, the soldiers of the Labyrinth Suppression Forces, Sieg, and, finally, her master, Freyja.

All of them nodded reassuringly at Mariela and Endalsia.

"That's plenty. We might make mistakes sometimes, but when that happens, just try to light our way a little. We can handle the rest; we can move forward on our own." It was with these words that Mariela offered the entire Transmutation Vessel with the Elixir to Endalsia.

—You have my thanks.—

The instant Endalsia touched the Elixir, the Labyrinth's sixtieth stratum filled with a gentle glow. A cascade of placid, warm light.

Before the light flowing from Endalsia blanketed everyone's field of view, Mariela saw Endalsia look at someone and smile.

—Thank you for guiding the children.—

The only ones who could hear what the spirit said were those closest to her.

Who is she— Sieg? No...it's... But the light engulfed their surroundings faster than Mariela could follow Endalsia's line of sight. After dazzling display subsided, the sixtieth stratum of the Labyrinth was nothing more than an empty cave. They could no longer

sense the ley line that had felt so close just a moment ago. Only the salamander atop Koo the raptor's head provided illumination for Mariela and the others. It was a small lamp in a pitch-dark cavern.

"Is it...over?" Leonhardt asked quietly of no one in particular.

In the middle of the sudden darkness, everyone's gazes naturally went to the salamander and the raptor, the sole source of light in the place.

"Rar?" the raptor asked at the sudden attention, as if to say "What should I do?"

"Raaawr—let's go home!" the salamander on the raptor's head said in reply.

"The salamander...talks?!" Mariela cried in surprise at the salamander's sudden use of human language.

"I see... Dominion of this place has been returned to the people. It's our land again..." Understanding that their desire had at last been fulfilled, Leonhardt looked back at the soldiers who'd come with him to this place and proclaimed, "Let's go home, my friends! Our wish has come true! This land is now ours!"

He paused for a moment and took a deep breath.

"This is our victory!" he shouted, thrusting his fist into the air. The stratum erupted into a chorus of cheers.

"Whooo!!!"

"Let's go home! We'll make our triumphant return!!!"

"A triumphant return! We'll have a feast when we get back!"

"Boooooze! I'll drink up the entire wine cellar!"

"...Master, you didn't have to say that."

"Rar!"

Thus, the hard-fought battles of two hundred years at last came to a conclusion.

The Alchemist Who Survived...

01

The celebratory feast lasted for three days and three nights.

A messenger bearing news of Leonhardt's victory was sent up through the Labyrinth and informed everyone in the City that their home had been rightfully restored to the hands of the people.

With the defeat of the boss, no new monsters were generated within the Labyrinth. What had supplied the monsters with magical power was no more. However, it seemed that it would take time for the magical power already permeating the Labyrinth to naturally diffuse. Likely, the Labyrinth's ability to maintain different climates would be lost as the magical power faded.

The swarm of monsters who had headed for the surface as though driven by some command made their way back to their original strata. Those that had been able to exist without eating anything probably wouldn't be able to survive as the magical power weakened. Monsters that had fully incarnated would eat prey and continue to live like their brethren in the Fell Forest.

When asked, the Sage of Calamity had stated that most of the monsters would be unable to deal with the shifting climate of the powerless Labyrinth and that most would probably die off within a few years.

Previously, the deep strata of the Labyrinth had not only maintained certain climates but had often even supported the entire place's physical structure via the magical power of the Labyrinth's boss. As such, the strata beyond the fiftieth had become rather perilous due to the influx of underground water and the collapse of bedrock. It seemed that Weishardt and the other mages had their work cut out for them ensuring the effects of the deep strata's collapse wouldn't reach the surface.

Although there was still more work to be done, both the collapse of the Labyrinth and the decline of the monsters would gradually come to a close, along with the fading of the remaining magical power in the Labyrinth. Eventually, the Labyrinth City would become a normal city, no different from the other territories in the vicinity of the Fell Forest.

The outskirts of the City, having been restored as a domain of people, no longer suffered frequent monster attacks, though there were still not as few as when the land had been known as the Kingdom of Endalsia. Perhaps monsters had started putting distance between themselves and the domain of humans so people wouldn't trespass on their dens. Just as animals had their own territory, this place simply became recognized as human land.

With the loss of the source of so many resources and materials, it was likely that the demand to cut through the Fell Forest for farmland and food would soon arise.

Now that the crisis of the Labyrinth had passed, the City would no longer be able to receive the special consideration from the Empire it had enjoyed up to this point. The City would have to learn to survive on its own, even more than it had before.

"Just as I'd hoped." Leonhardt was brimming with confidence in the bright future ahead of his home. He gazed at the people of the Labyrinth City and the comrades who'd fought alongside him, all drunk from the celebratory alcohol.

This city, its people, would now move forward by way of their own strength. After all, had not nearly every resident of the City, from children to the elderly, fought in the final battle of the Labyrinth's subjugation?

What promise. What magnificence. With such a nation, Leonhardt knew they could overcome any trial, no matter what is was. As he looked upon his people, aglow with newfound hope for tomorrow, Leonhardt felt the dawn of a new age upon him.

The drunken revelry and feasting lasted for three days and three nights.

Almost everyone in the city had gone into the Labyrinth. Most had been injured, but they considered alcohol more important than healing and had gone to the feast before they went to see Nierenberg or Robert.

Freyja sloshed and guzzled alcohol with a vigor that truly did threaten to empty the wine cellar of Margrave Schutzenwald's family. Inebriated, she chatted with Leonhardt.

"Tha'sh why Dropsh of Life flows through the ley line and all life. They alwaysh shaid everything'll fall into place riiiight when we need it."

The person in charge of watching Freyja was Mitchell, and he was so flustered he'd completely sobered up. Leonhardt appeared not to mind at all and interjected periodically to show he was listening to Freyja as he happily emptied his own cup.

Voyd and Elmera Seele were as amorous as ever, but even Amber, who preferred not to flirt in public, freely expressed her joy at Dick's safe return without worrying what others would think. Edgan had a lewd, idiotic look on his face, directed at the female adventurers he'd saved in the Labyrinth. The women squealed excitedly over him, while the other members of the Black Iron Freight Corps watched without enthusiasm. Even Haage, normally treated rather coldly by his staff, was surrounded by the top brass of the Adventurers Guild, and they all drank together. Caroline and Weishardt smiled at each other. Emily, Sherry, Pallois, and Elio all got to stay up late without getting into trouble. The regulars of Sunlight's Canopy, Ghark, Gordon and the other two dwarves, Merle, and the chemists, were all celebrating, too. No one was left out; everyone was having a fantastic time.

"We really owe Lynx this time," Sieg muttered next to Mariela.

"Yeah. Turns out I brought something incredibly useful into the Labyrinth without even realizing it."

Mariela looked up at Sieg, who was back to wearing the eye patch Lynx had given him.

The effects of the special-grade Regen differed for each person. In Sieg's case, the effects apparently focused on his Spirit Eye, and he'd lost his former power. Since Endalsia was no longer the warden of the ley line, Sieg's Spirit Eye held no importance in protecting the city, either. However, the Spirit Eye itself had also seemingly grown weak, as Sieg could no longer empower spirits simply by opening it.

Even so, the spirits still loved him, and if he channeled power to them through the Spirit Eye, they would show up to help him by strengthening his arrows or the like. However, it was only doable via Sieg's own magical power. Endalsia had become one with the ley line, so she no longer provided an endless supply of Drops of Life. Controlling the Spirit Eye was still difficult for Sieg, and just opening it rapidly consumed his magical power. That was why he wore the eye patch.

"I wonder if Lynx has found his way home...," Mariela murmured as she tightly grasped the pendant at her chest. She'd only heard Lynx's voice that one time. After the chain had snapped,

Mariela had gotten it repaired and was wearing it around her neck again. The tricky opening mechanism had apparently broken from the impact of the fall, however. Now the locket could be opened and closed at the mere press of a button.

Somehow, that fact led Mariela to believe that Lynx had finally completely returned to the ley line and that there was nothing left of him in this world anymore.

"Mariela, I'll never leave you. I'll stay by your side forever."

"Thanks, Sieg. I hope we stay together forever."

The feast lasted through the night, and the people of the Labyrinth City eagerly awaited the arrival of the next day.

02

Finally, dawn broke, blurring the stillness that followed the feast and the excitement that followed the drinking. It was a silent daybreak, as if the city had tired itself out from the ruckus and had fallen asleep. No figures lurked in alleyways hazy from the morning mist, and even the morgena birds that announced the dawn seemed to have quieted their cries.

On this quiet, picturesque morning, the back door to Sunlight's Canopy opened without a sound, and the Sage of Calamity, Freyja, emerged from the house alone. On this sleepy morning, Freyja, wearing the same lightweight equipment she'd come with when she'd first arrived in the City, approached the sacred tree.

"Illuminaria, take care of Mariela and the others." That was all Freyja said as she lightly touched the trunk, then headed through the garden toward the back gate. After a statement like that, who could say where she was going? Before Freyja could open the back gate and depart Sunlight's Canopy, however, someone stopped her.

"...Are you really going to leave without saying anything, Master?"

"Mariela... Shouldn't you be asleep?" Freyja answered with her own question and a wry smile. The sage had even sung Mariela a magical lullaby.

"I know you too well. I burned sleepless incense," Mariela revealed, sullen.

Mariela stood at the back door, refusing to budge.

Freyja approached her, smiling. "You've grown."

"You didn't fool me, Master. I told you not to disappear on me this time..."

"Haha, sorry, Mariela. I can't stand all the melancholy."

They'd talked previously about this when Mariela had spent the night with her master in the crystal cave. Ever since then, Mariela had had an unshakeable feeling that Freyja would leave even if they killed the Labyrinth.

"Are you really gonna go? No matter what I say?"

"Yup. I have thing to do."

Mariela didn't bother begging Freyja not to go or asking where she was going. She knew her master probably wouldn't answer even if she asked. Instead, she chose to value the time she spent saying farewell to her master. Freyja stroked Mariela's head like she had when Mariela was little, and the alchemist hugged Freyja tight.

"Will we...meet again, Master?"

"Yeah. I'll be sure to come see you again in your lifetime."

Mariela trusted Freyja not to break that promise. Her master was the kind of person who didn't make promises she couldn't keep. Surely the day would come when Mariela would see her again. Even knowing that, Mariela couldn't bear to part from Freyja and clutched at the hem of her master's clothes. There was still something Mariela wanted to ask.

It was something she had always desired to know, but the idea of it was frightening, so she'd never put it into words. However, if she didn't muster her courage and ask now, she risked never hearing the answer. Mariela steeled herself, raised her head, and asked the question that had long weighed on her heart.

"Hey, Master. Why...me? If you wanted a kid with alchemy skills, there were others. Others who could use not just alchemy, but magic and swords, too..."

Why had her master chosen her that day, when Mariela was still very young? Mariela had been a useless child with no skills but alchemy. No matter how much she thought about it, she didn't understand the reason she had been chosen. But despite her curiosity, she was terrified of the answer. This was a question that had been locked away in Mariela's heart since the day she'd come home with Freyja.

What finally enabled Mariela to ask this dreaded thing was the self-confidence she'd built up through knowing Sieg and the many other people she'd met in the Labyrinth City. All those kind, wonderful people who'd come into Sunlight's Canopy.

Freyja smiled gently and stroked Mariela's head with some nostalgia. "That's right, Mariela. You couldn't do anything at all besides alchemy. Yet you focused on what you *could* do without getting all sulky, even though you were still such a little thing. That's why, Mariela. Because all you had was alchemy, because you single-mindedly persevered at what you had the ability to accomplish, you were able to reach the peak of alchemy—the Elixir."

Freyja had been watching Mariela and had understood her. Mariela's master had known her strengths, even if she'd lacked the skills others had possessed.

"No one else was good enough. Mariela, only you could have gotten there. That's why I, Freyja, the Sage of Calamity, made you my pupil. Don't you ever forget that. Believe in yourself, Mariela. I chose you, and you've become the greatest alchemist in the world through nothing but your own hard work."

Those may have been the words Mariela most wanted to hear. Many people were born with alchemy skills, but those skills were difficult to master. Even then, only a very small number of alchemists ever trained enough to be able to make special-grade potions. Just working at it hard and long enough might've seemed simple, but it was by no means easy.

A useless child with no skills but alchemy.

That phrase did not describe the true Mariela. She practiced and practiced, continued to work tirelessly, and reached new heights. Above all, what Mariela possessed was an invaluable disposition that allowed her to overcome the obstacles in her life. That was why had Freyja selected, taught, and guided Mariela. She had crossed the span of two hundred years and lived up to every conceivable expectation.

"You're my pupil, and I couldn't be more proud of you," Freyja said, looking at Mariela's tear-stained face.

"Master... Masterrr, thank you, thank you sho muuuch."

Freyja had said she hated sentimental stuff like this, so why had she made Mariela start crying? Although she'd finally outwitted Freyja and caught her leaving, Mariela now suffered an utter defeat at the unexpectedly tender attack. Bawling, she clung to her master.

Freyja patted Mariela's back to comfort her. No matter how old Mariela got, it seemed she would always be a child to her master.

As Freyja soothed her, Mariela remembered another question that had long troubled her.

A little over two hundred years ago, Freyja had picked out Mariela from many other children and made the girl her pupil. Then, before Mariela had really been aware of how odd it was, Freyja had taught her something very unusual. She had made Mariela learn the Magic Circle of Suspended Animation, which by rights an alchemist shouldn't have regularly needed. She'd also provided Mariela with a cottage that had a cellar with no ventilation and a lantern with a large amount of fuel in it. Forcing the then-head of the Aguinas Family, Robroy, to buy rainbow flowers and proposing marriage between the prince of Endalsia and the beautiful princess must have both been by Freyja's design, too.

The fact that the princess was from a foreign country and didn't believe in the glory of the Kingdom of Endalsia and questioned the certainty of its survival was precisely the reason she'd believed the words of the spirit Endalsia. She'd trusted the spirit's visit in her dreams, and that was the reason she had been able to escape the disaster of the Stampede along with the twins she was pregnant with, the descendants of Endalsia. Freyja had likely had a hand in all of it.

Freyja awoke again in this era, when Mariela had been struggling to work through the grief of Lynx's death. She'd even guided

Mariela and the others to the very bottom of the Labyrinth, where Endalsia awaited. It seemed as though Freyja truly knew everything.

It was certain that Freyja possessed high-ranking appraisal skills, because she had the ability to access the Akashic records. Mariela hadn't harbored any doubts about Freyja's apparent ability to see everything, but Mariela had known her master for so long that she'd always been content to believe that Freyja knew so much because "she's a master," never giving it more thought than that.

But what if it was true that Freyja had the ability to predict the future? What was it, then, that Freyja was working toward? What did she hope for?

What was important to Mariela was the fact that her master lavished her with genuine love, and she'd never doubted Freyja's sincerity in that matter. To Mariela, Freyja was both her mentor and her parent, someone very dear to her. As she thought about it, however, Mariela had the vaguest sense that Freyja's desire, her true goal, wasn't just to save this world of two hundred years after her own time.

To Mariela's master, had rescuing Endalsia, saving the people of the Labyrinth City, and even taking Mariela as her pupil all been no more than a means for something else she hoped to accomplish? Mariela could only guess at the answer.

"M-Master. Um, here…" Having managed to stop crying, Mariela handed Freyja a long tube that had been set next to the back door.

"What's this?"

"A Magic Circle of Suspended Animation… I wondered if you might need it, so I made one for you."

Freyja accepted the tube with the magic circle inside from Mariela. "You're a lifesaver. Reproducing a Magic Circle of Suspended Animation with Bestow Flame Seal is just a liiittle bit tough," she said, laughing.

Watching Freyja, Mariela got the sense that her hunch about the sage was likely true.

Her master hated drawing such complicated magic circles by hand. However, if it was just for herself, Freyja should've had other ways of reproducing the Magic Circle of Suspended Animation. She'd made Mariela memorize it specifically so that she could escape the Stampede and survive. If her master had the ability to put herself into magical sleep, even if she disliked making the circle for it, that meant...

Mariela found herself at a loss for words, and Freyja seemed content not to offer anything on the subject.

"Well, take care of yourself." After embracing Mariela one last time, Freyja lightly waved good-bye, and the two parted ways. Freyja left with the same cheerfulness she would've had when she went out for a drink.

"Master! You too! Thank you so, so much for everything!!!" When Mariela rushed to the back gate to see her master off, Freyja had already vanished. All that remained of her now was the warmth from where she'd hugged Mariela.

In the end, I couldn't ask her...

Mariela had been able to ask the thing she'd wanted to know most, but she had hesitated to ask the question about her master. Though even if she had, surely all her master would've done was laugh awkwardly and not give a straight answer.

"Master. How long have you... How much longer do you need to live?" That was Mariela's second question. Mariela had heard that the name Sage of Calamity had existed in old stories and fairy tales. At first, she'd thought it was a different person with the same title, but now...

When on earth had her master been born, and how many times had she used a Magic Circle of Suspended Animation? And for what purpose? When would her job be done?

"Drops of Life flows through the ley line and all living things. So everything will fall into place in a time of great need." That was what Freyja had said during the celebration of the Labyrinth's defeat. If that was true, then surely she'd reach her goal someday, when everything fell into place.

I hope that time can come even a single day sooner, Mariela implored the ley line flowing deep beneath her feet.

03

There was a play that was gaining popularity throughout the empire titled *The Fangs of the Golden Lion Sleeping in the Labyrinth*. As one might've guessed, it told the story of Leonhardt's subjugation of the Labyrinth.

In the story, General Leo lay on his sickbed, suffering from a curse of petrification. In the grips of death, he was visited by the queen of the spirits. The queen of the spirits was the warden of the ley line, and although she was losing her power and was about to be devoured by the boss of the Labyrinth, she brought about a miracle to save General Leo.

At General Leo's side, his younger brother, Wes, along with Wes's betrothed, Cathy, offered prayers to the queen of the spirits. The queen connected Cathy to the ley line so that she could become an alchemist. Cathy came from an ancient line of alchemists and used knowledge that had been passed down for generations in conjunction with the spirit's blessings to create a potion to remove the curse, saving General Leo.

General Leo, grateful for his life, vowed in his heart to rescue the queen of the spirits.

Cathy received divine knowledge from the queen and crafted potions. General Leo led a stalwart army. Together, they made great strides in the fight against the Labyrinth. However, the Labyrinth was no ordinary foe, and it used every means to obstruct their path.

General Leo used melee attacks, while Lieutenant General Wes favored long-range tactics.

The two brothers joined forces to face the Labyrinth, but in the final hour, it seemed they were nearing exhaustion and defeat. With their backs to the wall, Leo, Wes, and all their soldiers partook of a forbidden potion. The effects of the forbidden draught were marvelous, and with the power of a thousand men in each of them, they managed to defeat the boss of the Labyrinth and release the queen of the spirits.

Although the queen had been freed before her life force ran out, the wounds the Labyrinth's boss had inflicted on her were deep, and she was fading away.

To save the queen of the spirits, who was slowly vanishing in General Leo's arms like a melting snowflake, Leo used the Core of the Labyrinth, a wondrous object they'd obtained after the death of the Labyrinth boss. Thus, the queen survived, and the land became the domain of General Leo and the other humans.

However...

The forbidden potion had robbed General Leo and others of their mighty power. And because the Labyrinth's boss had been consuming the queen of the spirits for so long, she could no longer take form. Even after risking his life to save the queen, General Leo could never see her or touch her again. The final scene of the play ended with General Leo kneeling on the earth before standing himself up with his sword. He stood flanked by his men, who gazed at him as one would a hero. In the background stood the silhouettes of an army of monsters. The image was symbolic of the hardships that still lay ahead of the soldiers but also spoke to their unshakeable determination.

—None doubt the glory of the valorous General Leo and his soldiers. They who killed the Labyrinth shall be spoken of in legend.

Sadly, those heroes have already passed from this world, the price for the power that came with the forbidden potion.

What survived were mere empty shells for the memories of those heroes. Nothing remained of the power that had surpassed even the Labyrinth itself.

General Leo and his soldiers, those who had each held the strength of a thousand men in their bodies, now merely pass on this story of the Labyrinth to future generations, as witnesses of the past and as storytellers of a heroic tale.

To this day, the broken fangs of the lion still sleep in the Labyrinth.—

04

"Well, it got the gist of it."

"I suppose it contained some portion of the truth."

In his room within the base of the Labyrinth Suppression Forces, Leonhardt discussed the letter he'd received from his son detailing *The Fangs of the Golden Lion Sleeping in the Labyrinth*. Weishardt had offered the occasional interjection to show he'd been listening.

Of course, they both already knew the details of this play. There had been no shortage of work to be done since the death of the Labyrinth. As such, the two brothers didn't have time to go to the imperial capital for a performance. However, this play held major significance for those who were involved in the subjugation, so Weishardt had taken time between busy moments to supervise its creation.

"And, Brother, what does the letter say?"

At Weishardt's question, Leonhardt again dropped his gaze to the letter from his son, who had seen the play in person.

"It seems he didn't like the ending. He said, 'Father, you killed the Labyrinth. You're still a hero the Empire should be proud of.'" Leonhardt gave a slightly embarrassed smile at the unreserved praise from his son.

"You've raised an honest boy." A smile appeared on Weishardt's face.

Of course the young boy didn't accept the ending. The protagonist of the play was his own father, a man who'd succeeded against all odds against the Labyrinth. It was natural for him to think Leonhardt deserved greater praise that befitted his heroic triumphs.

In fact, if Leonhardt's true strength hadn't deteriorated due to the side effects of the special-grade Regen potion, he probably would have been asked to serve as a general directly under the emperor.

If Leonhardt had A-Rank strength, the effects of his Lion's Roar would elevate any troops he led to roughly A-Rank power, even if their actual strength was only B Rank. True A-Rankers were rare, even in the imperial capital. With an army empowered by Leonhardt's Lion Roar, surely the Empire could defeat any enemies that dared to threaten it. Such an army would no doubt have been showered with both the praises of the Empire and the blood of their enemies until its final days.

"It takes more than honesty to survive in this world. I'll have to teach him about the kind of battles you don't fight with swords."

After Leonhardt folded up the letter from his son and returned it to its envelope, he carefully stored it in a drawer. Despite Leonhardt's harsh tone, he wore a calm expression; a smile even showed on his face.

The backlash from the Regen potions had reduced Leonhardt to B-Rank ability. In other words, his Lion's Roar skill would only raise his troops to B-Rank strength. The forces he commanded were strong, but since there were many B-Rankers among them already, it was hard to say his forces boasted outstanding military force within the Empire anymore.

The Labyrinth, a blight on the land for two long centuries,

had been destroyed. Leonhardt had earned great acclaim for the achievement and had been awarded the appropriate honors and a medal of merit from the emperor. However, just as the play described, Leonhardt's glory was already a thing of the past.

The fangs of the lion had already been broken and were now lying impotent in the depths of the destroyed Labyrinth. This had actually been a great comfort to the nobles in the imperial capital. They had feared that Leonhardt's military might would afford him influence and power within the capital now that he was no longer occupied by the Labyrinth.

While the nobles praised Leonhardt as a hero, they secretly took joy and relief from knowing that his power was a thing of the past. It also pleased them to know that the Fell Forest, still crawling with monsters, would continue to serve as a wall protecting the imperial capital from other territories.

"I learned from that master and pupil that the definition of success in life is different for each person," Leonhardt commented.

Contrary to what the nobles in the imperial capital expected, Leonhardt was extremely satisfied with continuing to remain in the Labyrinth City. His wife and child were planning to join him there once the situation stabilized a little more. For the man who had known only battle, it would be a new kind of life.

Before meeting Mariela and so many others, Leonhardt would have imagined himself serving as a general of the emperor once the Labyrinth was defeated. He would've seen success as a path paved with glory and blood as he struck down the enemies of the empire.

"Weis. What is glory? What is success in life?"

Weishardt didn't answer Leonhardt's question, trusting that his brother already had the answer.

"Everything we've achieved has been because of our wish to defeat the Labyrinth. It is the perseverance of two hundred years that has brought us here. Indeed, you could say this is one kind of success. But what about our ancestors and comrades, who fought alongside us? What of those who met their end before the Labyrinth fell? Did they fail? They never gave up. They continued to challenge the Labyrinth. In that way, I believe they succeeded. This triumph belongs to all of us, including our fallen comrades. Are they not also heroes who killed the Labyrinth?" Leonhardt asked Weishardt while peering through a window at a group of soldiers training.

In the base, Dick had joined the soldiers weakened by the side effects of the special-grade Regen potion in their relentless training. Dick himself was in particularly low spirits due to his newfound weakness. He was training desperately.

According to Malraux, Dick had apparently started losing fights with his wife, Amber, because of the side effects of Regen. If he reached out to sneakily snatch food, he could no longer avoid being pinched, and when he knew she was mad at him, he found himself unable to disobey Amber when she told him to sit in a corner.

"Maybe it isn't just my speed but also my resistance to magical power that's deteriorated," Dick reflected, consulting with Malraux. Yet, from the beginning, Amber had always been able to order Dick around, and he'd never won an argument with her. Malraux wondered how exactly Dick was measuring the strength he'd lost.

The amount and severity of the changes differed from person to person, but the soldiers trained hard every day to try to reclaim what they had lost, even if only a day sooner. Weishardt watched the training soldiers for a while with his brother. He felt the same way Leonhardt did about those who had fought and died.

"Indeed, Brother. This victory is an accomplishment for all of the Labyrinth City, and was only possible with two hundred years of history behind us."

If this victory, this accomplishment, was something everyone had achieved, what had the people who confronted the Labyrinth over the past two hundred years fought for? Surely not to get compliments merely for form's sake from nobles in the imperial capital—people they'd never met. Perhaps that was why Leonhardt and Weishardt cared so little for compliments from such people and why the greatest medal of honor was the arrival of peaceful days like these. The dawn after a long, dark night.

Nonetheless, the final moments of *The Fangs of the Golden Lion Sleeping in the Labyrinth* didn't depict General Leo as happy-looking at all. From the instant the Labyrinth was defeated, nothing but "past glory" remained for the story's protagonist. He couldn't do anything to help the queen of the spirits, who was implied to have a romantic relationship with the general. Plus, he'd used the Core of the Labyrinth. Although the defeat of the Labyrinth returned the land to human rule, the monster silhouettes suggested that peace was not assured. The danger wasn't necessarily past, but General Leo and his soldiers had lost considerable strength. It was hardly a happy ending to the performance.

Those in the capital who saw the play likely didn't find the ending agreeable, nor did they particularly like the overemphasis on the protagonist, General Leo. However, that melancholy, ambiguous ending was the very reason the play was gaining popularity. It seemed everything had gone exactly as Leonhardt and Weishardt had hoped.

"With this, the ill-natured nobles in the imperial capital will probably stay quiet for a while."

"Yes. I don't think there's anyone who accepts the events of the play at face value, but we also have the inspector's report: 'Leonhardt and the others who defeated the Labyrinth, as well as their now Labyrinth-less city, no longer have any particular value.'"

This had been the true purpose of the only somewhat factual performances: to make the people of the empire believe that Leonhardt and the Labyrinth City were no longer of use.

A great number of issues had been piling up in the City after the threat of the Labyrinth was gone. Some people flocked to Leonhardt and his people after their great achievement with smiles on their faces, hoping to gain favor with the newly minted heroes. Others jealously wished for the people of the Labyrinth City to suffer misfortune and lose their status of acclaim, even going so far as to plot against the people of the City. Leonhardt and Weishardt were already busy enough dealing with real problems; they didn't have time to deal with such riffraff.

The Labyrinth had been a threat, but it had also been a gold mine of resources like medicinal herbs and monster materials. With those all but gone now, the Labyrinth City needed to change its form of industry. They chose to clear farmland around the Labyrinth City, establish a highway to the imperial capital, and trade materials gathered from the Fell Forest.

The Labyrinth City, now the domain of humans again, was not afforded the same level of protection from the spirits that the Kingdom of Endalsia had once enjoyed. However, monsters surrounding the Labyrinth City at the edge of the Fell Forest had since moved deeper into the vast woods, meaning the City was in no more danger than any other village near the forest. Since the number of monsters attacking farmland during the day would probably also decrease, they would now be able to produce the food the Labyrinth City needed.

The location for hunting monsters and gathering medicinal herbs and other things was quickly changing from the Labyrinth to the Fell Forest. This was also something adventurers did in the Kingdom of Endalsia's time. While it wasn't particularly profitable, it also wasn't an especially difficult enterprise. It was something the villages around the Fell Forest were already doing.

With so many big changes coming to the city, the house of Margrave Schutzenwald had plenty of opportunities to demonstrate its political influence. Thankfully, Leonhardt had a number of reliable retainers, including Weishardt. Things were difficult, but it wasn't something those who had defeated the Labyrinth together couldn't handle.

Moreover, unlike in the past, this city now had *many* alchemists.

"Speaking of the inspector, he made an amusing blunder when we talked about the alchemist."

"Yes, truly."

Leonhardt and Weishardt recalled the inspector's appearance back when he'd asked about the alchemist who'd made the Elixir, and they both laughed.

05

"By the way, I happened to hear that an alchemist participated in the Labyrinth subjugation. Where is that person now?"

The inspector, a rather tactless man, was a famous noble so straitlaced he was a rare sight even in the imperial capital. It was probably a direct order from the emperor that had sent this fastidious man with an instinctive dislike of bribes to be an inspector. He was the first to be dispatched to assess the current situation after the Labyrinth had been defeated. It was thanks to this that the less scrupulous nobles, those who would seek to pounce on the Labyrinth City during its time of instability, were kept in check.

"You have sharp ears. Certainly, without the alchemist and the miracle of potions, we wouldn't have been able to defeat the Labyrinth and purify the ley line. Nor would it have been possible to train new alchemists so quickly." Leonhardt responded to the inspector's question with a bit of additional information about more alchemists.

"New...alchemists?"

"Yes. After the Labyrinth's subjugation, that person took on a large number of pupils and trained new alchemists. Weis, how many are we up to again?"

"I believe today's alchemist was the seventy-eighth?"

Seventy-eight people. The inspector's expression changed almost immediately as he heard the absurd number.

"Did you say seventy-eight?! That's so many! Are you not aware, my lords? When an alchemist allows a pupil to make a Pact with the ley line, they give their pupil part of their experience. With such a large number of Pacts, that alchemist's power will greatly weaken. They'll never be able to make the Elixir again!"

There it was, just as Leonhardt and Weishardt had suspected. The real reason for the inspector's visit was to measure the power of the City's alchemist and to discover the secrets of the Elixir.

"Yes, it's certainly regrettable, but this was an agreement made to ensure the cooperation of the nobles in this city, and above all, that's what the alchemist wanted. I'm sure I don't need to tell you that relying on a single person for potions has its drawbacks. Besides, without the material for it, the Elixir can't be made anyhow. We've deemed this to be both a profitable and a proper choice for the Labyrinth City."

The inspector took a moment to digest Leonhardt's logical reasoning. There was a look in the man's eyes like he was searching for the true meaning behind Leonhardt's words.

"...What was the material for the Elixir?"

An alchemist who could make the Elixir. An alchemist of the highest rank, beyond any that could be found even in the imperial capital. That alchemist had taken on pupils with reckless abandon, and in doing so had greatly diminished his or her own abilities. The Elixir was now out of reach.

It was an unforeseen circumstance, but only having that one alchemist would've been nothing but a risk for the City. Leonhardt's point was infallible, and from a policymaker's point of view, he'd made the correct decision.

Although perturbed for a moment, the inspector was a shrewd person, and the situation being what it was, he'd switched to asking after other bits of valuable information. By nature, alchemists couldn't use alchemy if they left the ley line they were connected to, so the City's alchemist posed no threat to the capital. Perhaps the inspector's true purpose really had been to gather information. If the inspector learned the Elixir's ingredient, no doubt the imperial capital alchemists would try to find it in hopes of making the potion themselves.

"The material for the Elixir? It's the core of a labyrinth."

The core of a labyrinth.

Despite how casually Leonhardt had revealed the ingredient, it was not something that could be obtained easily. One would not find such a core by killing a young labyrinth with shallow strata, and the subjugation of an older labyrinth of even fifty strata was a monumental undertaking.

When one factored in that the Elixir also needed to be made by an extremely proficient alchemist, the odds of all the necessary pieces coming together seemed too low to even be possible.

It had been neither a miracle nor an accident. Instead, it had only been out of necessity that the ley line—that Endalsia—had drawn all the pieces together at the right time. Leonhardt couldn't help feeling that it had all been by the grace of someone extraordinary. An alchemist survived the tragedy of the Stampede and awoke two centuries later. Then she went on to meet and save the life of Siegmund, a descendant of Endalsia. What other explanation for such circumstances could there have been?

If a person drank an Elixir, it was possible for that person to ascend beyond the mortal, gaining unprecedented power and eternal life as the warden of the ley line. But after seeing the state of the Labyrinth's boss with his own eyes, Leonhardt didn't think it possible that a being as insignificant as a human was capable of such an ambitious undertaking.

Leonhardt and Weishardt had readily accepted that they would never again obtain the Elixir, as well as the decline of the alchemist who had achieved the pinnacle of her craft. To the inspector, it seemed that the brothers were content to regard both as part of a predetermined series of miracles.

"I see... So that's how it happened, is it?"

The inspector stayed in the Labyrinth City for a few days after that but returned to the empire after concluding his innocuous observations. Likely, he would report that this Labyrinth City had exhausted its powerful forces and that its alchemist had lost her touch. Everything the City had gathered to kill the Labyrinth was seemingly gone, and the place had now become rather ordinary.

The play performed in the imperial capital had successfully transformed the story of the Labyrinth City into a heroic tragedy, all while concealing the existence of Mariela, the Sage of Calamity, and the Isolated Hollow. The performance's story would come to be the one remembered by history as the years went on.

Not Leonhardt, Mariela, or even the soldiers of the Labyrinth Suppression Forces once came to regret all that they'd sacrificed. They never lamented what the Labyrinth City had lost in exchange for the peaceful days the land had so longed for over the past two hundred years. They were all truly happy.

06

"It took a bit of time to distract the nobles in the imperial capital, but we must give you the honors you're due for your many contributions to the Labyrinth subjugation."

As this was a private meeting, Mariela and Sieg had been invited to Leonhardt and Weishardt's estate via the underground Aqueduct. Mariela had been secretly worried that the brothers were going to demand that she pay her master's tab at the pub. When Mariela realized that Leonhardt and Weishardt were going to give her something instead, she felt an overwhelming sense of relief. She looked as though a load had been taken off her chest, though there was hardly any "load" there to begin with.

"Miss Mariela, you refined the Elixir and are the finest alchemist in the Labyrinth City—no, the entire Empire. And you've already taken in so many young nobles as your pupils. You ought to have a fitting title."

"...Huh?"

Mariela had been excited, wondering what she would get, but Leonhardt had only offered Mariela something she didn't really want or understand.

"Of course that goes for you, too, Siegmund. We may be the only ones who know the secret of your Spirit Eye, but you are the rightful successor to the Kingdom of Endalsia. Although the kingdom is no more, a proper position is essential, even when considering your future with Mariela."

Weishardt offered the same honors to Sieg, and the way he coyly mentioned Sieg's "future with Mariela" was quite crafty.

As Leonhardt and Weishardt had said, Mariela had already helped dozens of pupils make a Pact with the ley line, and the Labyrinth City was enjoying an unprecedented alchemy boom.

"If you cooperate, we'll allow your children, should any have alchemy skills, to become Alchemist Pact-Bearers."

This was the card Freyja had played to sway the nobles of the Labyrinth City when potions had started being sold on the market.

Many people had alchemy skills. Even if someone's biological child didn't, it would be easy to adopt one that did. Up to now, there had been only one alchemist in the City. The potential benefits of having an alchemist in the family were unfathomable. Many nobles thought that way, and all of them had cooperated with the Labyrinth Suppression Forces.

In exchange, the sacred tree spirit Illuminaria in Sunlight's Canopy's rear garden led dozens of nobles' and officials' children to the ley line, and they connected to it with a Nexus, becoming alchemists.

Of course, it wasn't only the children of nobles who became new alchemists. Mariela had made an unbelievable number of potions, so she hadn't lost all that much experience. All the alchemists she helped were only connected to a shallow layer of the ley line because of the danger of not returning from making a Pact. As such, each Pact consumed only a little bit of Mariela's experience.

Incidentally, the thickness of each pupil's Nexus was the same as those of the alchemists in the imperial capital. Apparently, only Mariela's was unusually thick, and generally, thin ones connected only to the shallow layer of the ley line. Their Library information disclosure configurations were the imperial capital standard, so they could view information without memorizing everything first, and they also weren't prohibited from using magical tools.

A policy of mass-training alchemists by standard imperial capital methods was put in place because of the idea that a stable supply of potions was a top priority. Caroline had become worried by Freyja's unorthodox teaching style and gathered information from the Aguinas family alchemists in the imperial capital. There had been no problem implementing them.

Incidentally, Caroline was Mariela's first pupil.

Thanks to the manipulation of information done by the Labyrinth Suppression Forces, the popularity of *The Fangs of the Golden Lion Sleeping in the Labyrinth*, and rumors spread by those not in the know within the Labyrinth City, Caroline Aguinas was believed to be the "first alchemist." Her presence and aura matched that title far more than Mariela's did. When the two of them were introduced together as "the first alchemist and the first pupil," ten out of ten people believed Caroline was the first alchemist, and about one in ten was likely to ask "Where's the first pupil?," completely ignoring Mariela.

Putting Caroline center stage was one of the measures taken to support Mariela, whose behavior and influence were unreliable. Above all, Caroline had wanted to do it for her friend.

At seventeen, Caroline was a bit old for making a Pact with the ley line. However, perhaps due to the joy of achieving her heart's desire and Weishardt holding her hand and calling to her, Caroline connected her Nexus and returned surprisingly easily.

The "Master Mariela" title had been ruined. It seemed extremely unlikely that the unofficial title Caroline bore would ever be dropped

Knowing Lady Carol, she might have come back on her own even if no one called her, Mariela thought. Perhaps the very first alchemist had been someone like that, someone like Caroline. She really was something, able to create mid-grade potions in almost no time at all, thanks to her preexisting knowledge and strong work ethic. The road to high-grade potions would probably be a long one, but knowing Caroline, it was likely she'd be able to make them soon. This person was completely different from a certain drunkard master somewhere, who'd been satisfied with mid-grade potions and slacked off as much as she liked.

Although it was some time after the nobles' children, the children of the chemists in the Labyrinth City, too, made Pacts with the ley line and became alchemists. Despite the slight delay, they were helpful children who'd learned and studied medicinal herbs from their parents. When one looked back on it, the noble children had probably needed the head start.

It was impossible for Mariela to instruct her suddenly large number of pupils one on one. Instead, they studied in schools at the Labyrinth City. They didn't have just Mariela as a teacher, either: Aguinas family alchemists from the imperial capital who'd been involved with the new medicine were also summoned. They were in charge of classroom lectures, while Mariela handled practical skills.

Incidentally, Mariela's practical skill training had somewhat of a bad reputation: "She does difficult things like they're easy, and her explanations are too abstract and hard to understand." It seemed the novice teacher had her work cut out for her.

"I wonder if I should aim for a hundred pupils," Mariela would comment as she filled requests for special-grade potions between her lessons, unaware of her unpopularity among her students.

"If their numbers increase any further, you wouldn't be able to take care of them all, would you?" Sieg answered. He'd been accompanying Mariela to the school as her escort. He dared not express his true thought: that Mariela couldn't even handle the current number of alchemist students she had.

"Mmm, but you know, since there's the Library, I bet they could just learn on their own…"

As one might've expected from someone raised by Freyja, Mariela really had a rather laissez-faire teaching policy. Perhaps she needed "teacher training" before she taught her pupils. Fortunately, Mariela's best pupil, Caroline, was far more teacher-like than she and was quickly gaining respect for it.

The only one who actually called Mariela "Master" was the sole Sunlight's Canopy child out of the four—Emily, who actually had alchemy skills. Even then, she normally called Mariela "Mari" and only used "Master Mari" to butter Mariela up when she wanted something.

It was that complete lack of dignity that caused Mariela's students not to respect her. So much so that a particular portion of the nobles' children didn't take her classes; rather, alchemists from the imperial capital were summoned as private tutors for them. Even then, Mariela didn't seem particularly concerned.

"Those kids might be able to make new potions! They should check the Library!" she exclaimed, rather carefree. The idea of alchemists forming ridiculous cliques as the Labyrinth City was beginning its new era wasn't particularly welcome, however.

Even if Mariela was given permanent escorts in addition to Sieg, a lot of inconvenient things, like money, a title, and social status, would also be needed to ensure her physical safety.

Knowing this, Leonhardt and Weishardt had been considering proceeding with bestowing titles and establishing guardianship with regard to Mariela's and Sieg's futures.

I don't really get it... Mariela was completely unable to grasp the details or the importance of the conversation.

Earl? Viscount? Baron? What's the difference? They're all just bigwigs, right?

Mariela's carelessly lumping so many different titles together was dangerous. If she mistook a butcher for a fishmonger, all the butcher would say was "We ain't got that kinda thing here. What about this instead? It's tasty." However, the more important the person, the more you needed to be particular about their social position and title. Mistaking one title for another could prove disastrous.

Seeing that Mariela didn't really understand and that his plan wouldn't go as he'd hoped, Sieg said "With all due respect..." to urge Leonhardt and Weishardt to reconsider.

"...This is more than I deserve, and I'm grateful, but I'm just a hunter's son. My lack of ability would prevent me from adapting to an official title or the like."

"Why, even the royal family of Endalsia were originally hunters, were they not? Their blood is so strong within you that you even bear the Spirit Eye. It's not more than you deserve."

Apparently, Weishardt had taken Sieg's rebuttal as mere humility.

"However, Lord Weishardt, neither my father nor my grandfather had the Spirit Eye. But I've heard there has always been someone who possessed the Spirit Eye in the past two hundred years."

"Go on."

"Most likely, many other descendants of Endalsia exist."

At Sieg's response, Leonhardt instinctively looked up at the heavens. He'd believed for a long time that only his own house of Margrave Schutzenwald had inherited the blood of the Kingdom of Endalsia, yet the proof of that, the Spirit Eye, had never appeared in his family. Just how far had the blood of Endalsia spread in the past two centuries?

During the time of the Kingdom of Endalsia, the princess was praised as having the greatest beauty and hunting skills. Her son, who'd survived the Stampede and had lived the life of a commoner, apparently had suffered no difficulty finding a spouse. Neither did his descendants. There had been many unknown kin who had thrived. Perhaps Endalsia had smiled upon them all.

"However, your abilities and Miss Mariela's skill as an alchemist alone are worthy of a house." Weishardt refused to give in. Certainly, the alchemists in the imperial capital who could make special-grade potions were surrounded by many pupils and escorts and relished their own self-importance. The number of Mariela's pupils alone was enough to rival them, so why couldn't she enjoy the same benefits? However, considering Mariela's abilities, her noble amenities would likely have to include some amount of protection as well.

Still…, Sieg thought as he looked at Mariela. She was sitting across the room in complete "leave everything to Sieg" mode and was stuffing her face with the teacakes they'd been served. It certainly seemed like she was enjoying the sweets, but she didn't have an ounce of the elegance that befitted a noble. To Sieg, it didn't seem at all like Mariela would ever adapt to a lifestyle where she was given a title and social status.

Aren't Leonhardt and Weishardt getting the wrong image about Mariela being some fine and magnificent alchemist? Sieg wondered. He decided to use his ace in the hole. He'd prepared a certain document in an envelope, thinking that he might need it. Now that the time had come, he conspicuously extended the envelope and its contents to the brothers.

After Weishardt accepted the offered envelope with a puzzled expression, he opened it, and his face contorted with shock.

"Wha—? This is... It can't be..."

"Yes, Lord Weishardt. It's just as you see. Therefore, I don't believe we're suited to noble life... Because Mariela's intelligence is a three."

"Bwah?! Sieg?"

Leonhardt and Weishardt fell completely silent at Sieg's coup de grâce. Poor Mariela almost spit out her tea.

Within the envelope Sieg had handed over was Mariela's appraisal paper from back when the two of them had first arrived in the Labyrinth City. Although she was an alchemist, her intelligence was lower than Sieg's. Mariela had tucked away the appraisal form in the back of the dresser in her bedroom, and she could've sworn she'd secretly thrown it away when she'd had the chance, but...

"H-how? I thought I tossed that..."

"...It fell on the floor and I happened to pick it up. There was never a good chance to give it back, but that may have been for the best!" Sieg grinned. "It fell on the floor" was a total lie. Obviously, he'd noticed it in the trash bin, took it out, and kept it.

"Impossible... An alchemist possessing that much knowledge with an intelligence of only three...," Weishardt muttered as he looked Mariela's appraisal paper up and down again and again.

Although referred to as "intelligence," the term encompassed a variety of things. Memory and problem-solving were big factors, but the appraisal took the average of various skills like mathematical ability, spatial awareness, and writing ability. Even accumulated things like general knowledge and experience were taken into account.

Mariela had learned the effects and processing methods for a great variety of medicinal herbs, as well as potion-refining methods. Her memory and quantity of knowledge were beyond those of an ordinary person. Weishardt had never thought Mariela's behavior was an act to disguise her true character. However, he'd always assumed her uninhibited ways were the result of being raised by such an unusual master. Weishardt had believed it was merely Mariela's folksy personality that suggested a lack of wisdom. He'd always trusted that her intelligence score was at least the same as his own. Never would he have thought it possible that it was lower than a five.

Mariela only having a three in intelligence despite the exceptional amount of knowledge she possessed meant...

Unbelievable... Does this really mean that, other than her memory and knowledge, she's actually as dim as she seems?! Weishardt was speechless. If Mariela's ability to think was as poor as her memory and knowledge were exceptional, she was absolutely unsuitable for exchanges with her fellow nobles, those who read into facial expressions and the hidden meanings of words. Of course, foolish nobles existed, but they still boasted exceptional educations.

Sieg's sneaky decision to secretly hold on to Mariela's appraisal paper, choose this point in time to show it to Weishardt, and give a grin as he did so meant he could probably cut it as a noble. No one present believed Mariela was up to the task anymore, however. The girl herself had grown so flustered she'd almost spit out her tea.

Perhaps Mariela's drink had gone down the wrong pipe, as she was coughing with tears in her eyes. As Sieg gently patted her back, he said, "I would be grateful if you took this into consideration," and bowed his head to Leonhardt and Weishardt.

"Weis, different people find happiness in different ways...," Leonhardt said.

Weishardt, still gripping the appraisal paper in his hands, agreed to arrange an environment where Mariela and Sieg would be happy.

07

A certain small hill east-northeast of the Labyrinth City allowed a sweeping view of the city. This was the hill of parting. The place of farewells, where people who'd died in the Labyrinth City returned to the ley line. The dead were carried to this hill and were liberated from their bodies via flame.

The autumn sky was clear and vast, but a chilly breeze blew, cooling bodies flushed from the excitement of the Labyrinth. It was like waking from sleep.

"I feel as if I was in a very long dream," murmured Robert Aguinas as he gazed at the glass coffin on the cremation altar, leading Estalia, the woman now sleeping within the glass coffin, to the new world. It had been a marvelous dream indeed, although Robert had been stained with blood and curses along the way.

"At last, I was able to show you the way," Robert whispered. Behind him, his father, Royce, and sister, Caroline, watched in silence. He had long wanted to see off Estalia on this hill that overlooked the Labyrinth City. His wish would finally come true today.

The stairs leading to the cellar where Estalia had slept were so narrow that it would have been difficult to carry the coffin out as it was. Thus the coffin had been removed after major construction to tear away the floor of the level above the cellar. Estalia, who had passed into eternal sleep via the effect of an erroneous Magic Circle of Suspended Animation, was no longer of this world. Half of her body had already turned to salt and crumbled away. Even the slightest disturbance risked collapsing her whole body, so they had taken the utmost care when transporting her.

It would have taken too much effort to hold a memorial service for every single person. However, for Robert, and for Royce and Caroline, who attended, this ritual was necessary.

The Aguinas family's dearest wish—to lead Estalia to a new world—had at last been fulfilled.

To the three members of the Aguinas family beneath the clear blue sky, the Labyrinth City appeared reborn in a new era.

The future head of the Aguinas family, Caroline, descended into the ley line with the guidance of the sacred tree spirit Illuminaria, becoming the first alchemist born in the Labyrinth City.

In the past, fledgling alchemists in the Kingdom of Endalsia had become full alchemists by exchanging True Names with the spirit Endalsia and connecting a Nexus to the ley line. However, the ley line now had no warden, so Caroline gave her True Name and engraved it into the ley line to link her Nexus.

"I, Caroline Aguinas, swear this: as an alchemist, I shall heal the people and live here in this land with them and the ley line. O ley line, grant me a glimpse of your secrets."

This was how Caroline and the other new alchemists of the Labyrinth City formed Pacts with their ley line. Caroline and the others believed these kinds of Pacts befitted a city that would rely on its own power from there on out, rather than hide behind the divine protection of the spirits.

When asked, Illuminaria said that the ley line still seemed to be without a master. She said the spirits, none of whom had the individual power to become its master, shared the management of the ley line. However, they lacked organization, and they weren't very thorough with their handling of Drops of Life. So sometimes the land was hit with a natural disaster or an epidemic. However, though it might not have been the case in a previous kingdom, the people of the current era had managed to defeat the Labyrinth. They were more than prepared to overcome such hardships and live in harmony with the ley line.

Perhaps one with power great enough to become the new master would appear someday, or maybe the ley line itself would give birth to its new master. Apparently, even the spirits didn't know if such a thing was a few years away or a few hundred years.

At any rate, the current Labyrinth City was a place where humans could support themselves without the divine protection of their previous guardian. The Labyrinth had been defeated. Monsters no longer controlled this land.

*　　*　　*

Robert placed his hands on the lid of the glass coffin. The thin film that had been melted around the edges to create an airtight seal on the coffin broke with a light cracking sound, and the glass lid slid open.

Exposed to fresh air for the first time in over a century, the upper half of Estalia's body suddenly turned to salt and gently crumbled to pieces. The wind blew as though it had been waiting for the lid of the coffin to finally open. The autumn breeze swept the bits of salt and carried them high into the sky.

Robert reflexively stretched his hand out to Estalia as the wind carried her away, and then he pulled it back down to his side.

"Good-bye, Estalia," Robert gave his sendoff to the beautiful person who had so thoroughly enchanted him ever since he'd first seen her as a child.

Farewell, you who lived in my childish dreams, he thought.

Robert had once felt sorry for Estalia, imagining her trapped eternally within the glass coffin. And yet she'd long since returned to the ley line and become free. The one who'd been trapped was Robert himself.

As he thought about it, Robert realized he didn't even know what kind of person Estalia had been. He realized he'd attributed so many of his own ideas the dreamlike woman sleeping in the cold glass coffin.

"Good-bye, Estalia. You're free....and so am I."

The sky was clear and stretched endlessly into the distance as the breeze carried Estalia off. As he watched, Robert felt that even his own body might be lifted up and away.

"Brother, are you truly going to leave us?" Caroline asked

after Estalia's remains were out of sight, and Robert was no longer watching them.

"Yes. The Aguinas family will be safe in your hands, Carol."

The existence of an eldest son who'd been removed as the head of the family would only get in the way of the new Aguinas family. The one that Caroline, the first alchemist of the Labyrinth City, and Weishardt would manage. Understanding this, Robert had decided to depart from the City.

"But you could still stay if you like...," said Royce.

His son had committed sins, but many of them had been brought about because Royce himself he had been the previous head of the Aguinas family. He pitied his son for having to bear such a burden alone.

"Don't look at me with such sadness, Father. I'm free now. No, I was always free, but I was prisoner to my own desires. My heart was shut away in this beautiful glass coffin." Robert recalled what he'd been told by the Sage of Calamity after the Labyrinth had been slain. He'd been working so hard healing all the wounded adventurers that the Labyrinth had died before he'd even known what happened.

Adventurers and guards had hoisted him up on their shoulders and brought him out of the Labyrinth. They carried him like that into the celebratory party, where Robert's former patients poured him drink after drink and offered their gratitude, even though he had once used people as materials to make accursed medicine.

The livelier the feast became, and the more the adventurers expressed their thanks, the more Robert felt he was losing the place where he belonged. Here, nobody needed treatment, and that was no place for him. He was about to leave when he'd had an unexpected encounter with the Sage of Calamity.

"Rooob, you drinkiiing? Ahhh. You're not drinking at all, arrre you? Heeey, you a teetotaleeer? You look like a frooog. And frogs don't drink. Frogface, ribbit, ribbit, Rob the froggy teetotaleeer." Freyja's behavior had reached new heights of disgracefulness.

Freyja held a bottle of alcohol in one hand and put her other arm around Robert's shoulders. Robert had thought all women smelled like flowers, but the only scent that reached his nose was the intense odor of alcohol. Thankfully, he'd learned by then that if he said something like that, Freyja would launch a forehead poke attack, so he kept his mouth shut.

Besides, after treating adventurers in the clinic, Robert found himself preferring Freyja's alcoholic odor and arrogant behavior. Adventurers got just as intoxicated; they even started fights. Some suffered injuries and had to be carried into the clinic. Others drank too much and vomited up the valuable food they'd consumed. Worse, some even drank themselves to death.

For once, Robert didn't give his usual middling response. Instead, he replied, "I'm not drinking because some other drunkards might need medical attention."

Freyja stared for a moment; then she whispered in Robert's ear. "You've committed sins, and you have the motivation to atone for them. You've got the hands to create the future and the feet to move forward and reach it. Isn't that reason enough to keep living? From now on, you can determine your own path, walk freely."

Freyja was capable of saying wise things once in a while. Robert reflected on the Sage of Calamity's words. She really did have a knack for showing up when she was needed. Robert no longer thought of her as a demon, but she still seemed to him like some sort of nonhuman entity. Her parting words had burned themselves into his heart as if they'd been branded. Curiously, they seemed to erase the gloomy feelings lurking within his soul like a cleansing fire.

Until recently, Robert had believed he had nowhere to go. He had no family to lead, no tasks to fulfill, nor even a place he belonged. Now he was free from those bonds. He could go anywhere, do anything he pleased.

On the hill overlooking the Labyrinth City, Robert recalled Freyja's words. Though he would continue to carry his many sins upon his back, there were no shackles on his feet. As he thought on that, Robert marveled at what a vast place the world was and how small the Labyrinth City appeared, surrounded by its protective walls.

"The world is so vast, it leaves me dizzy...," Robert muttered rather spontaneously.

Edgan of the Black Iron Freight Corps, who'd been waiting for Robert at a distance, approached and called to him. "The view from here is like a speck compared to the rest of the world. And wait until you see the beautiful ladies in the imperial capital; you won't believe your eyes."

"Wouldn't it be nice if that was what finally made Edgan blind?" Yuric asked, harsh as ever. The demi-human had suddenly appeared behind Edgan.

"If I went blind, Franz would cure my eyes, right? I'm counting on you!" Edgan was in rare form and hadn't even flinched at Yuric's wicked remark. Had his period of newfound popularity strengthened his mental fortitude?

"If you go blind, get a specialized potion for eyes. Anyway, I think what Edgan needs more is treatment for his head." Ever since the Labyrinth subjugation, even Franz had been treating Edgan rather coldly, due to the "take all comers" attitude he'd adopted with both clients and women.

"Ha-ha, that's enough, you two. Mr. Robert, if we do not depart before long, we will not be through the Fell Forest by sunset tomorrow."

"We're gonna be making good time. The carriage has been remodeled for speed, so there's no problem. Even if the ride is a little bumpy."

Grandel and Donnino each called for Robert to come to the armored carriage. The Black Iron Freight Corps had been contracted to transport Robert to the imperial capital.

"Indeed. Let's go. I'm off, Father. Carol, I'm leaving the family in your hands." Robert boarded the Black Iron Freight Corps's travel carriage and departed the Labyrinth City. As she saw off her older brother, Caroline felt relieved that his parting words didn't connote permanent separation. She prayed for Estalia to illuminate and guide Robert's path.

08

"Pardon meee, I cut my hand."

"In that case, use a low-grade potion."

"Uuugh, my stomach hurts…"

"A low-grade potion for that, too."

"My skin's been kinda dry..."

"Here. Apply a low-grade potion to it."

Mariela had recently been recommending low-grade potions again and again with a kind of dismissive attitude.

"Yer customer service's been sloppy lately," Gordon commented in regards to Mariela's behavior.

"Whaaa? But they really all *can* be cured with low-grade potions...," Mariela protested, asserting that she was still looking after her customers in earnest.

It was another busy day for Sunlight's Canopy.

Low-grade potions were enough for common injuries and illnesses, and the potions themselves could now be bought anywhere, thanks to the sudden increase in alchemists who were working hard to produce the concoctions each day.

Mariela was still the only one who could make high-grade potions, but she didn't want to monopolize the market, so she supplied the ones she made to the Merchants Guild, who distributed them from there. Elmera of the Merchants Guild had become Mariela's contact as an intermediary for special-grade specialized potions. This meant almost all the people who ordered those more powerful potions didn't know who'd actually made them.

Maintaining that anonymity was why the product lineup in Sunlight's Canopy was no different from any other potion shop in the city. Most people still didn't know Mariela was the first alchemist. Curiously, however, there were many who came to Sunlight's Canopy claiming that Mariela's potions felt more effective than those of other shops. But then, most of the regular customers visited frequently to have tea in the sun, not to buy potions.

* * *

"Mariela, I got earth dragon meat today!"

"Welcome back, Sieg. Sounds like the joint expedition with Captain Dick and the others went well!"

Sieg returned home carrying a large mass of earth dragon meat, and Mariela greeted him with a smile. He had left before dawn that day to hunt down some earth dragons.

"Since you got so much, maybe we should have a barbecue for everyone," suggested Mariela.

Immediately, there were replies like "I'll get some booze!" and "I wanna have sausage or shrimp, too!" and "Buy some veggies and bread for us, too!" from Merle, Gordon, and the other members of the dwarven trio. The group of regulars all stood up together and left to prepare. It was still lunchtime, but since earth dragon meat was a high-class item, Mariela thought it was fine to overlook a bit of early drinking today.

"Well then, here you go, Gordon."

Amber quickly tallied up the ingredients they needed, wrote shopping lists that evenly divided the responsibilities, and distributed them among the volunteer shopping group. Such a thing had become almost common practice in Sunlight's Canopy.

"Sherry and the rest of you are eating, too, right? I'll contact Dr. Nierenberg and Ms. Elmera."

"Yeah! I'll help, Mariela!"

"I will too!"

"Meee too!"

"Hold on, Elio, Emily. Finish your homework first."

At Mariela's invitation, Elio and Emily immediately discarded their homework and offered to help, but Pallois scolded them.

Sherry had finished her homework and was already preparing the meat in the kitchen.

"Mariela, would it be all right if I joined you as well?"

"Of course, Lady Carol. But are you sure?"

"Yes, since you are the one holding our buffet, there is no problem. Lord Weis is a magnanimous person, after all." Caroline expressed her desire to participate while nonchalantly slipping in a compliment about her beloved.

Though Caroline had a good relationship with Weishardt and was a young noblewoman eagerly counting the days to her wedding, should she really be participating in a barbecue at a commoner's house? Even with guards from the house of Margrave Schutzenwald present, it seemed rather low class. Not to mention, the very act itself of continuing to regularly visit Sunlight's Canopy wasn't very becoming for the head of such an esteemed family.

Weishardt was lenient toward Caroline, however. And if Caroline wanted to turn the barbecue into a proper buffet, then a buffet she would get.

"All right, you guards over there. Sorry, but could I ask you to set up the venue in the rear garden?"

"Yes, ma'am."

The guards of Sunlight's Canopy did not hesitate at Amber's command. Among them were soldiers dispatched from the Labyrinth Suppression Forces and soldier slaves employed by Reymond the slave trader.

Now that the Labyrinth had been subjugated, there was less demand for manpower in the City. Adapting to the times, Reymond had started a new slave liberation business. Apparently, it allowed those who'd been falsely accused or those capable and possessed of relatively good personalities to be deployed for guard duty or monster hunts. That way, they could raise their rank and gain their freedom. Even after penal laborers and lifelong slaves were freed, they paid half of their earnings to their former masters for ten years, so it seemed a very profitable venture.

Expecting that the people deployed to Sunlight's Canopy would all straighten themselves up and take their work more seriously upon learning Sieg was a former slave, Reymond had sent soldiers there at a reasonable price. They seemed to be learning rather quickly, too.

Even though they were good people, many of them reminded Sieg of his younger naivete. He trusted they would come into their own in time.

Perhaps the body language Sieg had learned from Nierenberg and Haage helped in training the soldier slaves. Or perhaps it was because Sieg's policy was to use gentle persuasion with delicious monster meat. He was worthy of the old nickname Mr. Meat.

"Mariela, work finished early today, so I brought my husband and Grandpappy."

"Thank you for always looking after the children."

"Hello there, young lady, sonny. Ye can cook this, too."

Elmera, Voyd, and Old Man Ghark had come to the barbecue-turned-buffet. What Ghark offered for Mariela to cook was orc king meat that had been processed into sausages. Turning already-delicious orc king meat into sausages gave the stuff twice the appeal.

"Whoaaa, this is so good and hard to get!"

Ghark's present made Mariela's eyes sparkle. Orc king meat was still her favorite, it seemed.

"I'll go cook it right now!"

Since the Labyrinth had been subjugated and the Labyrinth City was now the domain of people, medicinal herbs hardly grew in the City anymore. Even in the backyard of Sunlight's Canopy, herbs only grew sporadically. Tables and chairs had been set up under the sacred tree. Several chemists had been working on selective breeding to try to create medicinal herbs that could be cultivated even within the city. Maybe someday soon, herbs would grow in Mariela's garden again, but for now the garden would be where they held their party.

"Ith tho good, Thieg! I wish Edgan and the other guys could've come."

"Ahh, delicious! ...Now that you mention it, we haven't seen Edgan for a while."

With earth dragon meat in her right hand and an orc king meat sausage in her left, Mariela was truly blissful. Sieg watched her with a happy grin.

Were Edgan and the rest of the Black Iron Freight Corps in the imperial capital? Apparently, Edgan was still enjoying the prime of his youth, as Mariela and Sieg hadn't seen him in a while. He'd been given the rather exaggerated nickname "User of All," seemingly because of his usage of multiple elements in battle. However, the truth was the nickname had been given to him because of his lack of integrity toward women. Sieg wondered if he should keep Edgan at a distance from now on, since Mariela wasn't very well educated in such things.

If Sieg's biggest worry was Edgan, truly the Labyrinth City and Sunlight's Canopy had become quite peaceful. Everyone at the party happily enjoyed themselves, partaking of meat, alcohol, and conversation.

A gust of wind surged through the yard. The gale extinguished the flames of the charcoal fire and shook the sacred tree as it went by.

"Illuminaria?"

Spirits were extremely fickle, and although the sacred tree spirit Illuminaria could have made many appearances, she rarely did so. She'd been leading quite a few fledgling alchemists down into the ley line recently, so perhaps she'd had enough of talking with children and had decided to become completely anti-social. Even today, despite the rare large gathering for the party, she hadn't shown up. Perhaps she hated smoke or the smell of meat.

"She sure is moody..." Mariela stopped herself from adding, "Just like master," and suddenly felt very lonely.

Master, where could you be? What are you doing right now? Freyja had promised to visit again, so where was she? Mariela couldn't help but wonder when she'd see her beloved master again. She wondered if it would be after dying and returning to the ley line.

"Young lady, I don't see Fire anywhere. Where the heck has she gone?"

Glint, shine.

Was it possible that the blade of the Limit Breaker could even cut through gloomy thoughts? Guildmaster Haage, like the house of Margrave Schutzenwald, had been extremely busy ever since the Labyrinth subjugation. Due to *actually* working hard at the Adventurers Guild for once, he apparently hadn't noticed that Freyja had disappeared.

"Master went on a trip," Mariela answered dejectedly.

"What? And she didn't even say good-bye? Awfully cold of her. You're feelin' down 'cause she left you behind, right? Well, this is Fire we're talkin' about. She's probably gettin' dead drunk somewhere. Why not give her some time to get in a fix from a big ol' tab at the pub and then go looking for her?"

At Haage's lighthearted tone, Mariela said "But I don't know where..." before choking on her words.

"What're you sayin'? You've been down in the deepest parts of the Labyrinth, where no one'd been before. Findin' someone as unforgettable as her would be a piece of cake for you, young lady!"

Bam!

Haage gave a snappy thumbs-up and a dazzling smile.

"Yeah... Yeah, you're right! I don't need to sit around and wait for my master to come back. If I want to see her, I can go find her myself!"

Mariela had traveled across two hundred years and to the very bottom of the Labyrinth. Wherever Freyja was, Mariela could find her.

"It'd be impossible by myself, though..." Mariela looked at Sieg, who was standing at her side.

"Yeah. You have me. I promised you, right? I'm always be with you. I'll follow you to the ends of the world."

Mariela saw her face reflected in Sieg's blue and green eyes. She looked around at all her gathered friends in the garden of Sunlight's Canopy. At the time of the Stampede, all Mariela had been able to do was escape alone. Now she'd made so many reliable friends, and she had Sieg at her side. Mariela took the hand Sieg offered to her, and they locked eyes.

"Shall we go look for Lady Frey?"

With Sieg, Mariela knew they could reach her master, even if she was hiding. Sieg smiled, and Mariela gazed back at him, feeling hopeful. She'd completely gotten her energy back, and she beamed with a smile of her own that lit up her face.

"Eventually! 'Cause you know, we can see her any time. Now that I think about it, that darn master is such a handful! I wanna go to a lot of different places and do lots of things with you, Sieg!"

"Oh, Mariela—"

Mariela's unexpectedly proactive proposal had caused Sieg's voice to jump an octave. Apparently, even he needed some more training.

Someone calling that more meat was ready brought the two out of their own little world and back to the rear garden of Sunlight's Canopy.

"Let's go, Sieg."

At Mariela's invitation, Sieg took a step forward with her. Toward the place they belonged. The place they'd built in the Labyrinth City and would defend with their lives.

"Aah, Guildmaster, you're here skipping out on work again!"

"W-wait! I haven't had any meat yet!"

"It's lunchtime, so your wife will have a boxed lunch for you. Or do you want me to tattle?"

"I don't remember trainin' you to be a snitch!"

Haage had been discovered slacking off at a party, and the Adventurers Guild staff members dragged him back to work just before he got his hands on some food. Some things really never changed.

Laughing, Mariela waved to Haage, then surveyed the garden and shifted her focus to the huge tree creating shadowy spots. Sieg also looked up, following Mariela's eyes.

The branches of the sacred tree climbed toward the sky. Its many arms and leaves swayed, adrift in the clear blue sky like decorations.

Commonplace, trifling, wonderful days.

Suddenly, a leaf from the sacred tree gently fell and landed on the top of Mariela's head.

The spirits weren't visible, but Mariela had the feeling that Illuminaria and Endalsia were smiling tenderly from within the sunlight pouring down through the canopy.

Appendix

Franz

⚥ Age: ?

Healing magic user of the Black Iron Freight Corps. His face, hidden by a mask, has pronounced demi-dragon qualities, so he worked in the slums of the imperial capital as something resembling a back-alley doctor to avoid the public gaze. He's Yuric's foster parent, and of an appropriate age for it, but perhaps because of his demi-dragon heritage, his face still seems rather young. Being able to use healing magic to cause harm makes him rather unusual, but it seems appropriate for a man of so few words.

Donnino

♂ Age: **38**

In charge of maintenance for the Black Iron Freight Corps. Loves crafting professions despite having no dwarven blood in his veins. Despite looking older, he's still in his thirties. However, he has a personality smacking of a middle-aged man that fits his appearance. Possesses a strong arm and can beat up small-fry monsters using his bare fists as weapons. His strength allows him to wield a giant hammer, but one gets the sense he's fastidious about choosing a practical size.

Elio Seele
♂ Age: **9**

Pallois Seele
♂ Age: **13**

Voyd and Elmera's sons. Pallois, the elder, inherited his father's impregnable defenses, while Elio, the younger, inherited his mother's lightning attacks. Neither sibling has mastered his power. Elio in particular is a considerate, introverted boy because he doesn't want to accidentally shock those around him. Thanks to the special education Freyja gave them, Sherry, and Emily, the two boys became founding members of the Youngster Bloodbath Squadron.

Robert Aguinas

⚦ Age: **24**

Caroline's older brother. A genius possessed of madness and love for a beautiful woman named Estalia, who was sleeping in the glass coffin. When he was at last freed from his nightmare, it was a delightful reality that involved, among other things, witnessing his sister's proposal scene while frozen in ice. He was also pushed around and torched a lot by Freyja. Freed from the fetters of his own making, he walks a path of healing. He is regretful that he does not possess any alchemy skills.

Teluther

♂ Age: **52**

Former colonel of the City Defense Squad. A man who possesses a skill called Empathy that specializes in letting him get ahead in life. He's the embodiment of a slightly disagreeable boss who seems to be everywhere. A big fan of adventurers and an expert in all things relating to them. He took responsibility for the giant slime incident and stepped down to an active role as an advisor to the current colonel, but he has no self-awareness. There's no doubt the esteem that people feel for Teluther when they're near him makes anyone who learns of it sense the warmth of the world.

Endalsia

♀ Age: ?

The queen of the forest spirits who fell in love with a hunter. She's protected the descendants of her son, to whom she granted the Spirit Eye, and she cherishes her children. The first thing she'd said after rescuing the hunter was "Give him to me." Likewise, the first thing Mariela had said after rescuing Sieg was "Sell him to me!" Apparently Endalsia had continued to meddle in things through Mariela's Nexus. After she was freed from the boss of the Labyrinth, she trusted Sieg and the others to make their own way, via their own strength. She's a mother who has let her children fly from the nest at last.

Master (*for real now!*) Mariela's
Alchemy Recipes
Special-Grade Edition

Special-Grade Mana Potion

Restores firepower with the magical power of the moon!

You can recover your magical power, so Fire with all your might! Since it deteriorates quickly, you need to drink it while it's fresh!

【Ingredients】 Ley-line shard: A physical crystal of the Drops of Life dwelling in a monster. It still carries some of the traits of the monster.

Magical power of the moon: Magical power dwelling in crystals that have been continuously bathed in moonlight.

【Quantity】 Ley-line shard: 1; Magical power of the moon: 1;
(per potion) Round crystalline lens: 1.

Special-Grade Regen Potion

A forbidden mysterious medicine passed down through the ages.

In addition to its continuous recovery effects, the dragon blood in this potion will increase ability scores. Unfortunately, it has some extremely serious side effects. Make sure to follow the directions to a tee and use the correct dosage if you want to carve your name in the annals of history.

【Ingredients】 Earth-element dragon blood: The blood of earth dragons, which live deep in the Fell Forest.

Fire-element dragon blood: The blood of the red dragon that lived in the Labyrinth's fifty-sixth stratum.

Water-element dragon blood: The blood of philoroilcuses that had been frozen in ice in the Labyrinth's thirty-third stratum.

Wind-element dragon blood: The blood of wigglertrills, small flying dragons that resemble migratory birds.

【Quantity】 Ley-line shard: 1; The four elements of dragon blood:
(per potion) 1 medicinal crystal's worth each

Secondary Materials for Special-Grade Regen Potions

Indispensable secondary materials for combining dragon blood.

The secondary material will differ depending on the kind of dragon blood you use, so do the research on your own.

【Ingredients】 Fibrous lava: A silicon life-form resembling a starfish that lives in the lava in the stratum where the red dragon used to be.

Frost tree flower: Made from blown-off fragments of ice-type monsters that blooms rarely on frost-covered trees.

Crystal flower from the Sacred Tree Cemetery: A mysterious flower that blooms when the magical power of a human is added to the mix of Labyrinth magical power and the sacred trees power within it.

【Quantity】 Fibrous lava: 1 pinch; Frost tree flower: 1 pinch; Crystal
(per potion) flower from the Sacred Tree Cemetery: 1 whole blossom.

How to Create Special-Grade Potions

《1. Mana Potion》

1-1 Collect the magical power of the moon

When the moon's magical power has accumulated in crystals over countless years, collect it in a crystal that's been ground down into a sphere shape. Since the amount of magical power a crystal ball can store varies depending on its material, one from a high-ranking monster is best. Items from stratum bosses in the depths of the Labyrinth are top quality.

1-2 Refine

Mix in the magical power of the moon when you dissolve the ley-line shard in Drops of Life. All impurities, including those in magical power, are prohibited. Since you can't use *Anchor Essence*, you need to drink it as soon as it's done.

《2. Regen Potion》

2-1 Add the earth dragon blood medicinal crystal to fibrous lava that's been cooled and crushed into a powder, then add Drops of Life after it's dissolved.

2-2 When you add the red dragon blood medicinal crystal, the whole thing will foam tremendously. The Drops of Life will fly away if the temperature changes, so manipulate the Transmutation Vessel to match the change in volume.

2-3 After soaking the frost tree flower in Drops of Life, add the philoroilcus medicinal crystal. Since the Drops of Life stick to the ice, melt it while slowly decreasing the pressure and increasing the temperature.

2-4 After you toss in the wigglertrill medicinal crystal, the mixture will turn into a gas and melt. It may even slip through the Transmutation Vessel, so keep the Transmutation Vessel thick and lightly increase the pressure so the mixture doesn't become volatile.

2-5 After you have the foliage of the crystal flower absorb the turquoise liquid of water and wind, place the flower in the reddish-brown liquid of fire and earth.

2-6 After shifting and rearranging the crystal lattice and unifying the crystal flower's petals and foliage, repeat the high-temperature maintenance and the rapid cooling to integrate them. When it becomes a transparent sphere, soak it in Drops of Life with a ley-line shard dissolved into it for three days and three nights to dissolve it.

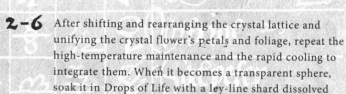

!
A Word of Advice

Both the side effects and the exact way of making a Regen potion differ depending on its dragon blood ingredients. Make a thorough observation of the materials' traits and find the optimal method!

Limit Breaker's Time

Did I keep ya waiting?! This is the start of my story! There are several key words that predict the future hidden throughout the Life of Haage story. My marvelous activities never end, and neither does *Limit Breaker's Time!*

It's as though everything was predetermined.
But the story people have the ability to learn is
only a fragment of the truth.

"Right then, young lady. I'm gonna borrow this one for a little bit!"
Bam!

Haage settled the matter with a snappy thumbs-up as the top of his head was burning. Well, actually, it was the *salamander* clinging to his head that was burning, and fortunately or unfortunately, Haage's head was a barren land of *famine*, with nothing to burn.

Haage had dressed for an excursion and was, as usual, alone. It wasn't that he'd had a *fight* and was *leaving* the guild. Rather, he was going on a routine survey of the Fell Forest to do some field research on gathering locations and monster distribution. The salamander on his dome was tagging along to both ward off monsters and serve as a source of light. This small *fire spirit* Mariela had summoned often did as it liked and didn't normally listen to people's directions, but perhaps it had taken a liking to Haage's head, as it stuck to the snappy adventurer like glue. Whether it had a *desire to help* people or its cooperation was coincidental, the spirit was a reassuring partner that kept deadly monsters away.

"Maybe this time I'll follow the main road to the stopover."

The main road the *Black Iron Freight Corps* had once used to travel to and from the imperial capital had undergone significant development. Now there were a number of places you could stop and rest along the way. Other roads hadn't been properly established yet, but adventurers were likely forcing their way through the brush as they'd clearly created a few small

Limit Breaker's Time!!

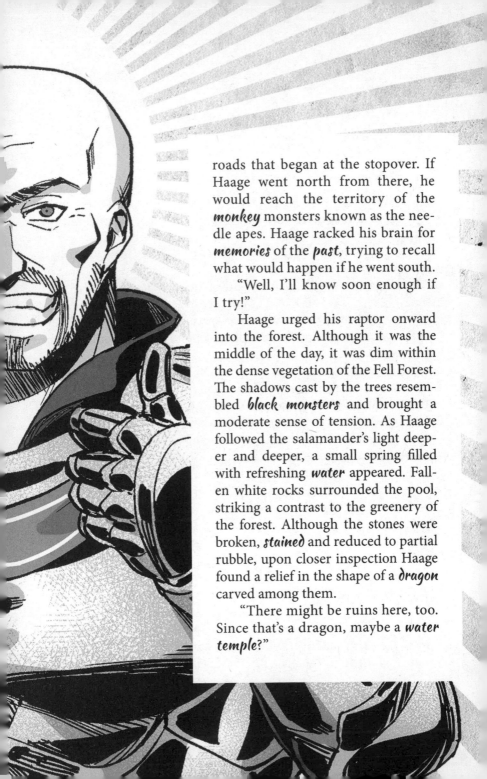

roads that began at the stopover. If Haage went north from there, he would reach the territory of the *monkey* monsters known as the needle apes. Haage racked his brain for *memories* of the *past*, trying to recall what would happen if he went south.

"Well, I'll know soon enough if I try!"

Haage urged his raptor onward into the forest. Although it was the middle of the day, it was dim within the dense vegetation of the Fell Forest. The shadows cast by the trees resembled *black monsters* and brought a moderate sense of tension. As Haage followed the salamander's light deeper and deeper, a small spring filled with refreshing *water* appeared. Fallen white rocks surrounded the pool, striking a contrast to the greenery of the forest. Although the stones were broken, *stained* and reduced to partial rubble, upon closer inspection Haage found a relief in the shape of a *dragon* carved among them.

"There might be ruins here, too. Since that's a dragon, maybe a *water temple*?"

As he thought about it, Haage remembered that the people of the imperial capital were supposed to have a legend about a sacred *lake*. Though he hadn't yet gone particularly deep into the Fell Forest, it seemed there were many ruins connected to the dense woods.

"It's been boring since the Labyrinth fell, but this could be interesting."

Just thinking about what lay in wait excited Haage. As if to welcome him, several monsters came flying out of a nearby thicket. Each had a tail as long as its body. The cute appearance of these weasel monsters belied the fact they were so formidable that low-grade monster-warding potions didn't even work on them. What made them even more troublesome was that sometimes they came to human settlements carrying *plague*.

"Limit-Breaking Cleave!"

Even so, such small monsters were no match for Haage. Even the salamander would have been able to drive them off. After felling them all at once with a single blow, Haage looked up toward the top of his head and found that the salamander was snoozing, perhaps even having a *dream*.

"I'd like to say 'Doing your work is like going to *war*; you may not like it but you gotta do it sometimes.' But *spirits* are fickle and no one holds *mastery* over 'em."

While Haage was lost in the excitement of the ruins, the sun had begun to set. He knew he ought to return to the City soon. Although the Labyrinth had been defeated, it seemed there were still plenty of adventures to be had in the Fell Forest.

Haage eagerly anticipated the next day's adventure as he made his way home to the Labyrinth City.

Limit Breaker's Time!!

AFTERWORD

In a little under two years since I started writing *The Alchemist Who Survived*, I've finally reached its conclusion, Internet version included. I'm glad I was able to write this tale from beginning to end, and that it all made it out into the world in book form. Although the words I use to express this are trite, I'm truly bursting with feelings of gratitude.

Mariela is the one who was able to reach the truth of the Kingdom of Endalsia and the Labyrinth, so her name was derived from "mari wo eru," which means to obtain the truth. Sieg was an empty man who grew to properly harness the power of the spirits. The origin of his name can be found by breaking down the second half of the kanji in the phrase "form is emptiness" into their readings of "shi" and "ku." There was no intention behind Lynx's name, but because he "linked" those first two together, the boss of the Labyrinth and the spirit Endalsia were finally freed, and the Labyrinth City truly became a place where people could live happily.

In terms of their growth as people, the pair still haven't quite lived up to their names, but they made it through this tale from beginning to end. I guess you could say they got through it by the skin of their teeth.

By the way, a ley-line shard was one of the key parts of the tale, and since it's crystallized energy, the design of the pendant

Lynx gave Mariela features a deformed $E = mc^2$. You can confirm this by checking the manga in Volume 2 or a certain illustration in Volume 4, if you're interested. I hope you'll check it out and get a kick out of it. As the author, the ability to pack the story with little details like that and funny bits while still reaching the end of the story really made the conclusion satisfying to me.

Last but not least, I'm truly grateful to ox, who drew such life-like illustrations that I can almost hear Mariela and her friends breathing when I look at them. To Kawana, the designer who managed to line up my work and the illustrations to make them a proper book. To the proofreaders who carefully looked over the typo-ridden manuscript. To my editor Shimizu, who compiled everything without letting me get too depressed or too full of myself over getting a book published, and took care of the manuscript without altering things. And to everyone else at Kadokawa for everything you've done for me.

Most of all, I want to thank everyone who picked up this book, and everyone who cheered me on while reading the Internet version. You have no idea how encouraging it was to see so many people pick up this tale, enjoy it, and to see your thoughts on it every week. It's thanks to everyone's support that I was able to finish the book without stopping for a break on either Obon or New Year's. Thank you all so much.

Nothing would make me happier than if everyone who read *The Alchemist Who Survived* enjoyed it, especially if they laughed at parts. It's my heartfelt wish that your future is full of hopes and dreams, just like the new era that has arrived for the Labyrinth City.

Usata Nonohara

NO, THAT'S NOT RIGHT.

THIS WAS MORE THAN JUST FATE.

WHAT A TURN OF FATE.

IT'S LIKE IT'S BEEN PREDETER-MINED.

SIEG, YOU'RE ALWAYS WEARING YOURSELF OUT, AREN'T YOU?

HMM?

THAT'S NOT WHAT I MEANT. SIEG, YOU'VE ALWAYS GIVEN YOUR ALL.

OU'VE ORKED UPER-UPER HARD.

AH, SORRY. I'M JUST RESTING A LITTLE SO I CAN RECOVER.

THAT'S WHY I'M ERE RIGHT NOW.

YOU ALWAYS DO YOUR BEST AND NEVER GIVE UP.

TRANSMUTATION VESSEL.

WHEN I FIRST LEARNED HOW TO MAKE SPECIAL-GRADE POTIONS, I WASTED MAGICAL POWER, DIDN'T I?

GOO (FWOOSH)

WHAT KIND OF MONSTER DID LYNX FIGHT...

I WONDER WHAT KIND OF CREATURE THIS WAS

...AND HOW DID HE FIGHT IT?

PAKAN
(CLICK)

AHHH, MY PENDANT!

YEAH, SIEG.

MARIELA, THAT PEN-DANT...

LYNX...

LYNX IS HELPING US.

PAKA (CHK)

GYU! (GRIP)

AHHH, WHAT SHOULD WE DOOO!? I JUST NEED A TINY BIT MORE EXPE-RIENCE...

......!? ...LYNX!?

YOU REEEALLY ARE A KLUTZ, HUH?

PUTSUN (SNAP)

ぷつん

KO (STINK)

KOKON (STATINK)

ONE MORE POTION'S WORTH?

YOU'VE STILL GOT MEDICINAL CRYSTALS, RIGHT?

SO YOU JUST NEED A LEY-LINE SHARD!

RIGHT, ALL OF YOU! EVERYONE! JUMP RIGHT NOW!

AAARGH, WHAT DO WE DO!?

BISHI (SNAP)

GRAR

RAWR!

CHARIN (CLINK)

HFF!

PYOIN (BOING)

HFF!

KASHAN (RATTLE)

GOSO (RUMMAGE)